THE COURIER'S APPRENTICE

The Divalian Chronicles

Book 3

S. T. Hobbs

ISBN: 979-8-9857217-4-4

First Edition: October 2022

10 9 8 7 6 5 4 3 2 1

Table of Contents
Prologue.. 1

Chapter 1... 6

Chapter 2... 10

Chapter 3... 16

Chapter 4... 21

Chapter 5... 26

Chapter 6... 34

Chapter 7... 38

Chapter 8... 45

Chapter 9... 51

Chapter 10... 57

Chapter 11... 63

Chapter 12... 69

Chapter 13... 76

Chapter 14... 86

Chapter 15... 93

Chapter 16... 95

Chapter 17..100

Chapter 18..106

Chapter 19..114

Chapter 20..120

Chapter 21..127

Chapter 22..131

Chapter 23..136

Chapter 24..142

Chapter 25..144

Chapter 26..150

Chapter 27..159

Chapter 28..163

Chapter 30...169

Chapter 31...175

Chapter 32...182

Chapter 33...192

Chapter 34...195

Chapter 35...200

Chapter 36...203

Chapter 37...208

Chapter 38...218

Chapter 39...228

Chapter 40...234

Chapter 41...244

Chapter 42...250

Chapter 43...256

Chapter 44...266

Chapter 45...274

Chapter 46...280

Chapter 47...286

Chapter 48...292

Chapter 49...299

Chapter 50...306

Chapter 51...312

Chapter 52...317

Chapter 53...324

Chapter 54...328

Chapter 55...330

Chapter 56...337

Epilogue...342

Prologue

THE INSIDE OF THE SLAVE CHILDREN'S hut reeked, and Halle wrinkled up his nose in disgust as he entered. The less time he spent in here, the better. Reaching the first form lying asleep on the floor, he nudged it with his foot.

"Get up."

The crisp note of command came easily to a son of the Chief and was recognized just as easily by a slave, even a young one. The boy he'd kicked sat up blinking and rubbing his eyes. He stared up at Halle for a moment, waiting.

"Come with me and be quiet about it."

Without a word, the boy rose to his feet and followed Halle out of the fetid room and into the cold white world beyond. Winter had a strong grip on the mountains and deep drifts of snow piled up against the windward sides of each structure. Even without the drifts, the snow lay piled knee deep. Halle avoided the deepest of these as he led the way toward the wooden palisade that protected the town of Illsen. The slave boy he'd awakened struggled through the deep snow, burdened now with the bundle that Halle had shoved into his hands.

The moon hung like a silver orb in the black sky, illuminating the bright white of the snow and turning the night visible. A full moon was the best time to go wolf hunting, but it was the worst time to try to sneak out of Illsen. Halle paused in the shadow of the last house before the open stretch of ground that lay between them and the wall.

"You know what happens to slaves who run away?" he said, turning on his companion.

"Yes, Master Halle. They are punished," the boy's voice quivered with cold and perhaps something else.

"They aren't just punished. They have a great, big mark cut into their chest like this," Halle leaned in close, tracing a finger from the boy's right shoulder to the bottom of the opposite ribcage and then repeating the action from his left shoulder, "and it stays there for the rest of their lives. And if they're ever caught running away again, having that mark means they're to be killed. If you make any noise and get caught, I won't say you're with me. I'll just let you be punished, and you'll be a runaway for your whole life. Understand?"

The boy nodded, his eyes downcast.

Slipping over the palisade itself wasn't challenging. Doing it without being seen or heard was. Halle waited another moment, scanning the empty space to see if anything was amiss. The guards passed by without noticing the two small figures hidden in the shadows and when they were safely passed, Halle made his move. Motioning for the slave to follow, he dashed across the snow as quickly as it would allow him to. The depth of the snow worked against him as he plowed through it. Glancing from side to side, watching for any sign of the guards' return, Halle reached the wall, with his slave right behind him.

"Climb over after me."

Halle didn't bother waiting for a response but found a handhold in the rough wood and started climbing. The frozen wood groaned softly beneath his weight but held firm. A moment later, his feet touched the other side and sank into a deep drift. No shout of alarm reached his ears. Only the soft whine of the wind and the almost inaudible clamber of the slave boy. With the bundle in one hand, the

2

boy did not land on his feet, but pitched forward onto his face in the pile of snow.

"Shhh," Halle hissed, laying a finger to his lips.

Pushing himself up, the slave nodded once more. The entire front of him was white but he made no effort to brush the flakes that clung to him away. Instead, he struggled out of the drift and fell into step behind Halle.

It was the steep, sloping side of the leeward mountain that Halle sought now. The rough, rocky earth was entirely hidden from sight and only the fact that he was familiar with the path kept them going straight. A copse of evergreens, protected from the wind and therefore standing taller than many of the other trees that grew on the mountain sides, offered the perfect hiding place for Halle's intent. He stopped when they were still at least twenty yards away and took the sack from the slave's hand. Loosening the strip of leather that tied it shut, he reached inside and pulled out several chunks of raw meat.

"Spread these out and then meet me at the trees."

"Yes, Master Halle."

It took the boy only a minute to toss the pieces of meat around at random and then he made his way to the cluster of pines where Halle stood waiting, a hunting knife in hand.

"I'll get one this time," Halle said quietly to himself. "Give me your arm."

Now, for the first time, the boy hesitated slightly. He gave an uneasy glance at the hunting knife in Halle's hand and took a deep breath before extending his limb. Halle took a hold of it with one hand, and in three swift motions left behind three red slashes in the bare skin.

"Ow! Ow!" The slave exclaimed but made no effort to pull away.

"Shut up. I need to get one, and fresh blood's the fastest way to bait it. Now go sit just beyond the trees where I can see you. And I'd better not catch you trying to stop the bleeding or cover them up."

As the slave moved to obey him, Halle climbed into the nearest tree, a short throwing spear in his hand.

Sitting out in the open, blood running in tiny rivulets of red down his arm and staining the white snow beneath him, the slave boy watched. With the brightness of the moon on the snow, it was easy to see a long way off. There was some comfort in that at least. He stared down at his arm. Although they weren't deep, the cuts stung, especially in the cold air. Bait. That's what his arm was. That's what he was. Living, breathing, thinking bait that had to sit quietly and wait for the approach of an animal that would shred him in seconds. All of the obedience ingrained in him from birth rose up in defiance, tempting him to bolt away to the safety of the nearest tree. It wouldn't be safety, though, not with Master Halle around.

The snuffling sound of an animal nearby jolted through the boy. He'd been sitting there in the snow for hours, knees drawn up to his chest to stay warm. The blood had long ago ceased its flow, but the ground around him was still stained with it and its scent still called to the roving predators. The boy lifted his head, and turned, trying to find the source of the sound. The moon was no longer high in the sky, its pale silver light no longer drenching the landscape. The boy squinted into the darkness, searching, searching for Halle's prize. When at last his eyes, well accustomed to the dark after so many hours, landed on the beast, he shuddered.

It was alone. Its gray body was only a few shades darker than the shadows on the snow. Crouched low, it slunk forward, its padded feet making no sound. Closer and closer it came. The boy could hear the low growl coming from deep within the animal as it crept towards him, its nose working to follow the scent of blood. He stiffened, clamping the hand of his uninjured arm over his mouth to keep himself quiet. Any moment now, Halle would throw his short spear and kill the animal and they could go home. He shut his eyes, waiting for the thud of the spear entering the wolf's body.

It never came.

With a spring that covered the remaining distance, the wolf attacked. The boy, sensing the sudden movement, scrambled back. The animal's jaws snapped shut with nothing but air between them.

"Halle!" He screamed, running for the trees, forgetting the title he ought to have used in his address.

Halle stood on the ground at the base of the tree he'd been sitting in. The spear still rested in his hand. His eyes

4

stared past the boy to the wolf, but his body refused to obey his will. He remained frozen as both the boy and wolf neared him.

Stumbling the final few steps, the slave boy came to the horrifying realization that Halle was incapable of movement. The same terror that caused him to run was turning Halle into a statue. With the wolf's breath hot on his own neck, the boy snatched up the hunting knife that still lay on the ground. Turning, he was met by a sight that nearly froze him as well. The gaping, snarling jaws of the wolf were only inches away.

He stabbed, sinking the knife deep into the flesh of the animal. His own panicked scream melded with the pained howl of the wolf as he stabbed again and again and again.

"Stop," Halle yelled over the din. The command stayed the boy's hand instantly. Halle, his face white with horror, stared down at the now dead wolf. "You killed it. It was supposed to be my kill."

The boy looked from the wolf's limp body to the bloody knife in his hand, confused. What did it matter who killed the beast, just so long as it was dead? Clearly it mattered to Halle, though. His face went red and before the boy could comprehend what was happening, he struck him.

"It was supposed to be my kill. It was my last chance. I needed to kill it," Halle said, kicking the unresisting slave over and over again until he exhausted himself. "What will Father say?"

Shielding his head with his arms, the slave boy dared a tentative glance up at Halle. "You could just say that you killed it, Master Halle."

It took a moment for his words to register in Halle's mind, but when they did the despair was replaced with cunning hope. His eyes narrowed as he considered the proposal.

"I could. What do they call you?"

"I'm called Aki, Master Halle."

"Well, Aki, if you ever tell anyone what happened here tonight, I'll make sure you die."

Chapter 1

THE WOODEN DOOR OPENED revealing the yawning black mouth of the entrance into the room beyond. Aki took a deep, trembling breath. A hand squeezed his shoulder and Aki turned and looked up at Stephan.

"Are you sure you want to do this?"

"I'm sure."

"Lead on then." Stephan motioned toward the open door.

Aki took a step forward.

"What's your name, boy?"

Aki jumped a little, startled out of his daydream, and found himself looking into the smiling eyes of the man Stephan called the Magistrate.

"Aki."

"Aki...any other name?"

"No, sir, just Aki."

"That's what you're here to change today, isn't it?" The Magistrate's smile widened and Aki, nodding, decided he liked the man. "Are you sure you want to go through with this?"

"Yes, sir. I'm sure. I want to have his name."

"Then let's get on with it." The Magistrate reached for a stack of papers and started shuffling through them. "I'm afraid this will be very boring for you, young man. Perhaps there is something you would rather do than sit here watching us sign papers."

Aki looked to Stephan, who frowned.

"I suppose you can wander around a bit outside, just don't go far and don't be gone long. Here" - Stephan held out a few coins - "Get something to eat, if you want."

"Thank you, Stephan."

Aki slipped out before Stephan could change his mind.

Outside, the bustle of the town beckoned to him and Aki wasted no time in answering. Turning from side to side and craning his neck to see everything, he wandered down the main road. The first buildings were mostly houses that would have been considered large if they had not been built in the shadow of the castle.

Aside from a passing curiosity, those weren't what Aki was looking for. He continued on until his eyes at last lit up with recognition. Beyond the houses were the shops. Aki looked down at the handful of coins in his palm. The first money he'd ever been given to spend on himself. Spotting a promising looking storefront across the street, Aki started toward it.

With a yelp of surprise, Aki fell to the ground beneath the weight of another body.

"Watch where you're going, boy."

Sitting up, Aki met the furious eyes of a girl who was at least two or three years older than him although she wasn't much bigger than him.

Rubbing his sore shoulder, Aki scowled. "You're the one who ran into me."

The girl's eyes narrowed dangerously, and an alarm went off inside Aki's head. The last thing he wanted was trouble. When she did nothing but glare at him, he started to get to his feet, dusting off the dirt that now adorned his clothes. The girl watched him a moment more before getting up as well.

"Where are you from, boy?"

"About a day's ride from here." Aki answered, torn between bolting back to the castle or continuing his search for something to buy.

The girl shook her head, a slow and not entirely pleasant smile spreading across her face.

"You're not from here. I know your accent. Karu?"

"I've never heard of that place."

The dangerous light came back into her eyes. "Aruuk." She spat the word out and Aki took a step back. "I should have known, you thinking you're better than me."

"I didn't say that."

"Didn't have to, boy."

Aki ignored her and began searching the road for the coins he'd dropped when she ran into him. Miraculously, none of them were to be found. Aki looked up at where the girl stood, now counting out a handful of coins.

"Those are mine."

"Says who? I picked them up, not you."

"But they were given to me."

"And now you're giving them to me." The girl tossed her matted braid of brown hair back over her shoulder.

Aki turned away and started back toward the castle. His feet dragged through the dust of the road and he didn't bother to look around at the same things he'd been fascinated by just a half hour before.

"Wait, boy." The girl's voice cut through the sounds of the town but Aki continued shuffling on. His day was ruined. And it was all her fault. "I said wait."

She caught up to him, out of breath from hurrying, and took hold of his arm.

"I'll make you a deal."

"What?"

"A deal. A bargain. For your money. I'll give it back to you if you buy some food and share it with me."

"Why?"

"You're not from here, boy. You don't belong any more than I do." Aki noticed her own accent for the first time. "People like us have to stick together. Deal?"

"Sure." Aki shrugged. Sharing food at least meant he'd be able to tell Stephan that he'd spent the money on something and not that he'd just been robbed.

"Come on."

Aki followed the strange girl through the streets. They sloped gradually downward, away from the castle and towards the sea. Aki was pretty sure this was farther than Stephan meant for him to wander but it was too late to change that.

"What's your name, boy?"

"Aki. Aki Turston, now."

"What'd you mean, 'now'?"

"I'm being adopted today. I get to have another name. What's yours?"

"Kezi or Kez." Kezi's hand darted out at a passerby and came away with a small leather pouch.

Aki raised an eyebrow but said nothing.

"Here's the place." Kezi stopped in front of a rather derelict shop. Its sign, unreadable to Aki, hung askew. Kezi counted out three coins and shoved them into Aki's hand. "Go in, buy a loaf of bread and then we'll split it. Then I'll give you the rest of your money."

Aki stepped inside, wrinkling up his nose at the smell. Most people would have left without a purchase, but Aki's ten years as a slave had taught him not to turn his nose up at food - regardless of the condition that food came in. A minute later, and he came out with a loaf of stale, dark brown bread in his hands.

Sitting in an alley within sight of the castle and out of the way of everyone else, Aki nibbled his part of the bread while Kezi devoured hers. The clatter of horses' hooves against the short wooden bridge that led into the castle drew a wistful sigh from Aki.

"Someday, I'm going to be one of them." He confided, drawing his knees up to his chest and watching the two men disappear inside the gray stone archway.

"A courier? Why?"

"They get to ride all over the place. They only answer to the King. And people respect them."

Kezi brushed the crumbs off of the front of her tattered shirt and snatched what was left of Aki's half out of his hands.

"Hey!"

"You weren't eating it," Kezi responded, her mouth already full again. "Someday, everyone in that place is going to know my name."

"Why?" Aki looked at her curiously. It seemed an odd ambition.

"Because if everyone in the castle knows my name, then everyone in this land will know it, and I want to be known. I want the whole world to know that Kezia Grimere was alive."

Chapter 2

3 Years Later

"THIS IS AN IMPORTANT DAY, Sky." Aki cupped the painted horse's muzzle in his hands. The mare snorted. Her name was in honor of her pale blue eyes that, as Alina said, looked like the sky was trapped inside of. Aki chuckled. "And you have no idea what that means. You just want me to feed you. But I'll tell you what it means anyway. It means that today we are going to Bren. And in Bren, I will start training as a courier. And..."

"Do you always talk to the horses like that?" Stephan stood in the doorway of the barn, nothing more than a silhouette against the sunrise.

"Haven't you gotten used to it by now?" Aki retorted.

"There are some things that I'll never get used to. It's a horse, not a person." Stephan came up to him, shaking his head. "Where'd you pick up habits like that anyway?"

Aki didn't answer right away. He picked up a saddle and laid it across Sky's back and reached beneath her belly for the cinch.

"You know where," he said quietly at last, tightening the girth.

If Stephan noticed the change in his demeanor, he didn't mention it. Aki gave Sky's girth a final test and pushed away all thoughts of habits and where he'd picked them up. Today was a new day, a fresh start.

"Ready?" He turned to Stephan, smiling once more.

"You haven't said goodbye to Alina yet. She'll never forgive you if you try to run off without that."

Aki acknowledged him with a brief nod and hurried out of the barn, leading Sky.

Alina was waiting for him on the front steps. Wisps of gray, the first signs of her aging, colored her otherwise brown hair. Aki dropped Sky's reins and came up the steps.

"You weren't in such a big hurry to leave us that you were going to miss saying goodbye, were you?" Alina teased, a gentle smile softening the wrinkles on her face.

"No. I mean, I am in a hurry, but I wouldn't have skipped saying goodbye."

"Are you sure you don't want to eat before you go?"

"I think I will be sick if I try to eat right now." Aki let out a nervous laugh. "I'll be fine. I won't starve by missing one meal. I used to do it all the time, you know."

"Don't remind me. I hate thinking of it."

"I hated doing it." Aki glanced over his shoulder to find Stephan waiting by Sky. "It's time. I'll miss you both."

Alina held her arms out and Aki obliged, returning her embrace.

"Stay out of trouble. Study hard. And make us proud."

"I won't forget the chance you both have given me." Aki promised, pulling away from her.

Sky stood patiently while Stephan said a few words to Alina.

"Not long now, Sky." Aki whispered to the mare as he stroked her neck. "Not long. You're going to be a courier's horse."

"If the only thing you're going to do is talk to that horse, it's going to be an awfully long ride to Bren."

Despite Stephan's worries, Aki had more than enough to say to keep the time moving quickly. It wasn't until Bren was within sight that Aki gave up on conversation. After a considerable length of silence, Stephan turned a curious eye toward Aki.

"Nervous?"

"No," Aki said too quickly. "What's it going to be like, do you think?"

"I would have absolutely no idea. It's not like I've ever been a courier. I just make sure the ones that stop at my place get fresh horses."

"Do you think it's hard?"

"I don't know."

"How long do you think it takes?"

Rather than answering, Stephan turned a very pointed gaze at Aki.

"There is one thing I know about couriers," Stephan said. "They are good at keeping secrets, which means they're good at keeping their mouths shut when they need to."

Aki frowned at the obvious jab. Unable to think of a good retort, he decided silence was the best option. It at least proved Stephan wrong. He could keep a secret as well as the next person, sometimes. Silence was boring, Aki decided after a few seconds had gone by.

"So, do you at least know where we're supposed to go?"

"Of course. What kind of a question is that? If I didn't know where we were going, we couldn't get there, now could we?"

"So, where is it? The castle?"

"Eventually, but not for you."

"Oh." Aki couldn't hide his disappointment. In the last three years he had ridden to Bren as often as Stephan had, mostly because he pestered Stephan into letting him come, and in all of those times he had yet to see any more of the castle than the Magistrate's office.

The first scattered houses that marked the outskirts of Bren were behind them now. Aki's eyes darted about, taking in the many people coming or going. As the houses gave way to shops, Aki smiled and raised a hand in greeting to a shabbily dressed girl standing just inside an alleyway.

"Who are you waving at?"

"Kezi."

Stephan shook his head. It was the same every time they came to Bren, ever since Aki took on Stephan's name. Aki liked having someone who spoke his own language and who knew what it was like to go hungry to talk to. Kezi was the one person, outside of the people he lived with of course, who didn't raise an eyebrow at his strange accent. That alone was enough to seal a childhood friendship for him. The fact that he always bought something for Kezi to eat sealed her part in it.

"Where are we going?" Aki asked when Stephan turned off the main road.

"To see an old friend."

"What old friend? Why?"

Stephan sighed. "An old friend of mine. And the fact that we are friends is reason enough for me to want to see him. Why do you have to ask so many questions?"

Aki shrugged and bit back the question he'd been about to ask. Instead, he turned his attention to trying to read the various signs that hung from buildings as they passed by them. It wasn't easy. Alina had taught him some words but mostly the letters just looked like senseless markings. Stephan was already off his horse when Aki realized that he had stopped.

"Wait out here," Stephan said as he rapped on the door.

There was a sign on this door as well, and Aki's face twisted up in concentration as he tried to decipher the markings once Stephan had disappeared inside. When that proved too difficult, he gave himself over to thinking about who Stephan was seeing and why and why he didn't want Aki with him.

Inside the building, a score of candles danced away from the slight gust of air that the opening door caused.

"It's been a long time, Stephan, a very long time."

"So it has, Atticus. You are," Stephan glanced around the front room, taking in the abundance of papers and books, ink pots and quills, "keeping busy, I see."

"Always busy, always busy. Some work never ends. It never ends." Atticus stared off into nothing as if remembering something. With a shake of his head, he brought his attention back to Stephan. "And what brings you here, old friend, after all this time?"

"A dilemma, and a favor."

"Ah, I see. A dilemma and a favor." Atticus made his way around a cluttered desk, leaning heavily on a thick, wooden cane with each step. "A dilemma and a favor. What else are friends for?"

"You know Alina and I adopted a boy."

"I'd heard mention of it. He's not from here, I believe." Atticus lowered himself into the chair behind the desk and motioned for Stephan to take the empty seat on the other side.

"No. Actually, he's from Aruuk. And here's my dilemma. He's had his heart set on becoming a courier since he knew what they were. Naturally, he is not as well," Stephan paused, searching for the word.

"He'd be starting behind everyone else?"

"Yes. He's learned our language, he's a good worker, does what he's told to do, does a job with the horses. But he doesn't read or write in our tongue. He doesn't have the same knowledge of the land as any of the others would. You're still training, aren't you?"

"One of these days, I'll have to give it up. But not yet. Not yet. I'm still an instructor."

"Well, then this is the favor I'm asking, and you have every right to tell me no."

"You want me to pick him?"

Stephan shook his head, "I have no right to ask you that. I only want you to at least consider him. Chances are, no one else will as soon as they realize where he's from. Will you at least do that?"

Atticus drummed his fingers across the thick knob on the end of his cane, staring past Stephan and out the small front window.

"You brought him with you?"

"I thought it'd be better for him to wait outside."

"So it is, so it is. Much better. If he really is what you say he is, I can promise you only this - where he comes from will make no difference to me. If his own merit makes him worth considering I don't see why his birthplace should change that." Atticus shifted his gaze back to the window, his fingers once more tapping a rhythm on the cane. "It might be good to have an outsider in the corps."

"Why's that?" Stephan leaned forward, resting his arms on the desk.

Atticus smiled. "Rumors, my friend, rumors. Nothing more than that. Shadows in the dark. The paranoid fancies of an old man, no doubt. But troubling, nonetheless. Very troubling."

"What kind of trouble?"

"Who can say? It's like trying to trap a shadow or ensnare a breeze. Beyond what I hear, there is no knowing." Atticus sighed. "We've known peace for several years. But there are those that miss the war. There are those that miss the chaos of war. They miss the power and profit it brought them."

"No one wants another war, Atticus. Maybe you spend too much time pouring over these papers and seeing shadows in places they're not."

"Perhaps. Perhaps." Atticus muttered, pushing his chair away from the desk and rising to his feet. "But not all wars are on the outside. Enough of this, though. You've kept the boy waiting long enough now and I'm sure I'm not the only business you had to attend to."

Chapter 3

AKI KICKED A CLUMP OF DIRT away and leaned back against the wall, his gaze intent on the road leading towards the castle. It was his last day to do as he liked in Bren. His last day before he took the first step to becoming a courier and he still had no clear idea of what to expect.

"You brought food, didn't you?" Kezi's voice came from directly behind him causing Aki to jump a little.

"Of course." Aki reached into the satchel he was carrying and pulled out a loaf of sweet bread. Tearing it in two and giving Kezi the larger piece, he sat down on an overturned crate and Kezi joined him.

"So, how long are you going to be here?" Kezi asked between mouthfuls.

"I'm staying." Aki answered, his eyes lighting up. "I'm going to be a courier, just like I wanted to be."

Kezi pulled her legs up and wrapped her arms around them, frowning.

"Aren't you happy for me? I'll be here all the time now."

"You'll be too busy to remember me."

"No I won't. I'll be able to buy you food more often."

Kezi turned toward him, smiling slowly. "I guess I won't mind more food. But you'll be working for the king."

"What's wrong with that?"

"Can you work for him and not tell on me?"

"You mean when you steal? I wouldn't tell on you for that." Aki met her eyes. In the three years he'd known Kezi, she was always too thin. Stealing meant food for her.

"You know, I used to steal too, when I had to. It's not a problem unless you get caught."

Kezi's smile grew when Aki pulled two apples out of his satchel. Instead of biting into it right away like she normally did with food, she rolled it back and forth between her hands. Her thin face turned thoughtful and sober.

"If you are staying here now, and you're not too busy to forget about me, maybe I could show you around sometime. There's so much of Bren that you never see when you come."

Aki, his own mouth full at the moment, nodded. He settled back against the wall behind them, content to watch the comings and goings of the people of Bren. Living here would be so different from Stephan's, he thought to himself. A group of horsemen coming up the road captured his attention and he sat up. It wasn't the noise they made, for that was barely noticeable in the crowded street. Nor was it the size of the group - there were many groups of half a dozen riders that made their way to the castle. It was their clothing, and their words as they spoke to one another. Aki understood them. And he knew at least one of them.

"Sasha!" Aki jumped up and called out when they were close. He was rewarded a moment later when the young man at the front of the group caught sight of him and pulled his horse up. A moment of bewilderment gave way to recognition on the man's face.

"Aki? Is that really you?" Sasha was off his horse and coming towards them. "I didn't expect to see you here."

"Of course it's really me," Aki laughed. "What are you doing here?"

Sasha glanced behind him to the other horsemen who were watching them with curiosity.

"Taking care of some business with King Darien. Look, I have to get going for now, but I'll see you around, alright?"

"Alright. I'll be here. I'm staying here now, actually."

"Oh?"

"I'm going to be a courier. Stephan's helping me."

"That's what you want to do, then? Spend your days riding around all alone. Good luck." Sasha started back to his horse. "I'll come find you when we're done."

Aki stared after them as they rode past. He hadn't needed to ask Sasha if he'd been successful. He was still alive. The men he rode with obviously deferred to him as their leader, their Chief.

"You know *him*?" Kezi, whom Aki had forgotten was next to him, asked.

"Yes. He's my brother." Aki frowned. "Actually, he's my uncle, who I thought was my brother because I was told that his father was my father and he wasn't really. I can't make myself think of him as my uncle, though."

"So you're related. I wish I didn't know that."

"Why?" Aki turned to her, noticing for the first time the change in her mood.

"Because I hate him. I belong to him."

"What are you talking about? No one belongs to him. He doesn't do that."

"He bought me in Karu and drug me here. If it weren't for him, I would still be back in my homeland, not scrounging for every bit of food I can here."

"Kez, I don't think he meant for you to end up like this." Aki picked up his satchel and slung it over his shoulder. "I should probably get going before Stephan comes looking for me."

"Fine." Kezi started toward a nearby alley. "You'll still share food with me, won't you, Aki? I don't hate you."

"Of course I will." Aki made a half-hearted attempt to smile and raised his hand in a brief wave.

The day dragged on after that until Aki thought he couldn't bear the boredom any longer. It wasn't until evening that he was able to throw the boredom off. Whatever business had been needing attended to was over and Aki was no longer left to his own devices.

The inside of the tavern was warm with the lingering summer heat. It was still early enough in the evening that the crowd was small and quiet. The smell of food hung heavy in the air and Aki waited rather impatiently for the arrival of Sasha and Hamo. Stephan, sitting across from him, was quieter than usual. Aki was on the verge of breaking the uncomfortable silence when the front door opened, ringing the little bell that dangled above it, and Hamo and Sasha entered.

"Sorry we kept you waiting," Hamo said as he sat down. "There was something we needed to take care of first."

"I think Aki's the only one who suffered for it." Stephan finally broke out of whatever troubled reverie he'd been stuck in and smiled. "Sasha, I think I can honestly say that I've never sat down to dinner with a Chief before."

"I hate to tell you, but you're not now either." Sasha grinned. Actually, Aki realized, Sasha hadn't stopped grinning since he'd followed Hamo in. "I've officially abdicated. I'm no one special anymore."

"Well, in that case, you wouldn't by chance be looking for work? I'm about to lose all my help."

"That's what Aki told me. Courier, huh?" Sasha turned to Aki.

"If I can make it. I'll find out tomorrow, I guess."

"Actually, you'll find out in about a week. You and all the others who've applied this year will spend a week working on some basics and after that your instructors will select. Whoever doesn't make that selection is out."

Aki's appetite deserted him. He stared down at the bowl of stew in front of him, the steam from it curling up into the air and carrying its savory scent with it. He picked his spoon up and pushed the food around with it. A whole week before he'd know. How was he supposed to get through that?

"Who was that you were with today?" Sasha asked him, drawing out of his anxiety.

"A friend of mine. Her name's Kezi." Aki had been hoping that he wouldn't have to say anything at all about her to Sasha.

"Really? Kezi? You're sure her name is Kezi?"

"You know her. At least, she said you did. She hates you."

Sasha's eyes widened. "For what? I never did anything to her. In fact, she tried to kill me."

"You bought her. You brought her here. At least, she said you did." Aki shifted in his chair. Accusing Sasha wasn't what he wanted to do.

"Boris bought her with the last of my money to throw suspicion off of us. And I gave her the choice of whether to come with us or stay where she was. She chose to come and took off as soon as we landed. I did nothing to hurt her or make her hate me. If anything, she's better off than any other girl sold in that auction."

"I know. I tried to tell her that."

Sasha shrugged and went back to eating.

"What would you have done to her if she hadn't run away?" Aki's curiosity got the better of him.

"Same thing I did with Dagmar, probably. I'd have set her free and found someplace for her to live."

Aki stopped stirring his food and finally took a bite. He'd managed, at least for a few minutes, to forget his own nerves. No doubt they would return tomorrow morning. While the other three talked amongst themselves, Aki stayed quiet. Stephan had said they would spend the first week working on the basics. What those were, Aki could only speculate.

Chapter 4

AKI'S FEET TOUCHED THE HARD packed dirt as he dismounted. He turned his head, trying to take everything in at once. Three long, gray stone buildings formed three sides of a square. Wooden doors broke up the stone at regular intervals, all of them opening out onto this dirt arena. The fourth side of the square, directly opposite the main entrance, was an open wooden stable. At least a dozen horses' heads hung over their stall doors watching the arrival of the newcomers.

Now that he'd taken in his surroundings, Aki turned his attention to the others who had arrived that morning. There were only six of them, all between fifteen and sixteen like him. And none of them looked any more comfortable than he did, which was a relief.

The entrance of several men interrupted a more thorough inspection of his fellow recruits. Scratching Sky's soft ear, Aki whispered, "This is it." Sky responded by rubbing her forehead against his arm.

One man broke away from the others and walked up and down the line of newcomers, his hands clasped behind his back.

"You all know why you're here so there's no need to go through all that. Presumably, all of you wish to serve as couriers for the king." He paused, scanning them once more as if expecting someone to argue. "And since that is what you are here for, you'll address me as Captain Lupin. The men behind him will be your instructors, if you are selected. As most of you already know, this first week is nothing more than a chance for these men to assess you."

Aki shifted at the reminder and glanced around at the others. None looked quite as nervous or unsettled as he was. "If, at the end of that week, an instructor selects you, you will move on in your training. If no instructor wants you, you go home. Simple as that."

Aki looked beyond Captain Lupin to the instructors. Without exception, all were older. They weren't exactly what he thought of when imagining a courier instructor. He'd expected them to be a little bit more like the young men who showed up at Stephan's. One of them, he noticed, was even walking with the help of a cane.

"You will have two instructors after selection. One of these men, who will be responsible for all of your academic learning - codes, map reading, and such. Your second one will be assigned, and they will be responsible for your field work. Between the two, they will determine if and when you will be tested and promoted. Now, you will be given the rest of the day to settle both you and your horse in. Rooms are assigned, normally two to a room but since we have an uneven number, one of you will have to room alone. Colin will show you where to put your horses and where your rooms are."

Captain Lupin stepped aside and a much younger man took his place. He motioned for them to follow him toward the stable. Aki didn't bother to hold Sky's reins as she followed him. Trained in Aruuk, she would follow him like a dog unless he dropped her reins to the ground.

"Where'd you get the horse, boy?"

Aki turned to see one of the instructors, the man with the cane, leaning against the wall of the stall.

"I brought her with me, sir."

The old man's eyes narrowed. "That's not an answer. Not an answer at all. Where are you from?"

"Up north, sir." Aki loosened Sky's girth and slid the saddle off her back.

"Vague. Still not really an answer, is it?"

Aki hesitated. Knowing that this man was one of the instructors making selections in a week didn't do anything for his own confidence. The second he told anyone where he was from was the second he could say goodbye to any hope of being picked. He looked up to find the old man staring at him still, his brown eyes boring into Aki.

"I'm from Aruuk and so is the horse." Aki admitted with reluctance when he realized that the man wasn't going anywhere without the truth.

"She's a good horse. A very good horse. Small but good." The man tapped his cane on the ground. "Did you train her?"

"No, sir. I wasn't allowed to train the horses when I was there, I just had to take care of them."

The man stood watching as Aki finished removing Sky's tack and hung it on the hooks meant for that purpose. Aki, normally quite at ease when doing anything around horses, found himself clumsy and uncertain. He splashed water on himself when he brought a bucket of it into the stall for Sky and fumbled the latch on the door when he was finally through. And all the while, the old man stood watching, his face impassive beneath the wrinkles that creased it.

A call from Colin put an end to the scrutiny as Aki hurried to join the others. Risking a glance over his shoulder, he saw the old man still standing there, still watching him.

Colin led the way inside and Aki forgot about the man as he took in his new surroundings. They were standing in a long hallway, the wooden floor of which creaked and groaned with every shift of weight. It would be almost impossible to sneak up or down the hallway. Colin stopped in front of the first unmarked wooden door and read two names off the paper in his hand. Aki tried to peek over the shoulders of those in front of him when the door opened, wanting to catch a glimpse of what to expect. Two more doors and Aki was standing alone with Colin.

"Aki Turston?" Colin looked up from the paper. "Any relation to Stephan?"

"Sort of. He adopted me." Aki started toward the door. It was likely just a coincidence that put his name there, but Aki couldn't rid himself of the notion that he was given a room by himself because of his nationality. When he was with Stephan and Alina, or Hamo and his family, or even Kezi the difference was not as acute. He'd been here less than half a day and already he felt it separating him from everyone else.

"He's a good man." Colin didn't seem to notice anything amiss. "Good luck."

"Thanks."

Aki set his things down and took stock of the room. Aside from two beds, two small sets of drawers and a single table with two chairs it was bare. The wooden floor matched the wood of the bed frames, drawers, table and chairs turning the entire room into one single shade of brown. Two small windows, one on either side of the fireplace and stone chimney, on the far wall looked out into the street that ran past the Courier Academy. He stood at the window, watching the people that went by for a few minutes before putting his own things away.

As much as Aki was dreading the first week, he was surprised by how little was actually expected of them. There were only two things that seemed to be of great importance to Captain Lupin and that was that his recruits kept to the schedule he laid out and took care of both their rooms and their horses. The men who would choose at the end of that time were always there, always hovering over their shoulders watching. Sometimes they would break away from their silent observation and actually address one of the trainees, as the old man had done the first day with Aki. By the end of the week, only one other instructor had approached Aki and he ended the conversation almost before it began when he heard where Aki was from.

"Are you ready for tomorrow?"

Aki, sitting in the common room with the others after supper, looked up from the paper he had been desperately trying to read and saw one of the other boys from his group sitting across from him. With bright red hair, Felix was hard to miss or forget. He also never seemed to notice Aki's accent.

"I guess so."

"I want Master Wehr to select me." Felix leaned forward on the table.

"You know their names?"

"Of course." Felix did not notice when Aki's face fell. "Everyone knows them."

"And why do you want Master Wehr to pick you? Does it matter who picks you?"

24

"Of course it matters. The better your instructor is, the better your position will be when you're promoted. And Master Wehr's the best. He's a legend among couriers. He served back when the old kings were alive and fighting." Felix leaned back again, clasping his hands together behind his head. "Being the best also makes him one of the hardest to please. Did you know, it's actually been three years since he selected anyone?"

Aki shook his head. The truth was, he didn't know anything at all about what Felix was talking about. It was on the tip of his tongue to ask who the old kings were and why serving them mattered, but that would surely send Felix away. So far, Felix had been the only one willing to say anything beyond polite pleasantries to him.

"He said none of them were worth his time. And he won't train anyone who isn't worth his time. He's never had a student fail. Which is part of what makes him a legend, I guess. Getting selected by him is a ticket to the best positions possible."

"What do you think they actually look for? They spent all week watching us, but we didn't really do anything."

"Who knows? Oscar and Archie got into a fight the other day, and I know they're both worried that the instructors might hold that against them."

Aki glanced over at the two Felix had named. He'd seen the entire fight from inside Sky's stall. Everyone else had, too. It was selfish, he knew, but he hoped that their fight would draw attention away from him in the selections. He might have a strange accent, but, thanks to his own upbringing, he knew how to stay small and avoid fights.

"I guess we'll find out tomorrow, won't we?" Aki folded up the paper in his hand. He was too tired to try anymore tonight.

Chapter 5

AKI RUBBED HIS EYES, trying to force them to stay open. Today of all days, he needed to be fully awake. But it was the importance of the day that had robbed him of sleep in the first place. It was impossible to relax when his fate hung in the balance. If he wasn't selected today...

Aki pushed the thought away. He couldn't bear to think about what it would mean to not be considered good enough to do the one thing, the only thing, that he'd wanted since he was capable of wanting.

When he was a slave, he knew he didn't get a choice. Even when he was Gundar's son, he had no control over his own direction. But here he did. Here he could want and dream and hope. He could also fail. And the possibility of failure hung over him like the gray heavy clouds of a storm.

Breakfast was a tense, solemn affair that morning. The usual banter that went on between the others was smothered by the importance of the day. Aki toyed with his food, his stomach too knotted up to eat. Felix, sitting next to him, dug his elbow into Aki's side. When Aki glanced over at him, Felix flashed him a nervous grin.

"I can't wait to get this over with. I just want to know who I'll be stuck training with for the next three or four years."

"You sound like you're sure you'll get picked." Aki raised a quizzical eyebrow.

"Of course I'm sure. My Father's a nobleman. They won't want to make him angry."

"Makes sense, I suppose." Aki started up from the table. Aside from heading into dangerous waters about family, the conversation was just another reminder of how much he didn't fit here. Although he hadn't spoken to them, a brief scrutiny of the others at the table showed that they shared Felix's firm belief in their own selections.

For being late summer, the sun was still quite hot when it rose. Aki shifted from one foot to the other, trying not to meet the eyes of the others as they waited in the dirt arena between buildings. A door opening and the sound of voices brought all seven boys to attention. Aside from Captain Lupin and the seven older men who had become a familiar sight around the compound, another seven men, all wearing the coat and badge of an active courier, entered.

Captain Lupin separated himself from the entourage and cleared his throat. It was an unnecessary gesture for everyone had already fallen silent in anticipation.

"Today is, of course, selection day. Before we get into that, however, I want to remind you all that just because you are selected does not guarantee you a future as a courier. At any time during your training, your instructors may reach the conclusion that you are not fit for the job. If that is the case, chances are that you're done." Captain Lupin paused, clearing his throat again. "We always start selections with the senior instructor and work our way down. This year will be no different. Atticus Wehr, the choice is yours."

Captain Lupin stepped aside a little, allowing Atticus Wehr to come forward. Aki choked back his surprise when the old man with his cane limped a few steps up. After hearing Felix talk about him, the frail looking man was disappointing. Aki stared down at the ground, trying to slow the hammering of his own heart. He wasn't going to be picked. Not by Master Wehr, not by anyone. The others weren't even worried about it. They knew they were in. They always had, he knew now.

"Aki Turston." Atticus Wehr's voice wasn't loud, but it carried and there was a collective gasp of surprise at his words.

Aki's head snapped up in stunned confusion. Everyone was staring at him. And everyone mirrored his own shock.

Everyone, except Atticus Wehr. Aki stared at him as he stepped back with the others, not quite believing.

The rest of the selections went by without Aki paying any attention at all. His mind was racing, going over Felix's words from the night before and trying to grasp that he had truly been selected.

Captain Lupin saying his name finally got his attention again and Aki looked up to find everyone staring at him again.

"Master Wehr will be responsible for all of the academic side of your training. Jasper Kunz will be your instructor in field work."

"Yes, sir." Aki followed Captain Lupin's finger and found the man. Jasper, in turn, acknowledged Aki with a brief nod.

Captain Lupin went through the remaining assignments quickly. "You will now meet with your instructors and they will take over all of your training. That includes your schedules. I'd suggest you adhere to those."

Avoiding Felix's eyes, Aki started toward the two men he was assigned to.

"I'm going to keep this very simple, unless Jasper disagrees." Atticus's voice, though firm, had the scratchy quality of age. "You will arrive at my place no later than eight o'clock every morning. If Jasper has field work for you, he will tell me and I will excuse your absence for that time. Agreed?"

The last word Atticus addressed to Jasper, who shrugged and nodded.

"Very well, very well. Let's get on with this then." Atticus started to walk away. Aki hesitated. "Come on. Come on. I haven't got all day to stand around here."

Aki half ran to catch up.

"Where, exactly, are we going?" Aki asked after several minutes of walking. They were outside the Couriers Academy now, out on the streets of Bren, although Aki hadn't been paying close enough attention to know where in Bren they were. "And what am I supposed to call you?"

"To my home, boy, to my home." Atticus did not slow his pace or turn his head to look at Aki. "And you may call me Master Wehr."

"Master? Like you own me?"

Atticus stopped abruptly and Aki nearly ran into him. Turning, he searched Aki's face with such intensity that Aki stepped back a little. For the first time, Aki noticed the man's height, or rather lack of it. Aki wasn't tall. He wasn't even average. Spending the first ten years of his life half-starved and scrounging for every bit of food he could get his hands on had taken its toll on his growth. But he was looking ever so slightly down on Atticus.

"Strange notions you have, boy. Very strange." Atticus turned around and started forward again, his cane thumping with every step. "You may call me Master because that is what I am, a master of my trade."

"I see. I'm sorry, Master Wehr. I wasn't trying to anger you."

"I am not angry. Not angry at all. Now, come."

Aki decided that silence was probably the best route for him at the moment. He didn't want to ruin his very first day.

The sign on the door was familiar. Aki stared at it hard while Master Wehr produced a key from his pocket and unlocked the door.

"Stephan visited you, didn't he?"

"He did, he did. Come in."

Aki stepped inside, taking in the dozens of candles that were burning at various levels. It all made sense now. He was here because Stephan had asked for Master Wehr to pick him, not because Master Wehr had seen anything worthwhile in him on his own. It hurt. More than Aki could have imagined it would.

"What's wrong with you, boy?" Atticus was shrewd enough not to miss the change in Aki's countenance.

"You picked me for him, didn't you? You picked me because he's your friend. That's why he came here, isn't it? That's why he wanted me to wait outside."

Atticus came close, and closer still, until he was standing mere inches from Aki. Aki leaned back away from him.

"Do you want to know why I chose you?"

Aki, quite sure that he was angry now and wishing he'd just kept his own mouth shut, nodded.

"I picked you because you were the only one out there today who thought you would fail. The others, they knew it didn't matter. They've known all week and they acted like it. They weren't afraid of being sent home. You were. I can work with someone who sounds a little different from everyone else. I can't work with pride. Not even talented pride."

"So Stephan didn't ask you?"

"He asked me only this - that I would be willing to look past your birthplace if I saw something of value in you. And that was a fair request. He did not ask for me to choose you. He would not have done that. He is not that sort of man." Atticus stepped back and made his way around the cluttered desk that dominated the front room. "Now sit, sit. You have a great deal of talking to do and I have a great deal of listening."

Aki lowered himself into the chair. Master Wehr's words soothed his wounded feelings enough for his curiosity to take over.

"What is it you want me to talk about, Master Wehr?"

"Yourself. I want to know about where you are from. I want to know what sort of connection you have to that homeland. I want to know why you left it, and why you are here. I want to know why you wish to be a courier."

Aki ran his tongue over his lips. He didn't talk about his past, not with anyone. Stephan knew only as much as he needed to know. Sasha knew more, but not much. And Kezi, of course, had only an inkling - the bits and pieces that had found their way out of him when she was around.

Atticus waved an impatient hand in the air. "Go on. Who were you before you were Aki Turston?"

"I don't really want to tell you. It doesn't matter. I'm not that person anymore."

"You will always be that person. We are many people in our lives, but none of them ever fully die. Now, begin."

"I don't know where."

"Who were your parents? That's easy enough to start with."

Aki shook his head slightly, but knew he couldn't refuse. Master Wehr was his instructor, and he had to obey him.

"I don't know who my mother was or where she came from. I don't even know what her name was," Aki said, his voice soft. His fingers picked at a loose splinter off the desk. "She was a slave girl, gifted to my father. My father was Anton, a son of the late Chief Gundar of Aruuk. I was their mistake and the reason they died. My father was supposed to kill me. Instead he let me live and he and my mother kept my birth a secret. Chief Gundar killed them for that." Aki had asked Sasha once during that first winter if he remembered anything about Anton's death and although Sasha admitted that he did, he refused to tell Aki any of it. Aki could only imagine how horrible it must have been.

"Go on," Atticus said when Aki stopped.

"I don't want to," Aki protested. When Atticus only stared at him, he sighed and went on. "Chief Gundar let me live, because when he gave my mother the choice between her life and mine she chose me and for whatever reason he decided to honor that promise to her, but he kept me as a slave. I was raised by whoever happened to be in charge of the slave born children, and that changed all the time. I didn't know anything about my parents at the time."

"You were a slave? You carry a brand, then? Let me see it."

"No. He didn't brand any slave children until they turned ten. My tenth year, I was waiting to be branded with some of the others when Chief Gundar sent for me. I don't know why, but he lied to me and told me I was his son. He moved me into his house and started training me as one of his sons, but I got in trouble a lot."

Atticus' eyebrows went up. "What did you get in trouble for?"

"Asking too many questions, annoying him, not obeying fast enough, being clumsy." Pretty much for just being alive, Aki thought wryly but didn't say out loud. In the years separating him from his life in Aruuk, he'd often wondered what possessed Gundar to maintain the lie of his origin. Gundar never acted without purpose but what purpose he'd derived from pretending Aki was his son, Aki couldn't fathom.

"And how did you come here?"

"The battle in the mountains, you know." Atticus nodded once. "There was a traitor..."

"Sasha Gundarson, correct?"

"Yes. Father found out about him after we lost. He found out that he was alive and where he was living. He took me and Lars, my brother..."

"Who was not really your brother?"

"Yes, but I thought he was. We were friends, sort of, and he took us with him and came here. He found Sasha and tried to murder him. He failed, and died instead." Funny how just a few words summed up the hours of what had to be absolute horror for Sasha and Boris and Ophelia, Aki thought. For his own part, he'd done everything he could to not remember that night or the days leading up to it.

"Leaving you behind."

"Well, yes, but I sort of almost died too. Chief Gundar didn't manage to kill Sasha, but he did torture his brother Boris to death. Sasha was obviously very angry and he almost killed me, he almost beat me to death. It was the girl he was with that stopped him." Aki hated talking about that almost as much as he hated talking about his parents. "In the end, though, he took care of me. He made me well again and looked after both Lars and I. When he went back to Aruuk in the spring to take his place as the new Chief, he let me choose whether or not to go with him. I stayed."

"Why?"

"Why would I go back? There was nothing to go back to. I hated my life there. Even when I was the Chief's son."

"I see, I see." Atticus leaned back in his chair, staring past Aki and out the window.

Aki, for his part, let out a relieved breath. Master Wehr wasn't pressing him for any other details. So far, the man knew no more than Stephan or Sasha. When Atticus continued to stare out the window and say nothing, Aki got impatient.

"Why did you want to know all that?"

Atticus smiled, deepening the wrinkles on his face, and continued looking beyond Aki.

"I wanted to know all of that because I wanted to know if you were really on our side. You will learn things that any of our enemies would gladly pay for. I need to trust you before I teach you. Now, I am going to ask you one last question about your life in Aruuk, and then we will not formally speak of it again."

Aki tensed. Something in Master Wehr's tone hinted at the uncomfortable nature of the question.

"What was the worst thing that was done to you while you were a slave?" Atticus turned his eyes from the window and fixed them on Aki, as if his gaze alone could draw the answer out.

"Don't ask me that, please, Master Wehr. I can't."

To Aki's surprise Atticus didn't press him. In fact, the intensity of his gaze softened and he nodded his head slightly.

"Then tell me this, do you hate the one who did it to you?"

"He's not here to hate anymore."

"He's dead?"

Aki nodded. It wasn't quite true. But Aki didn't care about the truth at that moment. He couldn't tell. If he told, he would be admitting to himself that it had actually happened and he'd spent years convincing himself it hadn't. If he admitted the man still lived, he would have to acknowledge that what he would not allow himself to believe happened could happen again. It was easier to believe the man was dead. Easier to believe such a comforting lie.

"Then there is no one you would seek vengeance on were you given the chance?"

"No. No one," Aki whispered, and hoped Master Wehr would not press him.

"Thank you, Aki, for your honesty. Now, I think we can get started."

Chapter 6

A SHEET OF PAPER, BLOTCHED and spattered with ink, lay in front of Aki. One hand cupped his chin, while the other held a quill.

"You can't learn it all in one day. You can't." Atticus moved around the room, snuffing out the many candles. Aki looked up, startled to find it so dark. "It's time for you to go. You'll need rest if you want to learn anything at all."

Aki set the quill down and stretched, massaging his stiff neck with one hand. After his conversation with Master Wehr, he had thrown himself into his work, eager to forget and lose himself in the effort of learning. He had no idea so many hours had passed. Now, stifling a yawn, he realized Master Wehr was right. He was tired. His head hurt from the hours of focus. His eyes burned from studying so hard. Blinking several times, Aki pushed his chair away from the desk and stood.

"Don't forget - eight o'clock. No later than eight o'clock." Atticus held the door open.

"Eight o'clock." Aki repeated, nodding, as he stepped out into the mostly dark street.

The door shut softly behind him and Aki started off. He made it to the end of the street before realizing that he had no idea where he was going. Although he had been to Bren several times over the last three years with Stephan, they always went to the same places. Atticus Wehr's home wasn't near the main road that Aki was familiar with.

Aki shut his eyes, trying to replicate the route they had taken from the Couriers Academy to here. It was useless. There were too many turns, too many times Aki hadn't been paying attention. Groaning in frustration, Aki thought about going back to Master Wehr's and asking him, but when he'd given it a moment's consideration, he decided it was a bad idea. He wasn't sure enough of the man yet.

"You look lost," Kezi said, stepping out of the shadows and startling Aki.

"What are you doing?"

"Waiting for you. I was beginning to wonder if you were ever going to leave."

Aki started down the street, hoping that it was the right direction, then paused and turned back toward Kezi.

"Wait. How'd you know where I was?"

Kezi shrugged. "It wasn't hard. I just followed you when you left earlier."

"Why?"

"You've been here an entire week and haven't seen me once. I just wanted to tell you I was right. You won't have time to visit."

"You sat out here all day just to prove you were right?"

Kezi shrugged again, tossing her hair over her shoulder. "I like being right."

"You're crazy. But it won't be like that all the time. Now that we have our instructors, we'll be leaving the Academy more, and I will have time. I can't spend all my time studying, can I?" Aki laughed a little. "Do you have any idea how to get back?"

"I might."

"Please, Kez. I'll make it up to you, I promise."

"A full meal?"

"Sure."

"Come on then." Kezi started off, and Aki tried to pay more attention than he had earlier with Atticus. In the dark it was harder. The street lamps only illuminated the larger streets, and for some reason, Kezi appeared to be deliberately avoiding those. She also seemed intent on steering away from the few other people who were out.

"I don't think this is the way Master Wehr brought me," Aki finally gave voice to his growing concern. They'd been walking a lot longer than he remembered them doing that morning.

Kezi laughed. "I'm sure it's not."

If she was trying to set Aki's mind at rest, her tone utterly failed. The sound of the sea, always present in Bren, increased, and the night air tasted of salt.

"Kezi, where are we going?"

"Didn't I tell you I'd show you around?" Kezi laughed again. "You don't have to look so worried, Aki. This won't get you in trouble. None of the other recruits stay in all night either."

"How do you know?"

"I watched for you, and while I was watching, I saw some of the others." Kezi rounded the corner and stopped. She swept her arm in an arc. "Look! No matter how many times I've seen it, it's still spectacular. And night is the only time you can see it like this."

Aki stepped up next to her. It was spectacular. Black water touched black sky in the distant horizon and the twinkling lights of a million stars in the sky were mirrored in the gentle waves of the sea. Ships bobbed up and down at their moorings, water slapping against their wooden hulls.

"You know you're not showing me anything new, right?" Aki whispered. "I've seen the sea before."

"I know. I just like coming down here at night. It reminds me of home."

"Do you actually miss it?"

"Of course I miss it. I don't think you'd be a normal person not to miss your home."

"Oh. I never miss mine."

The shuffling of feet behind him made Aki turn and look. A movement in the shadows caught his eye. Sounds of a scuffle, a cry that was cut off as soon as it began, carried across the night air. Aki stiffened. There was a reason Stephan never came down to this part of Bren after dark, or ever if he could avoid it.

"Don't, Aki." Kezi's voice held a warning note. "Just let it be. There's nothing you can do about it anyway."

"I should get back."

"If that's what you want." Kezi sighed and turned back away from the sea. "You'll have to come with me again, though. Your free time is your own. I know. I asked one of the others."

"I will." Aki answered absently. Free time that was all his own. He'd never had that before. Not as a slave, not as the Chief's son, not even with Stephan.

This time Kezi led him right and the long low building that marked the front of the Academy lay before him. Kezi disappeared once more into the shadows, so quickly and quietly that Aki was a little unnerved by it. For all of her hating it here in Bren, Kezi had certainly learned how to live on the streets.

Chapter 7

AKI RAN A FRUSTRATED HAND through his hair. He was seated on a high stool in front of an equally high desk that was pushed up against a smoke smudged window. Resting one elbow on the edge of the desk and holding his head in that hand, he poured over the work Master Wehr had assigned.

Alina's attempts at teaching him to read and write had been sporadic, mostly due to the fact that Aki inevitably found better, easier things to spend his time on. At the moment, he could think of a whole list of things he'd rather be doing.

For two weeks he'd shown up on Master Wehr's doorstep right on time. He'd labored tirelessly, but it was dull work, and his progress was not significant enough to encourage him. The window faced the street, and more than once, Aki found himself staring out it wishing that Jasper would appear and whisk him away for field work. So far, Jasper had disappointed.

The thumping of Master Wehr's cane coming across the floor made Aki turn around on his stool.

"Come," Master Wehr said, heading toward the door.

Aki slid off the stool and grabbed the light jacket he'd hung by the door. Whatever Master Wehr had in mind, if it wasn't slogging through stacks of papers that were, as Master Wehr put it, "Begging to be read," then it was an improvement.

Aki took a deep breath as they stepped outside. Compared to the smoky, stuffy front room of Master Wehr's, the fresh air was invigorating. Master Wehr didn't pause outside and Aki had to jog several steps to catch up with him. For an old man who limped along with a cane Master Wehr could certainly move fast, Aki thought as he fell into step beside him.

"Where are we going? Does Jasper want me for something? You know, he hasn't actually taken me out for any field work yet. Is that normal? Felix has already been out three times. He just came back again yesterday."

"Would you like me to actually answer your questions, or are you going to just keep talking?" Master Wehr finally interrupted.

"Sorry, Master Wehr. I didn't mean to say so much."

"We are going for a walk through town. I have errands to run that you need to accompany me for. Jasper has nothing to do with this. Typically, I would say it is strange that you have not gone out at least once. I imagine he's waiting to see how you do with me before doing anything himself."

"Why is he waiting?" Aki knew the answer. He was sure he knew it. But he wanted to hear it from someone else.

Atticus sighed and slowed imperceptibly. "You are from Aruuk. No one wanted to be assigned to you. He considers himself very unlucky to have been given you."

"Just because I'm from Aruuk doesn't mean I'm bad. No one thinks of Sasha that way. He's everyone's hero here."

"That, Aki, is not true."

"What do you mean? If it weren't for him, you'd have been destroyed. I've heard the story."

"True. But he was a traitor. He put his own conscience before his ruler, and that frightens people who want power. You cannot control a man who obeys his conscience first and his leader second."

Aki considered Master Wehr's words before deciding that the conversation was going too deep for his liking at the moment. "So, what exactly do you think Jasper is waiting for?"

"He is waiting for you to fail me."

"Am I? I'm trying as hard as I can. I can't make myself learn any faster. My head feels like it's going to burst as it is by the end of every day. It's just so much harder than I thought it would be."

"Did I say you were?"

Aki thought for a moment before shaking his head. "No, Master Wehr, I guess you didn't. I'm sorry. What happens if he never takes me out? Is he allowed to do that?"

"Instructors have a great deal of liberty in what they are and are not allowed to do. However, it must be through an agreement between both. As long as I wish to keep teaching you, he must as well. If both of us decide it is no longer worth our time, which has happened before, then you would be out."

"Just like that? How many times have you decided someone wasn't worth your time? Felix said you went three years without choosing anyone at all. Is that true?"

Rather than answering Aki's questions, Atticus turned a street corner and paused in front of a shop door. Aki looked up at the sign that hung over the doorway. It bore an engraved picture of a quill and inkpot above the words.

"Read it," Master Wehr said.

Aki's face wrinkled up as he concentrated on the letters. "Monica Cravin - Scrivener and Supplier."

"Very good." Master Wehr pushed the door open.

"What are we doing here?"

Aki looked around as soon as they were inside. A fluttering noise followed by the twittering of a bird turned his attention to a cage hanging off to the side of the doorway. A pair of songbirds shared a perch inside it.

"Good day, Mr. Wehr," a woman's high-pitched voice called out from the back room. A moment later, the door between rooms filled with the very round figure of that woman. Aki stared for longer than he should have before remembering that it was rude. He'd never seen anyone so corpulent. Her neck seemed to have disappeared entirely. She bustled forward with the air of someone used to running their own business. "What can I do for you today? And," her eyes seemed to fall on Aki for the first time, "who is this? Don't tell me, you finally took one?"

"Miss Cravin, you are correct, as usual. This is my trainee, Aki Turston."

"Fortunate young man." Monica Cravin smiled at Aki who looked up long enough to return it briefly. "You listen to whatever Atticus tells you and you'll turn out just fine. Understand?"

"I understand."

Miss Cravin leaned forward onto the counter that separated them, her pudgy face scrunching up as she studied him. "You're not from here."

"No, ma'am."

Miss Cravin looked from Aki to Atticus. Something about Atticus' face warned her against pressing any further.

"What is it I can get for you, Atticus?"

"The usual, nothing more. Just the usual."

Miss Cravin disappeared into the back room again and Aki relaxed and went back to looking the room over. Similar to Master Wehr's workspace, there were papers everywhere. Unlike Master Wehr's workspace, there was no order to the papers. Master Wehr kept his in neat stacks, divided by content. Monica Cravin tended to have them strewn about haphazardly. Beyond the papers that were scattered loose, there were the ones that hung from the walls. These were almost all accompanied by a picture. Aki stepped away from the counter and closer to these.

"What do they say?" Aki knew it was a mistake as soon as the words left his mouth.

"Read them."

Aki, his back to Master Wehr and his face safely hidden from his sight, scowled and made a face. He started to turn away when one in particular caught his eye. The picture on it was more than a drawing, it was painted in vibrant, enticing colors. And Aki understood what Master Wehr meant when he said that words could beg to be read. The words on the paper screamed silently for him to read them, to decipher their meaning. He had to know what it said, and Master Wehr wasn't going to do it for him.

"Harvest Festival." He whispered them in triumph a minute later. "What's a 'Harvest Festival'?

"A celebration of the harvest. The better the harvest, the greater the celebration. People get together. There's feasting and usually music, dancing, games." Aki turned to him, a single eyebrow raised in disbelief. "Didn't you celebrate anything in Aruuk?"

"Well, I guess we did. There used to be a celebration after the Spring Market, but it wasn't good. It wasn't fun at all, at least not for the slaves, especially the girls. I guess the raiders had fun, but it wasn't like that."

"I see," Master Wehr said, his face troubled.

"I said too much, didn't I? I'm sorry."

"You are free to say whatever you like, so long as it is not treason. I would advise you not to mention those sorts of things in public, though."

Aki turned back to the paper hanging on the wall. "Do you go to this festival? Is it fun?"

"I'm too old for such things. But I suppose, when I was younger I did find them fun."

Monica Cravin reentered at that moment, preventing Aki from questioning Master Wehr further although he would have liked to. Miss Cravin had a parcel in her hands that she set on the counter.

"There you are, Mr. Wehr, the usual," Miss Cravin said, sending one last searching glance Aki's way when he picked the parcel up.

They were only a few steps away from the shop when Aki opened his mouth to speak again. For once, Master Wehr put a hand up to stop him. Thrown off by the uncharacteristic gesture, Aki frowned, puzzled. Master Wehr generally exhibited far more patience for Aki's questions and conversations than pretty much anyone else in his life. That, if nothing else, endeared him a little to the old man.

"What is a courier, Aki?"

"Someone who carries messages."

"They do. They do. And that is a very important task. It is not, however, their only purpose." Master Wehr spoke as he walked and Aki found himself torn between listening and trying to memorize where they were going. After not knowing how to get from Master Wehr's to the Couriers Academy and back again, Master Wehr had made it very clear that he was to pay more attention when he was out. "The King is a powerful man. But his power does not come from himself or his position alone. It comes also from those who serve him. You've already sworn to protect the secrets of the Courier Corps. When you are promoted you will swear a new oath, binding your allegiance to the King.

You will become, not just a messenger, but the eyes and ears of the king."

"Sorry, I don't think I quite understand."

"A courier goes many places. He travels around more than pretty much anyone else in the kingdom. He is in contact with noblemen and other important people. He hears many rumors, some more true than others. He detects the mood of a place - whether the people are happy or upset, afraid or restless. Some of that can be ignored, and with time you will learn to decide that. Some of it will fester and become a problem for the king. Those are the things we listen and watch out for. That is what we make sure the king hears about."

"Sort of like spies?"

"A little. A little." Master Wehr hesitated. "Now, listen. Don't talk. Just listen. What are people talking about? What is foremost in their minds?"

Master Wehr's final words came as they entered the market square. Although shops lined many streets, the market square was the hub of commerce. It wasn't really a square, which Aki always found a little disappointing. It was a stretch of the main road that was wider than the other parts, allowing outdoor booths to be set up during the day. Things like fresh fruits and vegetables that couldn't be stocked ahead of time in shops were sold here. It was one of Aki and Kezi's favorite places to go. Aki always came away with less money than he started with, and Kezi always came away with more.

Standing behind Master Wehr as he went from booth to booth, Aki did as he said. It wasn't hard for him to shamelessly listen in on people. He'd made a habit of it while he was a slave. It helped to know the mood of those over him. So long as he kept his head down and didn't react, no one was ever the wiser.

It was late afternoon before Master Wehr was ready to return home. Aki, his arms laden with packages and parcels and his mind full of what he'd overheard, had been ready quite a while before.

"What did you hear?"

"People talking about how good the harvest was this year. The festival coming up. Someone's wedding."

Master Wehr nodded. "And given all you heard today, what would you say of the morale of the people?"

"They're happy, I guess. Content, at least. The things they complained about weren't big or important. One woman was complaining that her husband spends too many evenings at the tavern."

Master Wehr nodded, impressed. "That was more than most pick up their first time."

"I sort of already knew how to do that." Aki admitted. "It was the easiest way to stay out of trouble, you know. If you already knew someone was in a bad mood, you knew to be extra careful around them."

"Then in that at least, you are ahead."

Aki grinned. "So, if part of our job is to be the King's eyes and ears, we should probably spend some time out with people, right?"

"Are you asking for permission? You know you can go out whenever you like, so long as it is on your time and not mine or Jasper's."

"I was just making sure."

Chapter 8

A FIST POUNDED ON THE door, rousing Aki from his study. Laying on his back, with his head at the foot of his bed and his feet propped up on the wall above the headboard and a book in his hands, Aki contemplated ignoring it.

It was the first day of the week, the only day they had off. Off, as Atticus had explained it, was really just another word for a day to catch up on all the work that he hadn't gotten done during the week. In three weeks, he'd always had plenty to fill up his off day. The knock was repeated with more force. Sighing, Aki tossed the book aside and swung his feet down onto the floor.

The first thing he saw when he cracked the door open was a mop of bright red hair.

"Come on, Aki," Felix said. "Let's do something fun."

The book completely forgotten now, Aki waited only long enough to lace his boots up and throw on his jacket. Felix apparently didn't hold a grudge against him for being chosen by Master Wehr. He wondered if it was possible for Felix to hold a grudge. He'd yet to see him be anything other than painstakingly polite and courteous.

"What do you want to do?" Aki asked as they made their way down the hall toward the door.

"Did you know we're allowed to use any of the horses stabled here?"

"No. I didn't. What do you have in mind?"

"Well, first, we're going to try them out. And then we're going to take our own out of town and race them. And when we've decided who has the best horse, we're going out to the festival."

"That's today?"

"It's all week, but we're all going tonight."

"Everyone?"

Felix nodded.

"They actually want me to come along?" Time hadn't made him any new friends amongst his fellow recruits.

"Sure, why not?"

Outside now, Aki could see that Felix and he were the last ones to arrive. The other five were already gathered around the stables and they were laughing about something.

"Here they are!" Archie caught sight of Aki and Felix approaching and the laughter faded out. "Ready? Who wants to go first?"

The group fell into an awkward silence, no one wanting to be the first to volunteer.

"I think Aki should go first." Oscar said, smiling at Aki in a way that he couldn't quite read. "What do you say?"

Aki watched as six pairs of eyes turned to him. Feigning indifference and nonchalance, he shrugged.

"We already picked the horse out and got him ready." Oscar gestured to the animal standing saddled in the nearest stall. "Try him out and see what you think. I'll go next."

The others parted so that he could approach the stall. Aki ran his eyes over the animal. He'd noticed it before when he was taking care of Sky. Big and heavy, built more as a war horse than as a couriers, he'd wondered why it was even here. Aki slid the bolt back that held the door shut and reached for the horse's bridle to lead him out. The horse danced sideways, its head in the air, as Aki led it out of the stall. The others stepped back even further, spreading out along the stable wall to watch. Aki caught sight of Oscar and Archie exchanging a whisper and suspicion flared up within him. Something was off. He glanced at them again and caught Oscar's smirk before turning his attention to the horse.

Stephan would have told him not to get on it. Stephan would have said the horse wasn't safe. But Stephan wasn't here. Aki could ride. He could ride better than most. Aki took a deep breath. He couldn't back down now, no matter what Stephan would have said. Gathering the reins and a fistful of the horse's man in one hand and sliding his left foot into the stirrup, he pulled himself up. Before he even settled onto the horse's back, he felt the animal's muscles tense and bunch up beneath him.

The horse bucked.

Aki's hold on him was useless as the horse sent him into the air. For a brief moment, Aki felt suspended in the air, and then he was falling. The ground came up to meet him at an alarming speed. A loud crack rang in his ears as he hit the ground. Stunned, the wind knocked out of him, Aki lay for several seconds before the pain washed over him in waves. His ears were ringing. Black spots floated in his vision. From somewhere far away a voice was calling his name and Aki tried to move. He tried to push himself up on his arm but his arm refused to work and the action sent pain roaring through him.

"Aki, don't move." The voice that had been calling his name was closer now, although the ringing in his ears still made it difficult to understand. "Are you alright?"

Aki blinked several times, trying to rid his eyes of the black dots. In spite of the pain, Aki was tempted to laugh at the question. He was not alright, and he thought it was pretty obvious. He tried to sit up again.

"You're arm, it's..." It was Felix leaning over him, his face wrought with worry.

Aki turned his head enough to get a glimpse. Even with his impaired vision, he could see what Felix was talking about. Halfway between his wrist and elbow, his arm bent at an unnatural, grotesque angle. Worse than that was the jagged bone that tore through the skin and the blood now spilling onto the ground.

"It's broken," Aki finished for him, staring at the arm as if it was attached to anyone but him, watching the blood puddle on the hard dirt beneath him with a strange detachment considering the fact that every nerve in that limb was on fire.

"It's really broken. This is bad." Felix slid his arm beneath Aki and raised him to his feet. Aki gasped and nearly fell over again.

The other boys were there too, Aki saw, huddled around him. They slowly stepped back as Felix got him all the way onto his feet, giving him space. Their faces mirrored Felix's worry but there was something else there as well. Guilt, Aki realized. It wasn't an accident. Oscar didn't even look concerned, just smugly pleased, and that irritated Aki. They had set him up and he'd fallen for it, but he wasn't going to show them how much he hurt. That, at least, he could keep to himself. He'd had more than enough practice in Aruuk. Pushing Felix's hand away and cradling his broken arm in his whole arm, Aki staggered away. It would have been easier if his head wasn't spinning and his eyes would work properly. He'd made it halfway across the dirt arena when he heard footsteps running up behind him.

"Wait, Aki. Let me help you." Felix caught up with him easily.

"I'm fine."

"Uh...you're clearly not. Doesn't it hurt?"

"Not that bad," Aki lied through gritted teeth.

"I didn't have anything to do with that," Felix whispered low enough that there was no chance for anyone to overhear him. "You have to believe that."

Aki didn't answer. It was taking all his concentration to stay on his feet. When Felix put a steadying hand on his elbow he didn't pull away. He couldn't have, no matter how badly he wanted to.

"Where are you going anyway?"

"My room."

"Aki, you have a bone sticking out of your arm. You're bleeding all over the place. You need a doctor. Maybe we should tell Captain Lupin?"

"Just get me to my room, and then I don't care what you do," Aki rasped out. He didn't think he'd make it even that far but traveling to a doctor was out of the question.

His ears were slowly starting to return to normal, the ringing fading. His eyes, however, were no better by the time Felix pulled open his door and half dragged him to his bed. Aki lowered himself onto the mattress, suppressing a moan as his broken arm shifted slightly.

Felix stood watching him for a minute, chewing on his lower lip, clearly torn about what action to take. At last, he said, "I'm going to get help."

Aki ignored him as the pain became more acute, consuming all of his attention and thought. He barely noticed the door shut behind Felix. Alone, he no longer fought to conceal the depth of his pain. His arm was screaming with it, his head was spinning with it. There were only a handful of other times in his life when he'd been in such agony.

Now, staring down at the exposed bone, the torn skin, the blood that still flowed freely, a lightheaded queasiness washed over him. He blinked, trying to steady himself. It was a lot of blood. His blood. He went cold. He bent over and vomited. The black spots filled his eyes and the last thing Aki saw was the floor getting close, fast.

"What happened?"

Aki winced at the sound of the man's voice. It was Captain Lupin, and he sounded angry. Aki forced his eyes open. He was still lying on the floor, which meant the others had just gotten here and he probably hadn't been out for more than a few minutes. Captain Lupin, Felix, and a stranger were all staring down at him.

"We were trying out some of the horses and Aki was thrown off, Captain," Felix answered, and Aki was glad of it. He didn't think he could actually speak at the moment. Actually, he was quite certain he couldn't. His mouth felt like cotton.

The stranger, a middle-aged man who had a leather bag in his hands, pushed the other two out of the way.

"However it came to be, I think we can discuss that later. He's still losing blood."

So that's why I passed out, Aki thought to himself. He tried to sit up but couldn't manage. Captain Lupin and the man Aki assumed was a doctor lifted him up and laid him on the bed. Aki stifled a cry, biting down on his lip hard enough to draw blood.

The doctor pulled the broken limb away from his body to inspect it and Aki clamped his teeth together harder as another wave of lightheadedness threatened him. If it were just the doctor in the room, he might have given into the pain and cried. But with both Captain Lupin and Felix watching, he couldn't. He would not have stories getting out about how weak he was, not after what had happened today.

"Get him something to bite down on." The doctor turned to a wide-eyed Felix, who nodded and disappeared from Aki's sight. Pulling a chair over, the doctor sat down and took hold of Aki's arm once more.

"What are you going to do?" Aki managed to whisper although he was pretty sure he knew the answer.

"I have to reset it and probably stitch it closed where it tore out." The doctor's hands were busy while he talked, tying a strip of leather he'd pulled out of his bag onto Aki's arm a few inches above the break, and he barely gave Aki a glance. "I'll give you something that will help with the pain. It won't take it all away but..."

"I can't have it."

"Why not? Trust me, boy, you'll want it."

"Trust me, I know I'll want it. But it makes me sick," Aki said.

"Ah, I understand." The doctor gave him a sympathetic smile. He took something from Felix's hands and put it in Aki's mouth. The taste of leather filled his mouth and he grimaced. "Bite on this, it might help. Captain?"

Captain Lupin nodded and came forward. He rested one hand on Aki's shoulders and gripped Aki's arm with the other. Aki tried to draw in a deep breath, but it was shaky and shuddering and didn't relieve the tension that was building inside of him the way he'd hoped it would. Out of the corner of his eye he could see the doctor laying things out on the bed next to him. And then the doctor was turning toward him, taking his broken arm in his hands.

"This is going to hurt, but I'll be as careful and quick as I can."

Aki almost laughed, except the idea alone was painful. He'd been deliberately hurt so many times in his life, but almost never deliberately taken care of. Sasha had been the first.

Without any other warning, the doctor pulled. Aki heard a short cry, but couldn't decide if it was him or Felix, whose face had gone from white to green.

Aki passed out again.

Chapter 9

SHADOWS DANCED ACROSS THE ceiling in the light of a single lamp left on his table. Aki let out a heavy breath. They'd brought him around again only after the doctor had finished stitching his arm and securing a bandage and splint around it.

"You're off field work for at least six weeks, maybe more," the doctor had said. Aki should have been bothered by that, but since Jasper had yet to take him out, he didn't think he was actually missing much. "And you'll stay in bed for the rest of the day. I don't want you up again until tomorrow morning at the earliest."

Now, hours later, Aki stared up at the flickering shadows. His arm hurt. His head hurt. And something deep down inside of him hurt. It wasn't a surprise that he wasn't liked or trusted by the others. Most people didn't like or trust him when they found out where he was from. But most people didn't set him up just to see him hurt either. That was one of the biggest differences between here and Aruuk. Until today.

The dormitory had a hollow silence. It was empty except for him. The others, it seemed, had gone on with their plans and were now enjoying the festival. Everyone, but him.

Ignoring the pain that throbbed in his head, Aki eased himself up so that he was sitting. His eyes took several moments to work again after the movement and Aki shoved away the twinge of worry that accompanied their failure. He'd hit his head, but not that hard. Taliea had told him once that as much damage as Sasha had done to his head, there would very likely be some damage that lingered for the rest of his life. No doubt, that was what was going on now.

After waiting for the black specks to swim away, Aki got to his feet. His arm was not only safely immobilized in its splint, it was also held close to him in a sling. As long as he kept it there, no harm would come to it. Of course, that didn't mean it didn't still hurt, but Aki thought it would hurt whether he was lying in bed or walking around. The doctor had ordered him to stay in bed, but Aki was reasonably sure that was just something he said to every patient. Aki was bored. He wanted to go out. He wanted to see the festival.

He was trying, and failing, to put on his boots with only one hand when a soft knock came on his door.

"Aki, are you awake?" Felix's voice drifted through the door.

Aki thought about not answering and letting Felix think he was asleep. If he hadn't been so bored, he would have.

"I'm awake."

"Oh, good." Felix's voice was louder now that he was sure. "I was hoping you would be. Can I come in?"

"I guess so." Aki kicked his boots away across the floor. The last thing he wanted was for Felix to know what he was planning and tell on him.

The door cracked open, and Felix slipped in as if he were trying to hide. He stood, awkward and unsure, in the center of the room for a moment.

"How is your arm?" he asked finally.

"Hurts. I thought you were gone with the others."

"I was, but I came back. I brought you something." Felix extended his hand.

Aki took what was offered. He could smell it before he even unwrapped the napkin that was protecting it. Still warm, Aki didn't waste any time biting into the tart. The crust was flaky and tasted of sweet butter, the filling of spiced apples.

"It's good," Aki said, his mouth full of a second bite.

"I'm sorry about what happened today. I didn't have anything to do with it. It was cowardly. My Father would be furious if he thought I'd done anything like that. It would have dishonored him." Felix sat down on the edge of the empty bed across from Aki.

Aki raised a bemused eyebrow. "Really?"

"Of course, really. I wouldn't joke about those sorts of things."

"And who is your father that he cares so much about honor and all that?"

Felix looked genuinely concerned at Aki's ignorance and Aki regretted showing it.

"My father is Baron Orlander, lord of the king's cavalry."

Aki's mouthed a stunned and silent, "Oh."

"Anyway, I wanted you to know that I had nothing to do with today's incident and that I told Captain Lupin about it. He's promised to look into it." Felix started to get up. "I should let you rest now. The doctor said you needed it."

"No, wait, please. He says that to everyone. I'm not tired, not really. What was the festival like? Was it fun?"

"Of course it was fun. It'd be a poor festival if it wasn't. There were lots of vendors selling all sorts of things, like tarts. And there were musicians. And a bard."

"What's a bard?"

Felix frowned. "It's someone who makes up songs about glorious battles and heroic deeds and beautiful girls that need saving and monsters that need killing. Usually there's only the tiniest bit of truth to the stories, but they are fun to listen to. There was dancing too. And games. And lights everywhere, so that it was barely night at all."

"I wanted to go."

"You've never been to a festival before?"

Aki shook his head.

"Maybe you can go this week. I'm sure Master Wehr won't have as much for you to do since you've broken your arm."

"Maybe." Aki doubted it. Something told him Master Wehr would not be moved much at all by a broken arm.

"I really should go, Aki. We're not supposed to be disturbing you, Captain Lupin said." Felix stood and went to the door. "Will you need anything in the morning?"

Aki wanted more than anything to refuse and say he didn't, but his attempt at putting on his boots had already proven otherwise.

"I might need a little help," he confessed.

"I will come."

"Thanks, Felix. And I know you didn't have anything to do with what happened."

Aki returned to staring up at the ceiling when Felix left, certain he could never actually sleep.

Morning came before he knew it and Aki found himself wishing the doctor had told him to keep to his bed for another day. When he and Felix finally left his room, he was still rubbing his eyes, trying to wake himself up fully.

Sky's head swung over the stall door at the sound of his approach. He rubbed her forehead with his free hand before starting his chores. Here, for the first time, the full import of his broken arm came to him. His right arm hung useless in its sling, but he was right-handed. Taking care of Sky with one hand was complicated enough, doing it with his left hand was miserable. His arm was hurting again, as well.

"Aki!" Captain Lupin stood in the doorway of his office that overlooked the arena and, when Aki looked over at the sound of his name, beckoned for Aki to come.

Setting down the bucket of water he'd been carrying, Aki hurried over. The look on Captain Lupin's face wasn't promising. Aki thought he was upset yesterday when he came in with the doctor. Now he had no doubts about it. He had time to wonder if perhaps they weren't actually allowed to use the other horses, if that had been another part of the dangerous prank played on him.

"Come inside," Captain Lupin said when he reached the doorway. "Sit."

Aki saw as soon as he entered that they weren't alone. Oscar was already there, staring straight ahead. He didn't so much as glance over at Aki as he came in. Swallowing back the trepidation that filled him, Aki sat down.

"How are you feeling this morning, Aki?" Captain Lupin asked, his voice stiff as if he didn't actually care what answer Aki gave and was only asking because it was the polite thing to do. He sat down across from the boys.

"It hurts, but I'm fine, sir."

"You are, of course, removed from field work until Doctor Lamberse says otherwise. You will, however, have no need to postpone your studies with Master Wehr."

"I understand, sir," Aki answered then fell silent, sensing that Captain Lupin had a lot more to say than just confirming what the doctor had already said.

"In the meantime, it has been brought to my attention that what happened yesterday was no accident." Captain Lupin paused, his eyes resting on Oscar who shifted in his chair. "It was, in fact, very intentional. Oscar?"

"We put briars beneath the saddle so he'd buck as soon as anyone tried to mount him. It was my idea. I'm sorry."

Aki stared incredulously at Oscar. Oscar's jaw was tight, his eyes staring at the wooden top of the desk in front of him, his hands clenched into fists on his lap. Nothing about his posture supported his claim of sorrow. Captain Lupin cleared his throat loudly and they both turned back to him.

"Oscar, I cannot permit you to endanger anyone's life in such a callous, malicious way without punishing you for it."

Aki stiffened and stared down at his lap. He knew all about punishments and just how terrible they could be in Aruuk. But Sasha said that these people were different. He wondered what a different sort of punishment might look like. A sidelong glance at Oscar's face showed that he wasn't terrified of whatever was about to come. Just angry. Aki couldn't decide if that was a relief or not.

"Since you have temporarily crippled Aki, it is only fair that you make it up to him. You will move into his room until he has recovered the full use of his arm. You will assist him in any way that he requires. You will help him with the care of his horse. You will not go out anywhere and leave him alone. If he is here, you are here. And you will be exempt from field work for as long as he is."

"What?" Oscar's eyes finally left the desk and snapped up to meet Captain Lupin's. They mirrored the horror that Aki felt, although Aki was sure it was for very different reasons. "That'll put me behind."

"As far behind as you have put him. You could have killed him, in which case you would have been out completely at the very least. Now, go, move your things over to his room."

Shoving his chair away from the desk, Oscar slammed the door behind him loud enough that Aki jumped. Aki wondered how he had the nerve to. It was now Aki's turn to stare straight at the desk, suddenly very interested in the smooth wood.

"I hope, Aki, that you will not take it upon yourself to seek your own revenge in this matter."

"No, sir. I wouldn't."

"Good. Because not only will that get yourself into trouble, it will begin a cycle that has no good end. What my son did was wrong in every way, but I think it will not happen again."

"Your son, sir?" Aki looked up, confused.

"Yes. I forget how much you don't know around here." Aki winced at the unintended sting in the words. "Oscar is my son. And, given his punishment, I do think I can safely say he will learn his lesson."

Aki wanted to say that Oscar's punishment was just as much his punishment. Living the next six weeks with Oscar was like living inside a nightmare that you couldn't wake from, especially now that Oscar hated him even more.

"I have my own opinions as to whether or not you should be here, Aki, but those are irrelevant. You are here by the decision of my superiors and regardless of how I feel about it, I hope you understand that you will be treated as fairly as the others by me. And I hope one day that you will prove my opinions wrong."

"I'll try, sir," Aki said, unsure of why Captain Lupin was telling him this now.

"There is one other matter I wished to talk to you about before you go." Captain Lupin leaned back in his chair. "You haven't done any field work yet, have you?"

"No, sir. Jasper hasn't taken me out yet."

Captain Lupin nodded, his gaze drawn to something outside the window. "I will speak with him. You will go out as soon as the doctor says you can."

"Thank you, sir."

Chapter 10

YOU'RE LATE. VERY LATE." Master Wehr looked up when Aki came through the door more than an hour late. "And what have you done?"

"I broke my arm," Aki said. "That's why I'm late. I'm sorry."

"No doubt it was an accident and therefore nothing to apologize for. Now, to work."

Aki sat down on his stool. There would be no staring out into the street hoping for Jasper to show up and take him away. Not for the next six weeks, at least.

"I won't be able to practice my penmanship."

"Why not?"

"I use my right hand for it, and I can't now."

"Then it's a good time to learn to use your left hand."

"I can't."

"Nonsense, boy. You learned to use the right one just fine. Your left is no different, and you can't afford to take weeks off. You're already behind."

"I know." Aki slumped in his chair, the full weight of his anger finally coming to rest on him. "You don't have to remind me."

Master Wehr studied him for a moment, drumming his fingers on the top of his cane.

"What is the matter with you?" he asked finally.

"What do you mean? My arm's broken and hurts like crazy. It will be at least six weeks before I can even hope to go out with Jasper, and even then the only reason he'll be taking me is because Captain Lupin is going to order him to. I'll be so far behind I might never catch up. And I have to room with the person who's responsible for hurting me so that he can help me. But he hates me and his help isn't actually very helpful so it's more of a punishment on me then it is him. He just gets to make the next six weeks of my life miserable. And the only reason any of this even happened is because everyone hates me for where I come from. I should never have even come here." Aki paused for breath.

"Are you finished?"

Aki, taking note of Master Wehr's crisp tone, nodded once. He didn't dare bring his eyes up to meet Master Wehr's.

"If the best you can do today is sulk in your own self-pity then you might as well go back and stop wasting my time."

"What? That's not what I'm doing."

"Isn't it?" Master Wehr got to his feet. "One bad thing happens and you're ready to throw everything away. One person hurts you and you're ready to forget all the ones who haven't."

"You don't understand," Aki mumbled.

"I understand a good deal more than you think I do, Aki," Master Wehr snapped, and Aki lifted his eyes in surprise and alarm. Master Wehr had never spoken to him like that before. A moment later, Master Wehr sighed and his face softened. "You want the whole world to like you and that's not going to happen. And it has nothing to do with where you're from. Don't waste your entire life wishing you were born somewhere else, to other people."

"I'm not..."

"You are, Aki. You blame everything on where you came from."

"But that really is why he did it. And now I'm stuck sharing the same room with him. It's going to be awful."

Master Wehr shrugged. "Or it may not be. It may be exactly what you make it, just like everything else in your life."

"What do you mean?"

"I mean that it is as much of an opportunity as it is a punishment. Perhaps in six weeks you will have a friend instead of an enemy."

"I don't think that will ever happen with Oscar," Aki said doubtfully. He wasn't ready to let go of the anger that Master Wehr was completely dismantling.

"Whether that happens or not, make the best of it. And get to work. We've wasted enough time today as it is. Come, I want you to read this to me."

Aki spent the next hour doing just that. Even without Master Wehr saying it, he knew he was getting better. After everything else, it was only a small comfort. Then came writing, and any comfort derived from his improvement in reading was lost. While he could appreciate the importance of the skill, his left hand was completely uncooperative. The paper was blotched and splattered with ink and few letters, if any, were legible by the time he was done.

At last, he was able to move on to the one thing that wasn't nearly as challenging - mapwork. Here at least, Aki wasn't at a disadvantage. Maps made sense. The markings on them made sense. Maps were just another way of viewing the world. North was always north, south was always south, and the invariableness of them was comforting.

It was still fairly early in the evening when Master Wehr announced the end of the day. Aki, once again lost in the effort of reading to himself, looked up in surprise.

"So early?"

"For tonight, yes. Don't come to expect this, though. And don't waste the entire evening. Practice your reading and writing more. You're getting better. Soon, we'll move on to other things."

"Really?" Aki reached for his jacket. "What other things?"

"Codes, seals, things that every courier must know and use."

"Am I actually getting good enough for all that?"

"I wouldn't have said so if you weren't." Master Wehr helped Aki with his jacket.

"Thank you, Master Wehr," Aki said, both for the words and the help.

The streets were still busy and, although Aki's arm was aching, he was drawn into the busyness. It called to some restless longing in him that he'd been fighting to suppress since he'd come to Bren. He certainly wasn't in a hurry to get back to the Academy and face Oscar and his help. He could spend a couple of hours out and still have his normal amount of time to practice before bed. And he really did want to see the festival. Before he even knew he had decided, he found himself caught up in the steady stream of people heading to the market square.

The sound reached him first - music, singing, laughter - sounds that echoed with happiness and celebration. Aki slowed down, hanging back on the fringes of the crowd, suddenly shy and uncomfortable. It was like stepping into a whole other world, a world he hadn't even known existed. It was enough for now to just wander around the edge of it, smiling at other people's laughter, catching bits and pieces of others' conversation - a spectator to the celebration. That was something he was supposed to be practicing, too, he remembered.

Even as the sun went down, lamps strung between buildings were lit and the darkness of night was held back. Aki kept to the edge near the shadows. As late as it was getting, he ought to be heading back, but he lingered.

As his gaze wandered over the other people, a familiar face caught his eye. Shrouded in the shadows as much as he was, and deep in conversation with a man, Kezi's face was barely visible. Aki opened his mouth to call out a greeting when he saw Kezi's hand slip something from beneath her threadbare coat and into the hands of the man she was speaking with. A moment later, the man disappeared into the growing darkness and Kezi noticed Aki. She sidled over to him, avoiding the lights and people as best she could.

"How much did you see?" she asked as she joined him in leaning against the front of a shop.

"It's nice to see you too, Kezi," Aki laughed. "I didn't see anything worthwhile, though."

Kezi's eyes narrowed and the corners of her mouth turned down in a disapproving scowl. "And what would you consider worthwhile?"

"I saw you talk to someone and pass something to them. I have no idea who they were or what it was. Besides, you're not actually afraid I'd turn you in for something, are you?"

"Thought you'd be here yesterday, since it was your day off and all." Kezi's face changed as abruptly as she changed the subject.

"I was going to."

"What'd you do to your arm?"

"Broke it, yesterday."

"Ah, well, that explains it then. How'd you break it?"

Aki recounted the events, telling not only of how he broke it but of the aftermath and where he found himself now.

Kezi shook her head in sympathy. "Poor Aki. Not fitting in so well, are you? Can't say I didn't warn you, though. We don't belong here, either of us. It's why we have to stick together."

"You're encouraging." Aki kicked at a pebble in disgust.

"I'm being honest. Not something I am very often, so count yourself lucky."

Aki raised an eyebrow but didn't say anything. Nothing needed to be said. He wasn't Kezi's friend because of her honesty, he was her friend for the same reason that his arm was broken. Honest or not, he could trust Kezi to not hold his origin against him.

"Bet this is the first time you've ever seen anything like this, isn't it?"

"I guess so. How can you tell?"

"You're staring at it like a blind man who just recovered his sight," Kezi laughed but cut it off short, something beyond Aki's shoulder catching her eyes.

Aki turned to see what had happened and followed Kezi's eyes. A man stood framed in a doorway on the other side of the street. Although Aki hadn't seen his face earlier, he was sure it was the same man she had been talking to before she saw him. His posture, the way he moved were the same. And familiar.

"I have to go, Aki." Kezi started to move away. Turning back toward him, her face unreadable now, she said, "You should come around more, though. Obviously you aren't making any friends where you are. I can assure you, the people I hang out with don't care where you're from. They make good friends for people like us."

"I'll try. I've just had so much to catch up on."

Aki stood unmoving for a bit longer, watching as Kezi disappeared inside the building with the man. The man reminded him of someone, he just couldn't think who. Shrugging to himself, Aki decided that he'd put off returning for as long as he could.

Chapter 11

AKI EASED HIS DOOR OPEN, careful to avoid making any sound. It was later than he'd ever returned before, and he both expected and hoped that Oscar would already be asleep.

"The next time you decide to spend half the night out, you'd better tell me."

Aki's shoulders slumped at the sound of Oscar's voice. If he'd been angry this morning, he was furious now. Aki entered the room and shut the door behind him with a great deal less care than he'd been using. If Oscar was already awake, there was no sense in pretending otherwise. He found Oscar laying on his back on the second bed in the room, fingers laced together beneath his head, glowering.

"It's bad enough I have to stay in here with you. If you'd told me you were going to be gone so long, I wouldn't have had to sit here all evening waiting for you to come back so I can play nurse to you." Oscar sat up, swinging his feet over the edge of the bed and onto the floor. "So you'd better tell me when you plan on being gone."

"Captain Lupin didn't say I had to tell you anything," Aki said. "It's your punishment, not mine."

"Do you think I care? I've been sitting in here for hours while you're, what? Running around town, having a good time. You did it on purpose, didn't you?"

"Maybe." Aki sat down on his own bed and picked up one of the books Master Wehr had sent back with him to practice reading. He flipped it open to a random page, only pretending to read in the faint hope that Oscar would leave him alone.

"If you try to make my life miserable, I swear I'll do it right back," Oscar leaned forward as he spoke, lowering his voice in case anyone was in the hallway outside.

"You've already done that," Aki said without looking up from his book. He lifted his broken arm as much as he dared to draw Oscar's attention to it. Although he stared at the words, he was not reading them. He wasn't even trying to. It was impossible with Oscar glaring at him from only a few feet away.

"I haven't even started." Oscar's face broke into a smile that was as far from friendly as it was possible to be and he lay back down.

A twinge of worry filled Aki. He had to sleep in this room, and that idea was suddenly very uncomfortable.

Within a few minutes, Oscar appeared asleep and Aki breathed freely again. Setting his book aside, he struggled to take his boots off. The temptation to wake Oscar and make him help flitted across his mind, but was dismissed almost immediately when he remembered his uneasiness. It took several minutes longer than usual to undo his laces and work them off, but he did it without help.

Morning found Oscar sitting on his bed, arms crossed over his chest, watching as Aki struggled to get ready for the day. Aki tried to ignore the smug amusement on his face as his own grew more heated.

"You might as well just ask me," Oscar finally said.

"Ask you what?" Aki had freed his arm from its sling and was attempting to put on a clean shirt for the day.

"For help. He's going to ask you if I helped anyway, just to make sure. And I doubt very much that you'll be willing to lie to him for me."

"Who? Captain Lupin?"

"Who else?"

Aki winced as he pulled his sleeve over the splint. The seams strained threateningly over the bulge of it and, in spite of the fast approaching winter, he decided to roll it up above the splint.

"Fine. Will you help me?" Aki asked through gritted teeth. He'd half wanted to get through the six weeks without ever having to say those words. And of course,

Oscar was going to make him ask for it. He couldn't just offer like Felix had.

Oscar shrugged, watching him for another moment. "I guess so. What happened to your back?"

"Nothing." Aki pulled the shirt down the rest of the way, hiding the scars on his back. He'd forgotten that benefit of having a room to himself. In fact, now that he thought about it, he wondered why it had upset him so much in the first place. Having a roommate wasn't that great.

"Whatever. You didn't get those scars from nothing."

"Just help me get my boots on." Aki replaced his sling and rested his arm inside it.

Oscar's face darkened and for a moment Aki thought he would refuse altogether. It passed and Oscar crossed the room, picking up Aki's boots and bringing them over. Stooping in front of Aki with ill grace, he helped slide them on and lace them up. When he was finished, Aki was on his feet, scooping up the books and papers he needed to take to Master Wehr's. He couldn't get out of the room fast enough.

"Wait. Are you going to go out again tonight?"

Aki stopped halfway out the door. He considered not answering at all. Oscar certainly deserved being forced to wait, not knowing when he would return. It was only his promise to Captain Lupin that made him hesitate. There was, of course, another way to make Oscar suffer that wasn't as obvious. Smiling, Aki turned around.

"No, I'm coming straight back tonight, just as early as I can. I have a lot to do."

Aki fled down the hall before Oscar could throw whatever was in his hand at him. He heard it strike the door behind him and smiled again.

He reached Master Wehr's a little earlier than usual but Master Wehr was still ready for him. The old man studied him from beneath his thick eyebrows.

"You're in better spirits this morning. Much better spirits."

"I guess so," Aki sighed. Now that he was here, he had the distinct impression that Master Wehr wouldn't think his behavior this morning was making the best of things. And, now that he thought about it, Aki could hardly believe he'd done it. He'd spent his entire life avoiding anyone else's wrath. Goading Oscar was reckless and crazy, and he would probably pay for it.

"Let's get started then," Master Wehr said. Instead of sitting down at his desk, though, he went to the door.

"We're going out?"

"We are. And we'll see how well you remember the way to Miss Cravin's."

Aki's face twisted in a grimace of frustration as he followed Master Wehr out the door. It wasn't the first time Master Wehr had done this - taking him to a place once, and then days later requiring him to find it on his own again.

"It will force you to pay attention to where you're going," he had said when Aki inquired into the purpose of it. "A courier must not only know where he is going, but how to get there and you won't always have a map to do the work for you. Besides, stopping to study a map wastes time. It's better to just know."

It had been more than a week since they'd gone to Miss Cravin's. Aki hesitated outside the door, closing his eyes to better remember the route they had taken. He knew better than to ask for even the slightest bit of help. Master Wehr was perfectly willing to let him lead them astray just to prove a point. Finally settling on a course, Aki set off, the tapping of Master Wehr's cane assuring him that the old man followed.

Aki turned the final corner and read the sign hanging above the door, relief mingling with pride. He was getting better. Not once today did he have to turn around or backtrack.

"Well done," Master Wehr acknowledged as he gestured for Aki to open the door. "Very well done."

Miss Cravin was already in the front room helping another customer when they entered. The songbirds in their cage flapped their wings and twittered as tendrils of outside air reached through the open doorway. Aki watched them while Miss Cravin finished up her business with the only other occupant of the room.

"Poor birds. They're miserable all cooped up in a cage like that," Aki said quietly to Master Wehr. "I wonder why she keeps them."

"You may wish to keep your thoughts to yourself, Aki," Master Wehr responded, a note of warning in his tone. "Before others take offense where you meant none."

"Sorry, Master Wehr. I didn't mean anything by it."

Master Wehr nodded. "I'm quite certain you did not. But still, a little thought before you speak can't hurt."

Miss Cravin turned her attention to them at last, robbing Aki of the chance to answer.

"Back so soon, Atticus?"

"I'm afraid so. I'm in need of more ink and parchment."

"Keeping you busy, isn't he?" Miss Cravin winked at Aki. The effect made Aki want to laugh but after already being chided for saying too much he pressed his lips together and nodded. "I don't seem to recall your name, boy?"

"It's Aki, ma'am."

"Aki. Different sort of name." Aki stiffened and took an involuntary step backwards as she leaned forward across the counter studying him. "And not from around here. If I had to guess, I'd say from up north."

"And that would be a very good guess, Miss Cravin. Now, if you will, there is more that we need to attend to today," Master Wehr said.

"Of course you do." Miss Cravin didn't seem to take offense but instead disappeared through the doorway that looked too narrow for her frame. A few minutes later she returned. "I'm sure you've heard about what happened last night?"

"I have not," Master Wehr said, smiling a little. "But I'm sure you'll tell me all about it."

"It happened right in the middle of the festival," Miss Cravin leaned closer, a conspiratory tone in her voice. "And they've not caught whoever did it. One of the shops, a jeweler's if I remember correctly, was broken into and robbed. The criminals even started a fire to cover their tracks, though thankfully, it was contained quickly."

"That is fortunate indeed. A fire in town can be catastrophic."

"Can you believe it? Right in the middle of everything. Whoever it was had some nerve. It makes me afraid to sleep at night."

"I'm sure whoever did it will be found." Master Wehr counted out money and placed it in Miss Cravin's hand. "In the meantime, work must go on. Come, Aki."

Aki picked up the parcel and followed Master Wehr out of the door. It wasn't as hard getting back to Master Wehr's as it had been coming and Aki was glad of that. Thoughts swirled through his mind as he remembered his own time at the festival last night. Now that they were walking away, it occurred to him that he should have asked when the burglary and fire had happened. It couldn't have been while he was there, but how soon after? A thought wormed its way into his mind. Kezi had been there.

"You are quiet, Aki," Master Wehr said as they neared his home. "And that is unusual."

"Just thinking. And listening." Aki added the last part as an afterthought. It was what he was supposed to do. "I was there last night but I must have left before anything happened. My friend was there too. I wonder if she was still there when it happened."

"Perhaps she was. Many people stay quite late."

An awful idea popped into Aki's head. Kezi had been there, but she hadn't been there alone. She'd left him abruptly and Aki suspected that it had something to do with the man she'd slipped something to.

Aki shook the thought away. Kezi might live on the streets and steal in order to eat, but she wasn't the kind of person who would do something like that. She wasn't someone who would endanger the lives of others for a few pieces of jewelry.

Chapter 12

THE CANDLE ON THE TABLE was near its end, wax melting and spilling down the sides of it. In its light, Aki bent over a book. It was no longer one of the relatively easy and therefore boring books he'd started with. It was interesting enough that he could ignore the frustrated sighs and angry glares of Oscar only a few feet away.

In the last four weeks Aki had fought back his own desire to go out in the evenings and had spent every possible free minute here in his room - lingering just as long as he dared in the mornings, and half running to get back in the evenings. A few times, he'd caught sight of Kezi coming or going, but he'd ignored her. Master Wehr praised his industriousness and noted the improvement he'd made, but that was hardly Aki's motivation. All the motivation he needed sat on the bed on the opposite side of the room.

Turning a page, Aki risked a glance at his roommate. Oscar was as furious as he was every evening and he was bad at hiding it. Actually, Aki didn't think he even tried to hide it. Aki smiled to himself and returned to his reading. Someday, Oscar's anger would reach a breaking point. Someday, he would snap back and Aki continually shoved away the worry that clawed at him when he remembered that. Immersed once more in the battles of the great war between Dorsten and Dival, he barely heard Oscar's muttered words. His attention was only briefly diverted when he heard Oscar's feet thump on the floor.

"This is ridiculous." Oscar reached the table in two quick steps and snatched the book out of Aki's unsuspecting hands. "It's been weeks. All you do is come home and study. You can't possibly have that much to do. You're just doing it to get back at me."

"Give it back, Oscar."

"What are you going to do if I don't?"

"Tell..."

"Don't you dare run to my father. I've done everything he told me to."

"Then give it back."

"No. If you want it, you'll have to take it from me," Oscar said with a knowing smile. Even without a broken arm, Aki was no match for him. His smile disappeared a moment later, replaced by annoyance. "Come on, Aki. It's bad enough I have to take care of you all the time."

"You don't even do that much," Aki muttered under his breath.

"Can't you just go out once? You have to be as bored as I am." Without waiting for an answer, Oscar tossed the book onto his own bed out of Aki's reach. A moment more and he'd pulled Aki's chair away from the table.

"What are you doing?"

"I'm taking you somewhere, anywhere, just so long as it's out of this room." Oscar grabbed Aki's good arm and tugged him out of the chair.

"But I don't want to...," even as he started to say the words, Aki knew he didn't mean them. He was terribly bored. The only reason he'd even kept at it was to annoy Oscar. For some insane reason, he'd wanted to provoke Oscar and now he'd done it. Aki had thought he'd be afraid when that happened, but now he just found himself in grudging agreement with his reluctant roommate.

"I don't care. Seriously, Aki, just give it up. I'm sorry I ever did anything to you, alright?"

Aki jerked his arm free. He stood where he was rather than making any effort to sit back down, studying Oscar with mingled suspicion and curiosity.

"What exactly do you have in mind?" he asked.

"Anywhere. Anything. I haven't even gotten to go see my family because you insist on coming back so early and staying here."

"Wait. You can see your family?"

"Yes, they live here in Bren. Where'd you think they were? My father runs this place, remember?"

"I guess I hadn't thought about it," Aki said, shrugging. To be honest, family wasn't something he ever gave any thought to. Families weren't a thing to be missed, although Oscar surprisingly missed his. He hesitated a moment more, not because he was actually thinking of refusing now, but because it was very satisfying to see Oscar like this - half angry, half pleading. "Alright, we can go. But you have to help me get ready."

"Fine."

The days were growing shorter with the approach of winter and the sky was already darkening when they left the Academy. Aki followed Oscar through the streets, his time with Master Wehr forcing him to memorize every turn they took. He wasn't entirely sure where Oscar was planning on going and it didn't really matter. If Aki decided he didn't want to be there, he could just leave and Oscar would be forced to go back with him. For someone who'd had so little control of anything in their life, the power was intoxicating, and Aki considered using it even if he did like whatever they were doing.

They left the shops and marketplace behind and ventured into the neighborhoods beyond. The houses in Bren were built quite differently from the ones in Illsen, Aki noted. In Illsen, no house had a second story. They were built low, their roofs slanted steeply to allow the harsh weather of the mountains to roll off. In Bren, however, it was not uncommon for a house to have two, or even three, stories. Some of the richer ones even had balconies built into those upper stories that overlooked the streets below. It was before one of the two story houses that Oscar stopped. Since he didn't bother to knock, but opened the door straight away, Aki assumed it was his own home.

"Oscar, is that you?" a woman's voice called out from another room.

"It's me," Oscar answered and then turned to Aki. Aki was startled by the pleading in his eyes. He lowered his voice so no one else could hear him, "You'll wait out here, right? I won't be long."

"What, you don't want your family meeting me? I don't want to sit out here all by myself. That would be too boring. I'd rather just go back." Aki turned toward the door when Oscar's hand grabbed his shoulder.

"No. Stop." Oscar hesitated, clearly torn between his choices and for once Aki felt a twinge of guilt for what he was doing. He didn't even really want to meet Oscar's family. They would most likely be just more people like Oscar. He just wanted Oscar miserable and, looking at him now, he wasn't sure how to feel about accomplishing that. It definitely wasn't what Master Wehr thought he should do, and if Stephan were here, he probably wouldn't either.

Aki opened his mouth to speak, to say that he didn't care and he'd just sit out here and wait, but Oscar beat him to it.

"You're awful, you know," Oscar said, defeated. "Fine, just come in with me."

Aki still considered just waiting but the entrance of a woman took the chance away. She appeared to be around forty, a few streaks of silver in her hair, and Aki knew at once that she was Oscar's mother. He looked as much like her as it was possible for a boy to look, except that she had a kindness about her eyes that was missing from her son's.

"What's taking you so long, Oscar?" She hurried forward and pulled him into a hug that he stiffly returned. She looked over his shoulder and saw Aki for the first time. "And who is this?"

"A friend." Aki hid a quick smile at the way Oscar almost choked on the word. "From the Academy. This is Aki, Mother."

"Aki?" Just the way she said his name told Aki that she'd already heard about him. It didn't take any imagination to guess what she'd heard. If she felt the same towards him as Oscar did, she did a wonderful job of hiding it. "Welcome to our home. Come, come all the way in. Here I thought we'd get to see you all the time still, and it's been weeks. What's been keeping you?"

"Sorry, Mother, I guess I've just been busy," Oscar said, glancing over his shoulder long enough to glare at Aki. Aki shrugged and held his hands out innocently.

Aki followed behind them. He watched the way Mrs. Lupin slid her hand into the crook of Oscar's arm in a comfortable way. He listened to their words. He hung back when they came into the sitting room, totally unprepared for the familial scene and instantly out of place. Captain Lupin was there. Aki had always just assumed he stayed at the Academy as well. Seeing him here, outside of his uniform and without the stiff bearing of his position felt almost sacrilegious.

Captain Lupin's eyes widened slightly when he caught sight of Aki standing in the shadow of the doorway and, to Aki's surprise, the corners of his mouth pulled upwards in a smile. He glanced between Aki and Oscar, who was currently doing everything he could to avoid his father's eyes. With a brief gesture, he motioned Aki all the way in.

"Who are you?" A little girl of maybe six or seven asked him as he came in.

"Aki."

"I'm Helena. Play with me."

Helena was sitting on the floor, an assortment of dolls lying about her. Aki hesitated a moment, then shrugged and joined her on the floor.

"What are you playing?" When he'd first moved in at Stephan and Alina's he'd spent many hours playing with Hamo's younger daughters, Elenora and Adelaide, so the thought of spending the evening playing with Helena wasn't daunting.

Helena looked up at him, suspicion covering her freckled face. "You sound funny."

"Helena," Mrs. Lupin warned from across the room.

"Sorry, Aki. Mother thinks that's rude. Where are you from, anyway?"

If it had been anyone else, Aki would have stiffened and withdrawn, but Helena asked it with the innocence of a child. It wasn't a judgment, just childish curiosity. Besides, the other three occupants of the room didn't seem to be paying any attention to Helena's conversation. And they already knew where he was from.

"Up north, in the mountains."

Helena's eyes got wide and she leaned forward to whisper, "Are they big?"

"Very," Aki said and smiled.

"Bigger than the sea?"

"No. Big in a different way. They're tall, taller than anything you've ever seen before. So tall that the trees that grow on them look tiny compared to them. Some of them reach all the way up to the sky, past the clouds."

"Really? What was it like living there?"

Aki's face darkened briefly. How was he supposed to tell this little girl any part of his life in Aruuk? None of it was fit to bring into a home like this.

"Did something bad happen to your home?" Helena asked.

Aki shook his head.

"You miss it then," Helena stated with confidence in her own assessment. "Is it your family you miss?"

Helena, in her innocence, was determined to ask all the questions Aki could not and would not answer. Some hint of his predicament must have shown on his face.

"Helena, dear, Aki may not want to talk about those things," Mrs. Lupin interrupted.

Aki mouthed a silent, "Thank you," to her.

"So, Aki, what made you want to be a courier?" Mrs. Lupin asked.

"I like horses, I guess. It seemed like an interesting job, getting to go all sorts of places, seeing new things."

"And now that you're here, do you still think it's an interesting job?"

"Oh, yes, ma'am. Very interesting, although I haven't got that far into training yet. So far, I've just read about places. I'm sure it'll be more interesting seeing them."

"I'm sure. We've been around quite a few places ourselves, over the years. Although, I'm not terribly fond of traveling myself."

"The worst place was that smelly town." Helena looked up from rearranging her dolls. "Too many fish."

Aki laughed along with the others to be polite.

"It was a fishing town up the coast," Captain Lupin clarified. "And we weren't there that long."

"I see."

Aki spent most of the evening just sitting back listening and occasionally cooperating enough with Helena's game that she was satisfied. Guilt for keeping Oscar away from his family for so long tangled with an envy Aki thought didn't exist anymore. As the hour grew late and Mrs.

Lupin insisted that it was Helena's bedtime, Aki and Oscar said their goodbyes and started back for the Academy.

Walking through the dark streets, Aki half expected to see Kezi lurking in the shadows somewhere. He wrapped his good arm around himself, wishing he'd worn something more than his light jacket. The air nipped at them and he was more than happy to reach the warmth of the Academy once more. The creak of the floorboards in the hallway was loud in the nightly silence and Aki winced with each one. In Aruuk, he'd mastered the art of moving noiselessly through the halls of the Chief's house. As a slave, he hadn't wanted to bring down the wrath of anyone he awoke, and as a son just because the habit lingered. It annoyed him that he couldn't do it here.

Inside their room, Oscar stood in the middle, hesitating while Aki sank down onto his mattress.

"So, you're not going to keep me cooped up here every night anymore, are you?" he finally said, his face unreadable.

Aki struggled out of his jacket without answering. He wasn't sure how to answer. He wanted to go out again, but he didn't want to visit Oscar's family again.

"Come on, Aki. You can't keep holding onto this. I said I was sorry."

Aki shrugged. "I guess I won't. But I can't go every night."

Chapter 13

THE FIRE CRACKLED TO RENEWED life as Aki blew on it. He lingered, holding his hands over the flame, warming them. Just because he could, he flexed his right forearm, enjoying the freedom of movement and the absence of the splint that he'd worn for the last seven weeks. Piling up on the sills of the windows was the first snow of the year. Aki blew on the fire one last time before rising.

Oscar sat up, swinging his legs over the edge of the bed, rubbing his eyes.

"I suppose I can move back to my room today," he said at last. "Now that you don't need help anymore."

Aki nodded absently and started getting ready for the day. He wasn't about to complain about getting his room back to himself. Having the free use of both his arms was a luxury, even if his right one was a bit sluggish and out of shape. Outside the room, the hallway groaned beneath the weight of someone's footsteps. A sharp knock on the door startled Aki as he was collecting his books. Without waiting for an answer, the door swung open and Aki's surprise turned to anticipation as he recognized Jasper standing on the other side.

"It's off?"

Aki had only a moment's confusion before he understood. "My splint? Yes, it came off yesterday."

"Meet me outside with your horse in half an hour." Jasper turned to go but called over his shoulder, "And dress warmly."

Aki grinned and dropped the armload of books he was carrying back down on the table. Either Captain Lupin had kept his word and spoken with Jasper, or Jasper had given up waiting on his own. It didn't really matter to Aki. All that mattered was that the endless days of doing nothing but reading and writing and memorizing codes and maps without any reprieve were over. He rummaged through his clothes to find warmer ones, pulling them on with such haste that he nearly tripped over himself. The last thing he wanted to do was keep Jasper waiting on his very first time out.

"You haven't gone out before, have you?" Oscar watched him from his bed.

"No."

"Why? All of the rest of us have been, even before your accident," Oscar caught the accusation in Aki's eyes and corrected himself, "I mean, even before the incident."

Aki, his back to Oscar now, rolled his eyes. Even after seven weeks, Oscar was reluctant to acknowledge his own part in Aki's injury.

"I don't know," Aki lied. "Maybe he didn't have any runs."

Before Oscar could ask any more questions that he didn't want to answer, Aki slipped out the door and made his way out into the arena. It was still dark out. The air was frigid and a thin blanket of snow covered the hard packed dirt and crunched softly beneath Aki's feet as he crossed the arena to Sky's stall. Sky's head hung over the half-door at the sound of his approach, two little clouds of breath hanging in the air around her nostrils as she snorted a greeting.

"We're going out today, Sky," Aki whispered as he ran his hand up her broad forehead and scratched around her ears.

It took only a few minutes to ready Sky, and Aki found himself standing in the arena alone, waiting. He pulled his cloak around him and, as more snowflakes began to drift to the ground in the predawn gray, he lifted his hood up. Gloves and a scarf that Alina had made for him completed his winter clothing and protected him from the cold. Remembering all the winters he'd lived through without made the warmth of the clothes just that much more comforting.

"You're going out today?" Felix asked as he came across the arena to take care of his own horse for the morning.

"I am."

"Know where you're going?"

Aki shook his head. He hadn't even thought to ask.

"Lucky you," Felix said, glancing up at the heavy clouds that were already depositing their snow on the earth. He shivered. "Glad it's not me today."

Aki shrugged. "I don't mind it."

"You will when you have to ride all day in it. Sometimes I wonder why I chose to do this."

"I used to..." Aki started to say but caught himself. Felix was polite and kind, but he wasn't someone Aki wanted to share any details of his prior life with. "So, why did you choose this? You're a nobleman's son, aren't you?"

"With three older brothers. I wanted to do something different."

Aki wasn't sure why having older brothers changed anything but decided against showing his ignorance. He just nodded as if he understood.

The sound of approaching hoofbeats put a halt to their conversation. Lifting his hand in a brief wave, Felix moved on and Aki turned to see Jasper coming.

"Ready?"

"Ready," Aki said, confirming the words by sliding a foot into his stirrup and pulling himself up onto Sky's back.

Jasper turned his own horse around again and headed for the wide entrance. Aki couldn't keep the smile off his face, although it was hidden by the scarf he'd pulled up over the lower half of his face. Not only was he riding again for the first time in seven weeks, but he was going out on his first run. He was doing what a courier was supposed to do. Even Sky, usually so docile, sensed his eagerness. Her head went up as they started for the gate, her ears twitching and swiveling to catch every sound. She snorted in excitement as Aki nudged her into motion.

As they rode through the streets of Bren, the snowfall grew more dense. The splashes of black color that were scattered like patchwork over Sky's coat turned white as snowflakes clung to her fur. Aki pulled his scarf up even further and lowered his head to avoid the bite of the cold wind that blew. Ahead of him, Jasper did the same.

The road they took led through the heart of Bren, past the market square, past clusters of tall houses and squat storefronts, past the docks - all places Master Wehr had made him learn by heart. As it continued on beyond the town, it followed the coast and sloped upward as the safe harbor that Bren was built on gave way to rugged walls of rock upon which the waves of the sea broke, foaming and white, against. Bitter wind came gusting in from the open water, and Aki hunched over to avoid it. With the sea roaring in his ears, drowning out the hoofbeats of their horses, it was hard to notice anything else. Without exposing himself to more of the cold than necessary, Aki tried to take in his surroundings. It was as much curiosity as it was Master Wehr's training.

Now that they were out of town their pace quickened to a trot. With the thick snow falling around them, Bren was no longer even visible. Aki turned back around and reached a hand up to adjust his scarf over his face again. Jasper rode in front of him and hadn't bothered to turn around once since they set out. His silence and apparent disinterest evaporated a little of the anticipation in Aki. The cold and the new surroundings occupied enough of his thoughts at the moment to keep him busy, but if they were to be riding for very long his companion's silence would become boring.

Half the morning went by before Aki could work up the nerve to nudge Sky a little closer.

"Where are we going?"

"East," was the cryptic reply. Jasper never even deigned to turn his head.

Aki was glad Jasper's back was to him and missed the flash of annoyance that rippled across his face. He waited a few more minutes, falling just a little farther behind again.

"What's the message we're bringing?"

"King Darien's."

Aki stifled the groan of frustration that rose in his throat and decided to give up. As the sound of the horses' hooves pounding against the packed dirt once again took over, Aki went back to studying his surroundings. He'd never been this way and the land turned rugged faster than he'd imagined possible. The sea road that they followed rose higher and higher, pulling away from the crash of the waves.

The road didn't turn away from the sea until late in the afternoon. By then, the snow had stopped falling, although the wind was no less savage. The clouds that had covered the sky broke up a bit and a pale wintry sun shone down on them, doing little to warm them. The farther they moved from the sea, the more Aki could hear. He hadn't realized just how loud the waves breaking against the cliffs had been.

There was only an hour or so left of the daylight and Aki was just beginning to wonder if they were going to keep riding straight through the night when Jasper turned his horse off the road. Aki followed him without a question. A short distance from the road, the rough terrain offered some shelter from the wind. Massive rocks, covered with vines brown from winter, formed a barrier.

"We'll stay here for the night," Jasper said, speaking for the first time since that morning. "Go ahead and take care of your horse, then get a fire started."

Aki's fingers were stiff with cold as he worked at the straps holding Sky's saddle on and it was impossible to move around that much without loosening the scarf he'd kept tightly wrapped around his face. Sky, unfazed by the cold, pawed through the snow in search of grass.

It wasn't until later, after he'd built a large fire, that Aki decided to make one more attempt. He was sitting as close to the fire as he dared and Jasper sat just on the other side of it.

"How many days are we going to be gone?"

"We'll get there tomorrow, then two days back."

"Get where?"

Jasper didn't answer him right away.

"Am I not allowed to know?"

"You're allowed to know whatever I choose to tell you," Jasper said, leaning back against his bedroll. "We're going to Baron Orlander's tomorrow. He's the..."

"Lord of the King's cavalry. I know. Felix is his son, and he told me."

Jasper stared hard at him for a moment.

"Sorry, I didn't mean to interrupt you."

Jasper nodded and went on, "He is that. More than that, though, he runs one of the wealthiest estates in the country and that is the reason for our trip. We're reminding him of the amount of money owed to the king in taxes."

"Will he like that?"

"Does it matter? It's one of the responsibilities that falls to him. Part of running an estate and its surrounding land and towns is collecting taxes for the king. He won't be upset by it, although there are usually a few who will be."

Content at last, Aki realized just how tired he was. It had been a long time since he'd spent the entire day riding.

The landscape changed once more as they neared Baron Orlander's estate late the next evening. The rocky hills gave way to gentle farmland. Houses and barns dotted the fields. A mixture of stone and wooden fences divided the farms. They crossed several small streams, the horses' hooves loud on the wooden planks, and one large river before finally reaching their destination.

Aki tried hard not to stare. After having seen the castle in Bren, he didn't think any other building would impress him enough to make him stare. The estate of Baron Orlander changed his mind. It lacked the formidable height of the castle but made up for it in its sprawling expanse. Even in the dead of winter, the grounds were obviously home to beautiful and well-maintained gardens. Dried vines of ivy crawled up the stone sides of the manor. White stone steps led up to a wide porch that ran the entire length of the front. Beyond the main house were several outbuildings. It was toward one of these that Jasper turned and Aki followed.

"Wait until you see the inside," Jasper said as they dismounted, making no effort to conceal his amusement. Before relinquishing his horse to the stable hand, he untied the leather pouch that carried the king's missives.

Aki followed Jasper's lead and passed Sky's reins off to the stable hand.

"Are we going inside?"

"Of course we are. I'm not standing out in the cold all night. We're staying here tonight, and we'll leave in the morning."

"They'll let us sleep here?"

"Another one of those responsibilities' noblemen have. They're required to put up any of the king's men when they're passing through. Don't get too excited, though. He'll hardly give us the best bedrooms in the house."

Jasper was right, Aki decided as they stood in the entry waiting for a servant to relay the news of their arrival to the baron. The inside was even better than the outside.

"Aren't you related to the Chief in Aruuk?"

Aki nodded, more interested in inspecting an ornamental set of armor standing along the wall than in Jasper's question.

"Didn't he have some kind of home like this? He *was* the Chief, after all."

"Nothing like this," Aki said, finally tearing his eyes off the armored statue. "No one builds anything like this in the mountains."

Any further conversation was prevented by the entrance of Baron Orlander. It was easy to see the resemblance to Felix in him. His hair was the same bright shade of red. Jasper wasted no time in pulling out the sealed envelope that he'd carried in his pouch. The yellow wax that sealed it was imprinted with the king's seal.

"With His Majesty's compliments," Jasper said, tipping his head forward in a slight bow and holding out the envelope.

Unsure of what to do, Aki hung back watching. Baron Orlander did not appear to be either surprised or upset by the contents of the letter. After a quick glance at it, he glanced up and noticed Aki's presence for the first time.

"You're new, aren't you?"

"Yes, sir."

"You'll know my son, then," Baron Orlander said with a smile.

"Yes, I know Felix."

"I suppose it was too much to hope that he would have been the one coming here. He is well, though?"

"He was when I left, sir."

Baron Orlander gave them another quick smile before motioning to a maid to show them to their rooms.

If these were not his best rooms, Aki wondered what were. Stephan's entire house could fit into the room he was standing in now. Thanks to a large fire on the hearth and heavy curtains draped over the walls, the cold of winter could not permeate the room. Stripping off his winter clothes for the first time in two days, Aki threw himself down on one of the cushioned chairs sitting in front of the fireplace and propped his feet up on the hearth. The flames danced before his eyes, making him realize just how tired he was. He shut his eyes.

Aki groaned at the sound of a knock on his door. His own feet had barely hit the floor before Jasper pushed the door open. Aki started to rise but Jasper gestured for him to remain in his chair as he crossed the room and sat in the other seat only a few feet away.

"Is there something I'm supposed to be doing?" Aki asked without waiting for the silence to stretch out between them.

"No, not at the moment," Jasper leaned back, making himself comfortable. "I have to hand it to you, Aki. You surprised me."

"How? I haven't done anything," Aki blurted out without thinking.

Jasper eyed him for a moment as if considering whether or not to go on. After the brief pause, he said, "We just rode two days through the cold and snow, and you didn't complain about it. Most recruits would have."

Aki shrugged. "Is that a good thing?"

Jasper studied him again, his expression indiscernible. When he did speak again, it was as if he hadn't heard Aki.

He waved a lazy hand at the room around them. "You look like you could get used to living someplace like this."

"I suppose anyone could. It's...," Aki turned his head, taking in the entire room as he searched for the right word to describe it. "It's amazing. Makes me wonder why Felix ever chose to come to Bren. If I lived here, I wouldn't be in a hurry to give it up."

"Nothing like where you came from?"

"Nothing."

"Seems almost a shame for one person to have so much when so many have so little," Jasper said softly, as if speaking to himself.

Jasper settled his own feet onto the hearth and closed his eyes. The crackle of the fire filled the silence and Aki wondered if Jasper meant to just sleep in the chair all night. Night had settled over them and Aki slid out of his chair without disturbing Jasper and crept across the room to the nearest of the two large windows that stood in the outer wall. Pressing his face up to the glass so that he could see into the darkness beyond, Aki studied the grounds of Baron Orlander's estate. After only a few seconds, he sensed Jasper's gaze on him and spun around to find the man staring at him through half-shut eyes.

"What weapons do you know how to use?"

The question caught Aki off guard.

"Most, I guess. At least, a little bit about most. I've had some practice since I was ten."

"And what do you prefer to use?"

Aki didn't even have to think about that. "Anything that doesn't force me to get too close to anyone in a fight."

"That's unfortunate," Jasper said, cocking an eyebrow as he continued to watch Aki. "You need to be able to defend yourself. And that means close up, if needed. When we get back to Bren, we'll get started. More likely than not, you'll be behind the others at this point."

Aki fought back the urge to remind Jasper that it was his fault, and not Aki's, that he was behind. Jasper was the one who had waited to do anything with him. His chance to say anything at all was lost when Jasper continued after a brief pause.

"Did you bring any weapons with you to the academy?"

Opening his mouth to answer, Aki faltered. The weapons he possessed - the ones he liked the best, the ones he preferred to any other - weren't actually his. And every time he took them out, he thought of where they'd come from, of where he'd come from. So instead of saying anything, he shook his head. If Jasper noticed his hesitation, he didn't mention it.

"I'm surprised Stephan didn't send you with any. I'm assuming he at least kept you in practice. If not, you'll have farther to go than I thought."

"He did," Aki said, his tone more defensive than he meant it to be. Although Jasper hadn't said anything amiss, Aki couldn't shake the feeling that his instructor had yet to stop scrutinizing him and sizing up his every word and action. Nor could he quite get away from the sense that he was disappointing Jasper.

"Good. You've been pulling your allowance?"

Aki nodded.

"Hopefully, you haven't spent it all. If you haven't, we'll buy you some when we get back," Jasper said, starting to his feet. "Better get some sleep. We're leaving early tomorrow."

Chapter 14

"I SUPPOSE IT WAS TOO MUCH to hope for," Master Wehr sighed and shook his head.

Aki, startled out of his reverie by his voice, glanced guiltily down at the work he was supposed to be doing.

"What was too much to hope for?"

"That, now that you've gone out on your first run, you would stop daydreaming out that window."

"I'm sorry. I was just...," Aki hesitated, realizing that there was no real excuse. "I'm sorry," he repeated. "I'll do better."

He bent his head, forcing his eyes to read the words in front of him. It was too much to hope for. Master Wehr was right about that. Now that he'd gone out once, all he wanted to do was go out again. In spite of the cold, in spite of sleeping out on the hard, frozen ground, he preferred being out on a run to this. Stifling a yawn, he finished the task before him.

True to his word, Jasper wasted no time in adding to Aki's training. He was waiting outside Aki's room when Aki returned from Master Wehr's.

"Let's see what you know," was all he said as he led them to a room Aki hadn't been in before. It was a large, long room that housed a variety of weapons and their accessories.

An hour later, his right arm aching from the sudden demands placed on it, Aki slid the practice sword back into its place in the rack that stood against the wall.

"You're not terrible," Jasper said from the other side of the room.

Aki, his face turned away from him, rolled his eyes. It was the closest Jasper could get to a compliment apparently. Of course, he wasn't terrible. And if Jasper had known anything at all, he would have known that. His life had practically depended on him mastering the same skills in two years that Gundar's other sons mastered in several more. Then there was his time with Stephan, as well. Stephan was, more than anything else, a soldier and Aki couldn't live with him for three years and not pick up a sword.

"I thought you didn't like any weapon that got you too close to your opponent."

"I don't. But I did say I knew how to use them. I had to."

"Pick something you do prefer," Jasper gestured to the wall of assorted weapons as he spoke.

Aki wandered over to the wall. A quick perusal of his choices led him to a set of throwing knives. He lifted them, one in each hand, testing their weight and balance in his grasp. A glance back at Jasper revealed the man watching him curiously. By his expression, Aki assumed he hadn't anticipated that choice.

"Are you any good with those?"

"I'm not terrible with them," Aki said with a grin, turning Jasper's words into his own. "What target?"

Jasper jerked his chin toward a sawdust filled sack suspended from the ceiling. Aki shifted his hold on the knife in his right hand and stepped forward. In the smooth, fluid motion he'd practiced a thousand times before, he sent the knife spinning through the air. A soft thud marked the end of its short flight as it embedded itself into the center of the bag. The second knife was already on its way, slicing through the air before the first landed.

"No, you're not." Jasper stepped up next to him. "Guess if you carry enough of those with you, you can keep your opponents away. You still need a sword, though."

Aki pulled the knives free and put them away. "What now?"

"We're done for now. Your day off is in two days. I'll come by and get you and we'll get you your own weapons. In the meantime, feel free to come and practice as much as you can. It can't hurt and you need to get your strength back in that arm. Get some of the other boys to practice with you if you can."

Aki grimaced at the reminder. Already his right arm was stiffening up and throbbing. He followed Jasper out of the room and crossed the arena, making his way toward his room. Half of the room was once again bare. Oscar had moved back to his old quarters while he was gone, and Aki wasn't sorry about that.

Especially not tonight.

With the door shut firmly behind him, Aki pulled out the bottom drawer of the dresser and rummaged through its contents until his hands brushed against the item he searched for. It was a small, oblong parcel wrapped in a piece of old cloth. Handling it with an almost reverent gentleness, he slid onto his bed and unwrapped it.

There were only three things Aki still possessed from his life in Aruuk. There was Sky, of course. Around his neck, he still wore his wolf's tooth talisman, containing not one but two teeth - one from the first wolf he'd killed and another from the first wolf everyone knew he'd killed. And he was staring down at the other laying across his lap.

They were a beautiful set. He slid the largest of the three out of its leather sheath and balanced it on his forefinger as a corner of his mouth turned up in a smile. They weren't his. Not really. But Halle was hardly going to come all the way down from Aruuk to reclaim his set of throwing knives. And Halle owed him something anyway. The knives had been a suitable payment.

Deciding that he wasn't ready to settle down to study for the rest of the evening just yet, Aki pulled on his winter clothes and set off, leaving the academy behind as dusk fell. At his side, for the first time since he'd come to Dival, Aki wore the knives that he'd kept hidden away.

It didn't take long for him to find Kezi, or rather, for Kezi to find him.

"These are new," she said from the shadows just behind him.

Aki spun around to find her dangling one of the knives from her thumb and forefinger. He snatched it from her hand and returned it to its place, annoyed that he had not even felt her take it from him.

"I wasn't going to steal it," Kezi said, stepping out of the shadows. "You've been gone."

"I went out with Jasper for my first run."

"All the way to Baron Orlander's. That's a long way to go in this weather."

"How did you know that?" Aki turned to study her and Kezi shrugged.

"I have ways of knowing a lot of things, Aki. How else do you think I've managed to survive here?"

"I didn't know you needed to spy on everyone to survive."

"It just helps me keep ahead. How'd you like it?"

"Honestly, it wasn't what I thought it would be. Not entirely. I liked it well enough; it just wasn't as exciting as I thought it would be. I guess I'd always imagined it being more like rushing from one place to another delivering some earth-shaking message. And it wasn't."

"He's rich, isn't he?"

"Who?"

"Baron Orlander, of course. Who else? I've heard he's one of the richest men in Dival." Kezi started to move down the street. For once, she wasn't avoiding the soft light of the streetlamps. Without looking to see if Aki followed or not, she continued, "Can you imagine what it would be like to have so much money?"

"Yes, I can. I saw exactly what it was like."

"Tell me about it."

Master Wehr's training asserted itself even as Aki told Kezi about Baron Orlander's estate. No matter how many turns they took, Aki knew how to get back and that was a comforting knowledge, especially as they reached the lower parts of Bren, close to the sea. He'd been here a few times with Kezi now in the last few weeks, but he still didn't feel at ease with the place.

"Where are we going, Kez?" Aki finally asked as she crossed the street, angling for the entrance of a ramshackle building. The sign hanging above its door marked it as a tavern.

"To meet my friends, of course. You'll like them."

Aki raised an eyebrow as he followed her through the door. It was less crowded than he'd expected. The low hum of conversation didn't shift or change at all as they came in and Kezi led the way to a darkened corner near the back. Aki hesitated only a moment before following her, wondering who he was about to meet. Someone else who made their living on the streets, he supposed. He was not at all prepared for the face that greeted him.

"Jasper?"

"It seems you and I have a mutual friend, Aki," Jasper said, looking up. "Join us."

Aki lowered himself into the chair opposite Jasper while Kezi moved away toward the counter. He made no effort to conceal his own surprise and curiosity and Jasper smiled tightly in return.

"Kezi says you know when to keep your mouth shut. Is that right?"

"I don't understand."

"You know she steals," Jasper leaned forward, his fingers curled around a mug, "and you don't tell on her."

"I guess so."

Jasper studied him hard and Aki squirmed beneath the scrutiny. Whatever Jasper was looking for, he must have seen because a moment later he offered Aki another tight smile then leaned back, bringing his mug to his lips.

"I wouldn't have thought you'd be out like this. Oscar complained quite loudly that the only thing you ever did was hole up in your room every spare minute, studying. Or was that for his benefit alone?"

Aki grinned despite himself. "Maybe. He did break my arm."

"You got on a horse that you shouldn't have."

Unable to argue with that, Aki changed the subject, "How long have you known Kezi?"

"A few months. She and I share a common," Jasper paused, drumming his fingers lightly on the table, "shall we say, goal. And you would be wise to not ask any more questions, Aki."

Biting down on his lip to refrain from asking the questions Jasper had just warned him not to ask, Aki decided it was time to once again change the subject. Kezi's reappearance did that for him. Accompanying her were two others, a young man and woman who were clearly related.

"Aki, meet my friends, Phineas and Cassandra," Kezi said, gesturing to her companions and taking a seat, setting down a cup in front of him. Aki brought it to his lips and made a face as he swallowed the first mouthful. Kezi stifled a laugh.

Phineas' eyes shifted about the room, never stopping long enough to settle on anything. Cassandra, on the other hand, never took her eyes off of Aki and although she smiled, there was nothing friendly in her gaze. Aki lowered his own, finding a scratch on the table that demanded his attention.

"Is he safe?" Cassandra asked, still watching him.

"If he wasn't, I wouldn't have brought him. Really, Cassie, you're too paranoid," Kezi laughed.

"Better paranoid than in prison," Cassandra nodded to Phineas, seeming to finally notice that anyone else was at the table.

Phineas glanced around the room one more time before reaching into his oversized jacket and pulling out three bags that jingled softly as he slid them across the table to Kezi and Jasper. Jasper frowned but Kezi loosened the string that held the mouth of one closed and peered inside.

"I suppose *he* is too *indisposed* to join us tonight," Cassandra said, placing a twist on the words that added weight to their meaning that Aki could not understand.

"He was passed out, drunk, last time I saw. That's for the best, though," Kezi said. Aki pretended not to notice Kezi's pointed nod in his direction and took another drink instead.

"If he can't be more...,"

"He'll do what he needs to, Cassie. I promise. He needs this more than we do. He wants it more than we do."

"If you say so. Is it enough?" Cassandra waved a hand toward the bags still sitting on the table.

"No," Jasper spoke up for the first time since Kezi and her friends had come to the table. "But I know where we can get more." Phineas, Cassandra and Kezi all leaned in expectantly, but Jasper's frown only deepened. "Aki, I think you should be getting back. You wouldn't want to be late to Master Wehr's in the morning."

Understanding the dismissal, Aki pushed his chair away from the table and left the tavern. He couldn't say that he was sorry to leave. Whatever was about to be discussed was beyond petty theft on the streets. Besides, it was late. Very late.

Chapter 15

YOU DON'T TRUST HIM?" KEZI turned to Jasper. It was hours after Aki left, and Cassandra and Phineas had also taken their leave. Only a handful of people remained inside the tavern as the lamps burned low and the room grew dim. "I told you, he keeps his mouth shut. He won't tell. He'd rather keep his head down and stay out of trouble."

Jasper ran a weary hand over his face. "Perhaps not. But I don't want to give him everything at once."

"Is he as good as you thought he was?"

"Better. And he doesn't even know how good he is. He can hold his own with a sword, more than his own, probably. Whoever taught him knew what they were doing, and never bothered to tell him how much progress he made. He's quiet, can move around without making a sound. He could be useful."

"But you still don't trust him?"

"I have no reason to. Just because he keeps quiet about you doesn't mean he'll do the same about us. There's rather a big difference in what he knows you do and what we're planning, don't you think?"

"I want him on our side in this, Jasper. It's his side too, even if he doesn't see it."

"And have you told Halle?"

Kezi stared down at the empty mug in front of her, her thin, calloused fingers wrapped around it. Several seconds passed without an answer from her.

"You haven't," Jasper said flatly.

"He doesn't need to know. Not yet. Let me worry about Halle, Jasper."

Jasper snorted, "I'll happily leave that job to you. And wish you luck with it. But Cassie's right. If he doesn't start coming through on his promises, then he's nothing but baggage to us."

"He'll come through. He has to," Kezi sighed. "In the meantime, we need to keep Aki coming. Even if he won't join us, he's our best leverage with Halle. We can't afford to lose that."

"The only way Aki would be useful at all in controlling Halle is if you're planning on using him as some sort of bait. It's revenge Halle wants, not a family reunion. Has it ever occurred to you that you're playing a very dangerous game?"

"With Halle and Aki? Yes. But it can't be helped. And I'm not the one who started the game. We just have to keep them apart until it's to our advantage to bring them together. And Aki doesn't have to be bait. One of them has to be, and it could easily be Halle. I'd rather it be Halle. That's why I want him on our side."

"I meant more than just with the brothers. I mean with all of this. All the schemes, the planning. What happens if it all falls through?"

"It won't," Kezi said, although her voice cracked a little and her fingers tightened around her cup. "It's all I've ever wanted. And I will get it, Jasper. I will get it if it's the last thing in this life that I do."

Chapter 16

THE ARENA WAS QUIET AND deserted this early in the morning. Aki shivered a little as he stepped out into it from the dormitory. It was still dark out, but the moonlight on the snow provided sufficient visibility.

He reached Sky's stall before he realized that he was not alone. He turned to find one of the other boys following him. A fringe of red hair peeked out from beneath his winter cap.

"Felix?" The smile on Aki's face faded as he noticed the expression that Felix wore. "You're out early."

"So are you," Felix said. Lines of worry furrowed his brow as he caught up to Aki and fell in step beside him.

"I'm trying to get a head start. I've been late twice this week and Master Wehr wasn't happy about it." Aki decided not to mention that he'd been late because he hadn't returned to the academy until well into the night and had overslept the following morning. Although it had come as a surprise after the way he was dismissed the first night, Jasper had been the one to ask him to return the other two nights and it was so nice to be wanted that he couldn't bring himself to refuse. Besides, he'd figured it would pay to be on such good terms with at least one of his instructors. "I figure if I show up early for a change, it might make him forget about it."

Rather than making his way over to his own horse's stall, Felix stood outside Sky's stall, resting his elbows on the top of the half door.

"I had a letter from home," he said after a moment.

"Oh?"

"Something happened."

A chill ran through Aki at Felix's words. But Felix wasn't done, although, judging by the pause, whatever he had to say was difficult.

"Someone, or rather, several people broke into our house. They stole quite a bit of money, but that's not the worst of it."

When Felix didn't say anything more, Aki paused what he was doing. "What was the worst?"

"My brother. He heard them, but when he tried to stop them, he was injured. Badly."

Aki turned back to Sky, unable to look at Felix's face another second. He couldn't bear to see the concern and hurt there - because he knew. He wasn't even sure how he knew, but he did. Jasper and Kezi, Phineas and Cassandra - they were the ones responsible. That was why Kezi was so interested in him telling her about the Baron's home.

"I'm getting ready to go home now for a few days. I couldn't sleep anyway, so I figured I'd get an early start."

"I'm sorry, Felix," Aki said, trying desperately to convey the depth of what he felt in those words. It was impossible. "I hope your brother will be alright."

Felix nodded once then turned away to ready his own horse for his trip. Aki watched him for a moment before returning to work. He lingered in Sky's stall until Felix rode away and then started back across the arena, hands shoved deep into his pockets. He was halfway across when he caught sight of him.

Leaning against the wall near the entrance, Jasper was watching him. Aki lowered his head and hurried on. He shoved open the door to the dormitory and brushed against Oscar on his way outside. By the time he reached his own room, it was clear that Jasper wasn't going to be ignored. He followed Aki through the doorway before Aki could shut the door.

"What's wrong with you?" Jasper asked, his voice low.

"Felix just told me what happened."

"I guessed that was what he was talking to you about. I was sort of hoping to catch you first. You figured it out, didn't you?" Jasper's eyes narrowed as he studied Aki. "Of course you did. Sit down."

Aki obeyed, sinking down onto the very edge of his mattress, ready to jump up again in a second. Jasper lowered himself onto the opposite bed, the one Oscar had occupied only a couple of weeks ago. He pressed his hands together, then pulled them apart and rested them on his legs.

"Before you start jumping to conclusions, there are reasons for what we did, Aki. Good reasons. Reasons you'd understand if you knew them."

"You hurt someone. You hurt Felix's brother."

"You know Felix isn't your friend, don't you? Sure, he's polite and he doesn't ignore you the way some of the others do. But that boy would be polite to a fly. It's what he was raised to be. But he's not your friend."

Aki stared down at his hands in his lap and said nothing. All the things he wanted to say, he didn't dare to. And part of him believed Jasper. Felix was kind because kindness was the only thing he knew.

"Kezi said we could trust you. You've been her friend, and she yours, for some time. You wouldn't betray her, would you?"

Aki shook his head. No, he wouldn't betray her. He couldn't. She was one of the few people he could count on to be a friend. Especially here in Bren when he was so far from the people he'd grown used to.

"Good. I knew I could count on you to keep a secret. You keep enough of your own, don't you?"

At that, Aki's head snapped up and his eyes met Jasper's with a mingling of confusion and horror. Jasper caught the look immediately and smiled, the thin, tight version of a smile that Aki was getting used to seeing on his face. Aki wondered if it was the only way he knew how to smile, as if the act itself caused him physical pain.

"I don't know what you're talking about," he lied.

"Weren't you there the night Lord Bayner died? The night your father died?"

Aki shifted as his breath quickened. "He wasn't my father," he whispered.

"Another secret? Whoever he was to you, you were there when he was killed, you saw who did it, and you saw what happened before it," Jasper let the words hang between them for a beat, causing Aki's heart to speed up.

"Maybe you even had a hand in some of it. But no one knows. Because, for some reason, the magistrate's report of that night doesn't say a single word about you. Not one single word. Not even a hint that you were there. I wonder why that is?"

Aki's fingers brushed against the blanket beneath him, clutching it as he shook his head.

"It doesn't say what part you had in the hours of torture perpetrated against your brother. Boris, wasn't it?"

Aki gripped the blankets harder as blood fled from his face, leaving him white and shaken at Jasper's words. He couldn't know. He couldn't possibly know anything about that day. No one knew. No one except...

Jasper continued, cutting off the thought before he allowed himself to finish it, "There are other secrets you keep, too. Things that happened before you ever set foot in our country. No one here really knows you, do they, Aki?"

Blood pounded in Aki's ears, drowning out the sound of Jasper's words. He shut his eyes as if that act alone could deny what was coming out of Jasper's mouth. When he listened again, Jasper had moved on.

"And not only does the magistrate's report make no mention of you, it also doesn't say a word about what your own brother did to you. That alone was a considerable crime. I wonder if Sasha would be thought of as quite the hero still if people knew what he was capable of. Nearly murdered you in a fit of rage. That'd be a terrible secret to get out, wouldn't it?"

"Yes, sir," Aki murmured.

"You understand, then, why you must keep what you know a secret. Sure, someone was hurt but you couldn't have stopped that. You can stop Sasha from being hurt. You understand that, right?"

"Yes, sir," he repeated, his eyes refusing to meet Jasper's. "How do you know about any of that?"

"That, Aki, is my secret." Jasper stood up and crossed the room. He laid his hand on Aki's shoulder in a gesture that would have been comforting under any other circumstance. "I'm not your enemy here, Aki. I'm trying to be your friend. And as your friend, I think you have more ahead of you than just being a courier for our king.

98

You have more skill than you know, and our king doesn't deserve it. Say the word, and you can be anything you want with us."

"I want to be a courier."

Jasper nodded, slowly. "I hope Master Wehr can see that. Because when I spoke with him yesterday, he was rather disappointed in you this week. He's a patient man, but his patience does have its limits. It might reach its breaking point if, say, you were late, again."

At that Aki was on his feet, casting a helpless glance at the rising sun through the window. Jasper stepped back out of his way as he retrieved his satchel of half-done work that he was supposed to have finished the night before.

"Remember what we've talked about," Jasper said softly as he opened the door to leave. "Remember what can happen if you don't choose wisely."

Silently berating himself for not staying back and finishing his work the prior evening, Aki hurried out of the academy and into the street beyond. Even if he ran all the way, he'd never make it to Master Wehr's in time.

Chapter 17

AKI WAS GASPING FOR BREATH by the time he stood in the front room of Master Wehr's. His heart hammered against his ribs, threatening to pound its way straight out of his chest as he met the stern gaze of his instructor - partly because he had run all the way here, and partly because he was fairly sure that Master Wehr's patience was at an end. And if that was the case, he wasn't sure how he would ever go back and face Stephan and Alina again.

"You're late. Again."

"I know. I'm sorry."

Master Wehr shook his head. "Why?"

"I lost track of time," Aki said. He was tempted to mention that he'd lost track of time talking to Jasper but he didn't dare risk Master Wehr asking about that conversation. And since he already knew what the next question was going to be, he went ahead and answered it, "Also, I didn't finish my work."

"Why?" Master Wehr repeated.

"I was out again. And I came back late."

Master Wehr sighed, but there was more disappointment than anger in it and Aki loathed himself for having caused it. He would do better.

"What is going on with you, Aki?"

Any other day, the question wouldn't have bothered him. But coming on the heels of Jasper's not so subtle threat and the news Felix had given him, something was definitely going on with him. His entire world was falling apart, and he wasn't sure how to stop it.

He shrugged, "Nothing, I guess. I just wanted...," he stopped.

The weight of those words sunk into him. His entire life he'd been forbidden from wanting anything for himself and now that he'd dared to, he had the sinking feeling that things weren't going to work out the way he thought.

And the hardest part now was forcing himself to meet Master Wehr's eyes. If there had been any anger in them, he could have handled it better. He understood anger. He was used to it. Even Stephan had been angry with him from time to time. It was the disappointment and pity that he didn't know what to do with and so he looked away again.

"Come with me." Master Wehr stood up and made his way around the desk and towards the door, pausing long enough to draw on a thick coat and to place a heavy satchel in Aki's hands. Normally, Aki would have wasted no time in trying to satiate his curiosity over the contents of the bag. But not today.

Aki followed at a distance as they started down the street.

"You are quiet."

"I don't have anything to say," Aki said, which wasn't quite true. There was so much he wanted to say, but with Jasper's words hanging over him, they were choked up inside of him.

"Then something is truly wrong," Master Wehr paused and motioned for Aki to catch up with him, "because you always have something to say."

He waited for Aki to answer, but Aki remained silent.

Aki could feel his gaze boring into him, searching for the truth he could not afford to reveal. He had an almost unstoppable urge to confide everything in this man without a care as to the consequences. Not just what he knew about Jasper and not just about the threat that haunted him. No, he wanted to tell Master Wehr everything - all the secrets he carried with him, about himself. But he didn't.

"There is trouble?"

"No. There's nothing. Nothing's wrong."

"Tell me, Aki, do you always lie so easily?"

"I'm not lying."

"Really?" The look Master Wehr turned on him was scathing in its accusation and Aki knew that anything he said now would only make things worse. It was almost a relief when he realized they had reached the entrance to the academy, although he wasn't sure why Master Wehr had brought him back here.

Master Wehr crossed the arena and reached the stall of one of the older horses stabled there. He tapped his cane against the door in gesture.

"I'm afraid I'm not quite as capable of saddling him as I used to be. Will you?"

Aki lifted the latch and stepped inside. He was surprised to find out that Master Wehr rode at all anymore. For the first time that morning, his curiosity began to outweigh his concern.

"Are we going somewhere?"

"We are, we are. When you're finished, get your own horse ready."

Aki handed off the reins of the horse and moved down to Sky's stall.

"Where are we going?"

"I think I'm not going to tell you that just yet."

It was such an odd answer for Master Wehr to give that Aki paused what he was doing to look at his instructor. A grim expression adorned the man's wrinkled face, but there was a hint of amusement in his eyes and that chased away the last of Aki's worries for the time being. After all, Jasper was only asking for his silence, not his participation.

The road they took as they left Bren was one Aki had never been on. It ran along the sea, but in the opposite direction of the route he'd taken with Jasper to get to Baron Orlander's. The wide harbor of Bren gave way to jagged rocks and steep cliffs. Aki was surprised to notice a few cottages dotting the rugged coast, some built close enough that he thought they must be in the way of the tides and waves. He mentioned that to Master Wehr.

"Smugglers huts. That's what those are. They build them up off the ground, with enough room beneath them to store their boats and whatever they are smuggling. When the tide comes in and the sea is at its height, the water comes all the way up beneath the hut and they can sail out with the tide without ever hauling their boat anywhere."

"But," Aki said thoughtfully, "if everyone knows what they are and what they're used for, why doesn't the king just have them destroyed?"

"They have the terrible habit of looking quite innocent and abandoned whenever the king's men are around. He can't just arbitrarily order the destruction of property without proof, and proof can be a very difficult thing to acquire." Master Wehr pulled his horse up and gazed out at the sea a bit wistfully. "Sometimes, I forget how much I loved this part of the job."

Aki, his own horse halted, followed his gaze to where waves broke, white and foaming, against the rocks, the dull roar of their movement the only sound that could be heard.

"Why, exactly, did you choose to be a courier?"

Master Wehr nudged his horse forward again before answering, "Dival is a beautiful country. And I was restless. I hated the idea of being trapped in one place, tied to a trade for the rest of my life. I wanted to see more. I'd have gone to sea, but to be honest, it's always frightened me a little." Master Wehr smiled slightly. "This was the closest I could come to what I wanted. To ride all over the country. To meet men both high and low. To represent the sovereign of our country. And at the time, we were in the midst of a great war. There was purpose to be had in serving our king's cause."

They rode on until Bren was far behind them and nothing but wild country surrounded them. The sun was high and shining, blinding and bright against the unending expanse of snow-covered land. A single tree, enormous and devoid of its summer greenery, stood a way off the road and Master Wehr turned his horse's head toward it. When they reached it, Master Wehr motioned for Aki to dismount.

"Aki, there is one question I asked you many months ago, on that first day, that you did not answer."

Aki thought back to that day, turning his memories of it over in his mind, searching for the unanswered question. The only one he could think of, the only one he had flatly refused to answer - what the worst thing done to him as a slave had been - was one he still wouldn't answer. Bracing himself for it again, he was surprised when Master Wehr spoke.

"I asked you many things that day, not all of which you were willing to answer, and I will not go back on my word regarding your life before you came here. But I asked you also why it was that you wanted to be a courier. And I must now demand an answer for that question."

Aki took a deep breath, as much to sort out his thoughts as to express his relief that the question was not quite as dreaded as he anticipated. He opened his mouth, but no words came out and he frowned.

"I like horses," he said at last, although that was hardly the real reason and judging from the look on Master Wehr's face, his instructor knew it too. He tried again, "And I guess I didn't really want to be stuck in one place either. I used to watch the couriers come to Stephan's and wish I was one of them because they didn't have someone constantly looking over their shoulder telling them what to do. Mostly, though, I wanted to be one because it was my choice and not what someone else wanted for me."

"And is it still what you want?"

"Yes," Aki answered without hesitation.

"Then, I'm afraid, you need to prove it to me."

Aki searched Master Wehr's face for some hint of what he meant but found nothing.

"How?"

In answer, Master Wehr loosened the heavy satchel that he'd carried with him on his saddle and tossed it to the ground at Aki's feet.

"I have taught you a great deal since you've come to me and until recently you've been a good student. I'm going to give you a chance to show me that you have truly learned."

"What do I have to do?" Aki's eyes darkened with suspicion.

"Inside that bag are all the instructions you need. Follow them, and you'll be fine."

Aki picked it up and unfastened the buckle that held it shut. He pulled out the first paper inside and looked up at Master Wehr in dismay.

"It's in code!"

"Of course it is. What would be the test in this if it wasn't? You've learned that code."

"But I've never had to decode it without any help before."

"Then count this as the first of many times. If you decode my instructions correctly and follow them precisely, then you will be on my doorstep the morning after tomorrow. If you can't manage that, then don't bother to show up." Master Wehr reached for Sky's loose reins, "And you won't need your horse for this so I shall take her back with me."

"What? I have to walk?"

"Yes, that is exactly what I mean. Your horse isn't the one who didn't finish their work or showed up late."

Aki was too stunned to say anything until it was too late to say anything at all. Master Wehr disappeared down the same road they had just ridden up. By then, Aki was no longer stunned, he was angry.

Chapter 18

FOR A FULL FIVE MINUTES, Aki sat on a large rock near the tree. The sound of waves still filled the air. Aki had a strong urge to carry the satchel right up to the edge of the cliff rising above the sea and pitch it with all its contents into the swirling waters below. He could still show up at Master Wehr's in two days and just say that he'd followed his instructions.

He abandoned the thought almost as quickly as it came to him. If he threw it into the sea, he couldn't go back. And if he couldn't go back to Master Wehr and the academy, then there was no way he dared show his face at Stephan's.

As the five minutes drew to a close, only one choice made sense.

Opening the satchel once more, he pulled out the first piece of paper. A cold breeze blowing in off the sea forced him to tighten his grip on it as he bent his head to decipher it. He squeezed his eyes shut and tried to picture the cipher Master Wehr had made him learn. Although it took more concentration than he anticipated and at one point tossing it in the sea and running away and starting a new life somewhere else became a very appealing thought again, he managed, bit by bit, to discern the message.

They were directions. Very specific directions. Aki studied them several times over before getting to his feet. Leaving the road and the sound of the sea behind him, he started off. Master Wehr's directions made no mention of following a road, only a series of landmarks that Aki could only hope weren't too obscure.

Hours of walking did little to improve his mood and a good deal to strengthen his poor opinion of Master Wehr's plan. He kept his gait brisk enough that the cold did not bother him too much at first, but after so many hours in it, it began to wear on him. It managed to work its way beneath the layers of warm clothing he was wearing and made him shiver.

An empty gnawing in his stomach reminded him that he hadn't eaten since the morning, and it was late in the afternoon now. Tempted once more to give up on the entire endeavor, he found a fallen tree to sit on and decided it was as good a time as any to rest for a few minutes.

So far, he'd managed to find all of the landmarks Master Wehr had listed. He lowered the satchel to the ground between his feet and pulled out the next piece of paper. A faint jingle as the contents of the bag shifted grabbed his attention and he rummaged around inside until he found the source of the noise. He lifted a small purse of coins out and weighed it in his hands. Having at least a little money in his possession improved his outlook somewhat, although, so far he hadn't seen so much as a farmhouse so he wasn't sure where he could spend it anyway.

In the fading light of the sun, he ran through the first set of instructions one last time and realized that he was near the end - although the last line on the paper made little sense to him. Rather than telling him where to go, it simply gave him a name with an amount of money written beside it. Slinging the satchel over his shoulder again, he got to his feet.

The shadows were growing long across the snow when he caught sight of a faint glow in the distance and hurried toward it.

A small cluster of houses formed a tiny hamlet nestled into the wooded hills that he'd been hiking through half the day. There couldn't be more than a dozen, Aki realized as he approached it. By now it was almost completely dark and Aki knew he'd either have to rely on someone's hospitality here, or spend the night outside in the cold. The pangs of hunger in his stomach were enough to make him knock on the first door he reached.

When a middle-aged woman answered it a moment later, Aki thought he understood the last part of Master Wehr's instructions.

"Can I help you?"

"I'm looking for a Cornelius Raftle."

"Three houses past mine, on the right."

"Thank you, ma'am," Aki said as he hurried on before the smell of food wafting out of the open doorway proved too much.

Although it was dark out already, it was hardly late and from the windows of all the houses lights still shone making it easy for Aki to see the way. The third house that the woman had pointed out to him was as nondescript as any of the others. He made his way up the stone pathway that had been cleared of snow only recently. He had to knock twice before anyone answered and was a little startled to find that the person on the other side was a girl around his own age.

"I'm looking for Cornelius Raftle," he said without waiting for her to ask.

She gave him a funny look that Aki attributed to his accent then turned and called over her shoulder, "Father, there's a boy here to see you."

Aki thought that was a little unfair considering that she couldn't be any older than he was but bit his tongue to keep from saying so.

"Come on. You're letting in all the cold air just standing there," she said as she stepped aside, motioning him through the door.

Aki hadn't realized just how cold he was until he was standing in the warm entry of Cornelius' home. And apparently supper time in this village was universal. The smell of roasted meat hung heavy in the air. Aki's mouth watered and he was just beginning to wonder how rude it would be to ask for them to feed him when Cornelius stepped into the room. Although he was a large man, there was a kindness about his face that drove away some of Aki's nervousness.

"Let me guess," he smiled, holding up a hand to stop Aki from speaking, "you're from Atticus?"

"Yes, sir."

"Come in. We were just sitting down to supper. Join us and we'll talk afterwards." He turned towards his daughter, "Martha, set out another place."

Aki tried not to let his relief show as he followed them into the kitchen. It wasn't large, but a fire was burning brightly in the stove and it was comfortable. It reminded him a little of being at Stephan and Alina's and for the first time in his life, Aki understood what it was to be a little bit homesick. Martha set another plate on the table while Cornelius pulled a third chair up to the small table and gestured for Aki to sit in it.

It was all Aki could do to sit and wait patiently while Martha served each of them in turn, and she seemed to be enjoying taking her time with it.

"You are Atticus' new student?" Cornelius asked as Martha finally finished and took her seat.

Aki, a forkful of food already on its way to his mouth, nodded.

"It's been several years since he's taken any. You must be proud to learn under him."

"Very," Aki managed to answer, trying not to think of Master Wehr's warning and of how great a disappointment Aki had been in the last few weeks.

"You are not from around here, are you?"

"No. I'm from up north, in the mountains."

"Ah, I see. We are not from, either."

That surprised Aki a little since nothing about them hinted at being different.

"Martha's mother and I came here from Sondaru many years ago. We tired of the constant civil wars and the weakness of the emperor. When we lost our home there, Dival welcomed us and we've made it our home ever since. Of course, as you can see, Martha's mother is no longer with us."

"I'm sorry. I lost my mother, too. I have a friend who comes from Sondaru. Only she didn't choose to come here. She was a slave in Aruuk and was brought here before being set free," Aki said, before realizing that he was probably saying too much, as usual. Dagmar likely didn't want him going around telling everyone he met what had happened to her. Not that she would ever say so. Dagmar was the kindest person he'd ever met.

"And Aruuk is where you are from, as well?"

"Yes," Aki said. He definitely shouldn't have said so much.

"I have heard that many changes have come to that country in recent years. Is this true?"

"I think so, but I haven't actually been there for a while." Aki decided it was time to change topics. "Master Wehr directed me here, but I have no idea why. Do you?"

"Yes. I would imagine, if you look in that bag of yours, you'll find a note addressed to me and a sum of money."

Aki pulled the satchel that had been sitting at his feet up onto his lap and searched it again. Sure enough, at the very bottom, was a small stack of notes, each one bearing a different name. The top one had Cornelius' on it. He pulled it out and handed it across the table to the man, then reached inside the money purse and began counting out the sum that had been written down. He handed those to Cornelius as well and then sat back, waiting, as the man opened the note and read it.

"I'll see to this in the morning," Cornelius said, setting the note and the money aside. "I trust you'll stay with us tonight. What I have is not much, but it is out of the weather and comfortable." He pushed his chair away from the table.

Sitting in front of the fireplace after supper was finished, Aki wanted nothing more but to lay down and sleep. Cornelius and Martha, however, did not appear to be in any hurry to go to bed.

Without ever having witnessed it before, he was sure that this time in front of the fire was as much a part of their daily routine as waking up in the morning. Nor were they made the slightest bit uncomfortable by his presence. In fact, the opposite was true. Where others might fuss over a guest, they simply absorbed him into their habitual time.

"Martha, why don't you sing a bit?" Cornelius turned to his daughter in a lull in the conversation. Even that seemed to just be part of their usual evening ritual.

"I'm sure we could do without that for this evening," Martha said, and Aki was inclined to agree with her.

"There's no reason to do without."

With a thin smile Martha reached for a stringed instrument that Aki had noticed resting against the wall.

She plucked the strings a few times, made a face, adjusted tiny knobs and then plucked them again. Aki was just trying to stifle a yawn when she finally started singing. It was a song in another language. Taliea and Dagmar's language, he realized.

Aki squirmed in his chair a little. Martha sang well, but the sound of her voice tugged on an uncomfortable memory.

The first time he could ever remember hearing someone sing was when he was six. He'd been given over to work for one of Chief Gundar's wives, Mara, at the time. Mara was as spiteful and cruel as she was beautiful and she was a hard mistress to please, her orders often capricious and fickle. Aki ran afoul of her temper more times than he could count. In some ways, he'd learned to fear her more than Chief Gundar, who officially owned him.

She had a son, Halle, who was only a year or two older than him and who had inherited his mother's poor temper and his father's penchant for cruelty. It happened that he was in her room one day, scrubbing the floors or stacking logs for the fire, he couldn't remember exactly which and it didn't really matter. He was invisible to them, toiling away while they did whatever it was that Chiefs wives and sons did. Halle had come in, wailing over a scraped knee.

Aki's own work was forgotten as he watched Mara scoop Halle up onto her lap and fawn over him. She'd washed his knee and kissed his forehead and held him until his tears dried.

And then she sang to him.

Her voice matched her beauty, and the soft, lilting lullaby filled the quiet space of the room. It was the most enchanting sound Aki had ever heard. It was sweet and soothing and wove a spell of calm in a space that knew little more than simmering anger most of the time.

Being too young to control such impulses, he'd scooted closer and stared, soaking in the forbidden solace. For a while, Mara hadn't noticed him. And it might have stayed that way if Halle hadn't seen him and pointed him out to his mother.

Mara had been furious.

She'd beaten him until he could barely crawl away and scolded him for daring to look at her, which wasn't quite fair since he was so young that she wasn't required to hide her face from him. Halle had beaten him as well, an action that brought a look of pride to Mara's face, although he was too little at the time to do as much damage as Mara had.

Aki hadn't cried when he was beaten. He hadn't cried when Mara's icy voice berated him and threatened to tell Chief Gundar what he'd done. He hadn't even cried when, as part of his punishment, he had to scrub all of the floors in their rooms again and missed his evening meal. It wasn't until he was finally allowed to slip away.

He'd found a quiet spot behind a large woodpile where he was mostly hidden and then he cried. Not from the pain that radiated from the numerous cuts, scrapes, and bruises that covered his body. He was used to those by that point. He'd cried because there was a great big hole ripped open inside of him that he hadn't noticed until that day and he didn't know how to fill it. He'd cried because there was a longing in his childish heart so deep and painful that he didn't understand but felt. He'd cried because, for the first time in his young life, he was aware of something missing.

And when he was done crying, he started hating Halle.

Halle, who had a mother to tend his wounds, and soothe his pain, and sing him songs. Halle, who had the luxury of shedding tears over a single scrape. Halle, who had something that Aki didn't, and never would, have - a mother's love and care. Hating Halle didn't fill that awful void, but it covered it, hid it away, took away the sharpness of its ache. It was a bandage wrapped over the space of a missing limb, useless but comforting. Hating Halle was easier than living with that newfound pain.

When he'd finally made his way back to the hut that all the slave children shared, he'd asked their keeper if she was his mother. The old woman, a slave herself, had backhanded him for his impertinence. Undaunted in the strange way that only young children can be, he'd asked her who his mother was and why she wasn't there to take care of him. At that, the old woman had cackled and said he was the reason his mother was dead and that no one even knew her name. He hadn't understood what that meant then. He hadn't understood until years later but her words had stuck with him, gnawing at the emptiness he tried to cover.

Something of his discomfort must have shown on his face because when Martha finished her song, she was staring at him oddly and she set aside the instrument without another word.

"You're not done already, are you?" Cornelius asked, his eyes shut and a pleasant smile on his face.

"I think Aki is tired, Father," Martha said. Aki gave her a grateful smile that was lost in another yawn.

"Of course, I'd forgotten. You must have come a long way today, Aki," Cornelius, unbothered by his daughter's reminder, said. "Get your things and Martha will show you to your room."

Since the only thing he had with him was the satchel Master Wehr had given him, he was following Martha up the ladder into the attic a moment later. Cornelius was right on all counts regarding what he had to offer in the way of sleeping quarters. The attic room was small, its ceiling so low that he could not stand upright, but it was also warm and there was a mattress on the floor with several blankets and Aki knew he would sleep just fine there.

"You didn't like my singing," Martha said, her voice quiet so that it wouldn't carry down to the rest of the house.

"It was fine," Aki answered, and then realized that was the wrong thing to say.

Martha stiffened, "I only do it because Father likes it. It reminds him of Mother. Or at least, he says it does. I don't ever remember hearing her sing. I was too young to remember much at all about her when she died."

"I'm sorry," Aki repeated.

"Did you know your mother?"

Aki shook his head, fighting now to keep his eyes open and wishing Martha wasn't so curious.

"What was her name?"

And because Aki could not bear to say that she was nameless to him, he lied, "Alana."

Chapter 19

LIGHT STREAMED IN THROUGH the tiny window above his head, waking Aki out of a deep sleep. He lay unmoving for a moment, remembering where he was and how he'd come to be there.

The satchel still lay on the floor near his bed exactly where he'd set it the night before and he pulled it toward him now. He might as well figure out what he was supposed to be doing today. Deciphering the message was a lot easier to do in a warm house, he decided. More directions, mostly, and as detailed as the ones from the day before. There were two different names on the paper this time - Silas Dregan and Bela Ubert - and sums of money written next to both of them.

A rattling of pans and dishes coupled with the smell of food spurred him out from underneath his warm covers. Knowing Master Wehr, he probably hadn't left much time for him to lay around in bed in his plans.

Cornelius was coming in the back door, a whirlwind of snow and icy wind blowing in with him, when Aki made it down. A glance out the front window confirmed his suspicions. The sunny weather he'd traveled in the day before was gone. He wondered if Master Wehr had accounted for foul weather when he formed the schedule he meant for Aki to keep. The thought filled him with a great urgency. Perhaps he was already behind that schedule. Perhaps he'd slept too late, or shouldn't have stayed the night here at all. The memory of Master Wehr's words pounded through his head. If he didn't make it back by tomorrow morning, he was done. He was out.

"Ah, good, you're up," Cornelius said, stomping snow off of his boots as he stood in the doorway. A parcel wrapped in oiled canvas was tucked under one arm. "This is for you to take to Atticus, as he requested. You'll stay for breakfast, won't you?"

He added the last part when he noticed Aki pulling on his coat and boots.

"I think it'd be better if I got started. I have to be back by a certain time."

"But I'm sure Atticus didn't mean for you to starve. Come and eat with us, and then be on your way. It won't take long."

Remembering how hungry he was by the time he'd reached his destination the night before, Aki decided it would be a mistake to refuse food now. Slipping into the same chair he'd occupied before, he waited only long enough for all three of them to be served before starting in.

"You'd think they didn't feed couriers," Martha commented as he neared the end of his plate.

"Oh, they feed us. But, not like this," Aki answered with a laugh. "I really should go now, though. Thank you, for the food and the bed and for whatever this is," he picked up the parcel Cornelius had given him and stuffed it inside the satchel. It fit, barely. He grabbed his cloak from where it hung by the front door and pulled the hood of it well over his head and face.

Out in the cold once more, he wished he didn't need to be in such a hurry to leave. The wind tore at the paper in his hands as he read through the first steps of his journey one more time. Stuffing it back inside the satchel, he set off - a grim determination to not fail and to prove to Master Wehr that he did know what he was doing the sole motivation for putting one foot in front of the other.

Expecting to spend the entire day walking, Aki was surprised when his directions led him to a large town around midday. Although it was not as big as Bren, it was obvious that it was a prosperous and busy town. Houses gave way to shops and merchants as he got deeper into town. Here, he didn't think he could just knock on the first door and ask for a name. With this many people, he would likely have been wandering around for some time before finding someone who knew who he was looking for.

S. T. Hobbs

Fortunately, Master Wehr had been aware of that and his instructions led Aki directly to the door of the man he was seeking. Aki read the sign above the door, a feat he couldn't have accomplished months ago. Silas Dregan, silversmith. Before entering the shop, Aki found the note addressed to him.

A little bell rang above the door when he opened it and stepped inside, brushing the powdery snowflakes off his shoulders and throwing back the hood of his cloak. A man stuck his head out from behind a corner.

"What can I do for you?" he said as the rest of him appeared.

"Silas Dregan?"

"That's me." Silas studied him a little harder, then grinned. "And if I had to guess, you're Aki Turston. Atticus told me about you. First student he's taken in a few years. What'd you do to achieve that honor?"

"I have no idea, honestly," Aki answered, trying to hide both his bewilderment and consternation. He was beginning to understand that this trip was no last minute thing. Master Wehr had not only planned it out, but apparently shared details of it, and him, with whoever he was to encounter along the way. He held out the note and money, "He sent these along to you."

"Just as he said he would. Come back here a minute. You're a bit earlier than expected, but I'll have it ready to go shortly."

"Have what ready?" Aki asked as he followed him into the workshop in the back. He thought of the parcel Cornelius had given him. He was running errands of some sort for Master Wehr, that much was sure. And, apparently, he was a little ahead of schedule. That took some of the edge off of his nerves.

Silas smiled over his shoulder, "If he didn't tell you, then I won't. The last thing I want is him mad at me for spilling his secrets."

The workshop was considerably hotter than the front room. A furnace burned brightly in the center of the room and a boy around his own age who looked like a younger replica of Silas bent over it. Silas' son and apprentice, Aki guessed. He barely looked up long enough to acknowledge their entrance.

116

"Have a seat if you'd like," Silas motioned to a tall stool sitting next to a workbench.

Aki jumped up on it and took advantage of the workbench to set his satchel down, giving his tired shoulders a break. His eyes were drawn to the bulge of the package tucked inside and he debated peeking inside. After all, Master Wehr hadn't said he couldn't. He pulled it out and ran his hands across it, searching for some clue as to its contents. Whatever was inside was soft and supple, yielding easily to his touch as he turned it about in his hands. The temptation would have proven too strong if it hadn't been for Silas' interruption.

"Here you are, Aki. Just like he asked for," Silas held out a very small leather pouch and dropped it in Aki's hands.

Aki smiled when he read the next directive. Pulling out a few coins and finding the nearest shop that sold anything edible, he bought himself lunch and ate it as he walked through the town. Here at last, he was to follow an actual road, although, thanks to the weather, he was just about the only person on it.

He reached Bela Ubert's by nightfall. It was a solitary inn sitting just off the road. At that time of year, there were few visitors. Aki handed her the note from Master Wehr and spent the last of the money he had on a room and supper. When Miss Ubert, an elderly widow who wore her silver hair in a single long braid, showed him his room, he asked how far he was from Bren.

"It's about a five hour walk from here," she said, handing him the lit candle that she'd carried up with her.

Aki sighed. Five hours of walking to make it back to Master Wehr's the following morning. That meant a very early morning. His legs ached from walking all day, and the soft bed beckoned him. But if he laid down now, there was every chance in the world that he would sleep late into the morning and miss any chance of making it back on time.

All through supper he weighed the idea of pushing through the night and reaching Bren with many hours to spare against spending the night here and risking his very career. He pulled out his instructions one last time, hoping for some clarifying information but the final command

Master Wehr had written was simply, *"Be at my door by 8 o'clock, or not at all."* Not at all helpful, or encouraging.

With a groan that was probably loud enough for whoever had the room on the other side of the wall to hear, Aki stood up. He couldn't risk it. He couldn't take the chance of throwing everything he'd wanted away just for a good night's sleep.

It was late enough when he slipped back down the stairs that he hoped everyone else would be asleep. He froze when he realized Miss Ubert was seated at a table, doing absolutely nothing. Not nothing, he realized when she looked up and smiled at his appearance. She was waiting for him.

"I thought you might be back down. You are not staying tonight?"

"No. I won't get back in time if I do."

"But you are tired, are you not? You've traveled a long way in a day. Perhaps a few hours of rest would be for the best."

"No. I need to go."

She nodded, "Well, in that case, here is this." She slid some of the money he'd given her across the table towards him. "I can't charge you for a room you're not going to use. This is for you as well." She set a bundle on the table next to the money. "Don't eat all of them before you get back. Atticus is very fond of these tarts and he'll be quite upset if you don't bring some of them back to him."

"You knew?" Aki turned a bewildered gaze toward her as he added her bundle to the other things he'd collected. "You knew I was coming, and you knew I wasn't actually going to stay."

"I only knew what Atticus chose to share with me. Good luck, Aki. You have proven much about yourself, I think."

"I haven't proven anything yet. I still have to make it back to Bren on time."

"But you have decided to try."

"I guess so."

"Here," she lifted a lantern off its hook by the door, "take this. You'll need the light."

Aki set off into the night, thankful that he was at least no longer wandering across the country looking for landmarks. There was a road beneath his feet and the light of the lantern chased away the shadows in a small, dancing circle of yellow. Still, five hours of walking stretched before him and his eyes were already heavy with want of sleep.

After a while, he was pretty sure he was walking in his sleep. The landscape changed around him, but he didn't remember seeing it change. He just opened his eyes one moment and realized it was different. The hoot of an owl, the flap of wings, the rustle of branches shifting wove their way into his consciousness. Aki slid his free hand up to his neck, feeling for the wolf's tooth talisman that hung there. Pinching the two smooth teeth between his fingers, he reminded himself that he was responsible for the deaths of both beasts and that he had nothing to fear out here.

The night turned from black to gray in a gradual, almost unnoticeable shift. Against the soft, deep gray of the sky the welcome sight of Bren appeared. The wind picked up and carried the faint scent of salt and sea and Aki quickened his pace. He had no idea what time it actually was, but since dawn was not so far off he didn't have time to waste.

The streets of Bren were nearly deserted so early in the morning. Aki hurried through them, the sun's first rays now showing over the eastern edge of the world.

When he finally stood before Master Wehr's door, his courage abandoned him entirely. He didn't know if he was late or not. The only way to find out was to knock, but his hand refused to obey him. If he was late, if he failed, he wasn't really sure what he'd do. And now that he thought about it, he was quite sure he was late.

Chapter 20

MINUTES SLIPPED AWAY WHILE Aki stared at the door. At some point, he'd have to just knock and find out the worst. Delaying it wouldn't change anything. Drawing in a deep, steadying breath, Aki lifted his hand at last and knocked. It was softer than he usually did, as if he didn't really want Master Wehr hearing it.

"Come in," came the muffled response and Aki let go of his breath. He pushed the door open slowly. Master Wehr was sitting in his customary spot behind his desk. "I was beginning to wonder how long you were going to stand out there waiting. Come in, come in. All the way. You're letting in all the cold air."

"You knew I was out there?"

"Of course I did. I was waiting for you. I believe you have some things for me?"

Aki stepped forward and set the bulging satchel down on his desk. "It's all in there." He added under his breath, "I hope."

A brief smile flitted across Master Wehr's face as he noted the number of items Aki had returned with. Much to Aki's disappointment, he didn't seem to be in a hurry to unwrap any of them. After he assured himself they were all there, Master Wehr set them aside. Aki didn't think he was in a good position to ask about them, either, in spite of the curiosity that burned in him.

"You look tired?"

"I'm fine," Aki lied, unwilling to admit that he felt like falling over.

"You are tired. And that's alright. It's good to be tired sometimes. You know, we've enjoyed peace now for several years, in part thanks to Sasha. It's easy to forget what it's like to serve in times of war and crisis. As long as the peace holds, there will likely be no messages so important as to require someone to ride straight through the night. Most of our communications in peace are nothing more than routine. But peace is a fragile thing and it will break. Perhaps not this month or this year, but someday. And if you are to serve as a courier, then you must be ready to serve in all times."

"Is that what the whole point of this was? You just wanted to see if I could make it all the way through the night?" It seemed like an awful lot of trouble to go through for a single night. "If that's what you wanted, why didn't your instructions tell me to do that? They weren't at all clear about that. I almost didn't leave the inn last night."

Aki paused for breath and caught the knowing smile as Master Wehr's face. Whatever he was going to say next, he stopped.

"You needed to be the one to decide. I gave you very specific instructions. It was up to you to determine the best way to fulfill those. You chose well."

The tightness in his chest released a little at Master Wehr's words. Deciding that he really might fall over if he didn't sit down, he moved to his stool. The thought came to him that any learning he attempted at the moment was likely to be a waste of time. He didn't think he'd manage to stay awake for more than a few minutes now that he was sitting. He rubbed a hand across his eyes, trying to force them to stop burning. When he looked up again, Master Wehr was staring at him with an odd, bemused expression on his face.

"Do you know what day it is, Aki?"

Aki shook his head.

"It's your day off."

"Really?"

"Really. It is," Master Wehr said. "And there's someone here who came to see you. I told him to wait for you back at the academy."

"Who?"

Rather than answering him, Master Wehr made a shooing motion. Aki, his face clouded in confusion, started for the door. He stopped, one hand resting on the latch and turned questioning eyes to Master Wehr.

"I know I probably shouldn't ask this, but, did you think I would make it back here on time?"

Master Wehr's face held no hint of amusement and his gaze was steady as he considered Aki's words for a moment.

"No, Aki. I did not think you would." Aki's heart dropped. "I knew you would. Now go. Get some rest. And be on time tomorrow."

Aki couldn't stop the grin that spread across his face in spite of his exhaustion. With the weight of Master Wehr's disapproval gone from his mind, he hurried through the streets until the academy came into sight. It was a welcome sight after the last two days.

He entered the common room first and, since it was their day off, found it occupied by the others. Except Felix, of course. The memory of what had happened, and of Jasper's threat, came rushing back as he scanned the room quickly for the redheaded boy and found no sign of him. It wasn't reasonable to expect him back so soon, anyway. He would have barely had time to reach home.

"Oh, there you are, Aki," Oscar looked up from a game of cards that he was playing with Archie. "There's someone waiting for you in your room."

"Who?"

Oscar shrugged, turning back to the game. "Don't know. I didn't ask him."

It must be Stephan, Aki guessed as he hurried through the room and down the hall that led to his room. All thoughts of sleep gone now, he threw the door open and froze.

"Sasha?"

"Hello, Aki. I'm guessing by the look on your face that I wasn't who you expected," Sasha laughed.

"I just assumed it was Stephan," Aki said, shutting the door behind him. Jasper's words rang in his ears, reminding him of just how little Sasha knew about him, and how much trouble Sasha could be in if Aki slipped up and said something he shouldn't. He wasn't even sure what would happen if word got out about what Sasha did to him, but Jasper made it sound like there would be trouble from it. That knowledge sucked whatever happiness he ought to have had for Sasha's visit right out of him. With a wariness that he did not intend he asked, "What are you doing here?"

If Sasha noticed his tension, he ignored it. "I thought that was obvious. I came to see you. Stephan wants to know how you're getting on, but it's hard for him to get away. Besides, I wanted to be the one to tell you my news."

"What news?"

"I'm getting married!"

"Ophelia?"

"You're not even a little bit surprised," Sasha said, a bit disappointed.

"Oh, was I supposed to be?"

"I don't know. I just didn't realize that it was so obvious to everyone. It took me forever to figure out that I loved her."

Aki cocked an eyebrow, "Really?"

"Oh, shut up. You'll come to the wedding, won't you?"

"I don't know if I'm allowed to."

"You are. I already asked Atticus for you. He said that you just have to tell him and Jasper."

"When is it?"

"In a month. We were going to wait for spring, but neither of us really want to." Sasha threw himself back on the empty bed and laced his fingers together behind his head. "So, how is it going with you? Atticus told me about how you broke your arm."

"Did he?" Aki slumped onto his own bed, scowling. That was a story he would have preferred not to have told about him. "It wasn't that big of a deal and it's fine now."

"That's not quite the version Atticus gave me," Sasha gave him a quizzical look.

"Forget about it. It's fine."

"Is something wrong with you?"

"No," Aki turned away, hoping his face didn't give his lie away. Just as he had with Master Wehr, he fought down the temptation to tell Sasha. There was even more reason to keep his secrets from Sasha. Sasha would hate him if he knew what Aki had done. And since he couldn't tell Sasha the truth, he would have to distract him. "Come on, let's go somewhere other than here."

"Where?"

"Um, I can show you around here, if you want. And," Aki brightened as a thought came to him, "you can help me. I'm supposed to practice weapons with the others, but the only one I would ask isn't here right now."

"Sure, but I'm not that great, and I haven't practiced in a while."

Aki rummaged through his drawers until he came up with his set of throwing knives, grabbed his new sword from where it sat by the door and headed out the door. The sword he'd only had for about a week. He'd meant to practice like Jasper told him but going out in the evenings had cut into that as much as it had made him late to Master Wehr's. He couldn't afford to keep putting it off, not if he wanted to stay in.

"There's not actually a lot to see," he said as they crossed the arena to the door on the side that led to the weapons room. "Mostly just our rooms, and then the stables, and this."

Sasha pulled a practice sword off the rack on the wall and hefted it in his hand. He put it back and tried another and then another before he was satisfied with the weight and balance. In spite of his claim to not be good, he held it with the ease of someone who had grown up with one in his hand.

"I didn't think this would be part of your training."

"Me either. Jasper says that I have to be able to defend myself, though. Apparently, just being a courier doesn't automatically protect you." He pulled his own sword out of its scabbard. "Ready?"

Even though it had been a couple of weeks since his arm had come out of the splint, Aki decided that his right arm was still not as strong as it had been. Within thirty minutes, it was aching. Still, he was holding his own. At the end of the half hour, he lowered his sword and stepped back, breathing hard. Sasha did the same, wiping a sleeve across his face.

"You're good," Sasha said.

"Not really. I started behind everyone back home."

"No, I mean you're really good. You're not behind at all."

"You shoot better than me," Aki put his sword away.

"Can you use those?" Sasha motioned to the throwing knives Aki had brought out.

In answer, Aki slid one out. With a grin, he handed it to Sasha and took another one out for himself.

"Let's see who's better."

Aki won easily. Sasha stared at his own target in disgust.

"Guess that's not something I ever really practiced."

Aki collected the knives and then sat down along an empty space of the wall. Sasha joined him and held out his hand for one of the knives.

"These are nice. Probably the best set I've ever seen."

One corner of his mouth pulled up in a half smile as Aki spun the other around in his hand.

"They're sort of not mine," he admitted.

"What? Whose are they?"

"They were Halle's. I stole them right before we came here."

"You've had those since you came here? Where were they? I don't remember seeing them."

"They were in with my things when you gave them back to me, remember? I might have kept them hidden from you, though. I didn't think they were something you wanted me having back then."

"If I had known you had those, I definitely wouldn't have let you keep them. Why'd you steal them from Halle, though? If you'd asked Father, he'd have given you some. He always gave us any weapons we wanted. It was just about the only thing he was generous with."

"He always gave you the weapons you wanted. I was different," Aki sighed. "And Halle deserved to lose them."

Sasha's face grew serious as he stared at the knife in his hand. "Halle was trouble when I was back home. To be honest, if anyone is going to destroy what I did there, it will be him."

"Just so long as I don't have to see him again, I can't say I care that much."

"And what would happen if you saw him again? Does he know you're the one who took those?"

"Oh, he knows. He'd kill me."

Sasha eyed him for a moment. "That wouldn't have been part of the reason why you were so desperate to stay, would it?"

"Maybe. A little," Aki confessed.

Chapter 21

THAT'S IT? THAT'S ALL?" the young man slammed a fist onto the table as he spoke. Leaning forward, he hissed at his companion, "You promised more than this."

"And you promised us enough people and the use of your ship to do this job. Where are they, Halle?"

Rather than answer her, Halle got to his feet and made his way to the counter, limping slightly with each step. Kezi's eyes followed him as he ordered another drink and returned to the table, sitting down in his chair with too much force.

"You're hiding something from me," Halle said.

"No, we're not. You know everything there is to know about what we're going to do."

"That's not what I mean," Halle raised his voice enough to attract the curious stares of those nearby. Kezi shot him a warning glance. It was bad enough that they were meeting in a public place. The fact that Halle only spoke Aruuken drew far too much attention to their conversation. At times, Kezi wondered why they bothered with him. Actually, she wondered that every time she had to talk to him. If it weren't for the fact that he had a ship, she would have sent him away long ago. "If there was nothing you're hiding from me, then why do you tell me when I can and can't meet with you? Why are there times you refuse to let me in on your planning?"

Kezi considered his words for a moment, her thin lips turned down in a frown. When she did speak again, it was slowly, each word drawn out with a condescending exasperation, "There is nothing we are hiding from you, Halle. Our plans are your plans," she paused, her frown turning to a look of disgust as he tipped his cup back and emptied it of its content. "You're drunk."

"I'm not yet, but I have every intention of getting that way as fast as I can." He set the cup down hard enough that Kezi winced and glanced around them again. "Is that a problem for you?"

She gave an exasperated wave of her hand, "Come back when you actually have something worthwhile to say."

"How dare you speak to me like that! You know who I am."

"You are no one here. Absolutely no one. You're not a Chief's son. You're heir to nothing. Remember? Sasha took all of that away from you. You're not even a very intimidating person because you can't stand up right now without almost falling over," Kezi added the last part as he started to his feet and grabbed at the table to steady himself.

"If you were in Aruuk, you wouldn't dare speak to me like this. No girl would."

"But we're not in Aruuk. And I'm not some slave girl who has to bow and scrape every time you yell. If you want our help, you'll have to accept that. I'm the one who makes the decisions here, not you."

Halle slumped back down into his chair, staring down at the empty cup with bloodshot eyes as if staring at it long enough would refill it. He said nothing for so long that Kezi's expression softened a little. It wasn't often that she set aside that sharpness. And if anyone else had been there, she wouldn't have done it now. Reaching across the table, she laid a hand on his arm that he didn't brush away.

"You'll get your revenge, Halle. I haven't lied about that, and I never would. When this is over, people will know who you are."

"He had no right to take it from me. He had no right to make me nothing, no one. If he didn't want it, he should have just stayed here and not bothered to come home."

Kezi glanced around at the other occupants in the room. Even though there was no one in the room who could have understood a word that passed between them, she couldn't control the impulse to look over her shoulder. Satisfied that their attention was not on Halle and her, she leaned forward, keeping her voice low as she spoke, "If you'd wanted the power so badly, why didn't you just kill him and take it? That's how you all do it up there, isn't it? It ought to have been easy."

"Kill Sasha?" Halle snorted. "You can't be serious. He had the clansmen on his side. It was too late for me by the time he even showed up in Illsen. They'd already sworn to him. If I killed him then, they'd have killed me. No, murder only gets you the throne if you do it before the clansmen swear allegiance. He knew that. Besides, I tried. And failed. He kept me locked up for the first several weeks after that and when he did let me out I was given a choice between dying and swearing to him."

"So he outplayed you. Now's your chance to pay him back, but only if you can stay sober long enough to be of some use. Jasper's losing patience with you and the others aren't far behind him."

"Speaking of others, who are they? These others that you're always mentioning. Why are they never around when I'm here?"

"The less any of us know about the full picture, the less risk is if one of us is taken."

"Except, of course, you," Halle said with a bitter smile. "Because you know all of it, you're the one who decides what bits and pieces you'll feed to us and what you'll withhold."

"I don't need to explain myself to you," Kezi said with a huff, her sympathy at an end. "Now, go. We're done talking."

"I'm not. Where's Aki?"

The question caught Kezi off guard and it was a moment before she concealed her shock and uneasiness. "I have no idea. I didn't know you were interested in finding him."

Halle smiled slowly, "Oh, yes you did. I thought I was quite explicit in stating my interest in finding him. I have a favor to return to him and if he thinks he can run and hide from me, he's mistaken. I don't like owing people things."

"Dival's a big country. He could be anywhere. And your petty feud with him cannot take precedence over our plans."

Halle's eyes narrowed as he weighed her answer. Whether he fully believed her or not, he didn't press the issue. With a final shrug, he pushed himself away from the table.

"When will this plan take place? Or is that information you won't deign to tell me?"

"Not until summer, at least. And not until the right opportunity presents itself."

"Then I have plenty of time to drink," Halle said with a grim laugh.

Chapter 22

AKI HAD MOSTLY FORGOTTEN about the mysterious items he'd collected for Master Wehr. In truth, he'd hardly had time to give them much thought. After Sasha's visit, both Master Wehr and Jasper demanded so much of his time that he didn't devote his few free hours to such curiosity.

He was taking off his coat and sitting down for the day's work when he noticed Master Wehr watching him with unusual intensity.

"Did I do something wrong?" He tried to remember the last two weeks. He hadn't been late, not so much as by a minute. He'd stayed at the academy each night doing his work rather than going out. He'd even worked up the nerve to ask Oscar to spar with him since Felix had yet to return. To his surprise, Oscar had not only agreed but had seemed to enjoy it.

"Why is that always your first assumption?"

"Because it's usually the right one."

Master Wehr chuckled, "It's not this time. I have something for you."

"Oh? What is it?" Aki left his desk and came over.

"This," Master Wehr slid a bundle across to him.

His fingers worked at the knots that held the string around it and when it came undone, he pulled it open and gasped. Running his hand across the soft, light brown leather he looked up at Master Wehr. He'd seen Jasper wear the same thing every time they went out.

"Why?"

"It's a courier's coat. I think you've earned it."

Aki lifted it up and held it out at arm's length to admire it. It was only then that he noticed the small, silver pin on its collar. The craftsmanship was exquisite, the details of the horse head vivid despite its small size. A courier's pin. He'd seen one on Jasper's coat as well.

"When did you have this made?"

"You collected the materials for it yourself," Master Wehr said with a smile. "I will admit, your lack of curiosity was surprising, considering that you ask questions about absolutely everything."

"I collected them?" Aki gave him a puzzled frown before realization dawned on his face. "Oh, when you sent me on that trip. You know, I almost threw your instructions into the sea. Guess it's a good thing I didn't."

"I would say so. That would have been a terrible mistake."

Aki ran a finger over the pin. He felt Master Wehr watching him again and looked up to meet his eyes. All of the amusement from the moment before was gone. In its place, Aki was a little surprised to find worry. It wasn't hard to guess the source of that worry. Not only had Aki been unfailingly punctual in the last two weeks, but he'd also been quieter than usual. He didn't mean to be, but every time he started talking, he remembered Jasper's threats, he remembered what he knew, he remembered what he'd done, and words failed him.

"Aki?" Master Wehr said. "Something has clearly been bothering you."

"No, it hasn't," he denied too quickly.

Master Wehr shook his head, giving up. It wasn't the first time in the last two weeks that he'd tried to draw Aki's secrets out from him. Aki pushed aside the guilt that always accompanied disappointing Master Wehr. It didn't matter, he told himself. All that mattered was protecting Sasha and himself.

He sat down at his desk and pulled out his work but it was hard to focus. He found himself staring out the window, watching people as they came and went. A glimpse of someone standing in the doorway of the building across the street caught his attention. The figure was slouched against the doorframe, his face hidden in the shadows. There was something familiar about the way he stood. Aki lost all interest in the paper he was deciphering before him. Resting his chin in his hand, he tried to put a face to the familiar posture but it eluded him.

"Aki?" Master Wehr's voice broke through his trance and Aki turned his head to look over his shoulder. "You are leaving for your brother's wedding soon, are you not?"

Aki didn't bother correcting him on his relation to Sasha. He'd gone too long thinking of him as a brother himself to think of him as anything else now. "Yes, the end of next week."

"I think you should go sooner. I think you should leave at the end of this week and spend a few days at home. I believe it would do you some good and perhaps you will be less troubled when you return."

"I'm not troubled now," Aki protested. A few days at home weren't going to change anything. He'd keep his mouth shut there just like he was here. "Everything is..."

"Don't tell me everything is fine. Don't lie to me, Aki. Tell me you don't want to talk about it, tell me you can't talk about it, but don't tell me that nothing is wrong. You and I both know that's a lie."

"Alright. So there is something, but I can't talk about it, not to you or to anyone else, for that matter. Going home isn't going to change any of it because there's something I've done and I can't undo it. I wish I could. And if anyone finds out," Aki paused, horrified at how much he'd just said, at how close he'd come to spilling the one secret that he protected above all others, the one secret Jasper had hinted at already knowing. He murmured, "I can't let anyone ever know."

Master Wehr nodded slowly, absorbing his words. A troubled cloud settled over his face and he turned to stare out the window, lost in thought. Aki shifted in his seat, unsure of whether Master Wehr was waiting for him to speak again or not.

Finally, unable to bear the silence any longer, he said, "I'm sorry I said so much. I should have just stayed quiet."

"Was that helping? Staying quiet? Because that's what you've been doing for the last two weeks, and it doesn't seem to me like it's helping. I want you gone for at least a week, if for no other reason than that I need the time.

There's much you haven't said, Aki, but I can guess that there is someone else that is the source of this trouble."

Aki nodded, wondering how he was supposed to spend a week around Sasha and Ophelia without giving something away. It had been hard enough for one day with Sasha and aside from Stephan and Alina there were no other two people whom he wished to spare more than them.

"What'll Jasper say to my being gone so long?"

"Jasper will be fine with it."

Aki turned back around with a sigh.

"Won't I get even further behind then?" he tried one last time.

"Aki, you are no longer behind."

That at least made Aki smile as he went back to work. His smile faded when he looked out the window again and realized that the same person who had been across the street a few minutes ago was still there, and no longer alone. He didn't have to think about who the second person was though. He recognized Kezi immediately. She was deep in conversation with the mysterious man. No, not a conversation, an argument. He shook his head and returned to his work. When he looked up again, both were gone.

Leaving Master Wehr's that evening, Aki started for the academy before changing his mind. It had been two weeks since he'd gone anywhere in the evening, and he was getting bored again. Instead, he turned his steps toward the lower end of Bren.

As usual, he only had to wander around for a little bit before Kezi slipped out of the shadows behind him. It was impossible to hear her coming, a feat that Aki had tried to master most of his life but still didn't think he was that good at.

"I thought maybe you weren't coming back."

"Why would you think that?"

"Jasper told us what Atticus did to you. Aren't you afraid you'll get in trouble again if you stay out with us."

"It wasn't really a punishment. It was just another part of training."

"If you say so," Kezi said. She nodded toward the new coat he was wearing, "I guess it's working out for you."

"It is. Kezi, what is it you and Jasper are planning?"

"I can't tell you that. Not unless you want in, in which case I would be more than happy to let you in on it. We want your help, Aki," she stopped walking and turned to face him. "If this works, we won't have to answer to anyone anymore. We'll be rich enough to do whatever we want."

Aki considered her words. There was no denying the appeal in them. If she'd asked him sooner, maybe he would have said yes right away. But he couldn't now.

"I'm leaving next week to go home," he said. "When I come back, we'll talk about it, alright?"

"That's right. Jasper told me you were going. For Sasha's wedding, isn't it?" Kezi gave his name a bitter twist. Aki tried to ignore it.

Chapter 23

IT WAS LATE EVENING WHEN Aki neared Stephan and Alina's home. As much as he'd disagreed with Master Wehr's insistence that he needed extra time away, now that he was here, he was glad of the decision. Jasper hadn't been bothered by it, either. When Aki told him, he'd simply pulled him into a corner where no one could overhear them.

"I know Kezi talked to you the other night. And I'm sure you remember what you and I talked about. Never forget that. Never forget, Aki, that I know things about you and your brother that you don't want others finding out. Enjoy your time at home, but keep our secrets."

When Aki had only stared at the ground, unable to answer him, Jasper once again laid a hand on his shoulder. It was all Aki could do to keep himself from shrugging that hand off.

"I don't want you hurt," he'd said, his voice softening a little. "But we've worked on this a long time. I need what we'll get from it. I'm not asking for you to help. That's what Kez wants. I'd rather keep you out of this if I can. But I need your silence. You can do that much at least, can't you?"

Aki couldn't doubt the sincerity in his voice. He couldn't question the reluctance Jasper spoke of. He nodded, "You have it. I'll tell no one. But, I don't think I can be a part of it. Will you tell Kezi that for me? Tell her there're people I can't disappoint. I owe them too much."

"I'll tell her. She'll probably still ask you again, though."

That had been the last time they'd spoken before he left.

Now, coming up the lane to Stephan and Alina's, his thoughts turned back to that conversation. Jasper was a strange man, he decided. He wondered what it was that Jasper was after, what it was that he needed that Kezi could get him. And he wondered why Kezi was so desperate to have his help. All the many times they'd wandered together through the busy market square, Kezi picking pockets every chance she got, she'd never asked for his help. She'd never needed it.

As troubling as those thoughts were, they were almost instantly dismissed when he saw the glow of light still coming from the front windows as he approached. Slipping off of Sky's back before she even came to a halt, he bounded up the front steps. He hadn't thought to send them word about when he was coming but that didn't make him hesitate at the door. He pushed it open and found that they weren't alone. Sitting with them in front of the large fireplace and deep in conversation with them was Dagmar. All three looked up at his entrance.

"Aki!" Alina was the first to her feet, a warm smile on her face. She pulled him into a hug. "You didn't tell us you would be home so soon. We would have had something ready for you if we'd known."

"Didn't think to," Aki answered, pulling away.

"You look well."

"No broken bones this time," Stephan approached him, laughing.

"Sasha told you about that?"

"Of course he did."

Dagmar had sat quietly watching them, but she started to her feet now.

"Hello, Aki," she said, then turned to the others. "I should go now."

"No, wait. There's no need for you to rush off," Stephan said. "Aki will be helping anyway."

"What? What am I helping with?" Aki looked between them.

"You'll help move her things," Stephan said. "When it's time for you to go back, we'll be moving Dagmar."

"You're moving to Bren?"

"Yes," Dagmar answered. "I think I really should go. It's getting late and I'm sure you all have a lot of catching up to do."

When Dagmar was gone and Sky put up, Aki was surprised at how easy it was to slip back into his life here even for just a few days. He'd spent the day riding alone with his thoughts and was more than ready to settle back in his chair and tell them everything he could about his life in Bren. He'd given a lot of consideration to avoiding what he couldn't speak about and neither Stephan nor Alina seemed to notice.

It was still very early when he slipped out of the house the next morning. The air was almost warm and the snow was wet and heavy. Not many more weeks before spring, Aki thought as made his way through the woods. The dormant trees creaked and groaned under the breeze. Although he'd never been one to particularly enjoy solitude and quiet, Aki was glad to be alone with his thoughts out in the woods that morning. He'd gone this way only a few times in the last few years. For the most part, he'd tried to avoid coming to this spot but today was different.

It was easy to spot. A splash of dark green against the otherwise brown and gray forest marked it. The skeleton of a still very small tree stood in the middle of the evergreens, waiting for the warmth of spring to awaken it and bring it back to vibrant life. It was an odd custom, Aki thought, to plant something that came to life every year over the grave of someone who would never live again. It was almost like reliving the pain through each season of the year. Or maybe that was the point. Keeping the memory of the lost one alive, fresh.

Brushing the snow off a fallen tree, he sat down. It was wet and uncomfortable, but he had other things on his mind as he stared at Boris' grave. For the first time since that night, Aki tried to piece together the tattered memories that still existed in his mind. He'd spent almost four years pushing even the thought of them away. The moments before Sasha's beating were still lost, and Aki didn't mind that.

He'd been the first one into the cabin that day. Gundar had sent him to slip inside as soon as Sasha left. It had been so easy, although now that he considered it, Gundar had put him in the greatest position of vulnerability by sending him first. If Boris hadn't already been in a trance, Aki would have been in trouble. He'd been bait, again.

He remembered slipping through the half open door and finding Boris there, crouched on the floor, staring at nothing. He hadn't so much as blinked at Aki's entrance, although he was only a few feet away and could not have missed it. And that was when Aki told Gundar that they were clear, that they could enter the cabin without raising any alarm. He remembered the look on Boris' face when they all entered. His eyes were drawn instantly to Lord Bayner, widening with horror.

In that moment, Aki understood exactly what Boris was feeling. He'd known the same terror around certain people. But that wasn't even the worst part he'd played that day and night.

The soft crunch of snow behind him startled Aki out of his thoughts and he twisted around in his seat to see what had caused it.

"Do you mind if I join you?" Dagmar, her face half hidden by the hood of cloak, asked.

"No," Aki answered quickly.

"I didn't know you came out here."

"I don't, normally. It just seemed like something I should do while I'm here."

She sat down next to him on the fallen log, rubbing her mittened hands together in the cold. For several minutes, neither spoke. Aki, unable to take the silence any longer, and unwilling to talk about why he was out here, spoke first.

"So, you're moving to Bren?"

"Yes. Does that surprise you?"

"I don't know. I guess a little. What made you decide to? I thought you liked it here."

Dagmar didn't answer right away. She stared off into the distance, seeing things that were not there.

"I do," she said at last, carefully weighing her words as she spoke. "I like it here a lot. Sasha gave me an incredible gift when he brought me here, even if he didn't mean to at the time, and maybe someday I'll be able to repay him. In the meantime, with Meri and Phelie married, I need to be somewhere I'm needed. I can't just spend the rest of my life living off of other people's kindness. And I want to live near the sea. Meri and Karl helped me find a nice little house close to the sea, and there's a tailor that I'll work for. I'll be able to make my own way."

"Have you ever thought about going back home?"

"No," she shook her head.

"Me either," Aki stood up. "I should get going before they start wondering where I disappeared to."

Dagmar nodded, remaining seated. "Did you know that Lars is here?"

"Really? No, I didn't know. Sasha didn't mention him at all when he came to visit me. Where is he?"

"Staying with Sasha, I assume. At least until the wedding."

Aki hurried back to Stephan's. Without needing to be asked, he helped Stephan in the barn, falling easily into the old routine they'd had before he left. There wasn't any need for conversation while they worked.

He wasn't able to slip away again until after breakfast. Saddling Sky up, he set off across the forest once more. It had been a long time since he'd ridden just for fun and he pushed Sky into a canter along the trail. He reached Sasha's home quickly. Pulling Sky up, he swung down and knocked.

"You're back sooner than I expected," Sasha said upon answering the door.

Even though he'd already eaten with Stephan and Alina less than an hour before, Aki sat down with Lars and Sasha and ate again. For once, Aki wasn't the one doing the most talking. Lars barely stopped long enough to take bites between all the stories he had to tell. Since Aki had never had a chance to learn exactly what happened when Sasha had returned to Aruuk, it was all new to him. Sasha, apparently, wasn't nearly as interested in the retelling and as soon as they were finished eating, he left.

Alone with him now, Lars grew more serious. "I guess you're doing pretty well for yourself here," he said.

"I have. Better than I'd have done in Aruuk."

Lars picked at an invisible speck on the table in front of him. "You know, I didn't come here alone."

"What do you mean?"

140

"Halle came too. It was his ship we took to get here."

At the mention of Halle's name, Aki went rigid and his face paled. Not daring to look at Lars he asked, "Here? At Sasha's?"

Lars snorted, "No. Definitely not. He hates Sasha almost as much as he hates you, and that's saying a lot, because he hates you more than anything."

"He hasn't forgotten, then?"

"Forgotten? Have you forgotten any of the times you were nearly killed? I don't think he'll forget what happened on that mountain for as long as he lives."

"Where is he now?"

"Somewhere in Dival. Bren probably, but I don't know for sure. We split up when I wanted to come see Sasha."

"And why'd he come?"

"Why do you think?" Lars leaned forward, resting his chin in his hands. "He wants to pay you back for what you did to him. I think he wants to kill you."

"He's always wanted to kill me," Aki said, glaring at nothing as he remembered his time around Halle. "Dival's a big country. And Bren's a big city. He won't find me."

"Doesn't mean you shouldn't be careful," Lars said with a shrug. He pushed himself away from the table. "Come on. Let's find something to do."

Chapter 24

SINCE AKI HAD GONE TO KARL and Meredith's wedding two years before, he wasn't nearly as ignorant about how they went as Lars was. His side hurt from Lars' elbow jamming into it periodically to get his attention.

"Just watch," he'd finally hissed.

Lars sat back, annoyed but quiet.

It was less extravagant in its decoration than Karl and Meredith's had been, but Ophelia was a less extravagant person than her twin so that was surprising. The only plants alive at that time of year were evergreens and holly bushes. Sprigs of the dark green stuff bound in ribbon provided the backdrop. Ophelia, dressed in a gown of deep crimson, her dark hair coiffed atop her head and a thin golden chain woven through it, was the picture of a perfect bride.

"That's the one that stopped him from killing you," Lars whispered as Ophelia walked to the front of the room to join Sasha.

"Yes, I know. Shhh."

"Bet you're glad you told Father about her because if she hadn't been there, you'd have died."

"Shut up," Aki said, more desperately. He turned, white and wide-eyed toward Lars. "Don't ever say that here."

"Oh. They don't know?"

"Just be quiet. You're missing everything."

"I'm not missing anything. We can't hear this part anyway."

Aki didn't have a good response for that. It was true. Whatever vows Sasha and Ophelia made to each other weren't to be heard by anyone except Hamo and Edith. Sasha's parents ought to have been there as well, but that couldn't happen. Sasha didn't seem bothered by their absence. Looking at him now, Aki didn't think anything would bother him today. He'd never seen anyone smile so much.

Witnessing that happiness made Aki ache. It made him want to hide from all the others so that they would never find out what a terrible thing he'd done. He lowered his head and paid little attention to anything else that happened for as long as he could.

There was no way he could ever let them find out the truth – especially not now.

Chapter 25

AKI'S EYES WERE HEAVY WITH sleep as they entered Bren. Sky walked patiently behind them, tethered to the back of the wagon. Usually, Aki would have opted to ride her instead of sit in the back of the wagon for hours, but he and Lars hadn't bothered to sleep most of the night before and he'd decided to take advantage of the hours of boredom to doze. He was alone in the back since Dagmar was sitting with Stephan and Alina on the seat.

It wasn't so late that the streets were quiet. Plenty of people were still out and Aki pushed himself all the way up into a sitting position so that he could look around. It wasn't curiosity that made Aki suddenly vigilant. It was the words Lars had spoken to him a week ago and had repeated again last night.

Halle was most likely here. Lars thought that's where he was headed, at least. And it made Aki uneasy as he scanned the people around them.

It had been a long time since he'd given any thought to Halle. Any serious thought, that is. He thought about him every time he looked at the set of knives he'd taken from him. But he'd never considered the possibility that Halle would show up here.

No one they passed resembled what he thought Halle would look like after almost four years and Aki began to realize what a ridiculous idea it was that he would just spot him riding into town. He glanced up at the others. Alina and Dagmar were talking, their voices drifting back to him but their words indiscernible. Stephan was whistling the way he often did. Aki was tempted to move closer and join in but, with a sigh, he turned away from them and stared at the receding road. They'd been so kind to him, and they thought so well of him. If they knew the truth, he wasn't sure they still would.

Stephan pulled the horses to a stop in front of a tiny cottage. It was, as Dagmar had said, near the sea. The only thing between it and the water were the numerous docks and boat sheds. The crisp, tangy scent of salt water made the air feel more alive.

Aki wasted no time in hopping down and grabbing some of her things to carry inside. The three rooms that made up the interior were small but comfortable looking.

"Are you in a hurry to get back?" Stephan asked when deposited his load inside and hurried to get more.

"I just don't want to be late tomorrow morning," Aki answered, unwilling to admit that he wanted to get back to the academy before the sun went down because moving through Bren in the dark had suddenly become a very undesirable thing to do.

Dagmar didn't have much and there was still daylight left when they were done. Aki said a hasty goodbye and retrieved Sky from the back of the wagon. He led her through the streets, looking over his shoulder every few steps, until they reached the academy.

Felix was halfway across the arena, heading back toward their rooms, when Aki entered. When he saw Aki, he stopped and waited for him. Aki caught up with him and they walked side by side to Sky's stall. Felix didn't say anything, but Aki had the sense that he wanted to talk.

"How's your brother?" Aki asked when they reached Sky's stall and Felix still hadn't said anything.

"He'll be alright. They caught one of the ones who did it. Fergus injured him and he couldn't get away."

Aki bit his lip, and turned away, busying himself with Sky's tack so that Felix wouldn't notice the change in his demeanor. He knew it wasn't Jasper and the only other man in their group that he knew of was Phineas.

"Father's furious about the whole thing still. He wants the man hung, but since no one was killed it probably won't happen," Felix said. He was talking absently now, more to say the words than for Aki to hear them. "He says King Darien needs to make an example out of this. Mother's just plain terrified now. She says she can hardly sleep knowing that they're not really safe. She thinks it must have been someone Father made an enemy of. It was all I could do to convince her to let me come back here on my own. She was going to send a guard with me. Can you imagine that? A guard just so I can come back to the academy."

Aki gave him a rueful smile. "At least she cares about what happens to you."

"I suppose so, but she needn't fuss over me quite so much. I know how to defend myself. Goodness knows, Father made sure of that. He had a sword in my hand about the same time I started walking, I think."

"Your brother knew how to defend himself and still got hurt," Aki countered. He closed the stall door and started back across the arena.

Oscar and Archie were the sole occupants of the common room that evening and both looked up at Aki and Felix's entrance. They were sitting at one of the tables playing the same complicated game they always did. Aki sometimes wondered if they knew any other game to wile away their evening hours. It involved at least a dozen pieces on each side that moved all over a board. Oscar waved them both over and since Aki didn't really have any other plans for the evening, he followed Felix over.

"Thought you'd never come back, Felix," Oscar said, moving one of his pieces and causing Archie to scowl at the game board. "Guess since you're back your brother's alright."

Felix nodded, "Did I miss much here?"

Oscar shrugged, "You missed sparring with Aki here. Turns out he actually knows how to hold a sword. Who would've thought?"

Aki rolled his eyes but smiled. The last time they'd sparred, Aki had been the unquestioned winner of the match.

"Oh, and he got on Master Wehr's bad side somehow and had to take a three-day hike to who knows where," Oscar continued, looking up long enough to grin at Aki. Payback for all the long evenings spent trapped in the room with him, Aki supposed.

Here, it was easy to forget Lars' warning and the ever-present knowledge that Halle was close. Aki wished it was possible to keep it that way. There was the matter of all the things he couldn't say too. Talking to Felix made the weight of his knowledge even more burdensome. He lingered in the common room longer than he normally would have that night.

Despite his foreboding, the next several weeks slipped by without any eventfulness to mark them. After the first few days, it seemed a little ridiculous to keep looking over his shoulder, scanning every group of people he saw in hopes of seeing the one face he dreaded finding. Aside from making several short trips with Jasper, he avoided going anywhere near Kezi and her band's gathering places. Jasper on their trips was all business and made no mention of the scheme he and Kezi were working on.

In those few weeks, spring came in with a rush. Aki noticed it the second he set foot outside. The air was warm, the snow little more than gray slush, and the sun was shining from vibrant blue skies. The shift in the seasons awoke a restlessness in him that tugged him out into the streets instead of heading straight back to the academy when he was done at Master Wehr's.

He wandered around the market square for a while, listening to the usual banter and gossip that filled the air, before the thought came to him that he should visit Dagmar. He'd always gotten along well with her, so much so that he imagined if he had an older sister he'd want her to be like Dagmar.

He started toward the sea but hadn't gone far when a familiar figure appeared at his side. For a few minutes, Kezi walked beside him in silence.

"We've missed you," she said at last. "You haven't been around for ages."

"Didn't think you'd really want me around when you're planning something I'm not part of."

"You could be."

"I don't..."

"You said we'd talk about it when you got back. You're back, and I need you more than before." She paused, then added quietly, "We lost Phineas."

"He's the one they took?"

Kezi nodded, "So, you see, we need you. This will be the chance of a lifetime, Aki. Think about it. If we pull this off, we'll have whatever we want. The king will have to acknowledge our demands."

"King Darien? What does he have to do with this?"

Kezi laughed softly, "I can't tell you that. Not yet, at least."

Aki stopped walking and looked around. He hadn't been paying attention to where they were going, but Kezi had. She'd led him right to the spot where he'd seen the sea at night for the first time. It was dark again and the sky clear. The starlight danced up and down as the waves came sloshing against the sand and the wooden docks. He wasn't far from Dagmar's, he realized.

Kezi turned to face, her hand on his arm, "Trust me, Aki. I'm not planning anything that'll get you hurt but you don't want to tell me no."

"Why do you want my help so badly?"

"You're my friend. One of the only ones I have, actually. And you deserve more than just following someone else's orders the rest of your life."

Aki pulled away from her, something in her eyes making him uncomfortable. He looked out over the sea, one hand running through his hair and a deep frown on his face. He tossed her words around in his mind, letting the appeal of them sink in. He'd always, always had to follow someone's orders. He'd never been that free. But, now that he thought about it, he wasn't sure he wanted to be. Kezi might not answer to anyone, but he didn't envy her life. Her sort of freedom came with constant danger, which made it not so free in the end.

"Kez, I'm sorry. I just don't think..."

Kezi cut him off before he got any further, "You'll regret that, Aki."

Aki stiffened and started to turn toward her, not so much because of what she said but because of the language she said them in. Kezi had spoken in Aruuken. Kezi never spoke Aruuken.

He was only halfway facing her when the rush of movement and the flash of something silver caught his eyes. Kezi stepped back as someone else staggered forward, a knife in their hands.

"Halle?" Aki recoiled in horror, his hand going to his belt but finding no weapon there.

"Thought you'd never see me again, didn't you?" Halle's words slurred and he stumbled a little as he came toward Aki. He swung the knife in a sloppy arc aiming for Aki's heart. Aki jumped back. It wasn't fast enough. He yelped as the knife tore through his clothes and sliced into his side. He brought one hand up to the wound. Shoving Halle to the ground with the other, Aki did the only thing he could think of.

He ran.

Chapter 26

PAIN TORE THROUGH THE SIDE of his abdomen with every step he took, but the stumbling footsteps behind him forced him on.

Halle was drunk. The smell of alcohol emanating off of him was enough to let Aki know. It was a good thing he was drunk. If Halle wasn't, he'd have already caught up with him.

Aki swayed and gripped the nearest wall with his hand as a wave of lightheadedness washed over him. Halle hadn't cut him that deep. He shouldn't already be feeling this faint. At least, he didn't think he should be. Aki sucked in a burning gasp and pushed himself off the wall. The footsteps were getting closer again.

By the time he reached the door, he could no longer hear anyone following him. Leaning against the door frame, Aki pounded on the wooden door with all the strength he could muster, which wasn't much. He looked down at the hand he'd kept pressed to his side. Blood, inky black in the darkness, spilled over the hand and dripped onto the stoop beneath his feet. His fist slammed into the door again. This time, he was rewarded by a muffled voice from the other side.

"Who is it?"

"It's me, Dagmar. Aki."

The door opened and he nearly fell through it. He recovered himself enough to shove the door shut behind him and then sagged against it. The world was spinning. The floor pitching up and down like the sea. Dagmar's face was nothing more than a blur in the light of the candle she held.

"Aki, what are you...," Dagmar started and then gasped. "Aki! You're bleeding. What happened?"

Aki tried to push away the lightness that claimed him.

"Don't... don't," he tried to form the words, but they proved very difficult, "Don't... open the door... not for anyone."

If Dagmar answered him, he missed it. He started to slide down the door to the floor but Dagmar grabbed his arm and pulled him forward and his feet obeyed. At least, they obeyed for a few steps. It was too much to ask of his legs to stay beneath him. He sank to the floor, both hands pressed now against the wound.

When Aki managed to force his eyes open once more, he wasn't sure how long he'd been lying there. Or where "there" was. Dagmar was kneeling next to him, her large eyes even bigger than usual as she lifted his shirt and stared at the wound in his side.

"It's deep, Aki. I think you need a doctor."

He shook his head, "No. No doctor. Don't leave the house. It's not safe."

"Aki, you're bleeding to death on my floor. You need help."

"I'm alright."

Dagmar looked at his wound and then up at his face, shaking her own head in protest.

"Just bandage it. As tight as you can."

She bit down on her lip. Her hands pulled his shirt back up and she grimaced. Without another word, she got up and disappeared from his sight. Aki tried to push himself up on one arm to get a look at the wound but dizziness forced him to lie back again. Dagmar reappeared with something white in her hands.

"You have to sit up so I can get this around you," she said, tugging on him. He pushed himself up once more and braced one hand against the wall behind him. "I really think you need a doctor."

"In the morning. I'll see one. In the morning."

"If you're still alive then," Dagmar muttered under her breath.

Aki gasped as she pulled the bandage tight. She loosened it a bit but he shook his head.

"Keep it tight. Bleeding has to stop."

When she tied it off, he slumped back to the ground. He let his eyes shut, unable to keep them open for another moment. He heard Dagmar get up again and then felt a blanket settle over him. When she started to stand again, he grabbed her arm and forced his eyes open.

"Don't tell anyone. You can't tell anyone what happened."

Dagmar looked at him oddly and said, "That would be really hard for me to do, Aki, since I don't actually know what happened."

Aki was drifting. The fiery pain in his side kept him aware but not really awake. Sounds made their way into his mind - the gentle rhythm of the waves nearby, footsteps moving about the house, the crackle of a fire only a few feet away - but he was detached from them.

How many hours passed in this state, he wasn't sure, but when his eyes blinked open once more it was no longer fully night. A soft grayness had entered the sky, heralding the approaching dawn.

He lifted his head and saw Dagmar sitting in a chair not far from him, asleep. And the sight of her suddenly frightened him. He shouldn't have come here. He shouldn't have involved her in any of this. If Halle had somehow seen him enter here, if he knew where Aki had sought help, he would not hesitate to hurt her too. And however much he might deserve Halle's wrath, Dagmar did not.

Gritting his teeth and wincing as pain exploded through his middle, he inched himself off the floor and to his feet. A glance down at the bandage showed a large, dark patch that was turning brown as the blood dried. At least he wasn't still bleeding. He found his jacket lying on the floor next to him and slipped it on, hiding the blood-soaked shirt beneath.

Dagmar didn't stir as he crept across the room to the front door and Aki breathed a little easier because of that. She'd be upset when she woke and found him gone, but he'd make it up to her somehow. He'd make all of this up to her just as soon as he could.

The air was even warmer than it had been yesterday, but Aki shivered in spite of it. Somewhere out here, Halle still roamed the streets. He could only hope he wasn't watching Dagmar's house right now. He'd never forgive himself if something happened to Dagmar because of him.

It had never taken Aki so long to reach the academy. His steps weren't steady and they grew less so as he approached, but at least there was no sign of Halle. That didn't keep him from jumping at every shadow. By the time he reached the street the academy was on, his hand was coming away from his side wet with fresh, warm blood. The lightheadedness returned and Aki staggered the last few steps inside.

It was as far as he could make it. He sank to the ground against the wall and shut his eyes. In here, there was not much danger of Halle finding him but he wasn't sure how he was going to explain his current condition to whoever happened to come across him sitting there.

"Aki?"

A voice broke through his daze. Aki shifted and moaned. He blinked, clearing the cloudiness from his eyes. He looked up. Oscar stood in front of him, his face twisted in confusion.

"What are you doing just sitting there?" Oscar spoke again and his voice sounded a little closer to Aki's ears. "And what happened to you? You look awful."

It took Aki a few attempts before his tongue would cooperate and form the words he wanted. "Help me get to my room."

Oscar stood, hands resting on his hips, staring down at him for what felt like eternity. Aki wanted to snap at him and tell him that if he wasn't going to help then he might as well leave, but he couldn't muster the strength for it. Then Oscar bent down and slid an arm beneath his and pulled him up.

Aki bit down on the inside of his cheek to keep from making a sound but that didn't keep him from sucking in each short, sharp breath. Oscar half dragged him inside the dormitory door and down the short hallway to his room. Aki was conscious enough to be thankful that no one else was in the hallway at the moment. He wasn't even sure what he was going to tell Oscar.

Once on his bed, Aki lay back without another word to Oscar. He almost hoped Oscar would leave without any more questions. It wasn't like Oscar to go out of his way to be helpful to him. When he didn't hear his door open and shut again, he turned his head to find Oscar standing, arms folded across his chest, staring at him. And judging by the look on his face, he had no intention of going anywhere without an explanation.

"Don't tell anyone, please," Aki whispered.

"What happened? You're covered in blood."

In answer, Aki slid a hand down to his side and pulled his shirt up enough to reveal the blood-soaked bandage beneath. Oscar pursed his lips as he stared at it.

"How bad is it?"

"Don't know."

Oscar came closer and pulled away the bandage. Aki hissed a protest as the part of the bandage that had dried and stuck to his skin pulled free.

"Oh, shut up. It has to come off eventually anyway," Oscar said. "This looks bad. You need a doctor."

"No, Oscar," Aki grabbed his arm, "please listen to me. You can't tell anyone."

Oscar looked dubious but agreed. Nodding, he said, "But only if you tell me what happened."

"I made someone angry, and they had a knife." It wasn't even a lie. He had made Halle angry; it had just been more than three years ago but Oscar didn't need to know that.

Oscar laughed a little then shrugged. "That seems a bit over-simplified, but alright. I won't tell. But you need help." He sat down on the edge of the bed. With a quick look of disgust, he pulled the bandage back over the wound and frowned. "You've bled completely through this. You need a new one. I guess, since you don't want anyone else to know, that I'm going to have to get some. Why do I keep getting stuck taking care of you? Couldn't you have made it to Felix's door? He doesn't mind helping you."

Aki glared at him but couldn't actually speak. There wasn't anything for him to say, anyway. He did need help. And Oscar was the only one around, although he would have preferred Felix now that Oscar mentioned it.

"It really kills you to ask for help, doesn't it?" Oscar laughed again, shaking his head. "I'll be back, but you're going to owe me something when this is over."

Aki tried to smile, but the pain gnawing at him made it nearly impossible. As Oscar left the room, he closed his eyes and tried to rest. He hadn't lain there long before his door opened and Oscar slipped back in. He set most of what he'd brought down on the table, keeping only a small, glass bottle in his hand as he approached Aki. He twisted the lid off and Aki caught a whiff of alcohol. He turned away with a grimace.

"I don't know much about taking care of wounds, but this is supposed to clean it."

"It'll hurt."

"Yes, it will," Oscar said, seemingly not bothered by that fact. Rather than making Aki sit back up, he took his knife out and cut through the bandage. "Try not to scream. That would sort of ruin the secret."

Aki glared at him again. A second later, he turned to bury his face in his pillow to keep from doing just that as Oscar poured a generous amount of the alcohol onto the open wound. All his previous pain paled in comparison to the deep, stinging sensation that tore through him.

"Enough," he gasped when Oscar took a cloth and began to dab at it. "It's clean enough."

Oscar shrugged. "If you say so. You'll have to sit up now."

Aki struggled to sit up, wincing as all the nerves in his body screamed in protest. He kept his lips pressed tightly together while Oscar wrapped a fresh bandage around him and pulled it tight. Oscar tied it off with a flourish and sat back to admire his own handiwork.

"I think I did pretty well. Maybe I should have been a doctor."

"You made it hurt worse than when he cut me."

"Which is going to make it better. I hope." Oscar stood up. "I need to leave."

"You're going to be late, aren't you?" Aki was surprised to find that he actually felt a little bad about that.

"Wouldn't be the first time," Oscar said with a grin.

Aki drifted off again before Oscar had shut the door. Even as he faded away, he knew he ought to be doing something. Master Wehr would be expecting him soon. If he didn't show up, there would be questions. And the last thing Aki wanted was questions. None of that was enough to keep him awake, though.

He awoke to a stabbing pain in his side and a hand on his shoulder. Blinking slowly, he realized someone was bending over him, their face only inches from him.

"What happened?" Jasper's voice was harsh and urgent, drawing him fully into consciousness. "Tell me what happened right now."

"He cut me," Aki mumbled, too muddled by pain and the ever-present faintness that told him he'd lost too much blood to put together a more coherent answer.

Jasper pulled up a chair and sat down. He leaned forward, resting his elbows on his knees and folding his hands together. His face was creased with worry.

"How bad?"

"I don't know. It hurts but I'm not dead yet." Aki tried to sit up but gave up almost immediately. "How did you know?"

"Kezi told me. I've been looking for you. You didn't come back last night. Where'd you go?"

Aki opened his mouth to answer, but a warning whisper in his mind stopped him. They didn't know. They didn't know about Dagmar. Another secret, but one he had to keep. Another secret that protected someone. Instead, he twisted his head around to get a good look at Jasper and all the anger he had been too stunned and too weak to indulge in before rushed back.

"You knew," he said. "You knew Halle was here. You and Kezi both did, and you didn't tell me. He tried to kill me."

A long pause only confirmed his own words and Aki reeled from the hurt in that confirmation.

"Look," Jasper sighed, "I did know he was here. And I knew he didn't like you, but Kezi's the only one who can talk to him. I swear I did not know he'd try to kill you."

"Kezi did though?" That didn't make it any better. In some ways, it made it a whole lot worse.

"I couldn't tell you that for sure, either. Kezi keeps a lot to herself. Let me take a look at it," Jasper said, reaching for the bandages. Aki looked down long enough to see that bright red was seeping through the last layer. He winced but stayed quiet when Jasper pulled them loose and let out a low whistle. "I'm going to get you a doctor, but before I do I need your promise. You can't tell anyone about this. No one."

Aki decided not to tell him that he was a little late. Two people already knew that he was injured.

"I'll tell Atticus that you're sick today and you'll be back tomorrow."

"Tomorrow?"

"You're used to working in pain, aren't you?" It wasn't the first time Jasper had made any reference to his time as a slave and Aki's jaw tightened at the reminder - and not just the reminder of a time he'd rather forget, but at the reminder of how much Jasper appeared to know about him that Aki had never revealed to him. Yes, he was used to it, but it didn't make it any easier.

"Two days. Give me two days and I won't say anything to anyone."

Jasper studied him, his face clouded with something other than concern. After too long, he nodded. "Two days. And I'll take care of Halle. It won't happen again."

Jasper left but returned only a short time later with another man. It wasn't Doctor Lamberse who had seen to his broken arm, and judging by the man's skittish gaze, Aki was pretty sure he knew something was amiss.

Aki had the impression that he could have been a fish for all the man cared about him. He was an injury to the doctor, a wound to be treated and nothing more. The doctor said nothing at all as he went to work.

With Jasper leaning against his door, Aki tried to remain equally quiet and composed but it was difficult. It was even harder when the doctor began to stitch the wound closed. No matter how tightly he clenched his jaw shut, it couldn't prevent the tiny moans that forced their way up his throat.

When the doctor finished, he still said nothing to Aki but instead joined Jasper by the door where the two men held a whispered conversation. Aki strained his ears to catch their words, but they kept their voices soft and he finally gave up. It was too exhausting anyway. He turned his face into his pillow and shut his eyes.

The day passed with a miserable sort of slowness. The dormitory was utterly silent and empty aside from him. Sleep was elusive, coming in bits and spurts and interrupted often by the shards of pain that exploded through his abdomen at the slightest movement.

He'd managed to doze off again when the sound of footsteps slowing before his door roused him. Lifting himself up enough to see the door as it opened, he expected to see Jasper. Instead, Oscar's head poked between the door and the frame, a grin on his face.

"Well, you look miserable."

"Thanks." Aki lay back down on his pillow with a sigh.

"Since I can't tell anyone that you're hurt, I guess that means I can't expect anyone else to help you." Oscar came all the way in the room then, a tray containing what Aki assumed was dinner on it in his hands. "Thought you might be hungry from laying around in bed all day."

The smell of food quickly filled the room and Aki realized that he was, in fact, very hungry.

"I hope you can feed yourself because I really..."

"Yes, I can feed myself," Aki interrupted. He forced himself into a sitting position and Oscar handed him the tray. "Thank you, Oscar. For everything."

"You're going to owe me after this."

Chapter 27

WHAT WERE YOU THINKING?" Jasper demanded, pacing the floor of the old rundown hut.

Seated at a small table, her arms folded and resting on its worn surface, Kezi refused to meet his eyes. Aside from the rhythmic creak of the floor beneath the weight of Jasper's steps and the sound of water lapping at the rocks only a few feet outside the hut, it was quiet. None of the sounds of Bren reached this small house by the sea.

"We agreed. Nobody dies. I won't be part of murder."

"He's not dead," Kezi said. "And even if he was, it wouldn't matter."

"Wouldn't matter?" Jasper paused in his pacing in front of the table. Leaning forward, his hands pressed flat on the table, he continued, "Wouldn't matter? You've lost your mind! Have you any idea what you've just done? Have you any idea just who he is connected with? He's not like those orphan children you steal off the streets for smuggling. People will look for him. People who have the ear of the king."

"Of course I know that."

"One word. One word from him to the right person and we're done."

"But he won't talk. He's never talked."

"You never threatened him before, either," Jasper said quietly. "You're going to leave him no choice but to seek help."

Kezi let out an exasperated huff of air and sat back in her chair. She glanced toward the wall where Halle lay sprawled on the couch in a drunken slumber.

"Fine. We went too far. Is that what you want to hear?"

"What I want, Kezi, is for you to keep to the bargain, the plan we've been working on for months. Keep Halle under control. Keep him drunk if you have to until we need him, but he'd better not try to kill anyone else."

"I haven't forgotten the plan. And I'll speak to Halle."

"Good. Because our opportunity may have just opened up."

Kezi straightened, her eyes brightening. "How soon?"

"Princess Charlotte has, as you know, been staying at her mother's estate in Pellor. In three weeks, she will travel back here to Bren. It's being done quietly, without any unnecessary attention. The only reason I know about it is because I took the orders. That'll work in our favor."

"What's the road from Pellor to Bren like?"

"Quiet. Secluded in parts. There's a couple of places that would give us good cover for an ambush. Will Halle have everything in place by then?"

"He will. I'll make sure that he will."

Jasper pulled up a second chair and sat down heavily in it. He pulled out a tattered paper from his pocket and spread it between them on the table. It wasn't a real map, but more of a sketch. It was one Jasper had Aki make after a trip to Pellor just before he'd left for the wedding. Aki hadn't even questioned why he had to draw it after Jasper told him it was practice to see how well he remembered landmarks and directions.

"The only problem will be in getting Halle's ship in close enough anywhere along here. There are only a few places that might work. Here," Jasper tapped the paper, indicating a spot, "is our best spot. Terrain is rough, a lot of big rocks, heavy woods, plenty of places to hide. He can have the ship waiting just offshore, too."

Kezi cupped her chin in her hands as she studied the homemade map. Reaching for the inkpot and quill that sat near the edge of the table, she started scrawling out the details in Aruuken.

"You sure that's smart? Someone might get a hold of that."

"They couldn't read it anyway, but Halle can, and his men can. They need to understand exactly what we're doing."

Jasper nodded.

"Without Phineas, we're shorthanded."

Kezi waved his concern away as she finished her note. "Doesn't matter. We'll borrow some people from Halle's ship if we have to, but the smaller the number, the easier it will be to hide."

"They're going to hang him, you know."

"Who?"

"Phineas."

"No. They'll give him back to us. Just as soon as we have the princess, they'll give us everything we want. Either way, it doesn't matter. If he wanted to stay alive, he shouldn't have been caught."

Jasper sat back and ran a weary hand over his face. He'd spent most of the previous night out looking for Aki and he felt it now.

"Something's still bothering you," Kezi said, eyeing him shrewdly. "It's something to do with Aki, isn't it?"

"Why him? What is it with him?"

Kezi let out a laugh that was both soft and wild. "Why him? Because, Jasper, he told me no. I warned him not to. Besides, Sasha cares about him. And whatever happens to Aki will get back to Sasha."

"I thought you'd moved past that." Jasper scowled down at the table.

"As if I could ever move past that? When every day of my life here reminds me of what he did, dragging me here?"

"You're better off here than you were in Karu."

"Am I?" Once more, Kezi laughed without merriment. She cut it off abruptly, her face hardening. "Am I really? I've had to sell every part of myself just to survive here, as you well know. I've had to beg, steal and degrade myself to make any sort of life. And he's the one who forced that on me."

"You and Halle really are a pair, aren't you? I've put too much into this for your revenge to get in the way."

"You do realize that I can get more than just one thing out of this, don't you?"

"I suppose so. Still, I think you should leave him out of this. And if we're going to move in the next three weeks, he needs to be out of the way. He knows too much. Even if he doesn't mean to, he can give us up too easily."

Jasper wasn't looking at Kezi and missed the dark annoyance that shadowed her face momentarily. She hid it almost immediately and gave Jasper an indifferent shrug.

"So, get him out of Bren. That shouldn't be too hard for you to do."

Jasper leaned forward, resting his head in his hands and remained silent and thoughtful for several minutes.

"I'll need you to do something for me."

"Anything."

Chapter 28

AKI WISHED HE'D DEMANDED three or even four days. Each step he took sent a burning agony rippling through his body and no matter how hard he tried, he could only draw in short half breaths before he was doubled over in pain. He kept his head down as he made his way through the streets, silently hoping that Jasper had told him the truth and had taken care of Halle - whatever that meant. It took more willpower than he could imagine to keep from looking down each alley and searching every face he passed.

He made it to Master Wehr's without incident and on time - both facts that surprised him when he was standing on the doorstep. Master Wehr looked up at his entrance and leaned back in his chair.

"You're well?"

"Yes, I'm better. Sorry for having to miss like that."

Master Wehr waved his apology aside. "It's part of life, nothing to apologize for."

Aki had spent the last two days planning an elaborate story of his illness just in case Master Wehr needed extra convincing. More lies. He wondered just how many more he could tell before someone heard the wrong story. Thankfully, his instructor didn't seem all that curious about Aki's ailment. If, throughout the day, Master Wehr noticed him grabbing at his side and stifling a soft moan every now and then, his teacher did not mention it.

It was near the end of the day when Master Wehr set aside his own work and stood over Aki's shoulder.

"You seem distracted."

Aki, who hadn't heard him come up behind him, jumped a little and his hand flew to his side as his breath hitched in pain. He'd been staring out the window, watching the people outside, but that was hardly something new for him.

"I'm sorry," he said when he'd collected his scattered thoughts enough to answer. "I guess my head's still hurting."

"I see."

Rather than returning to his desk, Master Wehr continued to stand over his shoulder, staring out of the same window Aki had been. Aki shifted a little, trying to imagine away the throbbing in his side and hoping Master Wehr wasn't perceptive enough to notice the added thickness of the bandage or the deep red that stained his shirt in spots. In spite of being stitched closed, the wound wasn't sealing up well at all.

"You know, there's no harm in asking for help, Aki. Especially when you're lost. That was one of the hardest things for me to learn when I first started," Master Wehr said, a wistful smile on his face as he continued to stare out the window. "There was more than once when I lost my way and was too proud or ashamed to ask for help."

Aki watched him, knowing full well that Master Wehr wasn't really talking about getting lost on the road. He tried to think of something, anything that he could say that would end this conversation before it went too far.

"You know what never did me any good? Wandering around, pretending I knew exactly where I was going and what I was doing. There's no harm in asking for help," he repeated. He glanced down at Aki's bandaged side and his face grew somber. "I know you're hiding that." Aki covered it with his hand instinctively and hung his head. "And I don't know why, but I know you don't need to. Just ask for help."

"I can't," Aki said softly. "I can't or people will be hurt. I can't risk that."

"You're hurt now," Master Wehr pointed out.

"I don't matter. Pain doesn't bother me." Which was a ridiculous thing for him to say, since the deep gash in his side was very much bothering him.

"I see," Master Wehr nodded his head slowly. He laid a hand on Aki's shoulder and when Aki lifted his eyes to meet Master Wehr's, he was taken aback by the sorrow and pleading in them. If only he could tell Master Wehr. Perhaps he would understand and help. After all, Master Wehr had given him a chance when none of the other instructors would. The freedom of having someone else know everything, all that he'd done and all that he knew, was tantalizing. And terrifying.

Perhaps his expression would change to one of disgust and horror at what Aki had done, at what Aki had been capable of doing. It was that thought that kept him quiet.

Master Wehr didn't press him, either, which was a good thing. Aki would have broken down and told him everything if he had. He started to walk away and Aki breathed a little easier. It was short lived relief, however, when Master Wehr's next words reached him.

"Jasper knows, doesn't he? He's the one who told me you were sick."

Aki wasn't fast enough to catch himself and Master Wehr had been watching him closely for just such a reaction. He didn't even bother waiting for an actual answer from Aki.

"I thought as much. We're done for today, Aki."

Aki was relieved to escape any more questions as he slipped out the door and started back to the academy. He hadn't made it far at all before he realized he was being followed. Instinct told him to run, but the pain in his side prevented him. The hurried footsteps caught up with him and Aki turned to face his pursuer.

"What is wrong with you, Aki?" Dagmar asked, grabbing him by the arms, her eyes trailing down to the bandage around his middle. "You left without a word. I've been worried sick about you. You can't just turn up bleeding all over the place and then disappear again without a word. You could have died. You could have been laying out in the street somewhere, dead, and I wouldn't have known."

When she paused for breath, Aki said, "I'm sorry. I shouldn't have done that. I know. But I had a reason, believe me, I did. And," he started to pull away from her, "you shouldn't be here with me. Not right now."

"Why not?"

"It's just not a good idea." Aki cast a surreptitious glance around them and went cold when his eyes found Kezi standing in the shadows of a doorframe watching them, near enough to have heard everything. He stepped away from Dagmar as if she were on fire. "I have to go. I'm sorry I worried you, but I was fine, really. You shouldn't come back here."

Without waiting to see the effect his words or tone had on Dagmar he spun around as quickly as his side would allow him and walked away.

It came as no surprise when Kezi appeared in front of him only a few minutes later, but Aki still stopped walking altogether.

"You knew," was all he said.

"Just give me a chance to explain, Aki. It's not what you think. I had no idea Halle was going to try to kill you. That wasn't my plan."

Aki started to brush past her, but she grabbed his arm.

"Please, just listen to me. You're my friend. You can't possibly think I'd want you dead. Halle came to me asking for me to help him find you. He never said why, but he never gave me reason to think he meant you harm. I thought you'd be happy to see each other again - the way you were with Sasha. If I'd known he would try to kill you, I never would have helped him."

Aki regarded her with suspicion but stopped trying to walk away.

"Look, if you don't want any part of what we're doing, that's fine. I won't ask you again, I promise. Please, believe me. You've been one of the very few people that I can call a real friend. I'd hate for some misunderstanding to change that."

"It might be just a misunderstanding for you, but I'm the one with my side cut open."

"And I'm sorry for that," Kezi said. Aki had never heard her say that before. "I tried to help you after but you were gone and we couldn't find you. I even went to Jasper."

That much, at least, Aki knew to be true.

"Where's Halle now?"

"He left. I was so angry I told him to leave and not come back here, and since I was the only one he could talk to here, he did. I saw him leave on his ship, Aki, I know for sure he's gone."

Aki shut his eyes for a moment, trying to make himself believe anything she'd just said. Part of him desperately wanted to, no matter how unreasonable it was.

"Just leave me out of all this, Kezi," he said at last, pushing past her once more. This time she did not stop him.

Jasper and the doctor were waiting for him by the time he reached his room. Aki groaned internally when he saw them waiting. He wanted a few minutes to himself and the look on Jasper's face made it clear he was not about to get that. Crossing the room to his bed, he didn't wait for the doctor to say anything before pulling his shirt off. Only a few spots of red had shown through earlier. Now those spots had merged into one slowly spreading stain. Aki turned away and stared out the window, forcing his thoughts away from the pain, as the doctor unwound the bandage.

"It's not closing up," the doctor said, not to Aki but to Jasper. He'd yet to say anything to Aki.

"Maybe because I shouldn't be walking around pretending it isn't there," Aki muttered.

The doctor pretended not to hear him. Jasper didn't say anything, but his eyebrows shot up and Aki was sure he'd earned at least another few minutes of the man's presence in his room after the doctor left. It didn't matter. Aki was beyond caring after running into both Dagmar and Kezi. Jasper would repeat his same old threats, and Aki would listen because there was nothing else he could do, and he'd keep his mouth shut because less people were hurt that way.

With a fresh bandage wrapped about him, Aki lay straight back on his bed, his feet still resting on the floor. Jasper left the room with the doctor but returned in less than a minute. Aki kept his eyes shut on the slim chance Jasper would leave him alone. He heard the scrape of a chair being dragged across the room and knew it hadn't worked. Jasper sank into the chair heavily but didn't speak. Curiosity finally got the better of Aki, and he opened his eyes, sitting up just enough to get a look at Jasper's face. He flopped back down.

"Go ahead. Just say whatever it is you want to say, because I'm tired and I'd like to sleep."

"Does Atticus know?"

"No. I told you I wouldn't tell anyone." It wasn't a complete lie. Master Wehr had guessed he was hurt, but Aki had never told him.

"Keep it that way."

The sharpness in Jasper's voice infuriated him in a way that he wasn't used to. He sat up, ignoring the pull of the stitches on his skin. One look at Jasper, and what he was about to say died away. If he made Jasper angry, there was plenty the man could do in return to hurt him. Jasper was watching him, waiting for him to speak. When Aki remained silent, he stood up and put the chair back at the table.

"I'm sorry things have turned out this way, Aki, really I am. Kezi should have left you out of everything. Hopefully, it won't be for much longer," Jasper said. He hesitated, one hand on the door. "Get some rest. If you want, I can let Atticus know you won't be in tomorrow."

"I'll manage. I'm used to it, remember?" It was the closest he could come to venting his anger but Jasper ignored the quip and left without another word.

Alone in his room at last, Aki got up and made his way to the window. Resting his arms on the sill, he stared out at the darkening street. He was tired, but he was also curious. Jasper's words rang through his head. Whatever they were planning would happen soon. He wondered what it was. Something big. Something illegal. And something Aki couldn't help but feel he was going to be drawn into whether he liked it or not.

Chapter 30

JASPER MET AKI IN THE hallway outside his room. Aside from bringing the doctor to his room every evening for the first week, Aki hadn't seen him or spoken to him. Aki could only be grateful for that. There was nothing Jasper could say that would make anything better, and a great deal he could say that would make things worse. Now, seeing him in the hallway, Aki tensed.

"How do you feel?"

"Fine," Aki said.

"Good. We're going out today."

Aki hadn't gone out once in the two weeks since Halle had attacked him. Even now, the thought of pulling himself onto his horse was painful. He had no intention of letting Jasper know that, though.

Shrugging, he turned back toward his room. "When do we leave?"

"Now."

It took him only a few minutes to get ready but even that appeared to be too long for Jasper's liking. The man stood, drumming his fingers on the wall behind him until Aki announced he was ready. Aki wasn't used to seeing him so impatient.

Aki was a little surprised when, instead of riding straight out of town, they stopped first at Master Wehr's. Aki was already on the ground before Jasper spoke.

"Wait out here," Jasper said. "I need to let him know I'm taking you today."

Aki rubbed Sky's broad forehead. A hand on his arm sent him spinning around and he found himself face to face with Kezi. He hadn't seen her since she'd tried to explain herself. She raised a finger to her lips before he could say anything. Eyes darting to the doorway that Jasper would walk out of at any moment, she drew a tightly folded piece of paper out of her pocket.

"I know you're probably still angry with me but," she said, her voice low, "Jasper let it slip that you're going to Pellor. I have a friend who took work there and I thought, maybe, since you're going there anyway, that you could find a chance to give this to her."

"It's against the rules. We're not allowed to take any unauthorized messages."

"No one would have to know you took it. You could give it to her when Jasper's not looking. Please, Aki. I don't have any money to send it properly."

Aki absently ran his hand along Sky's neck as he glanced back at Master Wehr's. It was taking Jasper a long time to tell Master Wehr that they would be gone for the day. He turned back to Kezi and was surprised to find her turning away.

"I guess I'll figure something else out. I wouldn't want to get you in trouble," she said.

"It's fine. I can take it."

"You can? Thank you, Aki," she smiled and slid the folded paper into his hand. "I'll never ask you again. I promise. This'll be the only time."

She was gone before he could respond, disappeared down an alley just as the front door of Master Wehr's opened and Jasper stepped out.

"What was that about?" Jasper came and stood in front of him as Aki tightened his hand around the paper he hadn't had time to hide away.

"Nothing.   She   was   just   apologizing   for   what happened."

"I thought she already did that?"

"I guess she thought she needed to do it again," Aki attempted a smile, all the while wishing Jasper would turn the other way so that he could stuff the note into a pocket out of sight. His hands were damp with sweat as he fought to keep them still at his side.

"What's that in your hand?"

Aki gulped and ran his tongue over his lips as he scrambled for something to say. Jasper didn't give him the chance. His hand shot out and grabbed Aki's. Aki didn't bother to resist as Jasper pried his fingers open to reveal the paper resting in his palm. He might have tried to pass it off as a note Kezi meant just for him, except that it was addressed to her friend, the name and town of residence written quite plainly on the outside. The sound of someone clearing their throat nearby made Aki look up and his heart sank as he found Master Wehr standing in the still open door.

"You know you're not allowed to do this," Jasper said.

"I know." There wasn't any point in arguing that he didn't. It had been among the first lessons Master Wehr had taught him and Jasper had reiterated it many times since.

"Why?"

To that, Aki didn't think he had a very good answer. He couldn't say that he wanted things to be back to the way they used to be with Kezi so much that he was willing to break the rules to get it. He couldn't say that he hated himself for the disappointed look on her face when she thought he was going to refuse. And he definitely couldn't say that he'd never thought that keeping the rules was very important, so long as one didn't get caught. He glanced back over at Master Wehr and wished he could disappear the same way Kezi had only a few moments before.

"Come on," Jasper said when he remained silent. "We'll have to tell Captain Lupin."

"Do we?"

"Yes, we do."

Aki was quiet as they retraced their steps back to the academy. Once he thought he caught a glimpse of Kezi but it was only for an instant and he couldn't be quite sure. He'd have to find her and let her know what had happened. Jasper was equally quiet. Aki thought to ask him what Captain Lupin would do, but decided he was just fine waiting for that knowledge.

"Wait out here," Jasper said when they reached the academy.

Aki nodded and watched him disappear into Captain Lupin's office. They were only in there together for a few minutes before Jasper opened the door and waved Aki in. With a resigned sigh, Aki slid to the ground and made his way into the room. He hadn't been in here since Oscar had broken his arm and standing here now, he remembered what Captain Lupin had said to him that day. Well, so much for proving the man wrong, Aki thought ruefully as he took the seat Captain Lupin motioned him to.

"Jasper gave me this. He said you took it from someone and were planning on delivering it during your trip today. Is that true?"

"Yes, sir."

"I'm assuming this was from a friend of yours? A favor you were doing for them?"

"Yes, sir."

"I see. Jasper has also told me that this isn't the first time he's caught you doing this," Captain Lupin leaned back, tapping his fingertips together as he regarded Aki. "Is this true?"

A puzzled frown, followed by horrified understanding crossed Aki's face as he sat, head down, listening to Captain Lupin. He dared a glance in Jasper's direction, and Jasper nodded slightly, expectantly. With a sinking feeling of despair mingling with fury, Aki knew exactly what Jasper wanted of him now. And he knew what would happen if he didn't comply.

"It's true," he whispered, his voice dull, empty of any sign of the turmoil raging inside him at that moment.

Captain Lupin continued tapping his fingers together, apparently lost in thought. Aki shifted in his seat, trying hard to keep his face impassive as everything fell into place.

"I've had a request from one of our remount stations for some help. I'm thinking that would be a good place for you for now."

Aki gripped the chair beneath him, staring at the floor. "What does that mean? Am I out?"

"Out? No." Aki's grip on the chair loosened ever so slightly. "But I think some time away to think about the importance of following our rules would be good. If we can't trust you to follow those, how can we trust you with one of the most important duties in the kingdom?"

Aki didn't answer and he didn't think Captain Lupin expected one.

"You may remain in your room for the remainder of the day, and I will draw up your new orders with all the details by this evening. You'll leave first thing in the morning."

"Yes, sir."

Aki made it all the way to his room, Jasper only a few steps behind him, before he said anything else.

"Why?" Just the one word, but all of his anger and confusion and hurt were bound together in it.

"Believe it or not, Aki, I'm trying to help you. You stay here, and you're going to get hurt - worse than you already have been. Take the punishment and move on. You'll be able to come back and when you do all this will have blown over."

"And I'll be behind. And no one will trust me."

"Listen to me, Aki," Jasper's voice raised in frustration, "I don't know exactly how but Kezi's going to use you. Whatever friendship you have with her won't matter, because she hates better than she loves. I never wanted to get you involved in all this, she did. She wants revenge and she's going to use you to get it. And Kezi always gets what she wants. I'm trying to save you from that. Sure, it might not be the best, but it's all I can do."

Aki sat down on the edge of his bed and buried his face in his hands, trying to sort through everything Jasper had just said.

"It won't be forever. Just for a few weeks. I'm sorry. It shouldn't have come to this."

Aki didn't move when he heard his door shut behind Jasper. He didn't move for a very long time and when he did it was just to stand and stare out of his window for an equally long time. More than once throughout the endless day, he went to his door, determined to go to Captain Lupin and tell him everything. Each time, his hand froze on the latch, his mind wandering over the consequences of what he was about to do. He'd be out for sure if Captain Lupin found out what he'd done, and Sasha could be in trouble. It wasn't worth the risk. Better to keep his head down and accept his punishment as Jasper had said.

As the afternoon wore on, Aki resigned himself to leaving. It wasn't the worst thing that could happen, he supposed. Captain Lupin himself had said he wasn't out. With nothing else to do, he began packing. When he got to the set of throwing knives he stopped, fingering them, remembering the day he'd taken them. Remembering why.

Halle hadn't been able to stop him that day, even though he was in the room when Aki came in. He'd been confined to his bed, both legs shattered from a terrible fall. He couldn't even call out for help because of the bandages that swathed his head and a good portion of his face. Aki had not bothered to sneak in, either. He meant for Halle to see him there after all that had transpired before between them. He wanted to see the terror that filled Halle's eyes when he saw Aki enter. Only it hadn't been just fear in Halle's eyes, it had been hatred. Deep, black hatred that matched his own in that moment. And that alarmed Aki.

Aki hadn't entered Halle's room with the intention of stealing anything, but seeing that hate, seeing the mirrored reflection of himself in Halle's eyes, he had to do something to prove he was not afraid. Not afraid of Halle, or of anything else. With a calm that he didn't actually feel, he'd sauntered across Halle's room, feeling the intensity of Halle's glare every step of the way, and started going through his things.

When he got to the knives, Halle tried to protest, but all that came out of his mouth was garbled gibberish. Aki knew the knives. He'd had to sharpen them not two years before when he still served as a slave. They were a gift from Mara to Halle. A symbol of the love Aki could never have and he knew he had to have those knives.

Aki slid them into his bag now. He'd told himself and Halle that day that he wasn't afraid of Halle anymore, that he wasn't afraid of anyone anymore. Aki had never told a bigger lie.

Chapter 31

WHEN THE KNOCK CAME ON his door that evening, Aki was ready for it. He thought. Captain Lupin stepped inside his room and handed him a sealed envelope and Aki took it without a word. He held it in front of him, debating whether to tear it open right away or not. Captain Lupin lingered at the door.

"Is there anything you want to tell me, Aki?"

Aki looked up from the envelope. There was a lot he wanted to tell, but nothing that he was free to say.

"No, sir."

"Very well," Captain Lupin nodded and left Aki to himself once more.

Aki tore open the envelope but had not yet pulled Captain Lupin's orders out when another knock came on his door. Thinking it was Captain Lupin again, Aki answered, "Come in."

He was not prepared for Oscar to enter. And it wasn't just Oscar. Felix was behind him and both looked curious.

"What was that about? He never comes to our rooms," Oscar asked.

Tempted to lie, Aki shoved the torn envelope beneath his pillow without another thought. He had all night to find out what that paper said, anyway, and he wasn't in that big of a hurry to know. Of course, Oscar and Felix both saw the action, which only made them more curious. And they'd find out soon enough, Aki realized. And he'd rather they hear it from him than someone else. He didn't want to lie. There were so many already.

"I did something I wasn't supposed to. And he's sending me away for a while."

"So, what'd you do?" Oscar made himself comfortable on the other bed, clearly expecting a good story and not particularly bothered by either Aki's wrongdoing or punishment. Felix sat down at the table with more reservation but no less curiosity.

"I took a letter for a friend."

"That's it?" Oscar's face scrunched up in disbelief. "I mean, I know it's against the rules, but everybody does it."

"I don't," Felix said. "It *is* against the rules."

"Well, everyone but you," Oscar rolled his eyes but Felix missed it. "Most of us are smart enough not to get caught. Shame you couldn't manage that."

Aki bit his tongue to keep from saying anything.

"So, you're leaving? Where are you going?" Felix asked.

"Don't know yet. Some courier remount station, that's all I know."

"Aren't you mad about it?" Oscar said.

"A bit," Aki managed an indifferent shrug. "I did take the letter, so it's my fault."

"But we've all," Oscar glanced at Felix, "well, at least, most of us have done that. It's not quite fair that you get sent away for it. You could always fight it, you know."

"What are you talking about? They're Captain Lupin's orders. I'm not going to argue with him. That'll only make things worse."

"No, not my father. I meant, you could make an appeal."

"To whom?"

"The king. It's one of his rules, that anyone who works directly for him can come to him and appeal any decision made by their superiors."

Aki laughed a little at the idea.

"That would be an absurd use of an appeal," Felix pointed out and Aki was inclined to agree with him. "Aki broke the rules. An appeal is only supposed to be when you're accused wrongly or something like that."

"It's what I would do," Oscar said, with an emphatic nod.

"And King Darien would probably throw you out for wasting his time. Don't be ridiculous."

"But he can't. His own rule says he has to hear me out. And I'd tell him that I was no more guilty than anyone else and that if I was to be punished, all his other couriers ought to be too."

"You'd still be wasting your time, and probably ruining your chance of really becoming a courier," Felix said.

Aki listened to them argue and was surprised to find himself smiling. Having someone to commiserate with made things a little easier, he decided.

"It doesn't matter. I'm not arguing this. I'm leaving in the morning and that's the end of it." Because that's what Jasper wanted, and because he couldn't afford to defy Jasper.

Oscar shrugged. "I'd still fight it."

When Felix and Oscar finally left him alone for the night, Aki decided he'd waited long enough. He retrieved Captain Lupin's orders from their hiding place. The paper slid out easily and rested, folded, in his hand. It was only for a little while, he reminded himself. And then he opened it.

Blood drained from his face and Aki shut his eyes, refusing to believe what they read. He opened them again, willing the words to be different, willing the entire thing to just be his imagination. They weren't. And worse than what was written was the fact that he was sure Captain Lupin thought he was doing Aki a favor. But there was no favor in sending Aki back to Stephan. None at all. It didn't matter that it was only for four weeks. It didn't matter that he would get to come back here and pick right back up with his training. It didn't matter that there was no permanent consequence for his disobedience.

All that mattered was that he was going to have to go back and face Stephan. And Stephan would know why he was there.

Aki spent half the night contemplating a new future, far from anyone he knew. It had its merits. When he did finally fall asleep, it was well into the early hours of the morning. Although he expected to sleep restlessly, when he woke up, sunlight was streaming through the small window. It was far later than he usually slept but he wasn't upset about the delay. It meant he could leave quietly while the others were gone for the day and gave him just a little more time before he had to face Stephan.

Leading Sky through the streets, he kept his head down, hoping he didn't run into anyone. He hadn't gone far before an argument reached his ears. It wasn't their voices that brought his attention to them, it was the fact that they spoke in another language. They were arguing in Aruuken. Keeping Sky's body between him and them, Aki spotted Lars and Halle standing in the entrance of an alley. A chill ran through him as the realization came to him that Kezi had lied - Halle was not gone on some ship, he was still right here in Bren and within easy reach of Aki.

Whatever outburst he'd heard was over and their voices were lowered enough he couldn't hear them anymore. It didn't matter anyway, he told himself, although it was a little disappointing for Lars to be with Halle. That didn't stop him from waiting out of sight around a corner until Halle stormed away, a slight limp making his gait uneven, leaving Lars standing by himself.

"What was that all about?" he asked, coming up to Lars when Halle was completely out of sight.

"Oh, that? Nothing really. He wants to leave now, and I don't. What are you doing?"

"I'm just leaving for Stephan's," Aki answered, keeping his voice light. The last thing he wanted was for Lars to find out.

"I just came from that way. I didn't know you were going back."

"It was a bit of a last-minute decision."

After Lars had left in search of Halle, Aki waited a moment longer. With Lars' back to him, he bent down and picked up the tattered, folded piece of paper that had been his real reason for coming over to talk. Halle had dropped it when he thought he'd shoved it into his pocket. Rather than lingering in the street to study the paper, Aki slid it into one of his saddlebags and hurried away from the spot just in case Halle noticed it missing and came looking for it.

Once outside of Bren, Aki mounted Sky and kicked her into a trot. He'd wasted enough time and didn't want to show up at Stephan's too late. That could only make things worse.

Throughout the long, lonely hours of riding, Aki tried to rehearse exactly what he was going to say to Stephan when he got there. There would be no easy way to break the news, no way that spared Aki the humiliation of returning home in this manner.

All of his carefully thought out and rehearsed lines flitted away the moment he stood in front of the barn, Stephan only a few feet away from him. His timing couldn't have been worse, he decided. He'd managed to ride up at the exact moment Stephan finished taking care of the horses for the evening and started for the house.

Stephan was confused but not unhappy as he approached Aki, who found himself suddenly bereft of the ability to move or speak.

"Aki? What are you doing back here?"

Unable to come up with a single thing to say, Aki merely held out the paper with Captain Lupin's written orders on it. Stephan took it and there was silence between them as he read it. Aki stared at the ground while he waited for Stephan to speak.

"What did you do?"

"Does it matter?" Aki replied, not at all wanting to tell him.

"I think it does. Tell me."

"I took a letter for someone that I wasn't supposed to."

"Why?"

"I don't know. Because I wanted to, I guess."

Stephan waited for him to elaborate and with a sigh, Aki knew he had to. "Kezi asked me to take it, and I couldn't tell her no."

"You can always tell someone no."

"It's not that easy."

"You knew not to?"

Aki nodded, still staring at the ground. Stephan was angry. He could hear it in the tightness of his voice, in the way he clipped each word off. He could sense it in his weighted gaze and the heavy exhale as Stephan considered for a moment.

"I'm sorry, Stephan," Aki said quietly.

"Go on and put your horse up," Stephan said and walked toward the house.

Aki's fingers didn't want to work properly when he went to take Sky's saddle and bridle off. They fumbled with the buckles and straps, dragging the process out far longer than it needed to be. Aki wanted to be frustrated by that, but the truth was, he was in no hurry to go inside. No doubt Stephan would have shared with Alina why he was back and that was worse than Stephan knowing.

When he could delay no longer without incurring an even greater level of Stephan's wrath, Aki made his way to the house. A quiet air of displeasure hung over the place at his entrance.

"You must be hungry, Aki," Alina said by way of greeting, a thin, troubled smile on her face.

"A little, I guess," Aki said, although he had little appetite under the circumstances. He glanced toward Stephan who was busy with something in his chair by the fire. Stephan apparently didn't have anything else to say to him for now. Aki wished he would. Being yelled at would be easier than watching his face harden into grim, disapproving lines.

He ate little of the food Alina gave him. He evaded all of Alina's many efforts to draw him into conversation. She asked so many questions about the academy and his training and Dagmar. Questions he couldn't answer truthfully and so he chose not to really answer them at all. It was only for a little while longer, he reminded himself when he noticed the concerned creases deepening on Alina's face as he brushed aside query after query. At last, she gave up and Aki decided it was as good a time as any to go to bed.

"You'll need to be up early tomorrow," Stephan reminded him.

"I know."

It was hard to imagine that he'd lived here so comfortably for the last three years. There was nothing comfortable about being here now, Aki thought as he closed himself into his room. Sleep wasn't coming any time soon, he knew. He was too troubled to rest. The soft murmur of voices reached him from beyond the door but he couldn't make out the words and he didn't want to. Stephan made it very clear how he felt about the entire affair. And he desperately wished he could explain to

Stephan that the real reason he'd been sent here was because there were people who wanted him out of the way.

Out in the sitting room, Alina's hands were unusually idle as she sat staring at the fire, the lines of worry etched even deeper in her face than when Aki had been present in the room.

"You're too hard on him," she said softly after several minutes of tense silence had gone by.

"He broke one of their rules and is being punished. He knew better. He knows better."

"You don't have to add to it, though."

"He shouldn't have let Kezi talk him into breaking the rules. I've told him before that she's nothing but trouble."

"And he's the first boy to ever do something foolish because a girl asked him to," Alina said, a slight smile playing on her lips.

Stephan looked up from what he was doing long enough to shake his head. "Doesn't make it alright."

"No, it doesn't. But that's been dealt with already. Besides, I think there's more wrong."

"And why do you say that?"

"He was different tonight. Too quiet. Too troubled."

"He was probably just upset that he had to come back here."

"No. We've both seen him upset before. But when have you ever seen him so unwilling to talk?"

"When I tell him to stop talking."

Alina gave him a pointed look, "Exactly."

"I'll talk to him in the morning," Stephan said with a nod, "but it's probably nothing."

Chapter 32

AKI LAY IN THE DARKNESS, surrounded by silence. Stephan and Alina had gone to bed some time before and he was still wide awake.

He sat up swiftly and reached to light the candle on his table. In its golden light, he drew out the tattered piece of paper he'd forgotten about. He'd been so preoccupied planning out how he was going to explain to Stephan that all thoughts of the paper Halle had dropped had fled his mind until now. Unfolding it, two things were immediately obvious. The first was that it was a sketch of a stretch of road and the land that lay around it and not just any sketch. It was the one he'd made under Jasper's instructions. Secondly, and far more surprisingly, there were notes scribbled all over it, written in a sloppy, scrawling hand. And written in Aruuken.

The single flame of the candle flickered in the darkness, casting strange shadows on the walls and table as Aki bent over the sketched map. He'd barely learned to read Aruuken before Gundar brought him here to Dival and it took a great deal of concentration for him to decipher each word. As the candle burned further and further down, its wax running down its sides and pooling on the stand beneath it, he worked his way through the notes. An ever-growing sense of horror filled him as the full import of the words reached his mind.

He'd always known that whatever Kezi and Jasper were planning was big. Never in his wildest dreams had he conjured up the possibility of a plan this dangerous, this bold. And Halle was right in the middle of it all. Kezi had lied about him leaving. She'd lied about what she knew of Halle. Aki went hot with the realization and his breathing quickened as anger wormed its way inside him. She had known. All along, she had known.

Aki held his head in his hands as he bent over the table and reread the notes. This was what she'd wanted him to be part of. And he knew what his part in it would have been.

Bait.

She planned to use him as bait - the one who'd take the blame, even if all went as planned. The diversion that would undoubtedly be caught. Halle had that part now and Aki smiled grimly at the thought.

He continued to stare at the map for quite some time, letting his anger at her betrayal simmer and grow. At long last, a smile flitted across his face. They thought him safely away. They thought him too afraid to say anything. But a clear path lay in front of him. It would be his own destruction, as well. He'd be ruined, in the eyes of everyone he'd come to care for, but Kezi would be ruined worse and that made all the difference. And his downfall wouldn't be quite so terrible if he were the one to inflict it, he decided.

Pulling out the writing utensils he'd packed, he spread them out on the table and smoothed out a fresh piece of paper. He started writing, the scratch of the quill on the paper the only sound in the entire house. After a few lines, he balled the paper up and held it up to the candle's flame until it caught and burned. He pulled another piece out and started again.

It took two or three more attempts before he put down what he wanted and even then, he hesitated. It was a difficult thing to make such a confession. The words screamed up at him in silent accusation of all he had done wrong in his life. Those words would be his condemnation, they would be the final weight that would tip the scales of Stephan and Alina's favor away from him, and Sasha's if they ever chose to tell him. But Kezi had to pay for betraying him, and this was the only way.

He started to fold it up, then changed his mind. He scrawled a handful of words at the very bottom of the paper and then sealed it closed with a few drops of hot wax from the candle before he could change his mind.

It was an easy matter to pack up his few things. He hadn't really unpacked yet. Leaving the letter where it could be easily seen, he crept out of his room. He'd lived in this house long enough to know which floorboards to avoid and how to close the door so that it made no noise. He paused at the front door, turning to take in the house one last time. Even in the darkness, he could make out the familiar space. An ache he hadn't felt in years gnawed at him. In his nearly sixteen years of life, this house represented the only three years spent in relative happiness.

Shaking his head as if to shake away the urge to go back, Aki left. He'd already ruined whatever chance he had of a happy life here when he'd shown up this evening with Captain Lupin's orders. Besides, there was a tightness inside of him that had grown for weeks now and was suddenly released by the knowledge that, come morning, he would no longer be hiding any more secrets.

The rhythm of Sky's hoofbeats on the hard packed dirt road mingled with the sounds of the night. Crickets sang and a soft breeze rustled the growing leaves on the trees. It was an easy road to follow and Aki dozed off and on as Sky moved closer and closer to Bren. For the first time in a very long time, Aki knew exactly where he was going and what he was doing.

He was less tired than he expected when he finally reached Bren. It was midmorning and he'd ridden straight through the night, but his mind was whirling with what he was about to do and that left no room for exhaustion. He put Sky on a very familiar path and pulled her to a stop when he reached Master Wehr's door.

Master Wehr was the best person to speak to, he was sure. He knocked on the door but no answer came. Aki frowned and knocked louder. Still no answer.

It had never occurred to Aki that Master Wehr wouldn't answer his door. For several minutes, he just stood there, paying little attention to anyone or anything around him. It was too late to turn back. Stephan would have found the letter by now and, even if Aki hadn't ruined everything by running away, his words would have done it for him.

There was no going back to the kindness of Stephan and Alina's. Besides, as soon as Jasper found out what he was planning on doing, Jasper would cause trouble. And not just for Aki. Aki's face crumpled as he remembered the other part of Jasper's threat. He'd make trouble for Sasha.

Unless...

Aki left the doorstep in a hurry, tugging on Sky's reins as he hastened through the streets. There was one way, one course he could take that could keep Sasha out of trouble and still ruin Kezi's plan.

The academy was deserted this late in the morning and Aki put Sky in her old stall before heading towards Captain Lupin's office. Captain Lupin's muffled voice answered when he knocked.

"Aki? What are you doing back here?" Captain Lupin started up from his seat in surprise.

"I," Aki took a deep breath, steadying himself, "I want to make an appeal."

"An appeal?"

"To the king."

Captain Lupin raised his eyebrows and sighed. Aki knew it was madness to ask for this, but it was his best plan. He knew how to bargain, and he had something to bargain with. And who knew? Maybe doing this would win him back some favor with Stephan and Alina and Sasha. Maybe they would think of him better for this.

"Aki, please don't do this. It's just a waste of your time, believe me."

"I know, but I have to."

Captain Lupin nodded, his lips pressed tight together. "I'll write up the request and you can take it over, but you should know he is under no obligation to see you quickly."

Aki stood while he waited, ignoring the whisper in the back of his mind that he was making a terrible mistake. Kezi had to pay, he reminded himself. She'd lied to him and used him and planned on using him further. Captain Lupin finished writing and folded the paper, sealing it shut with yellow wax and pressing his own courier's seal into it.

"Hand this to any guard there and tell them it's for Jarvis. I wish you wouldn't do this. You'll just make things worse," he said as he handed it to Aki.

"I've already made things about as bad as they can be," Aki answered, shocked at his own impetuous honesty. Judging by the look on Captain Lupin's face, he was as well.

"Is there something more going on? Something I'm missing?"

"No, sir."

Aki turned and left before Captain Lupin could question him further. He had to get to the castle before his nerve abandoned him.

The academy wasn't far from the castle and it wasn't yet midday when he arrived, a little out of breath from half-running all the way. He passed under the great stone archway that marked the entrance of the courtyard. This was as far as he'd ever gone the times he'd come with Stephan. He found the door Stephan always used and headed for that one. Just as Captain Lupin had instructed him, he handed his request off to the guard, telling him who it was for. The man had motioned for him to wait on a bench inside.

Aki sat on the bench and watched the man walk away with his request in hand. The weight of what he'd begun settled over him and he wondered if he'd lost his mind. He'd just requested to see the king, and he wasn't even going to talk to him about his punishment like he was supposed to. Everything he'd ever heard about King Darien had shown the man to be just and understanding. Aki desperately hoped it was a true assessment.

He was not forced to wait long before being escorted to another room. Here he was told to wait again. It was a simple room with only a few chairs scattered around it and a small fireplace located on the back wall. Each of the other three walls had a door in them and Aki tried to imagine what was beyond each. Every now and then, the soft murmur of voices reached him from the other side of those doors but never distinct enough to help him. When that was no longer interesting, he pulled the hand drawn map out of his pocket and spread it across his lap. However insane he might be for coming here, one thing was certain. King Darien would want the information on this map. Aki just hoped he wanted it enough.

There was no way to tell time in the anteroom, but Aki felt the day slipping away hour by hour. Even so, when a man who introduced himself as Jarvis came in and asked Aki to follow him, Aki was surprised to see through the windows they passed that dusk was not far off. They walked through another, larger room and stopped at a door.

"His Majesty will see you now," Jarvis said, pulling the door open and gesturing Aki inside.

Aki had never seen King Darien in person, but he assumed the man sitting behind the large desk was him. He bowed low before King Darien waved him toward a chair. Aki fingered the map in his pocket with a sweaty hand.

"You are Aki Turston?" King Darien motioned him towards a chair.

"I am, Your Majesty."

"I'm afraid I must warn you, Aki, that I'm unlikely to take your side in this. To be honest, I wouldn't have made time to see you today had your request not shown up around the same time another visitor did. He convinced me that it might be worth my time to listen to whatever you had to say."

Bewilderment flitted briefly across Aki's face before he drew in a deep breath and began, "I'm not here to actually make an appeal to you. At least, not that appeal."

"Oh?" It was King Darien's turn to look bewildered. Strangely, Aki didn't think he looked surprised. "Then you are wasting both our time, I'm afraid."

"I'm not, Your Majesty. I have something, some information that you will want and this was the only way I could think of to get it to you."

"The correct way to get such information to me would have been through Captain Lupin."

Aki swallowed hard and pressed the palms of his hands against his legs.

"I couldn't do that because I need something in exchange for this information." Now King Darien looked surprised and perhaps a little upset. Aki looked down at his lap and continued before he could be stopped. "I want to make sure Sasha doesn't face any trouble because of this."

"Sasha? What has he got to do with this?"

"Nothing. But there's something he did that almost no one knows about, and I don't want him in trouble because of it."

King Darien frowned. "You are making little sense, Aki."

"I know. I'm sorry," Aki whispered, losing all his resolve. He pulled the map out of his pocket and laid it out on the smooth surface of the desk. "Here. This is what I have."

"Wait," King Darien said, rising from his chair. He went to a door that was almost hidden in the paneling of the wall and, cracking it open, whispered something to someone on the other side.

Aki almost jumped out of his chair when Master Wehr entered the room behind the king. He glanced from one to the other, King Darien's earlier comment finally making sense. It was the only thing that did make sense about this.

"Master Wehr?"

His instructor gave him a troubled smile before sitting down. King Darien resumed his seat as well and laid his folded hands on top of the desk.

"I told you I had a visitor that convinced me to hear you out today. Now," King Darien motioned toward the map, "since this is clearly not in Divalian, I assume we'll have to rely on you to read it. What is this about, Aki?"

Aki looked up to find Master Wehr's reassuring smile. None of this was working out the way he'd anticipated. He was committed too far, though. Committed and with no idea how to proceed now.

"You have a daughter?"

"I have three."

"But you have one named Charlotte, right?"

"Yes."

"This is a plan. To kidnap your daughter, when she's on the road here," he pointed out the spot on the map. "It's near the coast and they'll have a ship waiting. It doesn't say where they plan on going after that and it doesn't say why they want her..."

"That much, at least, is easy enough to guess. They want her to bargain with, although what it is they want...," King Darien didn't finish as he sat back in his seat, frowning. "They know I'd do anything I could to get her back."

Aki considered his words with a stab of envy. He wondered what it would be like to have a father like that. Stephan might have been that for him once, but not after last night and today. The few people who did care about him, he'd spent the last few months pushing away.

"Aki," Master Wehr spoke for the first time, his voice soft and measured, "there are a few questions that beg asking. Why don't you start at the beginning and tell us everything? How you came by this knowledge, who is involved, how long you've known."

"Can you at least promise me that Sasha won't get in trouble for anything before I do? That's the only reason I came straight to you," Aki looked toward King Darien.

"Kind of hard to make a promise for something I don't know. Is he involved in this somehow?"

"No. Not him. Another brother, I mean uncle, is. Halle is the one with the ship, these notes were for him. I happened to pick it up after he dropped it."

"Then Sasha's part in this is?"

"He almost killed me. I don't want him getting in trouble for that."

"Did he? When?"

"A little more than three years ago. The night Boris and Gundar and Lord Bayner all died."

"I see. Well, he's in little danger of trouble from that. You would have to be the one to initiate it."

"I would?" Aki sat up, scowling as he remembered Jasper's words, his thinly veiled threat. Jasper had to have known that and he'd used Aki's ignorance against him.

"From the beginning, Aki," Master Wehr gently reminded him.

"Right. From the beginning," Aki shut his eyes for a moment, trying to decide just where the beginning was. He started with the first time he'd met both Kezi and Jasper together at the tavern. Although he hesitated, he told them what he knew of the attack on Baron Orlander's and how he knew about it. He ignored Master Wehr's mild surprise when he told of Jasper's threats and the part he played. When he reached the night Halle stabbed him, he left out all that had happened between him and Halle while they were still in Aruuk together. That information, he decided, was not necessary to his story. When he finished, he finally looked up at the two men across from him.

"That was a very interesting story, Aki," King Darien said, getting to his feet and pacing the space in front of his desk. "But why are you coming to us now? You've known for quite some time and kept their secrets. What changed?"

"Kezi lied to me. She lied, and she was going to use me as bait. And they ought to be stopped."

"You should have come forward right away. Baron Orlander has been investigating the attack on his home and your information would have been valuable. Your silence up to this point has contributed to their plan, has it not?"

"Yes, sir. I suppose it has."

The king paused his pacing to stand and gaze out the window, his hands clasped together behind his back. The sun had set while they were talking and Aki realized for the first time since leaving Stephan's that he was exhausted and hungry.

"Here's what I want from you for now, Aki," King Darien said, still facing the window. "I want you to return to the academy tonight and to remain there quietly until you are sent for again. Do you think you can manage that?"

"Yes, Your Majesty."

"Good. Go on. And please do yourself a favor, and don't try to run off on us. It will make matters worse."

Aki got to his feet and started for the door.

"And Aki," King Darien called after him. "Thank you for coming to me. That was a very brave thing to do."

Aki nodded, unable to say that there was nothing brave in his motivation. He was terrified and angry, not brave.

Leaving the dark shadow of the stone archway, Aki yawned and rubbed a weary hand over his eyes, trying to force the sleepiness from them. It was hard to keep them open as he made his way down the street. Several times he caught himself walking forward in a half asleep daze, his eyelids too heavy. It would be nice to have nothing to do for a few days, he thought.

He turned onto the street the academy was on and his steps quickened. Only a minute more he could collapse into bed and sleep uninterrupted for hours. A shuffling sound behind him pierced his consciousness. A whisper alerted him to the presence of another. Before he could turn, something whistled through the air behind him, and pain exploded through the back of his head. He thought he cried out.

He was falling.

The darkness grew, swelled, and consumed him.

Chapter 33

A KI?" STEPHAN KNOCKED ON the bedroom door and waited for an answer that never came. "Aki, it's late. Come on, you should have been outside an hour ago."

The silence that met him caused Stephan to let out an exasperated breath before pushing the door open. His eyes were met by an empty bed. Stephan pressed his lips together as he surveyed the room. Aside from the unoccupied bed, there was a candle burnt all the way down on the table and a letter. An odd look came over Stephan as he picked the letter up and turned it over in his hands. He stared down at it, almost reluctant to open it for a moment. Breaking open the seal, he began.

Stephan,
I know you're angry with me and you have every right to be. By the time you read this, I will, hopefully, be long gone and you'll never have to worry about seeing me again. Since that's the case, I'd rather you hear from me why it has to be this way because you'll find out eventually anyway. You'll hate me when you know, but it's for the best.
I'm not the person you thought I was and I can't hide it anymore. I wish I could have been, I really do. But there are things I've done that I can't undo, no matter how much I regret them. So here goes.
When I was nothing more than a slave in Aruuk, all I knew was fear and hate. There were some who I feared and hated more than others. When Gundar made me his

son, I wasn't any better than any of the rest of them. In fact, I was worse. Certainly a lot worse than either Sasha or Lars. I tried to kill one of my brothers. I meant to kill him. It was only an accident that he survived.

But that isn't the worst thing I've done. That brother deserved much of what happened to him. No, the worst thing I've done is something I've tried very hard to forget about. Sasha made that a little easier when he beat me because I couldn't remember most of what happened that day.

Gundar's plan was to take Dagmar that day. He sent me to spy on Sasha and I found him in the woods talking with Ophelia. I followed Ophelia home. And then I told Gundar about her. I was the reason she was taken that day. Everything she went through was because of me. And more than that, I was the one to sneak into the cabin first and let the others in. I kept the fire going that they used to torture Boris. Sasha was right when he was angry at me.

When I first woke up after Sasha nearly killed me, he was kind to me. He was the first person to ever be kind to me and I knew, as my memories of that day returned, that if he knew the truth, that if anyone knew the truth, they would no longer be kind to me. I didn't, I don't deserve such kindness. I hope you can forgive me for not telling any of this the last three years. I didn't want to ruin the life you were giving me. But it is ruined now. It was ruined when I showed up here tonight. I can't have it back, so it's best that I just move on.

Aki

I hope you can someday forgive me for not being worth the trouble you and Alina have gone through for me. I know I will never forget the three years I had with you, they are the only ones I can look back on with any sort of pleasure. Tell Alina that she was the best mother I could have hoped for.

Stephan didn't move for a long, long time. He only stared down at the words, uncomprehending and unwilling to comprehend. It was more than just a letter, scrawled out late at night. It was a confession, an apology, a thank you. It was a goodbye.

Alina found him standing there. Without a word, he held it out to her. She read it.

"You're going after him, aren't you?"

"I can't. I can't just leave the farm unattended while I go off and search for him. What is he thinking?"

"That we don't want him anymore, obviously. You can't just let him go like that."

"I'll see what I can figure out. Sasha should see this."

Chapter 34

ADEEP THROBBING LIKE A second pulse filled his head and his stomach revolted against it. He swallowed down the bile that rose up as the pain crescendoed. There were other people around him. He was conscious of their presence, their breathing, their footsteps.

Twice before he'd surfaced from the black waves of pain that sucked him into oblivion. Both times he'd been moving, not on his own, but rather he was on something that was moving. This time was different. This time he was lying still, and by the sounds of it, he was no longer outside. Waves broke against the rocks nearby and the smell of saltwater filled his nose so he knew he was close to the sea.

He forced his eyes open although he kept his head down. His vision was blurred, black clouds closing in around the edges of his eyesight and threatening to drown it out altogether. A chair scraped across a wooden floor. The footsteps drew closer.

Aki tensed as a rough hand forced his head up.

"Hello, *brother*," Halle said, his soft voice defying the wild light in his eyes.

Aki tried to scramble back, but he was already propped against a wall and he only succeeded in hitting the back of his head against it. He pulled in a sharp breath as the throb deepened. Blinking in an effort to clear his vision, he tried to look around the room in the hopes that he wasn't alone with Halle.

His relief at finding he wasn't was short lived. Both Kezi and Jasper, and several men he didn't know, stood behind Halle. Jasper came forward and sat in the chair directly behind where Halle was crouched. Halle stood and moved over to the side. Aki knew what was about to happen. Jerking his head free of Halle's hand, he pressed up against the wall and forced himself to meet Jasper's eyes.

"Why'd you come back? Who have you seen and what have you told them?" Jasper asked.

"No one. I haven't seen anyone."

Halle moved before Aki could blink. His foot connected with Aki's side right where he'd been cut. Aki gasped and hunched over but Halle grabbed a fistful of his hair and pulled him upright again. He tried to move his hands only to find that they were tied behind him.

"Who did you tell?" Jasper asked again.

"No one. I looked for Master Wehr, but I never found him."

"Don't lie to us, Aki," Jasper warned.

"I'm not. He wasn't home. I don't know where he is, but I didn't talk to anyone."

He was ready this time when Halle kicked him, not that it made it any less painful. Several times, Jasper repeated the same question and Aki gave him the same answer. And with each kick from Halle, the pain spread deeper. But they couldn't know the truth. Not if he wanted them to pay for all this, and that desire was growing stronger every minute. He looked past Jasper to Kezi. If he was hoping to find some fragment of sympathy, he was disappointed. She looked on with cold indifference. Seeing that only spurred his defiance. It was just pain. He would survive pain, but there was no way he would give away his chance to pay her back for betraying him.

He was doubled over, coughing for air, when Jasper finally stood up and kicked his chair away in frustration.

"Maybe he's telling the truth," he said over his shoulder to Kezi who shrugged.

"Maybe."

The two moved out of earshot. By their gestures, Aki guessed they were arguing about something. Probably about what to do with him, he thought. If Halle had anything to do with it, they'd kill him. As slowly and painfully as possible.

As if he could read Aki's mind, Halle knelt back down in front of him. A knife was in one hand and his other still gripped Aki by the hair.

"You know how long I've waited for this?"

Aki stiffened as he brought the knife up to his throat. He shut his eyes as it bit into his skin. His body trembled against his will. This wasn't how he wanted to die.

"Too bad for you, they won't let me kill you. Jasper has a weak stomach when it comes to things like murder. It makes him feel like he's still better than us," Halle explained. "But they have agreed to give you to me. Which means that instead of a quick, clean death, I get to make your life just as miserable as I can. I may not be allowed to take your life, but I'm going to make you want to end it."

The knife was gone and Aki let out a shaky breath and opened his eyes. He wished he'd kept them shut when he saw the smile on Halle's face. He'd seen that smile so many times before. And it was terrifying. When Jasper and Kezi walked toward the door together, he wanted to scream for them to stay, to not leave him alone with Halle. But begging had never done him any favors and he wasn't about to start again now.

Halle, to his surprise, didn't do anything at first. He ordered one of the men to build the fire bigger and then disappeared for a while. Aki shut his eyes, hoping that the world would stop spinning and blurring if he just rested them enough. The pounding in his head was worse and he was conscious for the first time of a warm stickiness at the back of his head and neck.

He was left alone for so long that he began to slip away again. Aki didn't bother to fight it. While he was unconscious, he couldn't feel pain and that could only be a good thing considering how badly his head and side hurt.

A charred aroma filled the air as hands grabbed at him, pulling him out of the semi-conscious state he'd been hovering in. He was dragged from behind across the floor and deposited at Halle's feet, his eyes barely able to make out Halle's face as it swam above his own.

At a nod from Halle, his hands were freed from the thin rope binding them. Aki's chest tightened and quick, panicked breaths forced their way out of him as Halle knelt at his side, and pushed him flat on his back. He wanted more than anything to push that hand away, to get up, to run. But his body was frozen, no longer obedient to any command of his mind.

"What are you doing, Halle?" Aki couldn't keep his voice steady as Halle took hold of his right arm and stretched it out across the floor.

Halle pinned it in place with his knees. His smile was cold and frightening as he answered, "Doing what Father should have done to you a long time ago." Turning to the men who'd dragged Aki across the room in the first place, he nodded. "Hold him."

In the brief moment Aki had to sort out what Halle intended, two or three men took hold of him, pressing him against the floor. Aki's feeble attempt to struggle against their grasp was futile. Not only was he imprisoned between their hands and the floor, but pain bored through his head sending a wave of nausea sweeping over him. Out of the corner of his eye, he saw Halle grab something from the fire.

The branding iron glowed red at its tip as Halle held it up above Aki's arm. Aki shook his head, the only motion he was capable of at the moment. He tightened his jaw as the first tendrils of heat brushed against the bare skin of his arm.

Halle pressed it onto his skin.

No matter how hard Aki clamped his teeth together, he couldn't repress the awful sound that forced its way up his throat. It was halfway between a scream and a yell and a hand was pressed over his mouth to smother it just as soon as it escaped. Tears burned in his eyes. His body fought to pull away from the heat searing through it. He barely felt Halle's knees pressing into his arm even harder above the roar in his head.

Halle held the branding iron firm against him. Seconds that stretched out like an eternity ticked by and still he did not remove it, only pressed it down harder, deeper. Aki had no sense of time, but he was sure Halle was holding it on too long. It was burning too deep. Agony melted all the way into the bone. It traveled up the whole length of his arm.

"Halle?" a voice from his other side said.

At last, Halle pulled it away. Aki was trembling all over, shuddering breaths escaping through clenched teeth, accompanied by whimpers as the burning continued even without the iron. Halle leaned over him, his face mere inches from Aki's.

"You'll get more of those, I'm sure, but I've heard the first one's the worst. The first one's the one that stays with you the most. Every time you look at it, you'll know that the first person you truly belonged to was me."

Aki moaned and turned his head away but Halle grabbed him by the hair and forced him to look again. Halle smiled again, although Aki was so close to passing out again that his eyes refused to focus.

With a start, Aki realized that Halle was talking again. He missed most of it, only catching the last few words.

"...enjoy your trip, *brother*." Aki winced at the mocking twist Halle gave the word. Never, for one day, had Halle ever accepted that Aki was his equal as a son of Gundar. Otherwise, he couldn't make much sense of his words. Halle disappeared from Aki's vision and there was a flurry of movement. Hands sat him up again, pulling his arms behind him and tying them together at his wrists. The movement was too much and the faintness that he'd been fighting overcame him completely.

When he first awoke again, he lay for some time listening to the water slapping against the wooden sides of the hut before he realized that he was no longer in the hut. The wooden floor beneath him really was pitching and rocking with the motion of the sea. Suddenly, Halle's final words made sense. As realization swept over him, Aki sat up and regretted it immediately. Grabbing his head between his hands, he groaned.

"Aki?" A soft voice reached through the darkness to him and he turned to find its source. All he could see was the shadowed silhouette of another person. "Are you alright?"

He knew that voice.

He knew why she was here.

Chapter 35

THE FIGURE PACING IN FRONT of the door of the academy paused as Oscar approached leading his horse. It was late and Oscar had been riding all day. He wanted nothing more than to go inside and go to bed. Since the stranger was standing directly in front of the entrance, Oscar was forced to acknowledge his presence.

"Is there something you need?"

"You are a friend of Aki's?"

"Sort of, I guess. I mean, I know who he is. But if you're looking for him, he's not here. He was sent off yesterday and I don't have any idea when he'll be back."

"He's back now. I saw him this morning."

"Oh, then what is it you need? And who are you anyway?"

"Lars. His brother. He's in trouble and I need to get word to Sasha."

"Can't help you with that, I'm afraid. It'd be against the rules. What sort of trouble is he in?"

"The kind that's going to get him killed," Lars said, looking past Oscar into the street. "Isn't your job supposed to be taking messages?"

"Only the ones that are authorized," Oscar said. He started to move past Lars to the door.

Lars gave a defeated shrug and muttered to himself, "Halle's going to kill him."

"Wait. You're being serious? There's really someone trying to kill him?"

"Of course I am. Why would I make something like that up?"

Oscar shook his head and turned back to face Lars. "I'm going to regret this and he's going to owe me again but come on."

Lars followed Oscar inside. Instead of heading toward their rooms, Oscar crossed the arena toward the stable, his eyes taking in Sky standing quietly in her stall. She wouldn't be there without Aki, he knew.

"That's his horse," Lars said. "I told you he was here."

"That doesn't make sense. He was sent away, he left." They reached the overhang of the stables. "Wait here. I'll look to see if he's in his room."

"He's not. Halle took him. That's why he's in danger."

"Fine. Tell me what's going on."

Lars told what he knew as briefly as possible. He'd seen Aki in town earlier that morning. So had Halle. Although Lars hadn't been present when Halle and his men took Aki earlier that night, he saw them carrying him away to Halle's ship. Oscar listened quietly until he finished.

"Is this Halle the same person who stabbed him a couple of weeks ago?"

"He was stabbed?" Lars looked taken back by the news then sighed. "Yes. Probably it was Halle."

"I'd have told someone except that he insisted it had to be kept secret. Wait here, I'm going to get one of the others."

When Oscar returned a few minutes later, he had someone else in tow. And from the way he kept rubbing his eyes and running a hand through his hair, Lars guessed he'd just been woken up. He squinted in Lars' direction when they stepped beneath the overhang of the stables.

"This is Lars, Felix. He's Aki's brother."

In spite of still being half asleep, Felix managed to extend his hand to Lars.

"Oscar tried telling me what was going on but he didn't do very well."

Lars repeated the same story he'd just told Oscar.

"Oscar already said you can't actually do anything, but if you'd just let me take Aki's horse, I can go get Sasha."

"Why not just tell the city watch? They'll find him."

"Halle isn't in the city anymore, he's on his ship. He won't stay around here after what he's done. Someone will have to go after him to get Aki back, if Halle hasn't killed him yet. I don't think the city watch does that sort of thing."

"We can't do it, Oscar," Felix turned to Oscar and whispered. "It's against the rules."

"I know."

"But you're still thinking about it."

Oscar gave him a conspiratorial grin. "Running off in the middle of the night to save someone from certain death sounds a bit fun, doesn't it?"

"You can't break the rules, Oscar," Felix said with greater conviction. "You don't even like Aki that much."

Oscar shrugged, "I don't hate him. He doesn't deserve to die."

"I just need his horse. He'd let me have it himself if he could."

Oscar and Felix exchanged a glance.

"Go ahead," Oscar nodded toward Sky. Lars didn't wait for him to change his mind.

"Oscar...," Felix said in warning.

"The rules aren't going to help Aki, Felix. It's fine, I'll take the blame. Besides, I think I'll go with him."

"Why?"

"It's gotten a bit boring around here. This'll change things up a bit." Oscar grinned once more and punched Felix in the arm. "Come on, Felix, lighten up. All you have to do is cover for me 'til I get back."

"This had better really save his life."

"If we're not already too late," Lars muttered.

Chapter 36

ARLY MORNING LIGHT FILTERED through the windows of the cabin and Sasha turned his head away from it. Ophelia was already sitting up, running a hand over her hair to smooth it.

"You know how we talked before, about adding to the cabin whenever we had children?"

"Yes," Sasha said, trying to sound more awake than he was.

"I think maybe we should start working on that now."

Sasha turned to her. "You do? Why?"

"I think it's a good time to. You know, we have all summer," Ophelia answered, a small smile on her face. "And you never know when we might want to have it."

Sasha shrugged.

"You're still thinking about what Stephan said last night, aren't you?" Ophelia asked, her smile fading. "Where do you think he went?"

"Who knows." Sasha sat up all the way. "My guess would be back to Bren since it's the only other place here he knows. Stephan said he was acting strange when he came back. I just wish he would have talked to one of us."

"You're not upset about what he said in his letter?"

"How could I be? I could just as easily write a list of all the things I did when I lived there and, despite what Aki seems to think, it would be twice as long as his." Sasha paused, frowning. "Wait."

"What?"

"Why would you suggest that now?

Ophelia only smiled, mischief in her eyes.

"You're not saying... are you... are we going to have a baby?"

She nodded, her smile growing wider and turning into laughter. "Yes, yes we are."

Sasha lay back down in stunned silence.

"Aren't you happy about it?"

"Happy. Terrified. I have no idea how to be a father."

"As much as I know how to be a mother. It's the first time for both of us."

"Yes, but at least you..."

"Sasha, we'll figure it out together. And we'll make mistakes, but everyone does. You won't be like your father, because you're already not."

Ophelia got to her feet just as a knock came on their door.

"Were you expecting anyone?"

"No." Sasha got up as well. "Especially not this early."

Although he moved quickly, the knock was repeated before Sasha could reach the door. He opened it to find Lars with his fist in the air ready to knock again.

"Lars?"

"Sasha, Aki needs help. Halle has him, I think. I don't know what he's planning, but..."

"It can't be good. Come inside, both of you," Sasha added as he noticed Oscar standing in the background. "Tell me what's going on."

It took more time for Lars to tell what he knew to Sasha than it had for him to explain to Oscar and Felix because Sasha kept interrupting him with questions. Ophelia moved quietly in the background, listening while she put together a hasty breakfast.

"You're going to go after him, right?" She asked as she set the food down in front of them.

"I shouldn't leave you alone, not when you're..."

"I'll be fine. It's not like it's an illness. If anything, I can always go back to my parents' if I need something. He needs you."

Sasha nodded. "I'll leave this morning, then. Are you sure you'll be alright?"

"I'm sure. Go find him. And after you bring him back, we can get started on adding that extra room," she said with a smile.

Sasha returned it and nodded. "Right away. Maybe I can even convince Lars to stick around and help."

"Help with what?" Lars looked up from his food.

"Come on, we should hurry," Sasha said, ignoring his question.

Oscar fell asleep where he was sitting while Sasha made his preparations and had to be shaken awake when they were ready to leave less than an hour later. Rubbing his eyes, he pushed away from the table.

"Aki's really going to owe me for this," he said as he followed Sasha and Lars out the door.

They didn't reach Bren until it was almost dark and while Oscar returned to the academy, Sasha secured a room for Lars and himself at an inn. Lars sat down on one of the beds, watching as Sasha paced the floor.

"What are we going to do?"

"I don't know. I don't even know where to start exactly. Did Halle tell you where they were going to sail next?"

"No. He never really seemed to have much of a plan aside from staying as drunk for as long as he could."

"Of course. He gets his life handed to him and this is what he does with it."

"Hate Halle all you want, Sasha. He's certainly done enough to deserve it. But this thing between him and Aki isn't just his fault. Aki's just as guilty."

"How can you say that?"

"Because it's true. You've always thought Aki was better than the rest of us just because of how he was born, but he wasn't. And don't get upset with me for saying that. I don't hate Aki. We've always gotten along just fine. But I don't hate Halle, either. Have you ever noticed the limp Halle has?"

Sasha nodded, pausing in his pacing and finally sitting down as well.

"Aki gave him that. It was right before we came here. We were, all three of us, up by one of the falls. We were just messing around since it was our free time. Halle slipped. He went over the edge. I wasn't near enough to catch him, but Aki was. And he did. He caught hold of him before he fell all the way. He could have pulled him up or at the very least held onto him long enough for me to come and help."

"But he didn't?"

"He didn't just let go, Sasha," Lars looked up at Sasha then, "he shoved him off. He sent Halle down into the fall to kill him. He meant for him to die. And when Halle didn't, when someone found him washed up on the riverbank far below and dragged him back to Father's house alive, Father didn't punish Aki for trying. He punished him for failing. Aki's no better than the rest of us."

"Why are you telling me this? You're the one who came wanting me to help find Aki."

"I told you, I don't hate him. I don't want him dead. I don't want either of them dead," Lars sighed. "You know, Father was always pitting those two against each other. He was strange about Aki, too. I think that to him Aki was never just Aki. He was always Anton as well; he was always a slave girl who rebelled and a son who disobeyed. Aki always had the most brutal punishments for the smallest infractions, but Father also gave him favors he never gave the rest of us. In some ways, I think he thought he was raising Anton all over again and that if he was just hard enough, he could break him. But Aki never really broke. He was so good at everything he was supposed to learn. He was better than Halle at just about everything and Halle hated that. Father used that to make things worse between them."

"Why are you telling me this?" Sasha repeated.

"I guess because I don't really want to see this come down to one or the other having to die. Halle's not a great person, but he lives in pain every single day from what Aki did to him. It's why he tries to stay drunk. You know what they call you in Aruuk?" Without waiting for an answer, Lars continued, "They call you Sasha the Peacemaker. That's how everyone there remembers you. Which is a lot better than what they call Father - Gundar the Merciless. The first bloodless transition of power in as long as anyone can remember. You changed life for everyone in Aruuk. But you changed it here first. You changed mine when you decided not to hurt me. You changed Aki's when you decided not to kill him. Maybe there's still some way you can change Halle's?"

Sasha was quiet for a long time. "Look, I don't know what I can do about Halle, but first we need to find Aki. If he kept him alive long enough to put him on his ship then I think it's safe to say Halle doesn't plan on killing him right away."

"How do we find out where they are headed, though?"

"We start asking around. Was there anyone he talked to here?"

"Yes. Some girl named Kezi. They had some sort of agreement. He even brought her onto the ship a couple of times."

Sasha shut his eyes and slapped his forehead with the palm of his hand. "Kezi. Of course, Kezi's in on this. This isn't just about Aki and Halle."

"You know her?"

"You could say that. Where did they meet up, aside from his ship? Were you ever there?"

"They used a hut outside of town close to the sea. That's where he had Aki and put him on a boat."

"Could you find it in the dark?"

Lars shrugged, "I think so. There's only a few out there."

"Come on then. Let's get started. If we can find Kezi, we can find out where Halle's headed."

Chapter 37

AKI SLOWLY RELEASED HIS GRIP on his head as he adjusted to the movement of the ship.

"I'm alright," he finally answered, although he was as far from alright as he thought it possible to get. "What happened, Dagmar?"

"I don't know. They just brought you down a couple of hours ago and threw you in there."

"In there?" Aki repeated, confused. He reached a tentative hand out into the darkness. He didn't have to go far before it collided with an iron bar. It took only a few seconds to determine that he was surrounded by such bars. "What happened to you?"

"There were people waiting for me when I got home last night. Kezi, and three men. They brought me here."

"I'm sorry. This is all my fault. I never should have come to you that night. That's why they brought you here, I'm sure."

"No, I don't think so. I'm here because of Kezi. Besides, you needed help that night."

Aki stared through the shadows at Dagmar's silhouette. He couldn't comprehend how she sounded so calm still, so unafraid. He envied her that calm. For a few minutes, the only sound was the ship creaking and groaning as it rode the waves. Aki drew his knees up to his chest and rested his right arm across them. He tried to feel the brand with his other hand, but pulled it away again with a wince. The skin was still hot and touching it was unbearable.

"We aren't the only ones they've taken, you know," Dagmar whispered, her voice coming from a little closer.

"There's not many, and they're all children. I've talked to a few of them and I think they're all orphans."

"They're smuggling them out to take somewhere and sell as slaves. No one will even notice that they are missing."

"But people will notice us missing. They'll look for us." So she wasn't as unafraid as she sounded, Aki realized.

"You, maybe. I don't think anyone's going to come for me now," Aki murmured softly.

Dagmar didn't say anything but a moment later he felt her hand brush against his and close tightly around it. He wished his hand was not shaking so badly. The last thing he wanted was for Dagmar to know how utterly terrified he was just then. He hesitated a moment before he returned the same reassuring grip. Keeping his hold on her hand, he leaned his head back against the iron bars and shut his eyes. Whatever else Halle planned on doing to him, he could face it better if he rested.

The sound of heavy footsteps woke him some time later. He opened his eyes to find that it wasn't quite so dark as it had been. Sunlight poured in through two hatches, turning the floor into a checkerboard of yellow and gray. By its light, he finally got a good look at where he was. Beyond Dagmar, who was still sitting near him, there were several children - none older than ten and all looking filthy and haggard.

The nearest hatch was thrown open and two men descended the ladder. Aki scooted to the back of the cage he was locked in, as far from the door as he could get, which wasn't far. He was completely ignored as the men handed out food to the others. The sight and smell of it made him realize just how hungry he was. He lowered his eyes as the children scrambled and fought over it. The scene was all too reminiscent of his childhood.

When the two men ascended the ladder and shut the hatch once more, Dagmar slipped a chunk of the dry, hard bread she'd been given between the bars and into his hand.

"Here, you need it," Dagmar said, keeping an eye on the hatch.

"Thanks, but you need it too." It took all of his will power to push her hand with the food away. "They're not..."

The hatch opened again, cutting Aki off. This time, he was quite sure that they were coming for him. He balled his hands into fists at his sides to keep them from shaking too hard. The nausea in his stomach wasn't caused by pain this time. Pressed against the back of the cage, he watched as the same two men descended, followed by Halle.

Halle dropped to a crouch when they reached his cage and Aki forced his rapid breathing to slow, forced his eyes to meet Halle's unflinchingly. With a quick hand, Halle undid the lock holding the door shut.

"Come," he ordered. When Aki didn't move, he smiled and looked back at the two men who'd accompanied him. They grabbed Dagmar and pulled her to her feet. "You can either come with me, or she does. I'm sure you know how that will go. Your choice."

Aki's eyes met Dagmar's. She wasn't fighting their grip, but her eyes were wide and her face white. Aki wished he hadn't looked at her. There was no way he could unsee her fear and no way he could just remain here while she was taken. The cage wasn't tall enough for him to stand, forcing him to crawl to the door. The humiliation was enough to counter some of his fear and he managed to glare at Halle as he stepped out. He looked back long enough to see the relief on Dagmar's face, followed almost instantly with guilt when she met his eyes, as she was released, and the men grabbed him instead. He couldn't blame her. He'd have felt the same if their roles were reversed.

His head was spinning as he climbed up the ladder between the two men, Halle once again bringing up the rear, but it wasn't as bad as it had been the night before. And his eyes seemed to be working properly again. Until he was met by the full force of the sun, that is. He brought an arm up to shield his eyes from it as he stepped clear of the hatch. Hands grabbed him by both arms and pulled him forward. One of them clamped firmly over his new brand and Aki wasn't quick enough to stifle a cry of pain.

He was guided across the deck and into the captain's cabin. Aki stumbled and fell to his knees as the men gave him a hard shove.

"Leave us," Halle said from behind him.

"But, Halle...,"

"It's fine. He won't do anything. Not when he knows he's not the one who will be punished."

Aki had started to get up, but at Halle's words he didn't dare. He heard the door shut behind them and Halle came around in and sat on the bed in front of him. Halle folded his arms across his chest and watched. Aki refused to raise his eyes to meet Halle's. Instead, he studied the wooden floor beneath him.

"Afraid, Aki?"

Aki remained frozen and silent. Halle slapped him, sending him reeling back. He raised his hand to hit Aki again, but Aki was ready and grabbed his wrist before he could. Halle just laughed. He jerked his arm free of Aki's grasp and sat back.

"So, you've learned to fight back. We'll have to break you of that, you know. Can't have slaves that think that way." Halle crossed his arms again and studied Aki for a moment longer. "I think I know how to do it, too."

Aki kept his head lowered and shut his eyes. Whatever Halle was thinking couldn't be good.

"That girl down there is awfully pretty. And a friend of yours, too. Pity. She already bears a brand, Sasha's brand. You know how we feel about runaway slaves. She's too pretty to just kill, but she ought to be marked as a runaway."

"Halle," Aki shook his head, finally looking up at Halle. "She didn't run away. Sasha freed her. You can't do that to her."

"Who's to stop me? Everyone knows slaves can't be freed. Once a slave, always a slave. You forgot that, didn't you, Aki? You thought you could somehow escape, but you can't."

"Halle, this is between you and me, not her."

"I don't care. But if you do, you can take the mark for her. In fact, I'll do better than that. You do everything I tell you to, no argument, no fight, no hesitation, and I'll give orders that no one is to touch her until we reach our destination. She'll go to market just as she is now. The alternative, of course, being that you stay down there, and she comes up here. My men do get rather bored on these voyages. I'm sure they'd appreciate the diversion."

Aki was ashamed of himself for hesitating, but he couldn't help it. Halle had a nightmare planned, that much was evident by the smile on his face. There would be more pain, more humiliation - perhaps more than Aki could bear. Halle had finally won his chance for revenge and Aki had no doubt he would eke every last ounce of it out of Aki before he was through. He didn't hate Dagmar quite the same. He thought of her as nothing, something to be used, not necessarily punished. Maybe things wouldn't be quite so bad for her as they would be for him. And they wouldn't do anything to her that wasn't going to be done once they reached their destination. He had the awful feeling that if he laid the choice out in front of her, she would choose her own suffering over his. And because of that he knew he could never do that to her.

"I'll," he hesitated, letting out a trembling breath, his voice almost inaudible. His hands balled into fists at his side and he forced them open again. Halle leaned forward to catch his words. "I'll do it. I'll take the mark for her."

"And?"

"And," he shut his eyes, afraid of what he was committing to, "I'll obey you, whatever you tell me."

Halle nodded, the light of triumph in his eyes and Aki hated giving him that victory. "You know, it was Kezi's idea to get the girl. I didn't really want to since it would raise too much suspicion. But I understand her usefulness now. They tried to make you a good person, Aki. It's a shame they partially succeeded. Come with me, *brother*."

Aki followed Halle out of the cabin and onto the deck. Halle called everyone's attention to them and Aki dropped his eyes. He was right. Halle planned on making this as humiliating as he possibly could. There was no fun in marking Aki alone in his cabin, it had to be done in front of the entire crew. Once everyone had stopped their work and come to watch, Halle shoved Aki in front of him. Aki cringed at the weight of Halle's hands resting on both his shoulders.

"As you all know," Halle began, his voice loud in Aki's ear and carrying across the deck, "we've retaken a runaway. As is our custom, he is to be marked as such and you all are to be witnesses of it." Lowering his voice for just Aki to hear, he said, "Take off your shirt."

Aki fumbled to get out of it, his hands trembling so hard that they refused to cooperate. It would be quick, he promised himself, over before he really even felt it. And it kept Dagmar safe. That was his only purpose now. If he could keep her safe, he was at least doing something. He was at least worth something. It would be just about the only thing he'd done right.

He winced as Halle grabbed his hair and pulled his head back with one hand. The other hand brandished a knife. Aki started to pull away, the action involuntary, but Halle leaned forward and whispered in his ear, "Don't fight me, or the girl goes through this."

Aki froze.

It was just pain. He'd been in pain before and survived it. He could take pain. He could survive it again. He sucked in a sharp breath as Halle began, drawing the knife from his right shoulder to the bottom of his left rib cage. He wasn't in a hurry, dragging out that single slice as long as he could. Aki was sure Halle was savoring every moment of his pain. The cut wasn't deep. It didn't have to be. When Halle was done cutting, they'd rub salt into it and it would scar. Halle repeated the action on his other side, creating the cross on his chest that would forever mark him as a runaway. The mark that meant if he was caught running again, he was to be killed.

He nearly collapsed when Halle released his hold, not from pain, not from shock, but more from the horror of what he'd committed to. He stared down at where blood now ran freely down the front of him. This wouldn't be it. This wouldn't be the only thing Halle meant to do to him.

"We will be setting sail for Karu shortly. We wait only for our final guest. In the meantime, I'd like to thank each of you for your loyal, faithful service to me. I'm putting Aki at your disposal until we retrieve the princess. You may put him to work and use him in any way you like so long as he is alive and able to walk to the auction block on his own when we reach Karu. To start with, I think this ship needs a bit of cleaning before we host a princess. I think that would make a good first job for you, Aki," Halle said, turning Aki to face him, a wicked smile on his face. "I want every inch of it scrubbed."

"I'm going to kill you, Halle," Aki whispered in return, his horror turning into burning fury at the freedom Halle had just given his crew over him.

"You already tried, remember? And failed. Maybe I'm not that easy to kill. Best get to work. It's a long three days up the coast and I'm sure everyone has something they want from you."

Aki's legs wobbled and buckled with the movement of the ship. He slipped, again, falling to his hands and knees on the deck. The sun was already touching the western horizon, turning the sea around them every shade orange, red, and purple. The blood from his mark was finally thickening and scabbing over. He'd pulled his shirt on again in the faint hope that if the wounds were not seen, Halle would forget that he was supposed to reopen them and put salt on them to ensure their permanence. Now, though, he was regretting the move. The front of his shirt was soaked in blood and as it dried, it clung to his skin, pulling at the cuts every time he moved.

He was nowhere close to finishing as the sun went down but that didn't seem to bother anyone around him. The crew's treatment of him had been mixed. Some had ignored his presence entirely. Quite a few had interrupted the task Halle had given him to get a few minutes of their own work done by him. Still others hadn't been able to walk past him without giving him a blow that invariably made him flinch. There wasn't a part of him that didn't hurt by now and exhaustion dulled his ability to work efficiently. It was too much to hope for that he would be allowed to sleep that night. Or eat. The crew had already taken their supper, the smell of food enough to drive him mad with hunger.

With the coming darkness, it was impossible for him to continue cleaning the deck. Halle had disappeared hours before into his cabin and Aki hadn't seen him since, although his second in command had made sure Aki was obeying. The man had a terrible habit of stepping out from around corners or coming silently up behind Aki every time he tried to rest for a few moments. Aki didn't bother to make an excuse. He just shut his eyes and waited for the inevitable. It was a trick he'd learned long ago - the ability to let his mind wander wherever he wanted it to while his masters did what they liked to his body. It had always annoyed Halle, the way he shut down when the pain got bad enough, the way he disconnected from it.

He sat back just now, the rag hanging limp in his hand. A firm hand on the collar of his shirt hauled him to his feet.

"Halle wants you," the second in command said, shoving Aki before him towards the cabin.

Lanterns were lit inside the cabin, and Halle sprawled half laying half sitting on his bed. In one hand, he held a bottle. Two more sat on the small desk, one empty and one full. There was nothing imposing or terrifying about him at the moment. But the threat against Dagmar still hung heavy in Aki's mind. Halle looked up through heavy lidded eyes at their entrance. With a final drink from the bottle in his hand, he sat up a little.

"There you are, Aki. You didn't think I'd forgotten, did you?" Halle's face was flushed, but he spoke clearly enough. "Unfortunately, Nic here will have to finish the job for me. I don't feel like getting up. And I'd like to see your face for this."

Aki tensed but remained still. He'd made it so far, and aside from the bruises, aches, exhaustion, and hunger, he was alright. It wasn't anything he hadn't been through before.

"Go ahead," Halle waved an impatient and unsteady hand, "take your shirt off. You've got plenty of work waiting for you still, according to Nic."

Obeying, Aki pulled the bloody shirt off. His fingers fumbled with it, but it wasn't so much out of fear as it was exhaustion. He shut his eyes again, almost as much from fatigue as from a desire to distance himself from what was about to happen. He almost fell asleep standing there waiting for Nic to begin. As Nic painstakingly reopened the cuts, Aki forced his mind away from it. He let it wander over his happiest memories.

Those three years that he'd spent living with Stephan and Alina had been the best of his entire life. He remembered what it was like that first summer after Sasha and Lars left, when he was truly on his own with people he barely knew. It hadn't mattered much, because Aki didn't know many people very well. He'd learned what it was to play for the first time that summer, following along with

Nora and Adel as they tramped through the woods imagining great stories and heroics. And the comfort of coming home, of always having a meal and a place to sleep was like nothing he'd ever known. He'd worked hard that summer. Harder than Stephan told him to, because he wanted to make sure Stephan understood his usefulness.

He was never going to see Stephan again. Or Alina. Or Nora and Adel. He was never going to see Sasha again. Never going to see home again. And by now, everyone would know him for what he really was. Worse than not seeing home again was the knowledge that no one there would want to see him now anyway.

The thoughts brought him back to the present and he cried out as Nic rubbed salt into the open wounds. It stung and burned all at the same time. His eyes blinked open, and Aki was mortified to find that there were tears in them. They weren't from the pain that racked his body, but from the horrible weight of realization that he was lost for good. What was worse was that Halle was watching him intently, looking for just such a reaction. By the slight smile on his face, Aki knew he found exactly what he wanted to see.

Nic finished and Halle gestured with the bottle in his hand toward the door in a silent command for him to leave. Aki jumped a little as Nic's hand closed over his brand and the man made to pull him along behind him.

"Leave him," Halle said. Nic's hand held onto Aki for a second longer and Aki thought he might argue. Then his grip was gone, and the door shut softly behind Aki as he stood waiting. Halle looked him up and down. "Give me your arm."

Swaying, Aki held out his arm. Halle took it and jerked him forward a half step. He ran his fingers across the brand making Aki's face twist up in a grimace.

"I did do it a bit deep, didn't I? Not that you didn't deserve it. Tell me, Aki, do you remember what you said to me the last time you saw me?"

Aki nodded. Halle dug his fingers into the brand and Aki shuddered at the pain.

"Answer me properly. After all, you do belong to me now. I'm your master. This brand says so."

Aki could work up enough strength to tighten his jaw as he ground out the words he thought he'd never have to say again. "Yes, Master Halle, I remember."

"And what were they? Oh, and also, since I'm your master and all, don't you think it'd be more appropriate for you to address me from your knees?"

"Of course, Master Halle," Aki said, sinking to his knees. To be honest, it wasn't quite the punishment Halle meant it to be. Aki hadn't been sure how much longer he could stay on his feet. "I said that I wasn't afraid of you. Or of anyone else."

"What a lie that was," Halle scoffed. "But you always were good at telling lies, weren't you? Some of them served me very well, too. But you always had to hang that over my head, didn't you? Always had to remind me that a word from you could bring Father's wrath down on my head." Halle snatched the talisman that hung around Aki's neck off. He fingered the two wolf's teeth that were bound into it then tossed it aside on the floor. "You know, after what you did on the mountain, I made a vow to myself that I would return the favor and more. It was what kept me alive all those months when I couldn't even rise from my bed. Not a day goes by when I can forget that vow either. Do you know why?"

"No, Master Halle."

Halle leaned in close, his breath hot and reeking of liquor. "Because every day I live with the pain that never goes away. You made me a cripple that day. And you did it because you were afraid."

Aki didn't dare meet Halle's eyes for fear that he might read the truth in them. He was still afraid. He'd always been afraid. It made him a coward, he supposed, but brave people didn't survive where he'd come from.

Abruptly, Halle sat back and laughed. "You're just going to love to see who's waiting for us in Karu. It'll be like old times again. Now, get back to work. If you behave yourself enough, I might find some scraps to throw into your cage later."

Chapter 38

AKI WASN'T SURE HOW HIS feet were still beneath him as the evening of the second day approached. He'd scrubbed the entire deck on his hands and knees, twice. He'd cleaned every inch of Halle's cabin no less than three times - each time failing to meet Halle's expectations. He'd been dragged from one end of the ship to the other, doing the work of different crew members.

And not once had he been allowed to sleep.

The only times he'd gone below deck were when he was ordered to accompany the men in charge of feeding the other captives. It required almost more strength than he had to pass the food to each child and Dagmar without stuffing it into his own mouth. Harder still was avoiding Dagmar's worried gaze that followed his movements. He hadn't eaten the first time Halle had thrown the leftovers of his own meal onto the floor in front of him. The second time, he couldn't have stopped himself even if he wanted to.

He staggered up to the man he'd just finished cleaning a pailful of fresh caught fish for. The man looked ready to give him another job when Aki collapsed, sending both the pail and fish across the otherwise clean deck. Not bothering to try to get up, Aki curled up, waiting for the man to kick him. He saw the man pull his foot back to deliver the blow but before it came a door opened.

"Take him below, lock him up," Halle's voice came from above his head.

Strong hands grabbed him by the arms and hauled him forward, his legs and feet dragging uselessly behind him.

When the hatch was opened, he was tossed down like a ragdoll. It was only a fall of a few feet but Aki was in no shape to try to catch himself or break his descent at all. He landed in a heap of aches and bruises at the foot of the ladder and remained there until the men descended and took hold of him once more.

Barely conscious of being shoved into his cage and the door locked behind him, Aki gave in to the exhaustion that could no longer be ignored. He heard Dagmar gasp but couldn't force his eyes open, couldn't force his mouth to form any words of reassurance. Her hand was in between the bars of the cage again, this time pulling back the blood encrusted shirt. Aki moaned as it pulled at some of his skin but otherwise stayed inert.

"What have they done to you, Aki?" Dagmar whispered.

He couldn't answer.

Less than an hour went by before the hatch opened again. Aki didn't stir but Dagmar looked up to see Halle climbing down the ladder. He was alone this time, a man waiting just at the top of the ladder. After hanging a lantern on a hook that hung from the ceiling, he approached the cage and slid the key into the lock.

"Please, just let him be," Dagmar, still sitting as close as she could, said.

Halle stopped what he was doing to look at her, an odd expression on his face - delight and triumph, but something else as well. His eyes traveled over Dagmar and his face once more resumed its cold indifference.

"And why would I do that?"

"He's had enough. You're going to kill him."

Halle shrugged. "People die every day," he said as if that were sufficient reason to end another life. "And besides, he tried to kill me, so it's just fair. He's getting nothing that he doesn't deserve."

"Please, just leave him alone for a few hours at least."

"Would you rather I take you up?" Halle asked, sitting back on his heels. He cocked his head, watching her with an odd intensity.

Dagmar looked away, biting her lip.

"Ah, I thought not. But you should know that, to his credit, Aki chose differently." Halle looked pleased with himself as he watched his words take effect on Dagmar's face.

"What do you mean?"

"You've seen what we've done to him," Halle nodded to the mark across Aki's chest, "that was supposed to be on you. Apparently, all that time with decent people made something in him change."

"If those were decent people, what does that make you?"

"Oh, I'm not decent. And I've never claimed to be. So, if you're not going to come up in his place, then I suppose I'll just have to get him up now."

"You don't have to be like this."

Halle laughed. It was a hollow, sad sound. "You'd like that, wouldn't you? You lucked out your first time. Sasha was too weak and a fool. He could have put you to good use, but instead he thought he could give you your freedom. I don't intend to make the same mistakes."

"Please, just leave us alone. You don't have to hurt anyone."

Halle studied her, a frown pulling the corners of his mouth down. He turned away and stared hard at Aki's still form. After a few moments, his face cleared and he shrugged.

"I don't really need him right now, I suppose. But I'm bored. And you interest me," he said, sitting down all the way on the floor. "I've met one girl already who belonged to Sasha and she's not terribly interesting at all. The only thing she ever talks about is her revenge on him. Why don't you talk about that? Don't you want it? Don't you hate us? Do you hate me?"

Dagmar's face paled as he made it apparent that he wasn't leaving anytime soon. She couldn't decide what he was trying to get out of her, what answers he sought from her. He stared expectantly at her, impatient that she hadn't spoken yet.

"I don't know if I hate you or not. You do make it hard not to. But I don't hate Sasha. I couldn't."

"He must be so much better than me. I've always been the worst, you know. Even my father thought I was a waste and a failure. Yet here I am, winning."

Dagmar didn't know what to say. Apparently, Halle didn't expect her to say anything this time. He kept talking, his eyes losing focus of her altogether, staring off into middle space.

"He was going to kill me. My father. After Aki failed to, that is. He said if I wasn't completely healed by the time he returned, he'd kill me himself rather than live with the burden of a crippled son. I could walk by that spring, but I limped, and the pain never went away. If he'd come home instead of Sasha, I'd be dead. Funny, isn't it?" He laughed a little wildly.

"I'm sorry," Dagmar said, shifting so that there was a little more distance between them.

Halle did not seem to notice. He fell silent, still staring at nothing. For some time, he didn't move and Dagmar wondered if he'd forgotten where he was. She could smell the pungent odor of alcohol on his breath and decided that he was probably at least a little drunk. That could explain the utter absurdity of his behavior.

"Did your father love you?" He snapped out of whatever place his mind had wandered off to and stared hard at Dagmar as if to drag the truth from her through his gaze alone.

"Yes, he did. Very much."

"Mine never did. He didn't love anyone."

"I'm sorry," Dagmar repeated. For the first time, she looked at him openly and was surprised to notice that he was only a year or two older than Aki. "It must have been awful to never be loved."

"You're sorry for me? I doubt it. You'd be happy if I dropped dead right here." Halle laughed again but cut it off quickly. "It made me strong enough to be what I am today. Isn't that a good thing? Besides, since he never loved me, I didn't have to mourn his death. Makes life so much easier, you know. Tell me about them."

"Who?"

"Your family. Tell me what made you love them, what makes you miss them."

Dagmar inched even further away, leaning her back against the wooden wall behind her. The last thing she wanted to do was share any part of her family with Halle. But, at least while he was talking to her, he wasn't causing

Aki any more harm and she owed Aki that much. Closing her eyes to picture them, she started. If she thought only about the years before the raid, there were plenty of happy memories to share. There were the hours spent on her father's fishing boat, the wind tugging at her hair. There were the days spent with her mother, baking and sewing and cleaning the fish father caught. There were the market days, when caravans would stop at the oasis and the sound of bartering and bickering formed the background of everything else.

"Enough," Halle said, frowning. "I don't want to hear anymore right now."

She watched anxiously as he got to his feet. He was unsteady, swaying a little and grabbing onto the bars of the cage to balance himself. Bending down, he pulled the key out of the lock and then shuffled to the foot of the ladder. It wasn't until the hatch closed with a bang behind him that Dagmar allowed herself a sigh of relief.

It was many hours before Aki showed any sign of still being alive. He laid without moving for so long that Dagmar frequently placed her hand on his chest to see if he was still breathing. When he finally did stir, it was because of the ruckus that began above deck. Halle was shouting orders, and men were running to obey them. He tried to sit up. He gave up and instead turned to Dagmar.

"What's happening?" His voice was little more than a croak. "How long have I been down here?"

"I don't know. I think they're getting ready for something, but I can't understand what."

She dipped the cup they'd been given into the bucket of drinking water that had been left for their use and passed it between the bars to Aki. He tried to sit up again, managing to at last pull himself up with the help of the bars. Taking the cup in both his hands he guzzled it. She refilled it and he downed the second cupful as quickly as his first. Even then, his thirst wasn't fully quenched but he waved away her efforts to give him a third cup.

"Why did you do it, Aki?"

He looked at her in genuine confusion, his mind still muddled by sleep and his grueling ordeal of the last three days.

"Why'd you let them mark you in my place?"

He started to shrug then decided the motion was an unnecessary expenditure of precious energy. "The pain doesn't bother me that much. Besides, I kind of deserved it."

"That's not true. I can't let them keep hurting you in my place. I can't let you do this."

Aki gave her an odd look. "You can't stop me."

Before she could answer, the hatch opened and Aki slumped against the back of the cage. As much as he wanted to hide it, he desperately hoped they were here for anyone but him. His eyes were wary as they followed the two men down the ladder. He relaxed a little when he saw them pass out the daily fare to their captives.

Assuming that he would once more be ignored, Aki shut his eyes and tried to think of anything aside from the gnawing hunger in his gut. It didn't work. He was ravenous. Out of the corner of his eye he noticed Dagmar already breaking her bread into two very uneven pieces. Selfish as the thought was, he hoped desperately that she meant the larger part for him.

To his surprise, the men turned to him when the others were served. A large chunk of bread and another smaller piece of dried beef were tossed inside the cage to him. Aki snatched them up without waiting or caring that they were watching him as if he were an amusing spectacle. He didn't care. All he could care about was the food filling his mouth and the fact that he'd apparently been left to rest for most of the night.

When they were left by themselves again, Dagmar slid the larger portion of her meal to him.

"Here, I'm not that hungry and you need it. Don't bother arguing with me, either."

He didn't.

He couldn't.

Sleep crept up on him once more after he'd eaten and had more water to drink. Aki surrendered to it without a fight. Even in his sleep, he sensed the difference, though. The ship was no longer sailing. Although it continued to bob up and down in the water, it stayed put. After the constant motion of the last two days, it was unsettling. The fact that he knew it meant something important but was too weary to remember what was even more troubling. It sapped the restfulness out of his sleep.

"Aki, Aki," Dagmar's whisper pulled him awake. Her hand was on his shoulder, gently shaking him and he tried to pull away from it. "There's something wrong, I think."

Aki squinted up at her, making no sense of her words at first. Gradually, as his senses returned, he became aware of the uneasy shouts that came from above their heads. Half sitting up, he listened to the words. Most were indistinct, a murmur of voices lost in the sound of the sea around them. But a few he understood. A few brought an actual smile to his face.

Nic's voice boomed across the deck, loud enough that there was no trouble understanding him. "Halle's not coming back. Make ready to sail, or we'll all be sharing his fate."

Dagmar glanced at Aki oddly. "What exactly are you smiling about?"

"It worked," Aki whispered. "I told King Darien their plan, and he must have stopped them. It's why I got caught in the first place. They'd gotten me out of the way, but I came back."

"Why? You could have stayed where it was safe and escaped all this."

"Well, I didn't plan on this happening. And besides," Aki's face darkened, "Kezi shouldn't have lied to me. She shouldn't have tried to use me."

"At least with Halle gone, they'll leave you alone, right?"

At that, Aki sobered. He shook his head in defeat. "No. With Halle gone, it could be a lot worse. Especially for you."

"What do you mean? Halle's the one behind everything. If he's gone..."

"No," Aki said miserably. "Halle's behind what they were doing to me. He's also the one who ordered them not to touch you. We made a deal. And as long as I kept up my part of the deal, you were safe. If he's not here, the deal's off."

"I doubt he was going to keep up his end of it, anyway."

Aki shook his head again. "Halle's many things, but he's not a liar. If he promises something, he keeps his promise. He always has."

For a long time, neither spoke. Aki leaned against the back of the cage, listening to the commotion that was dying down. The ship was moving again. There was a slim chance, he supposed, that King Darien would send a ship after them. But Halle's had a head start and it was far more likely that they would reach Karu and the slave market.

He'd heard of Karu before, and not just from Sasha's brief experience of the place. It was the preferred refuge for those unfortunate enough to be exiled from Aruuk. The language was the same. Some of the customs were the same. The difference being that where Aruuk was stark and rigid, Karu was wild. Home to pirates and mercenaries who lived in a state of constant lawlessness. They were cruel, he'd heard, but not in the orderly way that Aruuk was cruel.

As night fell, they were fed once more. Aki braced himself for the men's return, expecting to be dragged back up and put to work as before, but they never came back. The hold of the ship turned black, only patches of the starry night sky visible through the grate of the hatch door.

Too tense and in too much pain to sleep now, Aki remained sitting up. He wasn't sure how long it would take for them to reach Karu, but he did know what would happen when they arrived. Although he'd seen them take place several times every year, Aki had never been in a slave auction.

The closest he'd ever come to the degradation of that experience was when Chief Gundar inspected the ten-year-old's right before the Spring Market. He did it every year, deciding which ones to keep, and which ones to sell.

Aki's recollection of that day was vivid. They'd been ushered into his great hall and undressed so that he could look them over completely. Even though he was only ten and he'd never known a different life, Aki had hated that day. No one needed to tell him that there was something wrong with the way they were examined and handled.

Chief Gundar had been accompanied by Mara, her face hidden beneath her veil, and the current keeper of the children - an elderly male slave who was no longer considered capable of hard work.

The Chief had paid Aki an unusual amount of attention that day, asking many questions about him - none actually addressed to him, of course, but to the keeper and even to Mara. Aki was used to being talked over by then. It wasn't until the next day when he was summoned out of the group of chosen children waiting to be branded that he understood what Chief Gundar's interest in him meant.

"Are you awake?" Dagmar's whisper came from just the other side of the bars, breaking into his thoughts. Aki was almost glad of the interruption. He didn't like thinking about that time.

"Yes."

"Do you mind if I ask you something?"

Aki's face scrunched up in confusion, but in the darkness, Dagmar couldn't possibly see the expression. "I guess not."

"What happened between you and Halle? He obviously sought you out and holds something against you."

"A lot happened," Aki said softly. He was quiet for a moment before deciding that since they were on their way to the slave markets he might as well tell at least one person the truth about himself. Somehow, talking to the darkness, unable to read Dagmar's face as he filled in details of his life that he'd never shared with anyone, was easier than he imagined. Dagmar didn't interrupt him, either. He'd almost forgotten that she was even listening until the end when he was finished. Even when he'd been silent for several minutes, she didn't say anything. He laughed a little, stopping quickly when he realized how much pain that caused. "You see, that's why I never told anyone. Now you think I'm as bad as Halle. And maybe I am."

"No," Dagmar said slowly, "no, I don't. I think you both are the same in a lot of ways and you don't even realize it. You both were really, really messed up and that man who called himself your father was a really, really terrible man."

"None of which makes any difference now. Halle's gone. We're on a ship bound for the slave markets of Karu. And no one is coming to save us, even if they did know where we were taken."

"Don't say that. Please, don't say that," Dagmar said, her voice breaking with despair.

"I'm sorry. It's just, I ran away from Stephan's to come back to Bren, and before I left, I told him a short version of what I just told you. I doubt he'll want me back now."

"That's not true."

"It doesn't matter. No one knows where we're at," Aki said dully, heaviness settling over him like a blanket. "I liked my three years of being free."

Chapter 39

THREE DAYS OF SEARCHING HAD been futile. Lars and Sasha had found the hut Halle had used, but it was completely abandoned when they arrived. Sasha had gone to Captain Lupin the very next morning, explaining what was going on. Captain Lupin was sympathetic and promised to send word to him if heard anything but there was nothing more he could do.

On the second evening, with no other idea, he'd wandered about the streets on the slim chance that he'd spot Kezi. The only person he did find, actually found him. He'd heard steps hurrying up behind him and had turned around in time to see Atticus Wehr approaching.

"You haven't found him yet?" the older man had asked.

Sasha had shaken his head, appreciating Atticus' concern. How he had known Aki was missing, Sasha wasn't sure.

"Not sure where else to look, honestly. Unless we know where Halle's ship was heading, we're lost."

Atticus had hesitated, clearly debating with himself whether to speak or not. Finally, pulling Sasha into a corner away from any listening ears, he'd said, "This isn't something that I'm supposed to share, but it may help you and after what you've done for Dival, I think it's a safe bet. The king is aware of the attack planned on his daughter - the attack Aki warned him about before he was kidnapped. He has decided that the best way to deal with it is to allow it to happen. Since we know exactly where and when it is to take place, he'll have soldiers waiting nearby. The intent is for them to catch as many as possible at one time, rather than having to hunt them down one by one while many escape. In the event that this plan is successful, there are likely to be prisoners taken who could point you in the right direction."

"That would be helpful. When is this supposed to happen?"

"That I really shouldn't tell you, but if you will tell me where I can find you, I will make sure word is sent directly to you."

Sasha had given him the name of the inn he and Lars were staying in. Atticus started to walk away but he seemed to remember something and turned back.

"If you find him again, Sasha, tell him," Atticus stopped, trying to put together the words he wanted. At a loss for what he wanted to express, he patted Sasha's arm and gave him a sad smile, "Just help him, will you? He's been lost awhile. And perhaps, you could mention to him that it's alright to tell others of one's troubles. It makes them a bit easier to bear sometimes."

Sasha had smiled and nodded, "I'll do that, just as soon as I get him back."

Now, a day later, Sasha returned to his room for the evening. In spite of Atticus' assurances of letting him know right away, he couldn't keep himself confined at the inn. Wandering the streets might not have accomplished anything aside from burning off the nervousness that plagued him with each passing hour. Lars was waiting for him and looked up at his entrance.

"You missed it," he said.

"Missed what?"

"There was some messenger looking for you about an hour ago. He said something about coming to the castle for information. You don't suppose they found Aki, do you?"

"No, but I bet they have someone who knows where he is. I'll be back in a bit."

"Can't I go with you?"

"No. They won't let you in where I need to go."

There were definite benefits to being the one who warned the king of impending doom, Sasha thought to himself, as he was escorted inside without hesitation. He followed his escort up a winding staircase that was very familiar. He'd climbed it a few times when Boris had been held here. Waiting at the top for him, Sasha was surprised to find Atticus.

"Ah, I see you got my message," Atticus said as Sasha joined him. "The trap worked quite successfully. Most of the people involved and captured have not yet been brought here. The ones we consider to be the leaders are here, though. I believe one of them was the girl you were looking for."

"And I'm allowed to talk to them?"

"You are. With the king's permission. He only asks that if they disclose any information, you will share it immediately. King Darien sends his thanks for Aki's warning and his condolences for his disappearance. It's the second time our country has been in debt to a foreigner. He hopes you will be able to find him soon. The girl is in there," Atticus pointed to a door at one of the three doors that surrounded the tower landing they were on.

Sasha approached it slowly. He was reluctant to face the person on the other side of the heavy door. Kezi hated him, but he'd always thought she was Aki's friend. Nodding to the guard outside of it, he waited as the key was turned in the lock and the guard held the door open for him.

The cell was dim and he stood in the doorway for a moment taking a good look at the room. It was identical to the one Boris had been kept in. The same small table mounted to the wall, the same stool, the same cot.

And sitting on that cot, her hair hanging down like a curtain in front of her face, was Kezi. She watched him from behind that hair, her eyes very much alive with hate as they followed his every move. Her legs were drawn protectively up in front of her body, her arms wrapped tightly around them. Remembering how quickly she'd tried to kill him that night in Karu, Sasha kept his distance and watched her with distrust.

"Kezi," he said.

"Look who it is," Kezi interrupted, unfolding herself and getting to her feet. "Have you come to gloat? To tell me what a despicable person I am? Oh, wait, I know. You've come looking for poor, little Aki, haven't you? He's alive, just so you know. Probably wishing he was dead, if Halle did half the things he talked about wanting to do to him. But alive nonetheless."

Sasha tried not to let his relief show. Kezi could be lying just as easily as telling the truth but the fact that Halle hadn't killed Aki right away gave her words credence. "Why'd you do it? Why him?"

"Because, Sasha, you cared about him. Because he was born nothing, and no one, and yet he found people who cared about him. Because he thought the world of you. And because he told me no."

"How can you possibly hate me that much? I did you no harm."

Kezi threw her head back and laughed until it caught in her throat and turned into a choked sob. "So you say. But surely you must know what a girl must do to make her living on the streets? It would have been better if you'd let me kill myself that night."

"You wouldn't have had to live on the streets if you hadn't run off the first chance you got."

"Nice try, Sasha, but if you think that saying that now makes up for anything I've had to go through, you're wrong. If you want me to tell you where Aki is, you'll have to help me out."

"Do you even know where he is?"

"Of course," she said, coming towards him. She placed her hands on his arms. "I'm the one who told Halle to take him. All of this happened because of me. And if you'll help me now, I'll help you."

"And what sort of help do you want?" Sasha pulled away from her and leaned back against the door.

"I don't want to spend the rest of my life locked up here. And I definitely don't want to die. You could convince your friends here that I'm innocent, that I wasn't the leader. You could convince them to let me go. Or," her voice dropped to a conspiratorial whisper, "you could just help me escape and then I'll go with you to find Aki."

"Absolutely not."

"Your loss," she shrugged. "Since Halle and Jasper both died, though, I'm the only one who knows where he is. Deny me, and he stays there forever."

Sasha's face darkened at the mention of Halle. "You're sure Halle's dead?"

"Positive. I saw his body when they were dragging me away. So, what do you say? We could both do each other a favor and I'd disappear. You'd never see me again."

"I don't think so. First of all, you're guilty and nothing I say is going to change that. And secondly, you've spent the last four years hating me and scheming to get your revenge on me. You're not going to give that up so easily." Sasha turned toward the door and called out to the guard that he was done.

Kezi grabbed him by the arm and pulled him around. Tears filled her eyes. "You can't leave me here, Sasha. You can't. I hate it. It's so cramped and dark. I'll lose my mind if I can't get out. Please, Sasha, you owe me that."

Sasha removed her hand as the door came open. "I owe you nothing, Kezi. You don't get to blame me for all the choices you've made since that day. You betrayed Aki's friendship and used him like a pawn to get to me. Goodbye, Kezi. Whatever happens to you here is what you deserve."

Kezi's scream reverberated through the entire floor of the tower. She pounded on the door as it locked back in its place and Sasha shoved away the memory of Boris and the way he used to go through fits of madness while locked up.

"I take it that didn't go well," Atticus said, his face tight with worry. "Sasha, there are two others here, but I don't know if it will go any better with them."

"I have to try," Sasha said, heading for a different door. While he waited for the guard to unlock it, he turned to Atticus. "Is it true that Halle and Jasper were both killed in the skirmish?"

"I know for a fact that Jasper was, sadly, among the dead. I would have liked to ask him why he did it. Halle, that's your brother, isn't it?" Sasha nodded. "Him, I do not know about. There were a few of the criminals who were killed, some of them were not from here and were unidentified. There were also some wounded and they were brought to the infirmary here, under guard of course."

"But you don't know if Halle was among them?"

"Unfortunately, Sasha, we have no way of knowing. The foreigners who were taken do not speak our language. They were kept together as far as I know."

"But I speak theirs," Sasha murmured to himself. "Where are they?"

"I'm afraid I couldn't tell you. They were not moved right away. We anticipate their arrival within the next day or two."

Sasha stood undecided. In the lull, he noticed that Kezi was quiet once more. He imagined she was just on the other side of the door, eavesdropping on his conversation. Not that it would do her any good.

"I might as well see if the others know anything," he said at last.

The first man he spoke to didn't even recognize Aki's name. The second, a young man named Phineas, had been imprisoned since before the attack and although he knew who Aki was, he had no useful information about him beyond the fact that Aki had joined them at times when they met together.

Sasha left the tower and made his way down to the infirmary, Atticus guiding the way. It was in a large room, with several smaller rooms attached, that was half-buried underground. Its placement kept the infirmary a moderate temperature year-round with very little effort. It had an unmistakable smell of herbs and tonics. Tonight, the scent of blood hung heavy in the air as well. There were several guards stationed in the room, but they didn't question Atticus' presence and by association, they didn't question Sasha's.

Sasha moved from bed to bed. There were a little over half a dozen men and none of them were awake at the moment. A complete circuit of the room revealed that Halle was not among the wounded.

"I'm sorry. I had truly hoped you would find what you needed tonight," Atticus said as they left. "I will keep you informed when the others arrive. Perhaps there will at least be one among them who knows where their destination was."

Chapter 40

A WEEK.

They'd been at sea for a week. At least, as far as Aki could tell. Aside from their meals twice a day, no other attention was paid to any of the captives in the hold. After being cramped inside the cage for so many days, unable to stand or stretch out fully, Aki desperately hoped they were nearing their destination.

It was the sound of waves driving against rocks that first alerted Aki to the presence of land. The ship slowed. Voices carried across the water. The sharp, pungent odor of fish filled the air. Above their heads, the crew had burst into frenzied action.

Aki stared up at the nearest hatch, watching the shadows of men flit past in the darkness. There were still several hours of night left. If he could have, he would have been asleep. But sleep didn't come easily after that first exhausted collapse. For one thing, there wasn't a position he could be in that didn't cause him some amount of pain. He was restless, too, from being unable to move freely, the close confinement almost worse than the hours upon hours spent on the deck working.

A soft scraping sound along the side of the hull told him that the ship had been pulled alongside a wharf. Unwilling to consider what that meant for him and the others, he rested his head on his drawn-up knees. The creak of the ladder as someone climbed down it a few minutes later made him look up. He couldn't tell who it was in the darkness, their face completely hidden in the shadows. When they reached his cage, he braced himself against the back of it. Without Halle to threaten Dagmar, he had no plans for cooperating.

The lock clicked open and without a word, his captor reached inside and grabbed the front of his shirt, hauling him out of the cage. Aki tried to resist, but he was weak and his muscles cramped from confinement. Spasms of pain awakened through him as he was forced to stand for the first time in seven days.

"Cap'n wants you to help," the man said by way of explanation.

Aki supposed he should at least appreciate the effort to keep him informed of what they planned for him. He would have preferred if the man gave him a few minutes to stretch out his limbs. Apparently, there wasn't time for that. He allowed himself to be tugged along.

The ladder was a challenge he wasn't prepared for. His feet seemed to have forgotten how to work and he slipped on its rungs several times trying to climb the short distance. As soon as his feet touched the deck, the man's grip on him returned.

Nic, the new captain since Halle's failure to return, was waiting for them. The other hatch was already open, a rope thrown over a beam and dropped through the black opening. Laying on the deck beside Nic was a pile of chains. Aki groaned internally when Nic jerked his head toward them and said, "Put 'em on him and get him to work."

"Why?" Aki dared to ask, staring at the chains.

Nic backhanded him, hard, before answering, "Don't think I've forgotten that you're a runaway. And we've reached land. You can do what I need you to just fine with those on."

Aki submitted with poor grace as the sailor shackled first his ankles and then his wrists. A long chain stretched between the two sets of manacles, restricting his movement almost as badly as the cage had. Nic noticed the look on his face and wasn't pleased with it.

"You're lucky you didn't spend the last week the same as your first few days. If I'd had my way, you would have. 'Twas only Halle's orders that the whole lot of you reach Karu unspoiled and fit that spared you."

That answered the unspoken question that had been puzzling Aki since they set sail. It had nothing to do with a change of heart on Halle's part, he was sure, just a desire to make the most money possible at market. Healthy slaves were worth more than wrecked ones. He wasn't given any time to ponder it, though.

Shuffling now because of the chains, which made an annoying amount of clanking with each step, he followed the sailor to the open hatch. Two other men, not bedecked in chains Aki noted, were already waiting.

"Pull it up," the man who'd brought Aki over ordered.

Aki took his place on the rope and pulled with the other two, slowly raising a crate from the cargo hold. Once up, it was grabbed by others and moved across the deck while the rope was sent down for another. Aki couldn't believe how many such crates and barrels the ship was capable of holding, nor how each seemed heavier than the last.

His two companions cursed him repeatedly for not pulling his weight, and he had to bite his tongue to keep from saying they would do just as poorly if they could lift their hands but a few inches past their waist.

It was daylight before the last of the cargo was unloaded. Without further direction, Aki simply sat down where he was. He watched as everyone around him scurried about the deck of the ship, putting the finishing touches on whatever job they'd been assigned. If they were anything like him, they were probably anxious to get back on land, even if it was just for a few days. Forgotten about for the moment, Aki managed to doze off, the morning sun warm and welcome on his face. He awoke to shouts a few minutes later.

"Where is he?" Nic was yelling to no person in particular while the sailors moved warily around him. "Where did he go? Who was in charge of him?"

It took a minute for Aki to realize that he was the subject of Nic's ire, and the thought made him strangely pleased. He hadn't noticed before that he was sitting, half-hidden, behind the open hatch door. Nor was he in any hurry to reveal himself. It would be satisfying to watch his poor escort punished for losing track of him. He shut his eyes again, pretending to be asleep still, while listening to the hapless sailor, who Nic had finally identified, receive a scorching beratement.

Rough hands jerked him upright and Aki blinked up at the man who'd found him, the picture of someone just roused from a deep sleep.

"I found him," the man called out and pulled Aki towards Nic.

It was only then that Aki noticed they were no longer alone on the deck. Dagmar and the other captives had all been brought up and stood now in a line. He caught Dagmar's eye briefly and saw her worry. Nic looked him over, face red with fury.

"If I find out you were trying to run again, I'll kill you myself and lose your profit."

"I wasn't, sir. I just fell asleep." Aki kept his eyes downcast as he spoke. If there was one thing his life had taught him, it was how to pretend submission and subservience.

Nic's anger melted away in an instant, replaced by relief. "Get him in line. She's on her way to inspect." Aki's ears perked up at that, remembering Halle's words, although he continued to keep his head down and his posture disinterested. "It's bad enough we have to tell her about Halle."

Aki's blood ran cold as he shuffled to a spot next to Dagmar. It was no pretense that kept his head down now. The pieces fell into place now in his mind and he knew exactly who was coming. She haunted his nightmares. And, although he had no idea how she had come to be here in Karu, he was about to be face to face with her.

"What did they do to you?" Dagmar whispered when no one was looking their way.

"Nothing. I just had to help unload the ship."

Silence fell over the crew and Aki knew without looking that she had arrived. Footsteps, soft and slow, crossed the plank and moved across the deck. A murmur of voices, one distinctly feminine, reached his ears. Although he could only catch bits and pieces of the conversation, it was clear they were breaking the news of Halle's loss to her. His heart raced. He balled his hands up but could not move them to his sides the way he was used to because of the chains that still held him.

She began at the far end. He watched out of the corner of his eye as she tipped the head of the first child back, the cold indifference on her face exactly as he remembered it. Her hands moved to the child's arms, firm as the frightened child tried to pull away. He knew exactly what it felt like to be grabbed by those hands, to be handled by them. She moved onto the next and Aki stopped watching. He had to. His stomach lurched at every memory of his time with her.

When at last she reached Dagmar, her indifference shifted slightly.

"You're a pretty thing, aren't you?" she said, her tone like that of someone talking to a favorite pet. Her eyes slid down to Dagmar's arm and noticed the brand on it. Her sharp eyes narrowed as she took it in. "You belonged to Sasha."

It wasn't a question, and Dagmar didn't answer. She only stood mute as the others had done.

Aki sucked in a sharp, shallow breath as she stepped in front of him. After so many years away, he could at least hope that she didn't recognize him. Instead of lifting his face up as she had done with the others, she gripped the top of his shirt and tore it open all the way down, exposing the still healing mark Halle had given him.

"A runaway? That explains the chains." Now she grabbed his face and tipped it up to meet her gaze. She turned his face from side to side. "You're familiar. What's your name?"

Aki clamped his mouth shut, staring past her. He'd spent too many years of his life giving this woman whatever she demanded. He was not about to start again now. Besides, it was taking every bit of his restraint not to jerk away from her hand. Just the touch of it was revolting.

She dropped his head and turned to Nic. "What do you call him?"

"Halle told us he went by Aki, ma'am."

"Aki?" she turned back to him. "Oh, yes. I see it now. So, Halle has had his revenge. And it has cost him his life." She turned away and spoke to Nic, "I'll take these two. Bring them to my house. The rest can go to market."

When no one was within earshot, Dagmar shifted slightly and whispered, "You know her?"

238

Aki nodded. "She's Mara, Halle's mother and Chief Gundar's favorite wife for years."

"And now our mistress," Dagmar murmured.

Any further chance for conversation was taken from them when they were shoved toward the plank. Aki tried not to fall on his face as the chain between his legs pulled taut. The chains were a consequence he hadn't anticipated when he agreed to take the mark of a runaway. He wondered what other unpleasantries were awaiting him as a result of that lie.

Karu only had one real town, the one built around the port. Its streets were narrower than the ones in Bren, more crowded. Once they left the docks behind, there were shops and houses all mixed up together in no apparent order whatsoever. At the very center of town was the marketplace, a large, open area that was home to the auction.

Aki was reminded of the market square in Illsen. There was a platform for the auctioneer and merchandise, raising them so that they were visible to whatever crowd of buyers showed up. And beyond that were the pens. Some housed livestock - cattle, sheep, a few horses. Two others contained the slaves, females in one and males in the other.

As they were led past the pens, a chill ran through Aki. For a moment he could be thankful that Mara had chosen him immediately. He was spared not just the indignity of the auction, but also the discomfort of waiting for it. The few men who were in the slave pen had no freedom of movement whatsoever. A beam ran across the length of the pen about three feet off the ground and from that beam, separated by about a foot and half, were short chains. These were fastened around the necks of the slaves. Having spent the last week unable to move freely, Aki couldn't imagine how much worse that would be.

Beyond the town, rocky hills rose up. Most of the island was made of rock, Aki noted. A road, full of rocks and stones jutting up out of the hard packed dirt, stretched out of town and up the steep slope of the nearest hill. Aki continued to struggle with each step he took as they began their ascent. Dagmar's soft gasp made him look up. A low stone wall rose up on the left side of the road. Another minute of walking brought them to a set of iron wrought gates and Aki got his first look of the house beyond.

House was the wrong word for it, he decided. Made out of white stone that could only have come from the southern continent of Sondaru, it was larger than any building he'd seen in town. A man was waiting for them at the gate and once Dagmar and Aki were safely through the gate, the sailors who'd escorted them turned and headed back down the road.

The lane up to the house was smoothed out and easier to walk on without tripping. Another set of iron gates were opened to allow them into the courtyard. The floor of the courtyard was made of the same white stone. A fire pit burned brightly in the center of the courtyard, despite the sweltering heat of summer. Their first stop was at that fire pit, where a branding iron was already heating.

Halle's brand hadn't even finished healing yet. Aki was more prepared for it this time and, although his face twisted in a grimace of pain, he managed to keep quiet for the few seconds it was pressed into the skin just above his first one. He was pushed off to the side while it was Dagmar's turn. And then they were both left standing in the middle of the courtyard, alone and ignored.

Aki noticed for the first time that Dagmar looked on the verge of being sick with fear. She'd said nothing since they left the ship, and he began to realize that it had more to do with fear than it did the lack of opportunity. He still couldn't help but feel as if the only reason she was here was because he'd shown up on her doorstep covered in blood that night.

"I'm really sorry about all this."

"You don't have to apologize, Aki. This isn't your fault. If anything, I should be thanking you for what you did for me on that ship. Besides," she took a deep breath, "it could be worse."

Aki laughed before realizing that laughing might not be the right response. He couldn't really stop himself, though.

"It could be a lot worse. We could have been tossed overboard and left for the sharks, or we could have been...," Aki paused, suddenly not sure what would be worse than the predicament they now found themselves in.

Still, he wanted to make Dagmar feel better. "It shouldn't be too bad for you here. Mara's always been nicer to her female slaves."

"I take it she wasn't very nice to you."

Aki fell silent. His attempt at cheering Dagmar had made him remember just how awful and bleak his own future appeared. Mara hadn't just not be nice to him as a slave, she was also the mother of the son he'd tried to kill. Halle likely wasn't the only one who wanted revenge. Before Dagmar could comment on the abrupt change in his demeanor, he gave his chains a little shake and forced a smile on his face.

"Mara never did this to me so maybe I remember her being worse than she was."

"You never let her think you were a runaway," Dagmar said quietly.

"I thought about running away, if that counts," which was a lie. As a child, he hadn't dared to even consider the option.

A door opened behind them. Mara stepped out onto the wide porch that skirted the courtyard. A man stood slightly behind her. Mara spoke a few low words to the man at her side and he bowed his head in acknowledgement. He started down the steps.

"You, girl, come with me," Mara called out.

Dagmar shot Aki a look of absolute terror.

"Good luck," he whispered, trying to muster a reassuring smile. And failing abysmally. "I'll see you around."

She caught hold of his hand and squeezed it, "You too."

When Dagmar disappeared through the doors with Mara, Aki was truly alone. He stared after the closed door without meaning to and was startled to find his vision filled by the man Mara had sent down the steps. Aki had to tip his head back to see the man's face and even then, most of it was hidden behind a large beard. There was no mistaking the look in the man's eyes, though. He was used to being obeyed.

"I'll only go over this with you once, so listen carefully. You are the property of Mara Wendlen. Your sole purpose now is to benefit her in whatever capacity she sees fit. As of right now, that's in the salt mines. My name is Sebastian and although I am not your master, I am your overseer. You would do well to remember that. Obey me and you'll be just fine. You're a runaway, so consider yourself already on my bad side. If you've any sense at all, you will never try to run from here." With that, and without waiting for a response from Aki, he turned Aki around and they started back out the gate they'd just entered.

Aki was glad Sebastian hadn't given him a chance to answer. The man's brief, terse speech had snapped something inside him, and he was afraid to let it out. He'd thought it would be a simple thing to slip back into the servitude required of him since he knew it so well, but as he listened to Sebastian's words, he realized there'd never been anything he hated more. Everything in him wanted to fight it and that was a very new feeling for Aki.

The trek up to the salt mines was long and slow of necessity. He kept his head down, picking out each tedious step to keep from tripping. His small, shuffling steps dragged their pace down to little more than a crawl. He waited for Sebastian to lose patience with him and strike him, but the man never did, and Aki felt a grudging amount of gratitude for the overseer's tolerance.

When at last they reached the crest of the hill that led down into the mines, Aki froze. He wasn't sure what he'd expected to see. Most of what he saw, he didn't understand, and Sebastian didn't give him the chance to even take it in. He guided him toward a gaping hole cut into the earth. A wooden platform was built around the hole. A wooden frame held a beam over the hole allowing a rope with a large bucket to be lowered into it.

Here, at last, Aki's chains were removed. Rubbing his wrists and discovering just how badly they had chafed in the last few hours, Aki listened as Sebastian explained his task. Sebastian held a pickaxe out for him to take, but before releasing it fully into his grasp, said, "Use this for anything other than cutting out rock salt, and I'll flog the skin off your back."

Aki nodded, not trusting himself to speak. Hesitating only a moment over the rope ladder that looked far too flimsy to hold up any significant amount of weight, he began his descent into the darkness.

He would die here.

He knew that.

Life expectancy in a salt mine was no more than a month or two, and he was hardly starting in peak condition. He was glad of the darkness for the moment. It hid how pale his face had gone. It hid the way his hands could barely hold onto the rope and ax. And it hid the tears of despair that threatened him.

For not the first time, he wondered how different his life could have been just now if he hadn't been so afraid. If he had told Sasha the truth from the beginning. If he'd told Stephan. He allowed his mind to wander over what everyone back home was doing, what they thought of him, if he was even missed or if they were glad he was gone. It was the first time he'd dared to allow himself such thoughts. And it was the wrong time to indulge them. By the time his feet met solid ground, his spirits were as low as his body was.

Chapter 41

THE CASTLE DUNGEON WAS A place Sasha hadn't even known existed or was in use until that evening. He'd been kept as a prisoner in the one in Dorsten and that was the extent of his experience with them. He found this one as unpleasant as Dorsten's. It carried the same damp, decaying odor and left him wanting nothing more than a breath of fresh, clean air. He wouldn't have come here at all if it hadn't been for Atticus' message.

It had arrived an hour before and stated simply that the others were available for him to question. Atticus himself was not present this evening, but Sasha was expected. He'd promised King Darien help in questioning the foreigners. A soldier led him down the hallway into a room not unlike the Chamber he'd known in Dorsten.

Although they were covered in dust from having sat so long in disuse, there were instruments of torture arrayed around the room. The center of the room, however, was a simple table and set of chairs. Two on the far side facing the door, and a third, with leather straps attached to the arms and legs, facing the back wall.

Sitting down with his face to the door, he waited for the entrance of the first prisoner. He didn't have to wait long.

Although the captive spoke Aruuken, he admitted that he was from Karu. Beyond that, Sasha could only garner the most basic information. The man claimed to be nothing more than a sailor for hire. He swore he had no knowledge of their purpose or who they were after. Nor did he know where they were going when the job was completed. When Sasha asked him to identify their leader, the man balked and said only that they followed their captain. Sasha waited until the soldiers came to take him away again before asking his final question.

"What happened to Halle?"

The man looked confused that Sasha knew Halle's name but insisted he was among the fallen.

Another three men answered his questions exactly the same as the first and Sasha's patience was at an end.

"Don't bother bringing another in," Sasha said as the soldiers took the last one out. "I want to look at the others."

Accompanied by two soldiers and carrying a torch in his hand, Sasha made his way to the large holding cell that contained the almost one dozen foreigners taken. As late as it was, and having been marched through the day to get here, most of the men were asleep. Sasha held the torch up close to the door, letting its flame illuminate the farthest corners of the cell. A grim, yet relieved smile flitted across his face as he caught sight of a sleeping prisoner in the back corner. He was nearly hidden by all the others, and Sasha was pretty sure he wanted it that way.

"Him," Sasha said quietly, pointing to the one he'd laid eyes on. "Bring him to me."

He hurried back to the room he'd questioned the others in, but instead of sitting at his place, he stood in the shadows by the door. He waited until the prisoner was secured to his chair, then motioned for the soldiers to leave them. For several minutes he stood, hidden from sight but fully able to see his younger brother. He was still waking up, Sasha saw, and the longer he sat, the more nervous he became, twisting his head around and trying to see what was going on. When he'd given up and slumped against the chair, Sasha stepped softly up behind him.

"Hello, Halle," he leaned down enough to whisper in Halle's ear, causing his brother to jump and jerk against his bindings.

"Sasha? What are you doing here?"

"I might ask you the same. But I already know the answer to that question, so it'd be very boring. Instead, why don't you tell me why all of your men claim you are dead? Why none of them would name you as their leader?"

Sasha rested his hands on the back of Halle's chair. "You know, I can't help but feel like we've done this before. Wait, we have. Back in Aruuk. My first night in Illsen as Chief. If I recall, you tried to murder me in my sleep. Lucky for me, I wasn't asleep."

Halle glowered in his chair, mute and defiant.

"Come on, Halle, help yourself out a bit. Tell me what I want to know," Sasha prodded.

"Or what?"

Sasha began to drum his fingers against the wooden chair back and Halle stiffened.

"It was your ship, under your command, that helped perpetrate an act of high treason against King Darien and his daughter, Princess Charlotte. Do you have any idea what happens to people like you?" Sasha let his words hang in the air for a moment, not really expecting an answer from Halle. "I promised the king that if I discovered anyone who helped lead or plan this sedition, I would tell him immediately. When I leave this room tonight, it will be with you. You will accompany me to the tower prison and remain there, in isolation, until your trial. At your trial it will most likely be determined that you are guilty and deserve a death sentence."

Halle's back remained rigid as he listened to Sasha, but his jaw began to work back and forth, betraying his attempt to stay calm.

"They have a few ways of carrying out that sentence here, not as creative, of course, as the ones Father used, but unpleasant, nonetheless. And effective."

"You're lying. You wouldn't even torture me back home."

"I won't be the one deciding or carrying it out, Halle," Sasha said quietly. "It'll be out of my hands entirely."

That thought seemed to strike Halle for the first time. He twisted around to get a look at Sasha's face. Sasha made it easier. He moved around the chair and sat on the edge of the table.

"On the other hand, King Darien likes me. And I'm friends with some of the people who will make the final decision regarding your fate. Help yourself out. Show them you're willing to cooperate."

"You want to know about Aki, don't you?" Halle's face darkened with suspicion. "I should have known. You don't really want to help me. You just want to know what happened to him. If our places were switched, you wouldn't be in such a hurry to run off and find me."

"I won't pretend that that wouldn't have been among my first questions."

"You don't know him. Not really. If you did, you'd hate him worse than me. Did you know he's the one who betrayed that girl you married?"

"What he did doesn't matter. Where is he now?"

"I'd rather die than tell you," Halle spit out. "He deserves what he got."

Sasha studied him for a moment before shaking his head slowly. "No. No, you wouldn't. Halle, you don't want to die. Do you think I can't see how afraid you are of it? That's why you were hiding amongst your men. That's why you gave them orders to conceal you, to claim you had died. Because you are afraid of dying, but that is exactly what will happen if you do nothing."

Halle recoiled as if Sasha had slapped him across the face.

"Should I give you some time with the guards waiting outside? I've heard they can be quite persuasive," Sasha said, hoping Halle wouldn't push it that far. It was an empty threat if he did. But Halle was as predictable as he remembered. He was as afraid of pain, and the anticipation of pain, as he was of death. The blood drained from his face immediately and he shook his head slightly.

"You've got to promise me something in return, Sasha," he said, defeated. "You can't expect me to give you whatever you want and get nothing in return."

"What do you have in mind?"

"Promise me I won't be killed. And get me something to drink."

Sasha snorted a laugh, "Why? So you can drink yourself into oblivion and forget the trouble you're in?"

"No. Because my legs hurt, thanks to Aki, and..., and yes, because I don't want to think about what's going to happen. It's going to be unpleasant any way it goes and I'd rather not have to dwell on it."

"I can't make either of those promises without speaking to the king."

"But you're going to go straight to him and tell him who I am," Halle protested. "I need you to promise me my life before you do that."

"I can't. I'll do the best I can, Halle. In the meantime, you are to come with me," Sasha said, standing up from the table and heading for the door. He paused halfway across the room. "You were wrong, by the way. I'd have looked for you, too, if you were lost. You're my brother, Halle, and I wish more than anything that I could undo the way you were raised. But you're the only one who can do that."

Sasha wasn't expecting a response from Halle and didn't wait for one. After explaining to the soldiers outside the door that he'd identified the leader, he waited while they brought him out and led the way as they escorted him back to the castle.

It wasn't until the next morning that he was able to get an audience with King Darien. After more than an hour with him in the same library where he'd first met the king, Sasha made his way up the tower stairs one more time. In his pocket was a small flask of liquor.

Halle was awake, lying on his back on his cot and staring straight up at the ceiling. Sasha pulled up the stool and sat down.

"Sit up, Halle. Let's talk."

"Well? Have you come to tell me that I must die? That there's no hope for my life?" Halle swung his legs over the edge of the cot and leaned forward, his elbows on his knees, his chin cupped in his hands.

"I've come to tell you," Sasha pulled the flask out, "I've reached a deal with the king."

Halle's eyes went straight to the flask and didn't leave it.

"When we're done here, Halle." Sasha noticed and shook his head. "Here's what he's offering - you tell me where Aki is, I go find him. You stay here while I do that. Your trial will be postponed until I return. The outcome of your trial will be determined in part by whether or not you told me the truth. If I come home with Aki, you'll live. If I don't, you die."

"But what if something's happened to him since I last saw him? He might be dead and I wouldn't know it. That's not a fair deal."

Sasha fixed him with a hard stare. "You'd better hope he's not, because then you'd be convicted of being an accomplice to his murder."

Halle paled and finally tore his eyes away from his prize. Sasha started to put it back in his pocket with a shrug.

"If you don't want to make the deal, you'll be tried with the others at the end of next week. I doubt your execution will be long after that. And you won't have anything to drink to forget your miseries in the meantime."

"He's in Karu," Halle blurted out. "That's where I ordered them. To Karu, to my mother."

"Mara? What has she got to do with this?"

"She lives there, ever since you banished her," Halle said, some of the sullenness slipping back into his voice. "She's made quite a life for herself there too. She thinks you did her a favor sending her away. And she practically runs the slave markets there. That's where Aki was taken. In the slave market or sold off already. Just like he was born to be."

Sasha got up and tossed the flask to Halle. "You don't deserve this."

Halle didn't bother to reply as he unscrewed the cap and took a drink.

"For your sake, I hope you're telling the truth."

"Unlike Aki, I don't lie. Ever."

Chapter 42

SHIFTING THE HEAVY SACK ON his back from one shoulder to the other, Aki almost lost his balance. It was an easy thing to do considering the fact that his right ankle was attached to another man's in front of him and so on down the line of twenty of them. The rock filled road didn't do them any favors, either.

For the first week and a half, Aki hadn't seen the light of day beyond what filtered down through the narrow shafts. The slaves who worked inside the mine itself also ate and slept there, trapped forever in the semi-darkness. Although he expected to be kept in chains down there as well, thanks to his mark, he was quickly disillusioned. No chains were necessary. Each evening after their work was finished and their food distributed, their overseers disappeared to the surface, pulling up the rope ladders with them and closing off each shaft, sealing the slaves in total darkness.

Quotas were everything down there, Aki discovered. Each slave was given one and their overseers were vigilant in making sure those quotas were reached. When, after ten days had passed and he had not once met his quota despite receiving a lashing for it every night, Sebastian finally decided he was more useful elsewhere.

Aki didn't argue.

Now, he was among the group of slaves entrusted with the task of transporting the refined salt all the way down to the harbor to be loaded on ships. Often, there were any number of miscellaneous items that they were required to bring back up with them on the return trip - materials and supplies needed to keep the mines running or the slaves fed.

Sebastian frequently accompanied them on at least one or two of the six to eight trips they made in a day. He was always on horseback, and never without his whip. For an overseer, Aki could remember worse. Sebastian didn't lash out randomly or out of malice, reserving his whip for only purposeful infractions.

Unfortunately, Aki had had quite a few of those in the two weeks since he'd arrived. Most of the time, he couldn't have said why he did it, why he flatly disobeyed, or intentionally did things the wrong way. It gave him the same insane, wild sense of control he'd had when he'd tried to goad a reaction out of Oscar. It was senseless and dangerous, reckless. And it went against everything that had ever been ingrained in him, but he'd slipped so far, he no longer cared.

Enslavement, that had come so naturally to him as a child, now felt like trying to squeeze into a shoe that was several sizes too small. He didn't fit. He didn't want to fit. He'd tasted freedom and it was sweet. It lingered with him, a craving he couldn't ignore. Bondage was a bitter substitution.

He hated it.

He loathed it.

And he fought it.

It was in little ways mostly. Slowing down the entire group. Dropping his sack of salt in the wrong place. Walking away when one of the lesser overseers was speaking to him as if he didn't hear their voice. Anything that proved to himself that he was still in control, that he was not owned by anyone. He wasn't getting back alive anyway, so nothing mattered anymore.

Sebastian was riding with them today, his horse plodding along behind them. Aki could feel the man's eyes on his back as he shuffled along. Their pace was grueling, thanks to his frequent stumbling and stopping. Already, he could hear the driver at the front yelling at them to pick up the pace. The driver was as malicious a taskmaster as Aki had ever seen but there was grim satisfaction to be had when he watched the man's entire face go red with fury - he was as bound to Mara's quotas as her slaves were and awaited his own punishment at Sebastian's hands if he failed to meet them.

"Halt," Sebastian's voice rang out over their heads.

Aki was the first to oblige, letting his sack fall to the road with a thud and then joining it on the ground. He looked up innocently as Sebastian rode past him. Sebastian eyed him with suspicion and pulled his horse to a stop. Their driver came hurrying down the line to see what the problem was. Aki lowered his head to avoid the man's attention but he needn't have bothered. He was too busy looking at Sebastian, worry plastered on his sweating face, his hands twisting together in nervous anticipation.

"Is there a problem, sir?"

"Unchain him." Sebastian pointed to Aki and Aki felt a twinge of worry, thinking he may have taken it too far this time.

The shackle fell away from his ankle with a clatter and Aki reached down to rub the spot it had been clasped around. The skin was raw, and his hand came away sticky with blood that oozed out of cracks and blisters.

"You may continue down with the rest of them and we will follow."

He'd definitely taken it too far. It didn't matter, he reminded himself. He was dead soon enough anyway and there was no one left for him to protect or care for now that he and Dagmar were separated. He'd rather die making his own decisions than mindlessly obeying others. He watched as the others moved off, their speed instantly greater than it had been with him in tow.

"I'd flog you here now, but then you'd bleed into the salt and ruin the whole sack." Sebastian's hard voice reached him, and he looked up once more at the man. He was no longer on his horse, and he held a length of thin rope in his hand as he came toward where Aki sat still on the ground. "And stop looking at me like you have no idea what you're doing. I've watched you for days now and you know exactly what you're doing. Get up and pick up your load."

Aki was sluggish to obey, and he discovered that even Sebastian's patience had limits. A savage kick in his side sent him sprawling across the road and gasping for air.

"I said, get up. I meant now, as fast as you can."

Aki decided he'd pushed it enough, considering he hadn't even yet received his actual punishment. Rising, he hefted the bag onto his back as before and stood before Sebastian. The man stepped close enough to him that he felt Sebastian's hot breath on his face. It took all of Aki's willpower not to pull away from Sebastian's uncomfortable nearness as it awakened a sense of dread Aki hadn't experienced in years. That could only make his position worse, and Aki had no desire to do that.

Sebastian either didn't notice or didn't care. His deft hands tied one end of the rope around Aki's neck, snug enough that Aki could not draw in a breath or swallow without feeling its coarse constricting fibers. Sebastian returned to his horse and mounted, the other end of the rope in his hand. He wrapped it around the pommel of his saddle and tied it off.

"I will not stop until we reach the harbor and neither will you, whether that means you're strangled or not," he said without even looking back at Aki. He kicked his horse forward and Aki stumbled forward at the tug of the rope.

If Sebastian had been more sadistic, he'd have kept his horse at a trot. Aki was thankful he was not. He followed along willingly enough until they reached town. Here, the humiliation of being led on a collar as if he were some sort of horse or dog was too much. He slowed a little, conscious of the stares that followed him and of his own blood rising to his cheeks.

The slight change in his gait was enough to pull the rope taut and send him stumbling and gasping and choking as the rope tightened around his neck. Without a second thought, Aki dropped his burden and his hands flew to the rope. He managed to right himself and loosen it a little, but by the time he regained his balance it was too late for the sack of salt lying in the street. He opened his mouth to call out to Sebastian. Remembering his words when they started, though, he decided against it. It was an easy matter after that to keep up.

They reached the wharfs a few minutes later and Sebastian pulled his horse to a stop. Aki dutifully halted behind it, his eyes downcast, waiting for the moment Sebastian realized something was amiss.

Sebastian didn't yell. He didn't shout or rage. With his face only inches away from Aki's flinching one, he said in a voice, soft and deadly, "Where is your bag?"

"In the street where I dropped it."

The first blow knocked him off his feet, the second sent him curling into a ball. He heard Sebastian's whip whistle through the air and suddenly realized that he was not quite so ready to die as he thought he was.

"You said you weren't going to stop," he cried out, bringing his hands up to shield his face out of instinct. "You never said anything about if I dropped it."

The whip landed its first strike, but Sebastian didn't hit him again. He stared down at Aki with a strange look on his face. If Aki didn't know any better, he would have thought it was a mixture of surprise and amusement and perhaps a touch of disbelief. The expression was gone with a shake of Sebastian's head. Hauled to his feet once more, Aki was shaken roughly while Sebastian cursed him.

Finally, Sebastian, in the same quiet voice he'd used before, said, "You'd better pray it's where you dropped it, or I'll take the price of it out of your hide."

It wasn't and Aki knew what he had to look forward to upon his return to the mines. Sebastian never lashed out in fits of anger, but he also never made idle threats. When he went to bed that night, his back was on fire from this last whipping.

For the next week, Aki made the same trip no less than nine times a day and always at the end of Sebastian's rope. They started earlier than any of the others and ended far later. On the occasions when he passed the group of slaves that he was supposed to be with, Aki kept his head down. Even if they were only imagined, he didn't want to catch any stares from them.

Aki had just returned from the final trip of the day, staggering the last few paces and falling over, exhausted, before they'd quite reached their destination. After a week of this, his neck was bruised and raw. And he was at the end of his strength.

To his surprise, Sebastian did not simply drag him along. He dismounted and made his way over to where Aki lay panting on the ground, his face pressed into the dirt. The small favor of not being dragged and strangled, as unexpected as it was, hit Aki harder than any blow could. He wanted to weep with relief for such a mercy. Sebastian crouched before him and, with a fistful of Aki's hair, forced his head up off the ground.

As the overseer untied the rope, he whispered so that Aki alone could hear him, "It's my job to break slaves like you. And I always do my job. There's no use fighting it, boy. This is your place now. The sooner you accept it, the better it'll go for you. No one can last forever without breaking."

Aki wanted to scream that this hadn't always been his place, that he knew what it was like to be free. He couldn't accept it. He wouldn't. But he was breaking, he knew. He'd broken before as a child, bent to the will of others without thought or opinion of his own. He never wanted to return to that.

He couldn't tell Sebastian that, and so he said nothing at all.

When Sebastian walked away, leaving him to crawl to the long, low hut that served as their sleeping quarters, he whispered the same thing he'd whispered to himself every other night since their arrival, "No one owns me."

Chapter 43

THE MORNING WAS HOT. The sun was barely risen and already its rays beat down on the world. Aki swallowed the thick, tasteless gruel-like substance that passed for their breakfast, wondering if he was still Sebastian's personal companion for the day. After last night, he wasn't sure. A horse's soft nicker alerted him to Sebastian's presence, and he hurried to scrape his bowl clean before the man came for him.

There was no rope in Sebastian's hands when he beckoned Aki to him. Aki was slow getting to his feet, although it wasn't in defiance this time. He simply didn't have anything left in him. Sebastian must have understood because there was no punishment this time for his sluggishness. The man simply waited patiently until Aki dragged himself to stand in front of the overseer.

Biting his tongue to keep from asking what Sebastian intended, Aki stood under the man's careful study of him. After a moment, Sebastian appeared satisfied.

"Come with me."

"Where?" Aki asked before he could stop himself.

Sebastian mounted his horse and started off down the road without answering. Aki ran several paces to catch up. He didn't bother asking again. Even if his curiosity wasn't going to be immediately satisfied, he could be thankful he was moving without the weight of Sebastian's rope on his neck. Just that tiny bit of freedom was a breath of fresh air.

When they stopped in front of the gates of Mara's mansion, his question was no longer where but why. He hadn't seen Mara since that first day, and he wasn't ready to change that.

The courtyard was almost exactly the way he'd seen it before, only this time there was no fire in the firepit, and the air was filled with the scent of the many flowers that surrounded the yard and grew from window boxes. The sweetness of their fragrance hung heavy in the hot, stagnant air of the courtyard, making it almost too heavy to breathe in.

Sebastian dismounted and motioned for Aki to follow him. They entered the same door Mara had come out of that first day and Aki found himself standing in a large room. The white tiled floor was cool beneath his bare feet, his boots having been destroyed within the first week, the leather so dried and cracked by the salt that they simply fell to pieces, and the air was mild compared to the heat of the outdoors.

Following Sebastian was difficult. Curiosity kept his eyes busy as they passed room after room. In one of them, he caught a glimpse of Dagmar, her hair done up in a headscarf and an apron covering her clothes. She saw him, too, and he tried to smile for her. She at least looked well fed and dressed. Better than I am, Aki thought.

Sebastian paused before a set of double doors, their polished brass hinges and knobs just another sign of the opulence Mara enjoyed here in Karu. Aki caught a glimpse of his own reflection in the bright metal and turned away in disgust from the bedraggled, filthy, half starved version of himself that he saw. A house slave opened one and ushered them inside.

The room was as cool and comfortable as the rest of the house. It was a parlor, he guessed, from the arrangement of stuffed chairs and low tables. Beautifully woven carpets, similar to those Gundar had used in his great hall, covered about half of the floor. Aki positioned himself to stand on one, its soft cushion a welcome luxury for his feet. A moment more and the temptation to sink down onto the soft carpet and rest would have been impossible to overcome.

"Thank you, Sebastian," Mara's voice, as cool as the air in the room, floated across the space, snapping Aki out of his exhausted stupor. "I will speak with you later."

Sebastian bowed his head and left without a word. Mara came forward and sat down in a chair. She motioned for Aki to sit as well. He looked dubious, comparing the amount of dirt he'd carried in with him on his clothes with the immaculate presentation of the room. With a shrug, he obeyed. What did it matter to him if her fine furniture were ruined?

Aki squirmed under Mara's appraising gaze. He'd forgotten the way she did that, staring at a person as if she could see all the way into their soul. It peeled away the layers of defiance and anger he'd built up and reduced him to the vulnerable little boy he'd been once in her service. Knowing Mara, that was probably exactly the way she wanted him.

A door opened off to the side, distracting him from her scrutiny and a serving girl entered balancing a tray in her hands. She was dressed almost identically to Dagmar, the same headscarf and apron, and she was equally beautiful. She set the tray down on the low table between Mara and Aki and dropped into a deep curtsy that Mara completely ignored. Aki's attention was immediately drawn to the contents of the tray - mostly the food, although he would thoroughly enjoy the tea as well.

"I've heard a rumor," Mara began, picking up one of the delicate pastries with two fingers. She frowned down at it as though it was the pastry she was speaking to and not Aki. "Despite the debacle Halle created by aligning with that girl in Dival, some of the men I sent with him have managed to make their way back to me. They tell a different story than the one I was led to believe." She paused, her dark eyes finding Aki's.

He shifted again, trying to ignore the food that was within arm's reach while contemplating how much trouble he'd be in if he just crammed some into his mouth before he could be stopped. He'd be whipped for sure, but it would be on a full stomach. The benefits were beginning to outweigh the punishment when Mara spoke again.

"Halle lives."

She stopped, allowing the silence to speak for her for a few moments, and took a bite of her pastry. Aki shut his eyes, as much to shut out her eating in front of him as to process what she'd just said. Halle alive. Somehow, he'd survived. Just like he had on that mountain. Aki remembered how stunned, and terrified, he'd been to learn that all those years ago.

"Why are you telling me this?" he finally asked when he could stand the silence no longer.

Mara's slender hand darted out, slapping his cheek. It stung and he sat back, blinking rapidly and fighting the urge to bring his own hand up. It was his fault, he supposed. He should have remembered how much Mara hated slaves speaking out of turn. Clenching his hands into fists at his sides, he forced his eyes down, away from her piercing gaze.

"I've been told he is held prisoner inside the home of the Divalian king. I'm sure you know the extent of love I have for my youngest son. He is the only one I have left." Aki's jaw tightened as he remembered. "I want him back, by fair means or by foul. Do you think an exchange would be possible?"

He hesitated this time before realizing that she really did want him to answer. "Who would you exchange?"

"Why, you, of course. You have friends who could and would pressure the king for your return."

"You're wrong. There's no one there that wants me now."

Mara raised her eyebrows in surprise but didn't push. Instead, she poured herself a cup of tea, the corners of her thin mouth pulled down into a thoughtful frown on her face. "Well, if not an exchange, then I will arrange for his escape. You lived in that town. Bren, isn't it? Tell me all about it, how I might get my people in and out again unseen."

"You think I'd help you free him so he can come after me again? I'd rather die."

"Oh no, Aki." Mara smiled at him. For once, there was nothing malicious in her smile. Only mild amusement and pity. Aki looked away. "You do not want to die. It's freedom you crave, not death - although, in some circumstances, I suppose those can feel like the same thing. Sebastian's told me stories of how you've behaved for him. You want to prove that you're still master of your own fate. I have to admit, Aki, I liked you better when you knew your place. Before Gundar filled your head with ideas of being something greater. You're finding it very hard to make yourself so small again."

"That's not..."

"Don't bother lying to me or yourself," she waved his words away, "I know what you want and I'm prepared to give you at least some form of it. I can be quite generous. What is it you would like from me? Food, a different job, a night with one of my girls?"

Aki wanted to say that if she was really generous she'd have offered him some of the food that she was eating or poured him some of the tea she was drinking. Instead, he folded his arms over his chest in a futile effort to create a barrier between himself and the devouring intensity of her eyes and said nothing. Mara could be very generous, but her gifts always came at a steep price. One he was pretty sure he couldn't afford.

"Do you hate me so much, Aki, that you'll refuse me?"

Aki's anger, coiled inside him like a serpent, sprang up at her words. "You beat me. You starved me. You worked me to exhaustion. How could I not hate you?"

"I treated you no different than any other slave." Mara's shock was genuine and that only fueled Aki's anger.

"I was a child," he cried. "As much a human as you."

Mara stared at him, stunned. It was quickly replaced by a cold smile that bore a strong resemblance to Halle's. "Do you know where you really come from, Aki? Gundar was never your father. Not really. Why he kept up that farce is beyond me."

"I know."

"Do you? The only reason you exist is because your father, Anton, raped a slave girl ..."

"Stop."

"... and felt so guilty that when she cried, ..."

"Enough," he whispered.

"... begging him not to kill her unborn child, he gave in to her. You were a mistake. You were the salve to his guilty conscience. And both your parents are dead because of you. No, you're not the same as me and you never have been. The only life you're fit for is the one I'm giving you. So stop fighting it and take it."

Aki pressed his shaking hands flat against his thighs in the hopes of stilling them. He stared at the colorful carpet on the floor in front of him as Mara's words rang in his ears. They were there no matter how he tried to shut them out, no matter how he tried to refute them in his head. And they were true. Every last one of them.

Mara must have taken his silence as defeat because her face softened once more, and she leaned forward. She traced gentle fingers down the side of his face, a caress he'd often seen her give Halle.

He recoiled, the memory of her slap still stinging his cheek. In a way, her soft touch was worse, more violating than her strike. It toyed with him, promising something kinder, something gentler. But it never lasted. Just enough to awaken a desire for such things and then it was snatched away again, leaving him wanting, always wanting. And he hated that craving. Better to never experience even a hint of kindness than to be left with a crumb of it and desiring more.

"You hate me so much, Aki, but I'm not the one who made you this. Your parents did that. I told Gundar he should have just killed you then and there. It would have spared you all of this. Let me show you that I'm not your enemy. Tell me what it is you want, and I'll give it to you, even if you never tell me what I want you to."

He pulled his eyes up from the carpet and met hers. They were just like Halle's - cold, calculating. There was something else in them too. Pity. Genuine pity. He considered her offer and decided it couldn't hurt to accept. She was right. This was his place, had always been his place. The years he'd spent in Dival were just a reprieve, not a reality.

"I want time alone with Dagmar," he whispered.

Mara's eyes widened a little. "The girl you came with?"

He nodded, unable to speak anymore.

"You'll have it," she said, sitting back and gesturing toward the tray, "but perhaps you should eat first."

Even despair couldn't stop his hunger. Aki didn't wait for her to change her mind as he devoured the remaining food and washed it down with two cups of the hot tea. He'd regret it later, he knew. It was too much food after weeks of so little, but the feeling of being full for at least a few minutes was worth it.

Mara watched him closely as he ate. "You're like him, you know."

Aki paused, his mouth too full to answer, but she understood the confused look on his face.

"Your father. Your real father, Anton. Always wanting what he couldn't have. It's why he had to die. Accept your place, Aki."

Aki understood the threat, understood the veiled meaning of her words. But he wanted desperately to ask her for more - more about his father, his mother, what they were like, and why they weighed his life against their own and found his worth more. He didn't dare ask and by then the food was gone anyway.

The room he was escorted to was a small bedroom on the second story. Compared to what he'd seen of the rest of the house, it was plain. It lacked all the lavish furnishings and bright colors that adorned the other rooms. A simple carpet, a bed, and a table and chair in front of the window made up the room.

Without a thought to the dirt he would leave behind, Aki sat on the bed, leaning his back against the headboard and drawing his knees up to his chest. His fingers traced the brands on his arm, the most recent one just barely healed. With a sigh, he pillowed his head in his arms and shut his eyes, stealing a few moments of rest.

He must have actually dozed off because he didn't hear the door as it opened, and Dagmar stepped inside.

"Really, Aki?" her voice was sharp as he raised his head a moment later. "I wouldn't have thought you'd do this."

"What?" Aki rubbed a hand over his eyes. Blinking, he took in her stiff posture and betrayed look and realized what she thought. He shook his head. "Oh no, no. It's not like that. Mara asked what I wanted, and I told her I wanted to see you alone. I just wanted to talk to you."

Dagmar sat on the bed, a rueful smile pushing away her offended countenance. She tipped her head to the side as she studied him.

"You look awful."

"Thanks."

"No. That didn't come out right. Are you alright?"

It was his turn to smile. It was a bitter one, even if he didn't mean it to be. "Never better. Don't I look it? You

262

look well, though. I guess Mara doesn't starve her house slaves quite the same as she does her mining ones."

Dagmar lowered her head. "It's not quite as good as it seems, Aki," she said softly. "She may keep us well fed but it's only because she gives us as rewards to her overseers. Anytime they meet their quotas or do something else that pleases her."

"I'm sorry, I shouldn't have said anything about it. I didn't know."

"I'd rather not talk about it. Besides, you are worse off, still. I've seen you a few times this last week in town. What did you do?"

"You saw that?" Dagmar nodded. "I guess I'm not as a good a slave as I used to be. That's over now, though. I think."

They sat quietly for a few minutes, Aki too disheartened and weary to think of something to say, his conversation with Mara too heavy to push away. Dagmar looked as if she wanted to say something but couldn't quite bring herself to do it.

"What is it?" Aki's curiosity finally won out and he asked.

"We should run. Ships leave the harbor all the time. It wouldn't be too hard to get on one. We could figure it out from there, find our way back to Dival. I can get out of the house easily enough. They send me to town for errands all the time."

Aki shook his head. "I can't. Remember?" He pointed to his chest where his torn shirt still hung open, gesturing to the scar on it. "If I'm caught running again, they'll kill me. And do you have any idea how they do it here? Sebastian told me, in great detail, yesterday when he thought I was staring at the sea for too long. And it's quite awful and slow and something I never want to go through. Besides, they might let you out easily, but I'm almost always on a chain, once again, thanks to this," he tapped a finger on the mark.

"I didn't forget, Aki. How could I? I just thought..."

"I know. I'm sorry. Maybe you can make it. You should. If you see a chance, don't worry about me, just take it and get out." He hoped she couldn't read the despair his own words caused him. The thought of her leaving him behind, leaving him to suffer, was unbearable. But he was too ashamed to beg her to give up the whole matter. He had no right to ask her to stay in this misery just so that he had company.

Dagmar drew her legs up under her and stared out the window. Without turning to look at him, she said, "If you won't run, why keep fighting them? It just makes everything worse. Wouldn't it be easier to just do what you're told without a fight?"

Aki couldn't explain that fighting was what kept him from despair. It didn't matter, anyway. After his conversation with Mara, Aki was done. If this was to be his life, he would have to find some way to swallow his own existence and accept that he was nothing more than property, born to serve and please those greater than himself.

There really didn't seem to be anything else to say on the subject after that but the silence was awkward and he knew Dagmar wasn't saying anything else because she didn't want to upset him, didn't want to make him feel worse than he clearly already felt. But even without words, he could sense her concern about him.

"Do you ever think about home?" Dagmar asked. She brushed the palm of her hand along the soft quilt spread across the bed, not meeting Aki's gaze.

"Yes. Mostly I just think about how I wish I'd have just told the truth. To everyone. I wish I'd just gone to Sasha and told, and to Stephan, and to Master Wehr. And then maybe we wouldn't be here. I was so afraid of what they'd think. And maybe they would have hated me, but they wouldn't have done this to me."

"They wouldn't have hated you...,"

"Maybe not, but it's easier to think that they would. It makes me not miss home so much."

"Do you want anything while you're in here? Food, maybe?" Dagmar asked, changing the subject abruptly.

"Am I allowed?" he asked, surprised.

"This is supposed to be a reward, or a gift. Mara is very generous with such things. So, now's your chance, if you do want something."

264

Aki smiled, "I don't think I could handle any more food at the moment. I ate everything in sight when Mara offered it a bit ago, and I feel like vomiting it up now."

"Get some sleep, then. I can see you need it. I'll make sure to wake you when it's time," she said, getting up and moving to the chair.

Aki didn't need any encouragement. He didn't even bother to lay down, simply leaning his head against the headboard and closing his eyes.

The only thing his impromptu nap did for him was make his body stiff and sore when he tried to move. It did nothing to clear his head, or shake the cloud of misery that hung over him, and it certainly didn't make up for the punishing work schedule he'd been forced to keep. Dagmar had slipped out of the room as soon as she was sure he was awake, whispering a goodbye that he was too drowsy to acknowledge.

Now, he was following his escort back down the stairs into the same parlor he'd been in before. Mara looked as if she hadn't moved in the last two hours. She didn't invite him to sit this time. She looked him up and down and he wanted to shrink away the same way he'd done as a child.

"I've given it some thought, and I believe I'll get the most use out of you if you are here rather than in the mines. Oliver here," she gestured to the man who'd brought him down, "will go over what's expected of you. I trust you'll give him more deference than you did Sebastian."

Aki wasn't sure if the move was supposed to be some gift on her part, or a punishment.

Chapter 44

AKI SCANNED THE BUSY wharf, looking for nothing in particular and finding exactly that. In his hands, he carried the large basket that was quickly filling with goods from the market. Dolores, the older woman in charge of Mara's kitchens, was ahead of him haggling over the price of fish.

Somewhere nearby, Oliver lurked. Mara had apparently forgotten that he was a runaway, agreeing immediately to Dolores' request for him to accompany her into town to help carry everything. Oliver had not. It didn't matter. After Sebastian's detailed explanation of Karu's slave execution practices, there wasn't a chance in the world that Aki would try to run. Mara was right about that, at least. He didn't want to die. Certainly not the way they would kill him.

A small smile came to his face as he thought of how annoyed Sebastian would be to see how much more compliant he was now that he was part of Mara's household staff. It didn't have anything to do with the move, though. Mara had been right again. This was what he was and there was no point fighting it anymore.

The sky was bright blue and cloudless, yet another day in a long stretch of days without rain or relief from summer's heat. If anything, Aki thought it was a bit hotter than the day before. He shifted his hold on the basket enough to bring one hand up and wipe away the sweat that was gathering on his forehead. Since his hand was equally sweaty, it didn't change much. The sweltering blanket of heat made the fish smell more pungent, the odor hanging in the heavy, humid air and overpowering everything else.

Dolores threw her hands up in exasperation ahead of him and started toward another fisherman. Apparently, they couldn't reach an agreeable price. Aki sighed. This was the fourth one Dolores had walked away from and his chores were still waiting for him when he got back. Oliver had made that very clear. At this rate he would be working late into the night to finish. Shifting his hold on the basket, he followed her at a distance, close enough to be there when she needed him, but far enough away that he didn't have to listen to every word of the bartering.

There were a lot of ships coming and going, thanks to the spell of calm weather. Aki watched out of boredom as a medium sized one pulled up alongside the dock, the sailors tossing their mooring lines to the men working the docks. They were close enough that he could catch some of their words as they shouted back and forth. The basket almost slid out of his hands as he realized that he understood the men on the ship and not because they spoke Aruuken.

All the times he'd been down to the wharfs, he had never seen a ship from Dival. He'd just assumed they had no trade agreements with Karu. But sure enough, when he looked up at the flag above, he recognized it was the same one that flew above the academy and the castle. His feet took him closer without his bidding, drawn to the familiar language and the comfort of being so near something from home. He tried to hear everything they were saying.

A hand clamped heavily on his shoulder and Aki spun around to find himself staring into the eyes of Oliver. With horror, he realized how far he'd wandered.

"I wasn't running," he said, but even as he said it he knew Oliver wouldn't believe him because Oliver had already decided what he believed. He looked around for Dolores in the desperate hope that she would vouch for him, but she was nowhere to be found.

As if reading his thoughts, Oliver said, "She's three docks down and hadn't noticed that you're missing yet last time I checked."

"I wasn't running," Aki repeated. He wondered if he would have, though, given the chance. If he had made it to the ship without being seen, would he have dared beg the crew to take him onboard and hide him and take him home again. Would he have been brave enough to risk it? Callous enough to leave Dagmar behind? He gave one last look over his shoulder at the ship. No one on her deck had even noticed him and Oliver.

"Let's go," Oliver said.

Guided through the crowd by Oliver's ever-present hand, they caught up to Dolores. Aki stood mute while Oliver told Dolores of his attempted escape - he made it sound like so much more than it was. Then they were headed back up the long road to Mara's, each step harder than the last. The heavy basket was still in his hands. Apparently, even a runaway had to finish their current task. Aki barely noticed its weight, though. Oliver's hand on his arm seemed the heavier of the two at the moment.

Oliver didn't bring him into the house but left him in the courtyard to wait while he went in. Aki knew he was doomed then. If Oliver had the chance to tell his story, Mara would never listen to Aki's. He was not kept waiting long. Mara swept out a few minutes later, her face a mask to anyone who didn't know her. But Aki knew the look. She was furious. And her fury meant there would be no chance to reason with her.

"This is how you repay me? After all that I've done for you?"

Since the only thing Aki wanted to say would only serve to make things worse, he remained silent. Mara had a funny idea about what kindness was. She always had.

"I should have left you in the mines."

"I wasn't running," he whispered in a voice that was hollow with impending horror.

"I wish I could believe you," Mara cupped his face in her hand, her mask changing slightly to let in a fragment of pity, "but you lie so easily. You always have." She looked past him to Oliver. "Take him. Turn him over to the magistrate."

Hands grabbed both his arms. He fought against them as he called out, "Mara, I wasn't running. Please, Mara. Believe me. You have to believe me."

Mara shut her eyes and turned away as if the scene pained her and maybe in some strange way it did. "There's nothing I can do. The law is clear."

Aki was dragged, struggling, backward toward the gate. The last thing he noticed before they passed through it and left the courtyard was a door flying open and Dagmar standing on the wide porch, staring after him in shock.

The road back to town was long and Aki made it even longer for Oliver and the other man who held him. He fought every step, pulling against their grasp. Several times he managed to drag them down with him when he let his entire weight sink to the ground. Each time he was hauled back to his kicking, scrambling feet. He barely felt when they hit him, which was often. All he could think about was the manner of execution that awaited him and how much he did not want to die.

When they reached town, Aki was drenched in sweat and gasping for breath, but so were the men with him. They went straight for the center of town, the marketplace. Aki hadn't noticed the whipping post there before but he did now. When he saw that they meant to bring him there, he dug his feet into the dirt road again and succeeded in freeing his right arm from Oliver's grasp. Spinning around, he tried to pry the other man's hand off. If he was going to be executed for an escape attempt that never happened, he might as well really try to escape.

Oliver's arms closed around him from behind, pinning his own to his sides, and lifted him back. The second man landed two punches on his stomach and he doubled over, gasping, heaving. By the time he'd recovered enough to stand upright, they once more had a hold of his arms. They dragged him inexorably toward the post.

Their hold shifted allowing Oliver to fasten both his wrists together with the rope that dangled down. Pulling the other end of it, he lifted Aki's arms high above his head until his feet barely brushed the ground and he was pressed against the wooden post.

While they went in search of the magistrate, Aki struggled to bring his breathing back under control. At the moment, every breath sent a stabbing pain through his side and he was heaving. Ignoring the fact that he was turning himself into a spectacle for anyone around, he twisted his wrists and pulled hard against his bonds, trying to free himself from the rough rope but there was no give in the knots. All he succeeded in doing was tearing open the skin of his wrists.

The magistrate and Oliver returned quicker than he expected. Apparently, runaway slaves were considered a great menace to the island of Karu and needed to be dealt with expediently. Aki was still panting, his limbs still trembling from the exertion he'd just put them through when he turned his head around to see the man.

"You're the runaway?" the man asked.

"I wasn't running away," he protested between gasps, still tugging against the rope.

"He is," Oliver said. "Delivered to you for punishment by Mara Wendlen. He already bears the mark of a runaway." Oliver twisted Aki away from the post a little and pulled away the remnants of Aki's shirt enough for the magistrate to see the crude, ugly scar on his chest.

Aki's protests were as useless as his struggles to free himself. He shut his eyes as the magistrate began speaking with the boredom of a man who'd repeated the same task a thousand times over.

"As this is your second attempt, it will be your final. You will receive the customary sentence of flogging and death by strangulation."

"It's a lie," Aki whispered, more to himself than for the benefit of the others. "It's a lie," he repeated, but no one was listening anymore, and even if they were, no one believed him.

What was left of his shirt was torn off and Aki braced himself for the pain he knew was about to come. He wasn't afraid of pain. Not the way Halle had always been afraid of it. But he couldn't keep his breath from hitching as he watched the magistrate unfurl the coiled whip in his hand. His back bore scars from enough other beatings that he knew exactly what to expect. As the whip whistled through the air, he tensed, sucked in a sharp breath and gritted his teeth. He wasn't sure if it was a comfort or not knowing that he would not be whipped to death here, that it would only be enough to weaken him for his execution.

When the magistrate finished, Aki leaned his whole weight against the wooden post, reeling from the agony.

Rivulets of blood trickled down his back, staining the dirt beneath his feet. He was left alone, the magistrate saying something about making preparations - Aki assumed for his own execution. The pain in his back was sufficient enough to cloud all his thoughts, even the ones surrounding the death he faced.

Without the motion of the whip to keep them away, flies descended on the open wounds in clouds. They were their own form of torment and Aki couldn't move enough to shake them off. All through the long, hot afternoon, he stood bound to the post, shifting as much as he could to rid himself of the swarms of flies. It was a losing battle. His blood called to them, promising a feast. It was almost a relief when the magistrate arrived near sunset to collect him. He had another man with him, a slave Aki realized as he caught sight of the brand on his arm. Between the two of them, they dragged him away from the whipping post and down towards the sea.

After the fight he'd put up coming here in the first place it was almost laughable how easily he went along with them now. Every step made all the nerves in his body scream and Aki couldn't fathom moving more than what was absolutely necessary. Besides, Sebastian had told him what came next, and if the man was telling the truth, Aki needed as much strength as he could muster.

Off to the side of the busy harbor, out of sight of the ships that came and went, a weathered wooden post stood about waist high. Surrounded by rocks that sloped away into the sea, it was sunk deep into the ground. There were two iron rings protruding from it - one at the very top, facing the land, the other a little lower and facing the sea. Aki took the sight in as they approached and determined that Sebastian had been honest with him and not just making an idle and exaggerated threat.

He was maneuvered to the seaward side of the post and forced to sit on the large rock there, his torn back pressed against the wood. He arched his back, trying to pull away from the splintering wood.

The magistrate worked quickly and efficiently, obviously experienced with carrying out this particular form of execution. He pulled Aki's arms up over his head and behind the post, chaining them to the hook with almost no slack. The strain created on his back and shoulders was enough to elicit a cry of pain from Aki who had otherwise managed to stay quiet.

A thin, short rope appeared in the magistrate's hands, and he knelt beside Aki to tie a noose of sorts around his neck. He pulled it snug but not tight and secured the other end to the iron ring just behind his head.

"You decide how long this takes," the magistrate said, his voice casual as if he were explaining how to perform a certain job. "Let your weight pull on this and it tightens like this," he gave it a quick tug to demonstrate. Aki's eyes widened as his breath was cut off. The magistrate loosened it again to where it had been.

"I didn't do it. I wasn't trying to run away," Aki said, unable to keep a tremor from creeping into his voice. "You don't have to do this to me."

The magistrate shook his head with the weariness of a man who had listened to the same words over and over again from different people. With a final inspection of his work, he rose.

Alone, Aki blinked back the tears of despair that stung his eyes.

He was going to die.

Here on this wretched island of rock. Here, alone, with no chance to make right any of the many wrongs he'd committed in his life. He was going to die.

Aki pulled his feet up, bracing them as close to his body as he could get them. The surface of the rock was rough and parts of it cut into his bare feet, but that pain was completely lost in the flood of terror and desire that filled him. Mara was right. He didn't want to die. Even as his shredded back rubbed against the rough wood and flies picked at his flesh, he wanted to live.

With the coming of darkness, the first cold waves of seawater lapped at his feet. The tide was rising. Each passing hour it came higher and higher, drenching him and making it near impossible to keep himself from slipping away. His arms were useless in holding him up. Any strain on them sent white hot agony tearing through him. The water tugged at his body, pulling him away from the post, pulling the noose on his neck a little tighter each time. It crept up his back and he hissed as the salt water stung in his open wounds. As exhaustion set in, Aki wondered how easy it would be to just let go entirely and let the sea and the noose work together to end his life.

But he wanted to live.

Chapter 45

DAGMAR DARED TO FOLLOW Mara inside.

"You can't do this to him. It's not like you think," she called out to her mistress.

Mara stopped walking and turned to face her, a bit surprised at her insolence in speaking out. Dagmar lowered her eyes immediately, unnerved by her own behavior. Keeping her head down was the only way to survive a place like this.

"Oh, please explain."

"The mark he has, he doesn't deserve it. It was supposed to be for me, but he made a deal with Halle on the ship. He only did it to protect me. He never tried to run."

"A deal he shouldn't have made but did. Now he has to face the consequences of it. Imagine if I let every slave come up with an excuse like that one. There'd be utter mayhem. Perhaps you'd like to take his place, instead?"

"No. I just... Please, I'm begging you, don't do this. He doesn't deserve it."

"It's out of my hands." Mara started to walk away again. She called over her shoulder, "And if you get any ideas of trying to help him, you'll take his place, understand?"

Mara didn't wait for an answer and when she disappeared, Dagmar had no choice but to resume her work. The other slaves who'd witnessed the exchange pretended they hadn't noticed, and Dagmar tried to copy their indifference. It was impossible to do after she asked one of them what awaited Aki. The answer was too awful to contemplate. She'd stared in horror at the woman explaining it to her. The woman shrugged and said, "He shouldn't have tried to run. One time is bad enough, two is unforgivable. Best if he ends it as quick as he can, though."

For the rest of the day and all of the next, Dagmar was not among those chosen to run errands into town. She suspected it had something to do with her protests. In a way, she was glad. She didn't want to witness any part of it. It was better if she didn't have to see him dying.

Her luck ran out the following morning when Dolores sent her into town with a list of things she needed for the day. Dagmar took her time on the road, the memory of Mara's threat fresh in her mind. The day was as hot as the last two weeks had been, the sun scorching with unrelenting strength and the streets were busy, full of not just townspeople but sailors from the ships that lay anchored in the harbor. Dagmar always hated walking through this town but it was worse now that the trading season was at its height.

Leaving one shop and heading to the next, she had to cross the marketplace square. The pens were filling up for the weekly auction that would be held the next day. She looked away and was met with a sight of the whipping post and the blood that had only recently dried there. Aki's blood. She hurried on, head down, until a conversation reached her ears. She froze. Oliver and the magistrate stood in front of one of the vendor's stalls, talking.

"She wants you to end it quickly. She's upset that he's still alive," Oliver was saying. Dagmar stepped closer to hear the magistrate's response.

"If he's still alive when I check on him at sunset, I'll break his legs. You can tell Mara he'll be dead by morning but that's the most I can promise," the magistrate answered. "She doesn't run everything here, you know."

Dagmar put a hand over her mouth and turned away. For a long time, she crouched against the wall, out of the way and hidden from sight while tears slid silently down her face. Part of her couldn't believe that Aki could possibly still be alive. She thought it would be over by now. Instead, it was only going to get worse.

"I'm so sorry. I'm so, so sorry," she whispered to herself. The words were empty sounds without their intended hearer, but it made her feel better to say them.

When the sun showed midday was nearing, she brushed the tears away with her apron and hurried to finish. She didn't want to come home late and have Mara think that she'd tried to help him.

She'd only just rounded the next corner when a hand gripped her arm. Too miserable now to make herself care about anything other than what she'd overheard, she didn't scream but turned and raised dull, red eyes to see who it was. He raised a finger to his lips and pulled her out of the street into a doorway.

"Sasha?" she whispered, stunned and then, before he had time to react, she threw her arms around him. He stiffened but didn't push her away. "Oh, Sasha. How did you find us?"

"Well," he pulled away now, his face troubled, "so far, I've only found you. But Halle's the one who told me where they were taking you both. Do you know where Aki is?"

Dagmar nodded.

Sasha looked at her more closely. "You were crying. Are you alright?"

"Aki didn't think you would come," Dagmar said, evading his question.

"Where is he? We'll get both of you out."

"It won't be that easy, Sasha. He's... they're killing him." She explained as quickly as she could what had happened and where he was now. Sasha listened without interrupting, only nodding along.

"We'll get him as soon as it's dark. There must be some way to sneak up without being seen."

"You don't understand, Sasha. He won't make it that long. He's been fighting it for two days and if he's still alive this evening, they're going to break his legs so he can't hold himself up anymore. Mara wants them to finish it quickly. He'll be dead by the time the sun goes down."

"Then I'll get him now," he said, turning as if to go that very second.

Dagmar grabbed his arm to stop him. She opened her mouth to speak and then shut it again, biting down on her lip.

276

"What is it?"

"There is a way," she said slowly, weighing her words carefully. "You'll need me to do it, but if it works, he'll either be returned to Mara's or put in tomorrow's auction if she decides he's not worth keeping - which is likely considering the condition he'll be in. Either way, you'll be able to get to him."

"What about you?"

"You'll have to come for me after you get him. Or better yet, I'll meet you here, in town. After tomorrow's auction. If he's sold there, we can leave then. If Mara takes him back, I'll figure out a way to get you into the house for him."

"Are you sure? Won't you be in danger?"

Dagmar didn't answer right away, but when she did there was no wavering or indecision in her voice. "I'll be fine. It's only until tomorrow. Just promise me, you'll get him first. Don't meet me until he's on that ship with you."

"Alright."

"Promise me? He comes first. No matter what."

"I promise, but we're getting both of you. I'm not leaving until you're both on that ship."

Dagmar smiled and nodded. "I should go and you should look like you're doing something other than planning an escape."

Sasha started away, but she pulled him back one more time.

"If he is in that auction, it might be better if someone other than you gets him, if you know what I mean. I don't think he'll have the strength to keep himself from reacting, and people could get suspicious."

"Like they did with my mother? I think I can arrange that. Don't forget, you're meeting me here when it's over."

"I won't. Now go."

Dagmar waited until Sasha had disappeared. Even after that, she didn't move. It took a long time before she worked up the courage that she needed to take that first step. Instead of heading back to Mara's she found a shop that sold writing materials. Using the leftover money, she purchased enough to write a single letter. Finding a spot suitable for the task was harder, but she finally found an upturned crate that provided enough of a surface for what she needed. When the ink dried, she folded the paper into as small a square as she could manage. Two more stops and the rest of Mara's money was spent.

Now came the part she dreaded. She'd wanted to get through this trip to town without having to see Aki, but that couldn't happen. Her basket resting in the bend of her arm, she started in his direction.

With a glance at the harbor guard who patrolled the area, she approached the post. The tide was receding and covered only a few inches of him as he sat there, his legs drawn up against his chest.

At first, she was afraid he was already dead. His chin had sunk to his chest and his body seemed devoid of any life. It wasn't until she was standing right in front of him that she saw the slight rise and fall of his chest and knew he was still holding on to his life. His eyes were half shut and each breath he drew in was shallow and wheezing. Blood, both dried and fresh, ran down his face from where birds of prey had come to stake an early claim. The water sloshing up against him came away red with blood from his back that never had a chance to close up.

She crouched in front him, her own feet getting wet in the process, and ran her finger across the thin rope around his neck. It was pulled so tight that she couldn't imagine how he was still drawing in any air. The skin beneath it was torn, the rope slowly sinking into his flesh, while the skin above and below it was swollen over top of the rope.

"Oh, Aki," she whispered in horror.

Her voice and touch seemed to rouse him. He lifted his head slightly and tried to open his eyes. "Shouldn't... here. Go," he rasped out, almost no sound left in his voice.

"Here," Dagmar unscrewed the cap of the water flask and held it to his lips with one hand. With the other hand she tried to loosen the rope on his neck. It only moved a fraction of what she wanted it to, its fibers too much a part of the swollen skin and bloody scab now. He swallowed only a little of it, most of it running down his chin and joining the sea water.

"Go," he repeated, his voice no stronger for the water and Dagmar began to worry that he wouldn't even make it long enough for her plan. "Please... go. Let... die."

Brushing away the tears that threatened again, Dagmar shook her head. When she spoke, her words were slow, measured. "You're not going to die, Aki. You're going to live. You're going to live and go home and you're going to get a chance to make everything right. You're going to live because you have a lot to live for. And when you see Sasha, you're going to give him this," she reached around and pushed the folded piece of paper into his swollen and unresisting fingers, forcing them to close around it with her own hand. Whether he comprehended her words fully or not, when she pulled her hand away, his fingers remained clenched around the paper and she was satisfied. She undid her headscarf and poured some of the water onto it, then lifted it to his face, wiping away some of the blood and revealing the deep red of the sunburned skin beneath. "It's going to be alright, Aki. You just have to hang on a little bit longer."

"You... can't... do this," he croaked.

Dagmar smiled through her tears, "You can't stop me."

And that was when she heard the harbor guard shout.

Chapter 46

AKI HAD NEVER WISHED TO die as much as he did now.

And yet, every time the rope constricted tighter, a desperate, wild desire to live filled him and refused to let him just give in. Every time the tide came in and pulled against him, he found a part of him that had to fight it. For two long, long days, he'd fought it. He was losing the battle, though. Whatever strength that kept him holding on was waning. He was no longer aware of anything save the dull sense of impending end.

Death was not far when Dagmar's voice pulled him back to the light. Seeing her there, although his eyes didn't see much of anything beyond a blur, he couldn't quite remember who she was. It had taken him far too long to think of her name, and even longer to think of why she couldn't be there. He'd barely comprehended anything she said until she mentioned Sasha. The name confused him, especially when she gave him instructions for when he saw Sasha. He wished he could speak enough to tell her that Sasha was a long way away and there wasn't the slightest chance of him ever seeing him again. And Sasha wouldn't want to see him again, anyway, not after finding out what he'd done. But the most he could do was tell her to go.

She didn't listen right away. She stayed and wiped his face with a cool, moist cloth. Since he'd done nothing but sit, unprotected, beneath the fierce rays of the sun, his skin was blistering and red with sunburn. The cloth brought cooling relief, even if it was only fleeting. He'd wanted to beg for her to keep it on him when she finally pulled it away, but by then the guard was there and his relief was at an end. He was only vaguely aware of the guard's yelling above his head. He hoped Dagmar wouldn't be in too much trouble.

He lost all sense of time after that, although his body continued to react every time he slumped in exhaustion and started to doze. He'd drop off just long enough to feel the pressure tightened and his body forced him awake, forced him to fight against it. Each time filled him with an uncontrollable panic until he managed to brace his feet once more.

The sun was getting low in the sky, its brilliance now directly in front of his eyes since he was facing west. He no longer bothered to turn his face away from it the way he had the first day. It no longer mattered.

Voices drifted towards him.

Hands that felt like both ice and sand against his burning skin undid the chains that held his wrists in place. Aki let out a breathless, noiseless cry as his arms, so long held in one position, dropped limply to his sides. The knot holding his noose to the post was released and Aki slumped over not caring that his head smacked against a hard, sharp rock in his fall. The same hands took hold of his wrists and dragged him across the rocks away from the post.

Aki screamed silently as his joints came alive with agony. The new sensation, while fiery enough to bring tears to his eyes, also brought him closer to awareness. And awareness was a horrible thing. It was a burning, throbbing, aching thing.

Lying on his side, his head resting on the rocks, he forced his eyes open. Through the film that covered them, he saw Dagmar held by the same man who'd helped put him there. She didn't look at him. She didn't look at anyone, only stared straight ahead at the sea as if there was something there that no one else could see. When the magistrate brought her in front of the post, she sat without a fight. Aki tried to push himself up but couldn't so much as lift his head.

"No," he mouthed the word over and over again, suddenly remembering why he'd gone through all of it. If he'd had anything left in him, he would have cried. He pushed enough air out to whisper her name but the breeze carried it away like a wisp of smoke.

The magistrate finished and came to stand over Aki. He heard the brief exchange that took place over his head.

"What are we doing with him?"

"Auction tomorrow. Mara doesn't want him back. Says he's not worth it anymore."

Although it was his fate being discussed, Aki could think only of Dagmar now sitting in his place. He stared at her, trying to figure out what had happened. Trying to figure out why.

His arms were pulled up again and draped over the shoulders of the two men as they half carried him. His feet, already cut to pieces, drug in the dirt behind them. He couldn't even manage an attempt at walking. The fragment of strength still inside him served one purpose and one purpose only. In his hand he held the letter Dagmar had put there. Whatever happened, he would not let go of that.

The sun was low when they reached the marketplace. Oliver was waiting for them, as was the auctioneer. Aki was dumped on the ground at Oliver's feet. The man knelt beside Aki, a wet cloth in his hand and began wiping away all the blood from Aki's face. He was rough and Aki's burnt, blistered skin suffered for it, but Aki could make no sound, could not pull away.

When Oliver was satisfied, he pulled a worn, threadbare shirt over Aki's head, forcing his arms into the sleeves. It was a pointless and painful gesture. Anyone who saw him in the auction the next day would be able to see how bad off he was even with a shirt covering the worst of his wounds.

Water was poured into his mouth but he could only swallow a small portion of it. A thin gruel came next and he fared even worse with it but it never seemed to occur to any of the men around him that the noose still encircling his neck needed to come off. Not even when he repeatedly brought his free hand up and feebly tried to pull it off himself.

The auctioneer exhibited the greatest amount of patience with feeding him, putting the tiniest of bites in his mouth so that he could manage to swallow them down.

Eventually, even he tired of the process and Aki was once again lifted up.

He recognized the inside of the men's slave pen as he was lowered to the ground and the iron collar fitted over his neck, completely covering the rope that was already there. The beam was just low enough that he could lean his head back against it.

For the first time in two days, Aki managed to sleep. It was fitful, interrupted often by a breathless panic that drove him to claw at the collar, trying to get his fingers under the iron band to loosen the rope beneath it. But it was sleep, and he was desperate for it.

Morning found him only slightly better off than the night before. He was given water and gruel again, getting a bit more down this time and he was attempting to doze again when voices interrupted him.

The auctioneer was moving through the pen with another man by his side. By his clothes, Aki guessed the man to be a sailor. He stopped at each slave and examined them. Aki turned away, listless and weary. He doubted very much that they would find anyone willing to pay money for him. His body was a wreck. But even if that was healed - a possibility that seemed very remote and impossible at the moment - he had nothing left inside him. Nothing but the empty, gnawing realization that his life was once again spared at the price of another's, and he wasn't worth that.

When they reached him, the sailor grabbed him by the hair and tipped his head back. Aki could only open his eyes about halfway and it was easier to keep them shut, so that was what he did as the man looked him over. At the moment, he couldn't even work up enough curiosity to study the stranger who might become his new master.

"What's the matter with him?"

"Not much, he got a beating the other day but otherwise he's fine," the auctioneer lied smoothly.

The man dropped to a crouch in front of Aki and lifted the back of his shirt up enough to get a good look at his back. Aki tried to pull away from that only because it caused him more pain. There was nowhere for him to go, and the man still had a firm hold of his shoulder.

"You won't get much for him. But I'll buy him now if you'll let me."

"No sales before auction. What's the hurry?"

"I lost a couple men in a storm before I blew in here. I didn't plan on having to replace them any time soon so I'm not looking to spend a lot of money and I'd like to set sail with the tide this morning."

"Sorry. Like I said, no sales before the auction."

The man nodded, frowning and Aki watched them leave the pen. Although the man had spoken Aruuken, he spoke it with the halting awkwardness of someone who had barely learned it. Aki wondered idly where he was from.

The auction was mostly abstract to him since he wasn't in a position to see anything that happened. When they came to get him, he was surprised to find that, although they were weak and trembled uncontrollably beneath him, he could use his legs. They tied his hands behind him before bringing him out of the pen, a wholly unnecessary action as far as Aki was concerned. He couldn't do anything even if he wanted to.

Aki stumbled twice climbing the steps onto the platform and once more as he was crossing it. If the auctioneer were trying to convince everyone that he was capable of working, Aki was destroying the facade. His eyes, which still saw everything through a thin film, took in the crowd before him. If he weren't already beyond caring, he would have been humiliated. But nothing mattered anymore. He was dead inside even if his body refused to accept it. Dagmar was dead or dying and he was alone and likely on his way to an entirely different country. The auctioneer forced his head up so that they could get a good look at him and then he started the bidding.

It hardly came as a surprise to Aki that he was sold for almost nothing to the same sailor who'd offered to buy him earlier that morning. It was fitting really, how little he was worth in that auction. Truthfully, the man was overpaying for him.

He allowed himself to be led down the steps again and to the money keeper's table where the transaction would be completed. Aki finally raised his eyes and studied the face of his new master as the man counted out his money. It was a weathered face, exposed to the elements for many years. To Aki's surprise, there was no lurking cruelty in his eyes. The man turned to him when he was done and took hold of one arm.

"Let's go," he commanded, and Aki obeyed.

Aki made it as far as the deck of the ship. As it rocked beneath his already trembling legs, he collapsed, his knees hitting the wood with a loud smack. He curled up into himself, waiting for his new master to kick him for his clumsiness.

"Get up," his master ordered, standing behind him.

When Aki tried and failed, his master reached a hand down and grabbed the back of his shirt to pull him up. Still holding him, he shoved Aki forward and into his own cabin.

His new master called over his shoulder to the men behind him, "Tell him I've got him in my quarters."

Here, his master released his tight grip and Aki dropped once more to his knees. There was a shuffling of feet behind him as someone else came through the doorway. A pair of hands worked to loosen the knots that bound his own. A moment later, the rope was off one hand and Aki brought it to his throat, clawing once more at the noose that still strangled him.

"Get it off. Please. Get it off," he whispered, hoping to find more pity from his new master. His fingers desperately searched for a way to pull it free. He grew more hysterical as his efforts proved unsuccessful. It was the only thing he wanted. He didn't care what happened to him afterwards, just so long as his throat was free of its strangling noose. "Get it off. Get it off."

"I'm working on it, Aki," was the quiet response.

Aki stopped struggling.

He knew that voice.

Sasha, Aki said the name in his head first, then, "Sasha?"

Chapter 47

S ASHA," AKI REPEATED, TRYING to twist around to see if his mind was simply playing tricks on him. It wouldn't have been the first thing he hallucinated in the last two days.

"It's me, Aki," Sasha said, moving in front of him.

A horrible trembling began from deep within him, rising to the surface and taking hold of his entire body. "Tell me this is real. Tell me this isn't a dream."

"It's not a dream. We're going home."

The shaking turned into mute, heaving sobs as Sasha pulled him close. His head rested against Sasha's chest as all the weight of those past weeks drained itself away in silent tears and Sasha held him until he quieted.

"It's alright, Aki. You're alright. It's over," Sasha said, his voice sounding exactly the same as it had when Aki was twelve years old, wheezing for each breath through a broken nose and swollen throat. It would have been comforting, except it only reminded Aki of how worried Sasha had been then. "Let's get this off and get you taken care of."

Aki sat, his hands quiet in his lap, as Sasha tried to work the rope free. He fought down the panic that surged up inside him every time Sasha accidentally pulled it a little tighter. It was too deep in his skin to slide a knife beneath and cut, and the knot was completely soaked and hardened over with blood.

For several minutes, Sasha worked at it until at last the knot came undone. That was only half of the battle, though. As Dagmar had discovered the day before, it had sunk into the skin and blood, sweat and seawater had dried the two together. Sasha poured fresh water over it to soften the scabbed over parts.

"This is going to hurt no matter how we do it," he said.

"Just get it off. I need it off."

"Alright. Here goes then," and Sasha yanked.

Aki screamed as it tore away bits of skin and flesh, but it was mostly breathless, and then he shut his eyes to take a full, deep breath. The first he'd taken in three days. His eyes opened, a new frenzied light in them, when he found he still couldn't breathe properly. His hand traveled to his neck, half expecting to find another rope still around it.

Sasha gave him a sympathetic smile. "It's probably swollen all the way through. It'll take a few days to go back to normal."

His shirt was as painful to remove as the rope had been for all the same reasons and Sasha called for a man named Lawrence to help him. Aki looked up when he came through the doorway and found himself staring into the face of the man who'd bought him. He looked from Lawrence to Sasha in bewilderment. Sasha caught the look and smiled again.

"It's alright. He's a friend. He did it to help you."

Aki took Sasha's word for it.

Both Sasha and Lawrence looked aghast when they pulled his shirt off. Aki himself had no idea how bad it was, but when he lowered his head he got his first real look at the damage two days in the full summer sun had done and the burning sensation that had crept up on him during that time finally made sense. His chest, stomach and arms were nothing but a mass of blisters, some oozing a bloody pus. Then they looked at his back. Sasha let out a slow breath, a hand resting over his mouth.

Lawrence looked him straight in the eye and said, "You should be dead."

He didn't mean it badly, but the words hit a memory and Aki slowly uncurled the fingers of the hand Dagmar had pressed the letter into. It lay there still, damp from his sweat, but intact. Lawrence was right, he should have been dead. The only reason he wasn't...

"Dagmar," he said, his voice still little more than a puff of air.

"I know. I'm going back to meet her just as soon as we get you taken care of," Sasha said.

"No. She's...," he couldn't finish the thought, but he remembered her instructions. Instructions that suddenly made complete, horrible sense. She must have known somehow, he realized. And that made it a hundred times worse. She'd known there was a chance of escape, but she'd given it to him instead. He held up the letter as best he could, which meant he let his open hand flop onto his lap where Sasha could see it. "For you."

Sasha took the folded paper but didn't read it just yet. He tucked it into his pocket and turned to Lawrence.

"I don't suppose you keep a store of medical supplies on here?"

"Some. Enough to see him through for a few hours, but beyond that I think you'll need to go ashore and get some more. I'll get what we have for now."

There wasn't a comfortable way for Aki to sit while they worked on him. He couldn't lay down on either his stomach or back. Eventually, he settled for folding his legs beneath him on the floor next to the bed in the cabin and resting his head, without turning it to either side because that caused excruciating pain to shoot up and down his neck, on the soft mattress. It was the best he could manage since he was too weak to actually hold himself up for any length of time.

It was probably for the best that he didn't have a voice worth anything at the moment. When Lawrence returned, the very first thing they did was pour alcohol onto his wounds. For not the first time, he wished that the pain numbing tea everyone used didn't make him ill. He grasped at the blankets on the bed, silent tears coursing down his cheeks as his whole body felt like it had been lit on fire.

When Sasha and Lawrence were satisfied that his wounds were clean, which was a long time after Aki thought they should be done, they began bandaging. There wasn't much of his body that didn't require a bandage, Aki realized. His feet certainly did after having been torn to ribbons on the rocks. For the most part, he didn't mind the soft fabric wrapped around him. Until it reached his neck, that is.

They didn't just wrap it in a bandage, either. They wrapped a brace in on each side and the back and bandaged it from the base of his neck all the way up beneath his chin and so thick that he couldn't move his head.

"Please don't," he'd begged, his words almost inaudible. "Get it off my neck. Please."

"We can't do that, Aki. You need it," Sasha had insisted. "Just try not to think about it."

That proved almost impossible. The minute they were finished, Aki's hand wandered to his throat and tugged at the bandage. It wasn't even something he had control of at the moment, just a reflex driven by the panic of having something closing in around his throat again. Sasha noticed and pulled his hand away. He held a cup of cool water up to Aki's lips and helped him drink as much as Aki could manage. Aki's mouth felt like sand from having so little water the last few days, but he couldn't drink enough to even begin to satisfy his thirst.

"I've got to go. But Lars is here, and Lawrence, and they'll take care of you until I come back. Alright?"

Aki tried to nod but his head was now immobile thanks to the brace on his neck.

"Where's Lars?" he succeeded in getting out.

In answer, Sasha pointed toward the door. "We weren't sure you'd be able to handle too much right away. Thought it best to have him wait."

Aki had to turn his whole body to see Lars, who was standing awkwardly in the doorway, fiddling with his hands as if they were new and he wasn't quite sure what to do with them. He smiled when he caught Aki's eye, but it was a worried smile.

"Try to get some rest," Sasha said, getting up. "I'll be back in a bit."

Aki let his forehead rest against the bed and shut his eyes obediently. Despite the pain, he sunk into a heavy, much needed sleep.

Lars stayed in the room with Aki, but Lawrence followed Sasha out.

"He's worse off than I expected. A lot worse. I honestly don't know how he stayed alive for as long as he did," Sasha said quietly when the door was shut.

"We could stay and get a doctor," Lawrence suggested.

Sasha shook his head. "There's too much risk. I'd rather not stay a minute longer than we have to. I'm going to get what we need for him first and then find Dagmar."

"What about that note he gave you?"

Sasha remembered it for the first time since placing it in his pocket. He pulled it out and looked at it. Now that it was in his hand, he hesitated. He had a horrible feeling he knew what was in it as he remembered her insistence the day before, the way she'd made him promise to get Aki first. Putting it back in his pocket, he decided to wait until he was off the ship and could find some place alone.

He was glad he did, when, a half hour later he ducked into a deserted alley and opened it.

> *Sasha,*
>
> *If you're reading this, I guess my plan worked. I'm sorry I lied to you. I knew if I told you what I was going to do, you wouldn't let me. You'd have tried something foolish that ended with Aki dead and probably with you in trouble. Trust me, this was the only way. Don't blame yourself. I wanted to do it. I don't think I could have gone back to a normal life after what has happened here. Consider it payment for a debt.*
>
> *Don't let Aki blame himself either. If he starts to, remind him that I know exactly what he put himself through on that ship to protect me. I owed him. Help him start over again, because he's going to need it.*
>
> *Don't bother coming to look for me. It'll be too late. Just get him home as quickly as you can.*

Sasha stared at the words for a long time, not quite willing to believe them. He should have known. He should have known the way she was talking yesterday. He should have insisted she come with him, then and there. He should have... with a start, he realized he was doing exactly what Dagmar said not to in her letter. He was blaming himself.

"It was her choice, you know," a woman's cool voice said over his shoulder. "You, of all people, should honor that."

Sasha turned around to find Mara standing in the entrance of the alleyway. Although Halle had told him she was living here, the sight of her was still a shock.

"How did you find me? And how do you know?"

"Aki was punished for trying to reach a Divalian ship. We don't get many of those here. It was a simple matter to discover who was on that ship. And as far as the girl goes, I knew I'd made a mistake the minute the words left my mouth. I told her she'd take his place if she tried to help him. She forced my hand, Sasha. I can't make idle threats."

"She's dead because of you."

"She's dead because she chose to die."

Sasha opened his mouth to argue, then realized it was a waste of time. Mara wouldn't see it his way and there was a far more pressing matter to discuss with her.

"So, what are you going to do? Refuse to let us leave with Aki? Board our ship and drag him away to finish what you started?"

"I didn't want him to end like that. He shouldn't have tried to run." Mara looked hurt at the sharpness in his tone, but Sasha had known her for too long to believe her authenticity. The look passed in a moment replaced by genuine concern. She stepped closer and said in a lowered voice, "Is Halle alive?"

"For now," Sasha said, shaking his head. Mara had always been like that - capable of the deepest love for her own, yet completely indifferent and callous to anyone else. It worked in his favor this time, a weakness he could exploit. "He dies if we don't get Aki back. And that's not an idle threat."

"And if Aki returns with you, he'll live? You'll give me your word that he will?"

"He will. You have my word."

"Then go. Your secret is safe with me," she said quietly before turning around to leave.

"Wait," Sasha called after her. "Dagmar's body, bury it."

Mara nodded once. "You spared my life and my son's when you came back to Aruuk. For that, I will always be grateful. She will be buried as you ask."

Chapter 48

AKI COULD NOT STAY ASLEEP for long before the now familiar sense of alarm set in. He couldn't breathe. His lungs screamed for air, but he could not satisfy them. He pulled away from the bed he was leaning against and brought his hands up to his throat. He got his fingers into the first few layers of the bandage and tried to rip it off. Hands pulled his own away.

"Take it off," he breathed, fighting to free his hands. "Please. I just want it off."

"Sasha said you can't," Lars answered him. He sat down on the bed beside Aki and loosened his grip on Aki's wrists. "You have to let us help you, Aki. You're just making it worse."

Aki let his hands drop to his lap. He had to fight hard not to bring them right back up to his throat. No one seemed to understand what a torment it was to still have something encircling it.

"Sasha?"

Lars had to lean down close to his face to hear him. "He hasn't come back yet, but he should be soon. You should try to drink something."

Holding the cup to his mouth, Lars tipped it just enough for Aki to take a small sip. Even swallowing that little bit hurt almost more than he could bear. The pain was different than it had been before. Before, it had been everywhere, a single sensation drowning his entire body, preventing him from noticing just about anything else. Now, he could pick it apart, identify where each shard of it was coming from, sense the subtle differences between them. Some weren't as bad as others; some were beyond anything he could imagine. He tried to sit up a little. His muscles refused to obey him. His body had given everything it had to keep him alive and there was simply no more strength left for him to call on.

When he could stand the pain of swallowing no longer, Lars pulled the cup away. The door opened behind him and Sasha came and sat on the floor beside him, his back to the bed Aki was facing.

"Dagmar?"

One look at Sasha's face confirmed Aki's fear. He shut his eyes with a whispered, "No."

"Think about it later. Right now, you need to heal," Sasha's voice was unusually quiet and reserved. He began to undo the bandages around Aki's torso. "Here, I have something that will help with the burns."

Lars left them alone while Sasha opened a small tin and a heavy, earthy odor filled the small space of the cabin. The salve brought instant relief, cooling his hot skin until the pain was little more than a memory. Even if it didn't last long, Aki was glad for the respite. It gave him space to think. He waited until Sasha finished with that and had started bandaging him up again.

"Sasha?"

"Don't try to talk. You need to give it time to heal."

"No. I have to tell you something," Aki said, wishing it didn't take so much effort to force out even a faint whisper.

"Save it, Aki. Try to get some sleep." Sasha finished and started to get up but Aki clutched weakly at his arm, stopping.

"Please. Just listen."

Sasha sighed and nodded, sitting down again on the floor next to him, his back against the bed. "Alright, what is it?"

"What I did... I told him about Ophelia. I helped him."

"I know."

"But you still came?"

"Of course I did. Aki, you were a child raised by a madman. We all were. I can't hold anything you did then against you. Besides, if you recall, I almost killed you that night. Now, get some rest."

With the weight of that gone and a considerable portion of his pain relieved, Aki managed better than he imagined he would. He slept most of the rest of the day, waking only when panic took hold of him and he tried, unsuccessfully, to remove the brace around his neck or when Sasha insisted he eat and drink. At some point during the day, he was aware of the fact that they were moving.

Inside the cabin, Aki had no sense of the days coming and going. He was rarely left alone, thanks to his constant efforts to pull the bandages off his neck. It didn't matter how many times Sasha explained to him why they needed to stay on. The need to have them off wasn't reasonable and when he was fully awake, he could stop himself. But there was no controlling when his heart started racing wildly and his lungs burned with frenzied desire as he sensed the constriction in his sleep. He would tear at it then until he was stopped.

He woke in the middle of the night after they had been several days at sea, too restless and hurting to sleep any longer. Lars was in the cabin with him, but asleep and not likely to wake unless Aki made a lot of noise. Aki almost smiled to himself at the thought. Lars had always been a very sound sleeper. Aki tried to take in a deep breath, like he did every time he woke up. He couldn't do it.

The walls of the cabin were especially tight that night and he was desperate to get out of the confined space. Aki attempted for the first time to reach the door. He couldn't actually stand, but he could crawl. Despite everyone's best efforts to feed him, he simply wasn't able to endure the pain of swallowing for longer than a couple of minutes at a time and so he ate almost nothing and was no stronger than the day they'd first brought him on board.

Once outside, he sank against the wall of the cabin, ignoring the wave of agony it set off in his back. The freedom was worth it. He shut his eyes, taking in the fresh, sea breeze that cooled the air. It was such a welcome difference from the musty smell of blood and medicine that lingered in the cabin. One hand trailed up to his neck and he found the end of the bandage. There was no one out here to stop him. It was hard to unwind, the motion pulling at his barely healing back but he persisted. That is, until a calloused hand rested gently on his wrist.

"You're not supposed to be out here, are you?"

Aki jumped at the voice coming from just over his shoulder. It took too much effort to turn his entire body, but the man helpfully stepped into his line of sight. It was Lawrence. Aki looked up at him, the hand he'd been using to remove the bandage on his neck frozen in place. Guilt. That was the first thing that flashed through him.

"Don't tell Sasha. I just...,"

"Hey, it's alright. But you'd best leave that on," Lawrence crouched down and pulled his hand all the way away, forcing Aki to give up his hold on the unwinding bandage.

"Please. Just for a few minutes. I need it off for a few minutes."

Lawrence hesitated then nodded. "Alright. But just for a few minutes."

When it came free at last, Aki couldn't actually breathe any deeper, but there was a freedom even in his shallow breaths that he craved as the night air cooled the hot skin on his neck. He leaned his head back again, relaxing as fully as it was possible for him to do.

"Thank you."

"Let's just hope Sasha doesn't find you like this. He'll be furious with me."

Aki smiled at that.

"I should probably apologize for how I treated you back there. We didn't want anyone getting suspicious."

"I know. Thank you," Aki repeated. "How long until..."

"Until we're home?" Aki nodded. "Tomorrow morning. Not long."

Aki's eyes refused to stay open any longer. Lawrence must have noticed because he stopped talking. Aki wasn't sure if he got up and left or if he stayed with him. He wasn't aware of anything, including Sasha's approach. Sasha stared at him in surprise.

"What's he doing out here? And why'd you let him take that off?"

"Just let him be for a bit, he's not making anything worse just sitting there. And you know that's the best he's slept since we left Karu."

"I suppose so. He's not healing well."

"Well, I don't reckon a ship in the middle of the sea is the best place for a recovery like that. Nor are any of us exactly experts of the job. Once we're in Bren, you can get him some proper care," Lawrence got up from where he'd sat. He laid a hand on Sasha's shoulder. "I'm sorry about the girl. She seemed like a very good person."

"She was. A very good person. She didn't deserve most of what happened in her life."

It was the longest Aki had managed to stay asleep and when he did wake up, it wasn't because he felt like he couldn't breathe but because of the warm, bright sunlight hitting his face. It was morning. He sat up a little and noticed that Sasha had taken Lawrence's spot by his side. Sasha had been dozing and Aki's movement woke him as well. With wary eyes, he watched Sasha's face, searching for any sign of annoyance or frustration at what he'd done.

"I'm sorry. I had to get it off. And I wanted fresh air."

Sasha brushed his apology aside with a half-smile. He shifted so that he was in front of Aki. With one hand he tipped Aki's head back to get a better look at the thin wound that encircled his neck. He ran his fingers across it and Aki winced and pulled back.

"It's going to scar."

"So is everything else," Aki said.

"That, unfortunately, is probably true. Especially these," Sasha gestured at the brands on his arm. "Who put that one there? They went too deep."

"He meant to," Aki said, wishing for the thousandth time that he could actually speak and not just push out barely audible whispers that everyone had to lean close to catch. Even producing a whisper was hard and excruciating. "Halle did it."

"Halle," Sasha repeated, a hint of disgust in his voice.

"I deserved it. I tried to kill him."

"So I've heard. I should warn you, before we get back." Aki turned his head stiffly to look at Sasha. "About?"

"Halle."

"He's alive. Mara said."

"He is. He was taken when they stopped the kidnapping. When Lars found me, all he knew was that Halle had taken you. We had no idea where. The only people who did know were Kezi and Halle."

Aki's face darkened instantly at the mention of Kezi's name. Halle had always hated him and never pretended otherwise. And he still hated Halle. Hated what he'd done to him. But there was no treachery in his action. But Kezi, Kezi had been his friend - he thought.

"Kezi refused to tell me unless I helped her escape. Halle agreed on a deal. They're holding off his trial until I get back. If I come back with you, they're going to let him live."

Aki absorbed the words quietly. Everything in his head was chaos still. His execution, Dagmar's death, his rescue - all things he didn't want to think about right now. He added Sasha's words to that list. He'd think about Halle, and what Sasha's deal with him meant, later. Later, when everything else was better, if such a time could exist again.

There was one thing he wanted to ask Sasha about, but it took more courage than he had and so he stayed silent. He hoped that Sasha would mention it first. So far, Sasha hadn't said much of anything at all about home and what awaited him.

"Are you ready to let me wrap it again?" Sasha gestured toward his neck.

Aki wanted more than anything to refuse, but he'd succeeded in keeping it off for the last few hours. Trying to steel himself for it, he whispered, "Yes."

Sasha had no sooner finished tying it off when the lookout spotted land. Aki tried to sit up enough to see it but couldn't. Sasha noticed his attempt, however, and slid an arm under his shoulders, lifting him to his feet. Aki's legs wobbled and shook under him.

"Don't let go. I'll fall over," he said to Sasha.

"I won't," Sasha said and pointed toward the thin brown outline on the horizon. "Look, you're home."

Aki tried to share in Sasha's enthusiasm. He'd thought he'd never come back. All of those weeks, he'd just assumed there was no way home for him, or even a home waiting for him if he did come back. He kept his thoughts to himself though. Sasha was clearly enthusiastic about their return.

"I'm sorry," Aki said, realizing for the first time what Sasha had left behind to come find him.

Sasha turned to look at him. "For what?"

"All of this. It's my fault. You had to leave Phelie. If I'd just...," Aki stopped, partly because it was too much effort and pain to keep going and partly because he wasn't sure how to finish.

Sasha didn't seem to take notice of most of his words, smiling widely when he mentioned Phelie. "You know, we're going to have a baby."

"What?" Aki stared at him.

"I'm going to be a father. Phelie told me the morning I left to find you."

"Then why'd you come for me?"

"You needed saving. Besides, if I hadn't come, Stephan would have. And whether he admits it or not, he's getting a bit old for these sorts of adventures."

Aki stiffened a little at the mention of Stephan. "Does anyone know we're coming?"

Sasha shook his head and Aki relaxed a little. He still had time. Time to get to all the things on the list of things he wasn't ready to think about.

"Come on, you should be resting."

Aki didn't argue as Sasha moved him back into the cabin and set him down once more. It would still be a few hours before they actually reached land and he was tired.

Chapter 49

THE ROOM WAS COOL, QUIET, and dark. Aki thought it was familiar, but it had the same medicinal smell that the cabin on the ship had so he wasn't sure. The floor wasn't moving up and down beneath him, so he knew it wasn't just another part of the ship. He lay for several minutes trying to place where he was and what had awakened him just then. He heard the sound again and recognized it. Someone was whispering nearby, the sound muffled by a wall.

Pushing himself up and wincing, Aki looked around. There were heavy curtains over the window, blocking out both the light of the sun and its heat. He sat on the edge of the bed, staring down at his feet still wrapped in white bandages. An odd, overly sweet taste lingered in his mouth. A glance at the table next to the bed reminded him why. A small jar full of whole dried leaves sat on it as well as a cup of water. Meredith had brought the jar, telling him it was something new for him to try for the pain. Although the leaves were too sweet when he chewed them, they worked. They hadn't just separated him from the pain, they'd put him into a deep, much needed sleep.

Seeing the jar of dried leaves also reminded him of where he was. They'd come ashore in the late afternoon and Sasha had brought him here, to the home of Karl and Meredith. Aki was more than a little surprised by the choice, although it made sense. Karl had never been anything more than distant with him, and only barely tolerated Sasha. Still, Aki remembered Karl helping him up the stairs and into the bed while Sasha went in search of a doctor.

He reached for the water now and took tiny sips of it. Someday, he told himself, someday he would be able to guzzle a whole cup of water without giving it any thought. Today was not that day. Today it hurt. Today he could only tolerate a few sips at a time.

A soft knock came on the door. He tried to answer but his voice wouldn't carry that far. It didn't matter, though. The door was already opening and the first thing he saw was a shock of bright red hair.

"Can we come in?" Felix asked.

Aki gave the slight, stiff nod that he was restricted to. Since Doctor Lamberse had agreed with Sasha, much to Aki's consternation, he still wore a thick layer of bandages all around his neck.

Felix opened the door all the way and stepped in, followed by Oscar. Aside from Karl and Meredith, who'd brought him medicine, and Doctor Lamberse, Aki hadn't seen anyone since coming ashore two days ago. Part of him wanted to keep it that way but it was too late now.

"You look dreadful," Oscar said as he threw himself into a chair.

"Oscar," Felix chided, looking appalled at his lack of politeness.

"What? He does. Did you know," Oscar turned back to Aki, "I think I might have witnessed the very first time Felix broke a rule. It was quite entertaining, I can tell you. I thought he was going to faint, just from the shock of it."

Aki smiled, but in a confused, bewildered way. There was clearly a story behind Oscar's words and it was just as clear that Oscar wanted to take his time telling the story. Aki listened without interruption as Oscar talked, although Felix pointed out more than once that Oscar was exaggerating. "It's all part of making a good story," Oscar responded, waving aside Felix's concern.

"We'd have gotten away with it too, if Felix hadn't gone straight to Father and told on us."

"You told on yourself?" Aki asked incredulously. The other two had to lean forward to catch his words.

"Of course. We might have had a good reason to break the rules, but we still broke them."

"You got in trouble for me?"

"It wasn't much. Father made us tell him everything, and he said we did the right thing. Although, we probably should have told him first. He also said you could have just told him in the first place and saved yourself all the trouble. Why didn't you?"

Aki felt an overwhelming sense of gratitude for the interruption of a knock just then. It saved him having to answer Oscar's question. Doctor Lamberse didn't wait for any answer before coming in, his leather satchel in his hands. He motioned for Oscar to get up and took the chair instead.

"You know you can tell them to leave if they're too much," he said to Aki, a slight smile on his face. "You're the invalid. They have to listen to you."

"I like the distraction," Aki confessed.

"I see. Well, I think it's time for them to leave you alone for now."

In spite of Doctor Lamberse's words, neither made any move toward the door as the doctor began unwinding the bandage from Aki's neck. Felix let out a gasp and even Oscar looked unsettled when Doctor Lamberse removed the bandages. Aki had yet to see his own neck so he had no idea how awful it looked but since everyone's reactions had been along the same lines, he had a good guess. As to the rest of him, he was well aware of how appalling his injuries were.

When Sasha had first brought Doctor Lamberse to see him, the doctor had required a full explanation of how each injury had been attained. It was a difficult half hour to get through, not so much because of the pain of talking, but because there was a certain horror in recounting those events. He hadn't even told Sasha exactly how it happened. They never spoke of it on the ship.

Once he'd finished, Doctor Lamberse shook his head, looked Aki in the eye, and repeated Lawrence's words, "You should be dead now."

"I didn't want to die," Aki had whispered. It was as simple as that. His mind and body had refused to accept his end.

"I guess you didn't."

Now, he tried to disconnect himself from the pain as Doctor Lamberse turned his head slightly from side to side. His thoughts inevitably strayed into the forbidden territory of things he wasn't ready to face yet.

"You're not going to need me to take care of you this time, are you?" Oscar asked from across the room. "Not that I'm not good at it. It's just getting kind of old. You never let anyone else have a turn at being the invalid."

Aki shot him an annoyed look that changed into a smile. With everyone else treating him with such care, Oscar was a much-appreciated change.

"You're welcome to it anytime. I would be happy to switch places with you."

Doctor Lamberse finished, this time deciding that a bandage would do Aki's neck no more good. The skin was sealed up and healing. So was the rest of him. He'd managed to actually lay down all the night before, a welcome relief from all of the nights and days spent sitting up, propped gingerly against a bed or chair or wall.

"Now, out, both of you," Doctor Lamberse made a shooing motion with his hand. Oscar and Felix filed out of the room with mumbled goodbyes and promises to come again. Doctor Lamberse only stayed a few more minutes, going over the rest of his injuries with the same meticulous yet efficient care.

Aki eased himself back down, lying on his stomach. He was just starting to doze off again when the door opened. He didn't hear it. His first clue that someone was in the room with him was the sound of footsteps crossing the wooden floor. A hand rested on his shoulder.

"I'm sorry, Aki," Meredith said softly. "They insisted, though. I couldn't tell them no."

He sat up again, confused by the expression on Meredith's face. He didn't have much time to ponder it though. The door opened wide behind her, framing two men - members of the city guard by their uniforms. Meredith stepped away as he lowered his feet to the floor. One of them entered the room and cleared his throat.

"Aki Turston?"

Aki nodded once, already knowing what the man's next words would be. Now that they were here, it seemed he'd always known.

"You're to come with us. The magistrate has some questions for you regarding the late attempt on the princess's life."

"He's not well enough to go anywhere," Meredith spoke up. "Can't the questions wait? It's already been over a month. Another week or so won't hurt."

As grateful as he was to her, Aki shook his head. "It's fine. I'll go. Just tell Sasha, alright?"

Meredith bit her lip but nodded. Aki eased himself up off the bed, holding onto the bedpost for a moment to steady himself. A glance at the guardsman showed Aki that the man was mildly surprised. Maybe he hadn't realized how injured and weak Aki was. Or maybe he'd expected more of a fight. Aki wasn't sure.

"How far is it?" he asked. Because I won't make it far, he finished in his head.

"Not far. We'll go slow," the man promised.

It wasn't far and they did go slow, but by the time Aki stood outside of the magistrate's office he wanted to collapse and never get up again. Compliance had its rewards though, and the men who'd brought him hadn't lost patience with him.

The magistrate's office was the same as he remembered it all those years ago when Stephan brought him, when he'd taken Stephan's name. It had been the start of a new life then. Now it felt a bit like the end of one. The end of the only good life he'd had. It was fitting. After all that he'd done, it deserved to come to an end.

The desk was as large as he remembered, covered in papers. The magistrate was bent over a small stack of them when Aki was ushered in. Aki started for the chair nearest him, hoping no one would stop him. He slumped into it, trying not to grimace at how much pain he was in from the walk. The magistrate glanced up at him but then went back to his reading. One of the guardsmen left while the other took a spot by the door.

"You are Aki Turston?" the magistrate asked after several minutes had gone by. He set aside what he'd been reading and stared hard at Aki.

"I am."

"Speak up, please. I can't hear you if all you do is whisper."

Aki's hand inched its way up to his throat. He pulled away the collar of his shirt enough to reveal the hideous scar beneath. "I can't. I'm sorry."

The magistrate leaned forward to look at the scar and nodded his understanding. "You know why you're here?"

Aki nodded. "Yes, sir. I think so."

"You were aware of the plan to kidnap the princess?"

"Yes, sir."

"We have done our best to get to the bottom of this attack. And, unfortunately, your name has come up many times when questioning the others." The magistrate pulled out a familiar piece of paper. It was frayed around the edges and had been folded over many times. Aki recognized it immediately. It was the map he'd given King Darien, the map he'd drawn for Jasper. "I've been told that this was your work. Is that true?"

"I drew it. I didn't know that was what Jasper wanted it for."

"But you knew they were planning this?"

"Not exactly."

"What do you mean?"

Aki blew out a deep breath. "I knew some things."

"You knew that this group was the one responsible for the break-in at Baron Orlander's? Both Phineas and Kezi said you were aware of it."

Aki stared down at his hands resting in his lap. After everything that had happened, it shouldn't have come as a shock that Kezi was using him again. He'd avoided asking Sasha anything about her. Now he was tempted to ask the magistrate what was going to happen to her.

"What did Jasper tell you?" he asked. Jasper, at least, might be honest.

"Jasper?"

"My instructor, Jasper Kunz. He was part of all this. He could tell you the truth."

Understanding dawned on the magistrate's face. "I forgot. You've only recently returned, haven't you? Jasper Kunz was among those killed. Whatever truth you think he can tell died with him. Now, were you aware of who was involved?"

Aki brought his hands up to his face. Jasper, dead. He let the knowledge of those words sink into him. Jasper was the only one who'd wanted to keep him out of this. Whatever else he believed, he believed that. Jasper wanted him safe and now Jasper was dead. Just like Dagmar. Just like his parents. When the magistrate cleared his throat, Aki realized he was still waiting on an answer.

"I knew."

"And you chose to keep that information to yourself?"

"I had reasons to," Aki said, knowing that no reason in the world would be sufficient. Thinking about them now, they seemed trivial compared to the knowledge he'd concealed and lied about.

The magistrate pulled one last paper out of his stack. This one was folded up like a letter. Aki recognized it as well. It was the letter Kezi had asked him to take. A chill ran through him as he realized he had no idea what she'd written in it. The magistrate opened it.

"This was written by Keziah Grimere. It names you as an accomplice to the plot. This is the same letter she requested you to take as a favor to Pellor. True?"

"She asked me to take it, but I didn't know what was in it."

"Regardless, you were aware of multiple crimes committed against both the crown and citizens of this country. By remaining silent for so long, you made yourself an accomplice. At least, as far as I'm concerned. Perhaps the council will judge differently."

"You're arresting me, aren't you?"

The magistrate nodded. "Do you have anything you want to say?"

Aki just put his face in his hands again, shaking his head.

Chapter 50

AKI PICKED APART A PIECE of straw that had come out of the mattress, scattering the pieces on the floor between his feet.

He should have been trying to figure a way out of this mess, but all he could think about was what he'd left behind in Karu. Dagmar shouldn't have saved him. He wasn't worth it. Nothing he'd ever done was worth saving. It was a debt he had no way of repaying. She'd been so calm, then. Aki shut his eyes and leaned back against the wall. She'd faced death like it was nothing, while he'd fought with everything he had to keep his miserable life going.

If he hadn't fought so hard, she wouldn't have tried to save him. It would have been too late. Sasha would have come and taken her to safety. No doubt they would have mourned his death, but it would have been better that way. If he could have just accepted his fate, she'd still be alive. If, if, if..., they never ended. So many ways he could have been different, been better. And he'd picked none of them.

No, he wasn't going to even try to get himself out of this mess, because this mess was exactly what he deserved. Footsteps coming up the stairs broke him out of his reverie. He stared at the door, trying to guess if it was going to open or not. Sasha would come, he was sure of that. Sasha had come all the way to Karu to get him, he wouldn't just leave him alone now.

The door opened and Aki wasn't at all surprised when it was Sasha who crossed the threshold. He covered the distance between the door and the cot in a few steps and sat down. Aki looked down at the bit of straw still between his fingers. He hated the look on Sasha's face.

"What happened?"

"What's supposed to happen. I'm going to be tried as an accomplice."

"After everything you went through? You're the one who told the king about it."

"I didn't tell him quite everything. And I don't think it matters what happened in Karu."

"It ought to. Aki, you've been through enough. I'm going to talk to..."

"No, please. Don't talk to anyone about me. This is my fault. It's all my fault. If I'd just...," Aki's voice dropped off. There it was again, that elusive "if". "I'll be alright, Sasha."

Sasha studied him, his eyes still worried. "It will be a bit before your trial. They'll give you time to heal first."

"You should go home to Phelie. I've kept you away long enough. And, she'll need you when she hears about Dagmar," Aki's voice broke over the last word. Forcing his eyes to meet Sasha's, he went on, "And when you get home, tell Stephan and Alina that I'm alright. Just don't tell them how badly I messed everything up. Please."

"You haven't messed everything up, Aki."

"I lied. I lied over and over again because I was scared. And I thought I was doing it to protect people, but in the end, Dagmar died. She's dead because of me, Sasha. So, please, just tell them I'm sorry. Tell them not to worry about me."

They sat quietly for a few moments, Sasha taking in Aki's words. As if sensing that arguing wouldn't change anything, he finally stood up.

"They'll have a doctor come and take care of you still."

"I know. They told me."

"Hamo's on the council. I won't talk to anyone else, but I will talk to him."

"Does he know?"

"Know what?"

"That it's my fault what happened to Phelie that night?"

"He knows. And, trust me, he doesn't hold it against you. If he did, he'd have never let me marry her." He reached the door and paused. "I'm coming back for the trial. You and Halle are the only ones they haven't finished with yet. You don't have to face that alone. I'll be here for you."

"Thank you for everything. I'm sorry you had to go through all of this trouble for me."

Once Sasha's footsteps faded, Aki laid down. Without the leaves Meredith had given him, the pain was coming back as bad as ever. At the moment, he welcomed it. It made it impossible to dwell on all the things he kept shoving away, saving them for a better day.

For the next week, he did little more than sleep while his body healed. Twice every day, a doctor was brought in to see him. The first couple of times, the man had been accompanied by a guard who remained in the cell. Since Aki hadn't once put up any sort of fight, however, their vigilance had slackened. Now the doctor generally came in alone or accompanied only by the older jailer.

There was something strange about the nothingness. His time had no demands made on it. All that was required of him was to stay in that room. It was the first time in his life when there was nothing he needed to do, nothing he needed to escape. He wasn't even dreading the approach of his trial. Whatever the outcome, it didn't matter. Not anymore. All the things that had mattered, he'd destroyed for himself. He didn't think anyone else was going to do a more thorough job.

It was well past dusk when he became aware of someone climbing up the stairs. Since he'd already eaten, and already been seen to by the doctor for the evening, Aki lay back on his cot and tried to fall asleep. The rattle of keys just outside his door had him sitting up again in a moment. When the door opened and he saw who his visitor was, he scrambled to get to his feet.

"Your Majesty, I didn't..."

"Sit down," King Darien said. Inside the cell, he looked decidedly out of place. He looked around the small space before sitting down in the chair. "I almost never come up here."

Aki gripped the edge of his cot to keep from falling over in shock. On the list of people he thought might visit him, the king hadn't even been a thought.

"I must admit, Aki, that you are something of a puzzle to me. Enough that I felt I had to come and speak with you myself before your trial tomorrow."

"I don't understand."

"You, by your own admission, were fully aware of many things that were of a nefarious nature. You kept their secrets for many weeks, even from the people you were closest with. And yet, I do not find you to be particularly treasonous. Your warning saved my daughter and saved this kingdom. As both a father and king, I can only be grateful for that. If that was all and it was up to me, I would say no more about it, especially considering what you were put through because of telling us. Unfortunately, that is not how a country is run. The magistrate has collected reasonable evidence against you, and it is out of my hands."

"I understand."

"Do you? Good. Because, although I don't think you will be handed a harsh sentence tomorrow, you will, of necessity, bear some of the responsibility for what has happened. But you are probably wondering why I brought myself all the way up here to tell you just that." Aki nodded. "I simply want to know why. If you harbored none of the ill-will that the other conspirators did, why take up their part? Why tell their lies? Why keep their secrets?"

Aki sighed. That single word could rival *"if"* in his mind for how many times he said it to himself. If it was anyone other than the king sitting in front of him, he would have found a way to say nothing at all.

"I was afraid. Of what would happen if I told. Of people finding out the truth about me. Of losing my friends."

King Darien nodded. "I see."

"I'm so sorry for everything."

"As am I. Fear is quite a crippling thing, isn't it? It makes a poor master." King Darien held out his hand. "May I see your arm?"

Aki thought it was funny that he asked. He could have just as easily demanded and Aki would have obeyed. He held it out now. He watched as King Darien pushed the sleeve of his shirt up far enough to reveal the brands there. The fact that he was sitting in a cell, talking to the most powerful man in the country still had him too stunned to think too much about anything else. The king ran a calloused thumb over Aki's brand. As much as he tried to push the thought away, the action made him feel like he was being inspected again. King Darien didn't mean it that way, he knew.

"These will never go away."

"That's sort of the point of them."

"And what do they remind you of?"

Aki pulled his arm back towards himself. "That Halle owned me. That Dagmar's dead. That I'm not worth all the trouble people have gone through for me."

If it wasn't the answer he expected, King Darien did not let it show. His face remained impassive. He stood up, motioning for Aki to remain where he was at the same time.

"Thank you, Aki. I think I understand a little better than I did before. I'll see you tomorrow."

Aki found it impossible to sleep after that. He tried to tell himself that it had nothing to do with finding out that his trial was the following day. And, in part, that was true. But his mind was in turmoil after his conversation with King Darien. What about him had prompted the king to make the rare trip up here? And what information had he gleaned from their brief conversation? Aki didn't think he'd said much worthwhile. He certainly hadn't revealed any great secret.

Morning came slowly, with Aki watching out the small window as the sky shifted. He massaged the sides of his head with his palms, trying to force away the sleepless headache that had crept up on him in the long night hours. When his breakfast was brought to him by the old, balding jailer, he only managed a few mouthfuls. That was all he was getting down from any of his meals still, much to the doctor's chagrin. Swallowing was just too painful to attempt more.

When he heard the key turning in his lock sometime later, Aki was already on his feet. Two guards stood in the doorway waiting for him. As he stepped out between them, he saw that the door opposite him was already open, the room's occupant already taken away. Halle, he realized with a start. He'd prepared himself for the trial, but he hadn't prepared himself for seeing Halle again.

Aki was out of breath by the time they reached the foot of the staircase. Of course, it didn't take much for him to get out of breath, but it was a very long staircase. His cooperation had earned him the privilege of walking on his own between the guards, free of their grip and of any shackles. That alone made the short walk down the hallway in front of people a little easier. They stopped outside a large door. By the murmur of voices that came from the other side, Aki assumed it was the meeting hall of the council.

They were not waiting long. The door was thrown open and Aki looked up just in time to meet Halle's eyes as he was led out. He'd imagined Halle would sneer or at least look smugly pleased to see Aki like this, but Halle seemed to barely notice him. Aki didn't have time to wonder about that, though, before he was escorted through the same door and into the presence of the council.

Chapter 51

THE COUNCIL ROOM WAS LARGE, and the sound of their footsteps echoed off the stone walls as he was led to a chair in the center. A glance around the room made him go hot all over. There were too many people here that he knew. Too many people whose eyes he was ashamed to meet. Hamo and Baron Orlander both sat at the table. Beyond them, he saw Sasha and Master Wehr and Captain Lupin.

The only person who he thought might be there but wasn't, was Stephan. Aki tried to be glad of that.

The trial itself was startlingly quick. The magistrate seated at the king's right hand, told what he knew. Hearing it spelled out so plainly was damning. Aki sank down in his chair. His fault. This was all his fault, he told himself. He glanced briefly in Baron Orlander's direction when the magistrate disclosed the fact that he knew who had broken into his home and injured his son. And wished he hadn't. The warm, friendly face that he remembered from his only trip there was now hard and cold.

There were questions afterward. Aki couldn't speak loud enough for anyone to hear him except the guard standing at his shoulder, which meant that the man had to relay his answers to everyone else in the room. His answers didn't matter much anyway. Nothing he could say could excuse his silence in the eyes of those around him. Even in his own mind, his reasons sounded trivial in the face of what had happened.

When asked if there was any final thing he'd like to say, Aki was tempted to apologize once more. The words had lost their meaning, though, ringing empty and trite against his actions. No one in this room had any reason left to believe a word that came out of his mouth.

"You will wait outside while we reach a decision," King Darien spoke for the first time, although his eyes had never left Aki.

Aki nodded, following his escort out of the room. There was a bench in the hallway outside and without waiting to be told what to do, Aki made his way over to and sat. In spite of the time he'd been given to heal, his body was still weak and his head was throbbing from his sleepless night. On the other end of the bench, Halle sat waiting as well. His head was in his hands, though, and he hadn't bothered to look up when Aki sat down. Aki decided to keep it that way.

Although he could hear their voices, Aki couldn't understand any of their words. His hand traveled up to his neck, searching for the talisman that used to hang there. Finding nothing but the scar, he fingered that instead. Shutting his eyes, he could see her. Dagmar kneeling in front of him, speaking, wiping away his blood. Her voice drifting in and out of his consciousness. Her words sliding into his ears, making little sense. She was gone, then back again. She was taking his place. He didn't understand why or how, but there she was, bound to the same post he'd just been freed from. She never even looked at him, her eyes staring out at the sea, her face peaceful in a way he still didn't understand.

"These people aren't very grateful, are they?" Halle's voice cut into his thoughts.

Aki glanced in his direction then turned away again. There was nothing he wanted to say to Halle.

"You're the one who told them our plan. I know it was you, even if you deny it. And yet, here you are in just as much trouble as I am."

Aki wondered if he would be in even more trouble if he reached over and strangled Halle now. More importantly, he wondered if it was worth it. Before he could make up his mind, there was a shuffling of chairs and feet in the council room and Aki sat up straighter. He didn't fail to notice Halle's mocking smile replaced with a worried frown.

The door was opened, and Aki's eyes found the ground again as it emptied. Most didn't even pause in front of him, disappearing instead down the hallway. The two people who did pause, Aki refused to look at. Master Wehr and Captain Lupin were the last people he wanted to talk to right now. His demeanor must have conveyed his deep reluctance and after a moment, they both moved on without a word.

Aki jumped when a hand rested on his shoulder. It was only Sasha, who sat down next to him. Hamo stood nearby as well.

"Just tell me," Aki said quietly. "I'd rather know and get it over with."

"It's the lightest sentence they give, if that makes it any easier."

"And what's that?"

"Indenture. For one month."

"So, I'll be a slave again. Well, at least they picked something I'm already good at."

It was a poor attempt at a joke, but Sasha smiled a little anyway. "It's not quite the same, and it's only for a short time. Halle's is worse."

Halle heard his name and looked over, but he didn't understand anything that had been said otherwise. Aki turned away as Sasha spoke to Halle, but he still caught at least some of the words. A year. That's how long Halle's sentence was. If it hadn't taken too much effort, he would have smiled at the thought of Halle working for a year. It was better than he deserved, Aki decided.

"Come on. We'll go out there with you," Sasha addressed them both in Aruuken.

The courtyard was mostly empty when they stepped out into it. A jolt of alarm went through Aki as he noticed where they were being led. They stopped just outside the open smithy. The blacksmith looked up from what he was doing and sighed. Clearly, this wasn't something he enjoyed doing. Aki supposed he could take comfort in that.

"Who's first?" the man asked.

Aki didn't have time to even consider an answer before Halle was pushed forward.

"He's the only one getting it," Hamo said, and Aki realized he'd been holding his breath. He let it out again slowly as Hamo's words sunk in.

Turning to face him, he whispered, "Thank you."

Hamo shrugged. "You have enough marks on you, I think. And so does the king. When your month is up, it's all over. You can start fresh."

Any hope for a further conversation was dashed by Halle's scream. If it was anyone else, Aki would have turned away, would have pitied them. But it was Halle. Halle had pressed his own branding iron into Aki's arm, burning deep into his flesh. His fingers felt for that brand now as he watched Halle fight against the grip of the two guards holding him. Halle deserved the searing pain. Halle deserved a permanent mark in payment for his cruelty.

The band was on and sealed closed around Halle's wrist and his scream ended in a choked cry as he placed it in the barrel of cool water. Aki bit his tongue. He wanted to remind Halle of the fact that he'd offered Aki no such comfort after his branding, but decided it wasn't a good time. After several minutes, the guards moved them toward a large, windowless room built off the side of the castle. Aki started inside the door after the others. Here, Sasha put his hand on Aki's shoulder once more.

"Hang on a minute, Aki." Aki turned and faced him. "This is going to be very hard for him."

"But not for me, because this has been most of my life," Aki finished for him. He couldn't help the bitterness that tainted his words.

"Yes, it will be harder for him than you. And not just because you're used to this. You will understand everything that's said to you, he won't."

"What are you trying to say?" Aki asked, although he had an uncomfortable feeling he already knew.

"I'm saying, it's time to end whatever this is going on between you two."

"There's nothing...,"

"Aki, I saw the way you watched when they put that band on him. You want him to suffer. I understand." Aki stared down at his feet. If it were anyone else saying this, he'd brush them off easily. But not Sasha. Not after he came all the way to Karu to find him. "Just try, Aki. That's all I'm asking you. Just try to put it behind you."

Aki only managed a nod, unable to speak. That was enough for Sasha, apparently. He went on, "I'll try to be here when your month is up. If I'm not, come to my home. We'll start over, find you something to do."

Again, Aki could only nod. He wasn't ready to think about a month from now. He wasn't even sure he was ready to think about the next hour. Turning back to the room, he heard Sasha make Halle the same offer for when his time was done. Halle didn't answer, either.

Inside the room, they were both given a change of gray, ill-fitting clothes and shown a space. It was empty for now and once they were dressed in their new prison garb, he and Halle were left alone. Aki sat down on his straw mat without bothering to look at Halle. Leaning his head back against the wall, he tried to rest.

In the ensuing silence it was impossible to ignore the tiny whimpers coming from the mat beside him. Cracking his eyes open, he glanced sideways at Halle. He was hunched over, cradling his arm with its new band. Aki ran a finger over his own brands and couldn't resist any more.

"Who would have thought putting hot metal on your skin would hurt so bad?"

"Shut up," Halle said, turning away from him.

Aki willingly obliged. He shut his eyes again and this time managed to doze in spite of the noise Halle made. The afternoon passed quickly while he slept. He didn't wake up again until they were joined by the others. Most of the men only gave them a passing glance, too tired to care about newcomers. A few engaged in quiet conversation but Aki made no effort to hear what they were saying.

"Aki?" Halle spoke for the first time since their brief exchange many hours ago.

Aki turned to see what he wanted.

"You're the only one I can even talk to here, aren't you?"

"Yes. I suppose I am. But I don't really want to talk to you."

Halle didn't say anything after that.

Chapter 52

A KI KICKED AT A STONE AS HE stood waiting. The sun was only halfway over the eastern horizon, but they were already outside. Coming towards them was a man Aki assumed was in charge. He'd already spoken to the other men and sent them on their way under guard. Now he stopped in front of Aki and Halle.

"Which one of you understands me?"

"I do, sir," Aki said.

"And you can speak to him?"

"Yes, sir."

"Good. You two will stay together then." Aki tried not to let his annoyance show. It was worse than having to stay with Oscar for six weeks. "I've been told neither of you are up to much hard work. Is that true?"

Aki knew he wasn't. Just getting through the trial the day before had been an exhausting ordeal. He wasn't sure about Halle, but if they had to stay together anyway, it didn't really matter. He shrugged. "I guess so."

The man ran a hand across the back of his neck as he considered. He scanned the courtyard as if searching for some task that he could assign to them that would meet the requirements of their sentence but not cause him too much trouble.

"Come with me," he said, turning away.

The room he led them into was familiar to Aki, and not because he'd ever actually been in it. One armory looked much like another and he'd spent many, many hours in Gundar's. It wasn't hard to guess what they were going to be doing in here, either. He only listened partially to the man's instructions, letting his eyes wander over the weaponry hanging off the walls. He had to wonder if the man knew anything of the history between him and Halle. It didn't seem like a good idea to leave them alone together in a room full of weapons. Of course, there was a guard just outside the door who would no doubt be upon them at the slightest hint of trouble, but still, Aki thought there had to be safer places for them to work.

"Aki?" Halle's voice broke into his thoughts. "What did he say?"

Aki allowed himself a tiny smirk as he turned to face Halle. "He said you have to listen to what I tell you to do."

Halle's eyes narrowed. "No."

"Suit yourself. But I'm the only one who can talk to you. That means, your orders come from him through me. It also means that whatever I say to him, you won't be able to argue."

Blood drained from Halle's face as his eyes darted to the weapons hanging around them.

"Go ahead. I'm better than you with any of those anyway, and if you try to start anything, I will tell."

The words seemed to arrest Halle's vengeful thoughts and leave him shaken. All at once, Aki realized exactly what Sasha had been talking about. Aside from Aki, Halle was completely on his own. That very knowledge seemed to be sinking into Halle at the same time. Any pity Aki might have felt, though, was lost when he traced the brand on his arm and remembered his ordeal on Halle's ship.

"Let's get started."

Aki settled into a spot and got to work. The work of polishing armor and sharpening weapons wasn't terribly difficult. There was a rhythm to it that Aki fell into easily, allowing his mind to wander wherever he chose. He steered it carefully away from anything that had to do with Dagmar, Kezi, or Stephan. Now wasn't the time to indulge in those thoughts. He ignored the many times throughout the day when Halle tried to speak to him. This was worse than being forced to share a room with Oscar, Aki decided. At least he had a few hours away from Oscar each day. Besides, Oscar had never been as horrible as Halle.

As the day drew to an end, Aki glanced at the pile of work Halle had finished. It was less than a third of what Aki had done.

"That's it? That's all you could do?"

"I was trying. How can they expect me to work when this hurts so much?" Halle held up his banded arm.

"It's what you expected of me. Or did you forget what you did?" When Halle looked away, Aki went on, "I should just tell him that you refused to do the work. It'd serve you right for what you did to me."

"You wouldn't..."

"Maybe I wouldn't. Or maybe I would." Aki shrugged.

Halle looked torn between arguing and pleading. Neither would do him any good, Aki decided. He just wished he didn't remember Sasha's words at that very moment. They were jarring and he turned away with a frown.

When their overseer came to collect them only a short time later, Aki caught the wary way Halle watched him, waiting for his lie, waiting for him to take his revenge. Aki couldn't do it.

For days, the only thing that changed was the jobs they were assigned. Sometimes, they cleaned the stables, sometimes they worked in the armory, sometimes they were sent to the castle kitchens to wash the stacks of dishes or to scrub floors. No one ever seemed to care how much they did or didn't get done and, by the end of the first week, Aki was pretty sure their overseer had decided that as long as they were out of sight and occupied, his job was complete.

Aside from telling him what they were to do for the day, and commenting on how little Halle managed to accomplish, Aki ignored him. After being completely ignored for the first couple of days, Halle finally stopped trying to talk to him. Aki would have been grateful for that except for one thing. Halle never left his side. Even when they were finished with the day's task, Halle was never more than a few steps away. He was a shadow Aki couldn't rid himself of.

On the last day of that first week, they were out in the courtyard, a mountain of tack laying in front of them waiting to be cleaned and oiled. Aki sat on the ground and picked up the first bridle. His hands worked deftly at the leather as his eyes wandered around the yard. There wasn't much to see that he hadn't already seen. Except for Master Wehr. Aki started when his eyes fell on the man. His old instructor wasn't doing anything, just sitting on a stone bench on the other end of the yard, watching him, Aki realized. He felt his face go hot and lowered his head.

"Aki?" It had been days since Halle had tried to start a conversation.

Aki ignored him and rubbed the bridle harder.

"Aki, listen to me," a hint of frustration and command crept into Halle's voice.

Aki gave another surreptitious glance in Master Wehr's direction and found he was still watching. His fingers slipped, dropping the bridle onto the stone. Even across the distance, the intensity of Master Wehr's gaze could be felt.

"Aki?" The command was gone this time, replaced with pleading.

"What?" Aki snapped, turning to face him.

"Your sentence isn't as long as mine, is it?"

"No."

"You'll be leaving soon, won't you?"

"Yes."

Halle fell silent again. Aki managed to regain enough of his composure to continue cleaning the bridle but his eyes kept darting over to where his old instructor sat. The man was watching for something, that much was obvious. Aki just wasn't sure what. And he wasn't sure how it mattered. When his month was up, he'd return to Sasha's and probably never see Master Wehr again.

The approach of horses drew his attention away from both Master Wehr and Halle. Aki looked up long enough to see that there were two riders coming through the gate into the courtyard. One had a familiar head of red hair.

Felix.

He didn't turn away fast enough. Felix caught sight of him. Aki had never known shame like what he felt now as recognition registered on Felix's face. He watched as the boy leaned over and said something to his instructor. The man nodded and Felix dismounted. Aki wanted to run.

Instead, he got to his feet, the bridle still in hand and waited for Felix to approach.

"You knew," was all Felix said. It was all he needed to say. The accusation was undeniable.

"I'm sorry."

"You knew. All that time, you knew. You listened to me talk about it, and you just pretended like it was nothing. Like you knew nothing. How could you?"

"I had reasons, Felix. I guess they don't really matter now, though. They weren't nearly as important as I thought they were, anyway. I'm sorry. I'm sorry your brother was hurt and that you and your family got dragged into all of this."

"I trusted you."

"I know. I'm sorry."

Felix stared at him for a moment before turning sharply on his heel and returning to his horse. Aki sat back down, his work forgotten for the moment, and buried his face in his hands. In those final words Felix had stated the most bitter truth that had arisen from this debacle. Trust was a thing of his past. No one would ever trust Aki again. They had no reason to.

"Aki?"

Aki was tempted to fling the nearest object at Halle's head. Instead, he picked his work back up and started over as if Halle had never spoken, as if Felix had never shown up, as if Master Wehr wasn't watching him this very instant.

"You should have just left me to die," he whispered to himself, to Dagmar who was no longer alive to hear him. "It should have been you that came home."

The day dragged on after that, the work not nearly demanding enough to distract Aki from his thoughts. Master Wehr eventually left, but Aki wasn't sure when - he'd stopped glancing in his direction after Felix had ridden away.

His appetite was gone when they were given supper and he only pushed the stew around in his bowl instead of eating it. Eventually, he gave up on that and set it aside. Leaning back against the wall, he stared at nothing at all, his fingers mindlessly tracing the brands on his arm. All around him, the others were either eating, talking or laying down to sleep. He had no interest in any of those things.

"Are you going to finish that?" Halle asked him.

Aki broke off his staring long enough to see what Halle was gesturing towards - his barely touched bowl. Any other day he would have been tempted to upend the bowl and its contents onto the floor, making Halle scrape it up if he wanted it. Tonight, he couldn't muster enough anger to even consider it.

"If you're not, I could...,"

Aki started to lay down, turning his back to Halle. "Just take it and leave me alone."

They were back in the stables the next day, cleaning stalls. This was one job that Aki truly didn't mind, mostly because of its familiarity. The same couldn't be said for Halle. The first day, his hands had been blistered from all the shoveling and he'd tried to complain to Aki that it made his legs hurt worse. Already, this morning, Aki could tell he was limping more than usual. A seed of guilt for being the cause of that stuck inside him.

He was lost in his own work when Halle came up behind him.

"Can you listen to me?"

"What?"

"You said yesterday that you'll be leaving soon." He paused, as if waiting for a confirmation from Aki. Aki kept shoveling. "I won't understand anything."

"No, you won't. Guess you should have thought about that before you decided to come here and help commit treason."

Halle stood behind him, quiet for too long and Aki set his shovel down and turned to face him. Halle twisted his hands together, avoiding Aki's eyes completely.

"What is it?" Aki asked impatiently.

Halle ran his tongue over his lips. "You could teach me. Not everything, but some. Enough that I can understand a little when people talk to me."

"Forget it. Give me one good reason why I should help you with anything."

Halle couldn't. He returned to his work but Aki stood still, watching him. In his entire life, he'd never seen or heard Halle ask for anything. He'd always demanded, always expected to be obeyed. It was a side of him that Aki hadn't thought existed and was a far cry from the gloating, swaggering Halle he'd known on the ship. By the slump in his shoulders, it had obviously taken a lot out of him to ask now. Aki thought back to Sasha's words. So far, he'd done the exact opposite. Aki swallowed the lump that rose up in his throat as he left his spot and started forward. Halle looked up in confusion when he cleared his throat. It was as hard for him to offer help as it was for Halle to ask for it, apparently, because the words clammed up inside him at first.

"I guess I could teach you a little," he said.

"You could?"

"It won't be much. I'm only here for another three weeks. But, yes, I could."

Without waiting for a response, Aki went back to his work.

Chapter 53

H E WAS ONLY A DAY AWAY from being done. Only a day away from being tossed back out into a world where he had to decide what to do with himself next. Aki had kept careful count of the passing days but that didn't make the approaching day of freedom any easier to contemplate. If anything, it was harder. There was an ease to getting up every morning and being told exactly what to do. It had allowed him to exist without consciousness.

He frowned down at his food as if it were responsible for his uneasiness. In the last three weeks, he'd tried, with varying degrees of effort, to teach Halle the language of Dival. And to Halle's credit, most days he did really try to learn. But it didn't come easily to him, and Aki knew his absence after tomorrow would leave Halle virtually deaf. In the last three weeks, he'd also seen plenty of Master Wehr, although the reason for the man's presence was as elusive as ever. He never tried to come up and speak to him, just watched him from a distance. In the last three weeks, Aki had not worked up the courage to ask about Kezi and what her fate was. Just the thought of her betrayal was enough to turn him hot all over. If he never saw her again, he would be happy.

There was a commotion at the other end of the room and Aki finally looked up from his food. For the first time, he realized Halle was not sitting only a couple of feet away the way he always was. That was strange since Halle had been his shadow for the last four weeks. And now he was the source of the commotion, Aki noticed. He'd been just behind Aki in line for food, but now he was cornered by some of the other men. Aki tried to go back to eating, but his eyes returned to Halle again. Aki wasn't sure what they were doing, but Halle was terrified. He didn't need to be close to see that. Probably because he couldn't understand what the men wanted, Aki thought.

He didn't need to get involved.

He shouldn't get involved, he told himself.

Tomorrow, he'd be gone and Halle would be on his own. And Halle deserved to be on his own. He deserved to suffer. But that look, that look on his face was exactly the same one he'd worn when he was dangling from Aki's hand over the fall.

Aki shut his eyes, but all he could see was that day - the day he'd finally given in to the darkness inside himself and tried to end Halle's life. He could hear Halle's scream as he plummeted into the dark waters below. And there was the horror in Lars' eyes - not at the death itself, because death was no uncommon thing to them - but at the fact that Aki had been the one to deliver it. Worse still was the realization as he stood on the edge of that cliff that Halle's death changed absolutely nothing about his life. It didn't take away the pain, the anger, the hate. If anything, it magnified them until they were all that Aki could see. It had come both as a shock and almost a relief when Halle's broken body was dragged back to Gundar's house, barely clinging to life.

"Leave him alone." Aki could scarcely believe it was his own voice that carried across the room. He should be keeping his head down, getting through this last night of captivity like most of the men in the room were doing.

"Stay out of this," one of them turned and said.

Aki wanted to. He did. But the very fact that he was standing here alive prevented him. Dagmar had told him that he would get the chance to make everything right, and there was nothing Aki needed to make right more than his attempted murder. A second chance. That's what she'd gifted him. That's what his parents had gifted him. So far, he'd done a spectacular job wasting it. Not anymore. Pushing to his feet, ignoring the heady pulse thrumming through him, Aki shook his head. "No. Leave him alone. He doesn't even understand what you want."

The entire cluster of men, which amounted to four, turned to face him now. The two that had a hold of Halle shoved him to the ground. All around the room, conversation had stopped, everyone's attention now fixed on them and Aki.

"That's exactly why we can do what we want with him. He can't tell."

"But I can. Leave him alone, or I will."

The speaker laughed. "No, you won't. I know who you are. You're in here because you wouldn't tell, remember?" He glanced at the men beside and jerked his head in Aki's direction.

Aki knew what was going to happen before it did, but that didn't make it any more pleasant when two of them grabbed him by the arms and pinned him against the wall. His stomach twisted in anticipation of the pain he knew was about to come. It was just pain. He could survive it. Just like he'd always survived it before. Aki questioned his own sanity when the man's fist connected with his stomach. Once, twice, three times. He gasped, hunched over, held upright only by the men on either side of him.

"Why would you stick up for him? You hate him."

"Maybe I do but," Aki said through gritted teeth, "he's my brother and you need to leave him alone."

That earned him a fist in his mouth and probably more but the door was flung open just then. A shout echoed across the room. The hands gripping his arms fell away. Aki leaned against the wall but managed to stay on his feet as their overseer, accompanied by a guard, entered the room. Aki realized he was actually grateful to see the man. He brushed the back of his hand across his mouth and pulled it away bloody.

"What's going on in here?"

"Nothing," the man who'd hit Aki said, glaring in Aki's direction.

The temptation to stay quiet, to say nothing, pressed in on Aki. But he'd started this. And, in spite of the pain that stabbed him with every breath he took, there was a certain satisfaction in what he'd done. When the overseer's eyes swept the room and noticed him bleeding, there wasn't any sense in pretending he wasn't. Aki spoke up, "They were tormenting Halle, and I told them to stop. Then he hit me."

The overseer looked at some of the others, most of whom nodded in confirmation.

"You had no part in starting it?"

"I only told them to stop."

"Why would you believe him? He's in here for lying, isn't he?"

The overseer turned to one of the men who'd watched the entire affair. "You saw what happened? Was it any different than what he just said?"

"No."

"Very well." The overseer pointed to the man who'd hit Aki. "Take him out. And if there's trouble from any of you," he gestured at the three who'd helped, "you'll join him." Finally, he approached Aki and held out a clean handkerchief. "Clean yourself up. You're being released tomorrow. I'd rather not turn you loose looking like we beat you."

Aki waited until the door shut behind the overseer before sinking down to the floor. He kept the cloth pressed against his bleeding lip and drew his knees up to his chest. Halle had, at some point during all the talking, crept back to his own mat. Neither of them said anything as the low hum of conversation resumed across the room. When Aki was done nursing his bloody lip, he laid down to sleep.

Just as he was almost asleep, he thought he heard Halle whisper two words that he was sure he'd never heard Halle say before, "Thank you."

Chapter 54

H E'S BEING RELEASED TOMORROW," Alina said, without looking up from the bread she was kneading.

Stephan grunted in response, suddenly too preoccupied by the task of putting his boots on to actually speak.

"We should go to Bren. You know, to be there for him," Alina continued. "Sasha said if we wanted to, he would take care of things here."

"Sasha also said he would go if we didn't want to."

"But we do. Or I do, at least."

Stephan finished putting his boots on and straightened. The momentary idleness took away his excuse for not talking. He rubbed a hand over his face.

"He should have just told us. He was here, he could have. If he hadn't got it into his head that he had to do everything alone, Dagmar wouldn't be dead now and he wouldn't be convicted of participating in treason."

It was a conversation that had been repeated many times in the last month, ever since Sasha had returned with his news. Alina stopped her kneading and crossed the room. Wiping her hands off on her apron, she sat down in the chair across from Stephan's.

"Remember how angry I was at you when you took Al?"

"How could I forget?"

Alina smiled. "In the end, that was what Al needed and he's been a different person ever since. But this is different."

"You're right. It's very different. Al didn't plot treason. Al didn't sit in this room pretending a lie. Al never did anything that ended with someone dead. Aki sat here, knowing what he knew, and said nothing. He let Kezi talk him into whatever she wanted even after I warned him that she was trouble. And then he ran away and dragged Dagmar into his mess. She didn't deserve that."

"Al never thought we'd stop loving him because of what he did, either," Alina added quietly.

"Aki will always have a home here if he wants it. I wouldn't deny him that."

"I doubt he'll see it the same way."

Chapter 55

HOPEFULLY, THIS WOULD BE the last time he'd see the inside of the magistrate's office for a very long time. Aki stood, trying not to let his impatience show, as the man searched for the paper that spelled out the details of his sentence. He hadn't miscounted the days; he was sure of that. Still, there was the nagging worry that the date written on that paper would be different. Aki didn't think he could bear the disappointment of being told he had to return to work for even one more day.

A dull pain had settled in his stomach from the beating he'd taken the night before, and his jaw ached. Neither of those things mattered when the magistrate pulled out the paper and smiled in satisfaction.

"Your time is finished." Aki let out a long breath. "You'll be provided with new clothes and enough money to see you through a couple of days. Do you have any idea where you'll be going?"

"Yes, sir."

"And would you like us to try to arrange for you to be taken there?"

"No, sir, I can manage on my own."

"Very well. I do have a note from Captain Lupin saying that he has some of your things. I assume you know where to find him?"

"Yes, sir."

Less than half an hour later, Aki took in the castle courtyard one final time. His clothes weren't the best but they were better than the gray suit he'd had to wear during his sentence and he had enough money in his pocket that he didn't need to rush home right away. He turned to leave when he caught sight of him.

Halle stood just outside the stable, his hands empty and his head hung down. Aki knew the look. He'd seen it a thousand times. It was the look Halle had every time he'd been in trouble with Gundar, which was almost as often as Aki was in trouble. Aki started to walk out the gate then stopped. He frowned. A chance to make everything right. That's what Dagmar had given him, and he'd made a start. But there was still something unfinished.

His feet reluctantly turned away from the beckoning gate and brought him before Halle.

"I have the knives I stole from you. When you get out, come to Sasha's like he said and I'll give them back to you. Alright?"

Halle nodded, not meeting his eyes.

"I'm sorry for stealing them. And for trying to kill you."

He turned and walked away before Halle had a chance to respond. It wasn't until he was out from under the shadow of the gate that he breathed freely again.

It made the most sense to collect his things from Captain Lupin and that was where he headed first. After the last few months, just walking down the road was a strange sensation. He fought back the urge to constantly look over his shoulder and tried to blend in with the others on the road even if he felt out of place.

It was late enough in the morning that he hoped to find the academy deserted aside from Captain Lupin. There was nothing but dust in the arena and Aki hurried across it. With only the slightest hesitation, he lifted his hand and knocked on the door.

"Come in," Captain Lupin called from the other side of the door.

Pushing it open, Aki stepped into the office. He'd only stood inside it four times, and none of those times were ones he enjoyed remembering. But with a pang, he realized he'd never stand in here again. This was a chance he wasn't getting back.

Captain Lupin cleared his throat and Aki realized he'd just been standing there lost in his own thoughts for an awkward amount of time.

"The magistrate said you had my things still, sir. I've just come to get them back."

"Wait here."

Aki appreciated the moment alone. He hadn't prepared himself well enough for this, he realized. He'd known since he ran away from Stephan's that he was giving this up, but standing here now there was nothing he wanted more than to stay.

Reentering the office, Captain Lupin set a bundle down on the desk near Aki.

"Sasha took your horse home with him to ensure she was cared for. You were just released today?"

"Yes, sir. Less than an hour ago."

"And what are your plans?"

"Go home to Sasha for now, I guess. I'll figure something out from there."

"Have you spoken to Atticus Wehr yet?"

"No, sir. I haven't seen him."

"You should try to speak to him before you leave," Captain Lupin said. "He would like it if you did."

"I'll try to," Aki promised, not sure that he really wanted to. He picked up the bundle and bid Captain Lupin goodbye before heading back out into the arena.

The road beneath his feet led out of Bren and up along the rocky coast. It wasn't the direction he needed to go to reach Sasha's, but he wasn't quite ready to take that step yet. No, today he just needed time to himself, time to sort through the myriad of tangled thoughts that assaulted his mind. So instead of heading toward Sasha's, he followed the coastal road that he'd ridden once with Master Wehr. It had been deep winter when he made that trip and now summer was coming to its close. Even in a different season, though, the scene was breathtaking. He didn't make it nearly as far as they had gone, only coming abreast of the smugglers' huts before deciding he'd gone far enough.

He found a spot on the edge of the cliff and sat down, letting his legs dangle over the precipice, and leaning back against his bundle of belongings. In his hands, he held a small, oblong parcel wrapped in an old, dusty cloth. Pulling away the folds of the cloth, he slid one of the knives out of its sheath. He toyed with it, spinning the perfectly weighted blade around and around with his fingers. Not afraid. That's what he'd told Halle the day he'd stolen them. Not afraid of Halle. Not afraid of anyone. Not afraid of anything. And yet, every decision he'd made since that day was because he was very, very afraid. Even when he chose to stay with Stephan and Alina, it was in part because he was afraid of going back to Aruuk and facing Halle, facing what he'd done.

"Is your life worth so little to you, boy, that you'd throw it away now?"

Aki started at the voice just behind him. Turning he saw Master Wehr standing only a few feet from him, concern etched all over his aged face. How his old instructor had known to find him here was beyond him.

"It's not like that."

"You're sitting on the edge of a cliff, playing with a knife. Doesn't that seem a bit reckless to you?"

Aki scooted away from the edge enough to abate the old man's worried expression and tucked the knife back into its place.

"How did you find me?"

"You say that like you were trying to hide."

"No. No, I wasn't. I just wanted to be somewhere quiet, to think."

"And now I've intruded on your thoughts. I apologize. But to answer your question, quite simply, I followed you. Do you mind?"

"No."

"Good," Master Wehr said, smiling a little as he sat on a rock a few feet away. "What are you planning to do now?"

"Go back to Sasha's..."

"Not Stephan?"

"I don't think he wants me back," Aki admitted. "I ran away from him and he hasn't come to see me since Sasha brought me back. I don't really know what my plans are after that. I'll figure something out, I suppose."

"You're not even going to ask to return to the academy?"

Aki didn't answer right away. In truth, it had never occurred to him to ask. It was over. It was easier to accept that it was over rather than hope for another chance. "I have no right to ask for that."

"No. No, you do not. Were you aware that that decision was placed in my hands? They trust me to make the right decision about you."

Shaking his head, Aki turned back to stare at the sea.

"Well, at least I've made it easy for you. I think I created a great enough disaster to settle the choice for you."

"Oh, no, Aki. You have done anything but make it easy for me."

"Sorry."

"You would apologize for your very existence if it would make people think better of you, wouldn't you?"

Aki had no answer to that, mostly because it was true but also because he thought it was a bad time to point out that a considerable number of the people in his life would, in fact, prefer if he didn't exist.

"Truthfully, this is one of the most difficult choices I've ever had to make."

"I really am sorry for that. Would it make it easier if I told you that I don't want to come back?"

"I can see quite plainly that it would be a lie, so no, it wouldn't help. Come," Master Wehr said, getting to his feet. "I must return, and I'd like for you to walk with me."

Aki slowly stood, wincing at the pain the motion caused. It was worth it, though. He didn't have the slightest regret for his actions the night before. That, at least, had to be a step in the right direction.

Master Wehr was in no hurry to reach Bren again and Aki kept up easily. After they had walked in silence for several minutes, Master Wehr turned to Aki. "Will you tell me about your time in Karu?"

"What if I say I'd rather not?"

"Tell me anyway, please."

Aki obeyed with a sigh of resignation. It was the most thorough account he'd given anyone, even Sasha. There was relief in telling it. Master Wehr listened without question or comment until Aki fell silent again.

"I'm sorry you went through that," Master Wehr said softly. "It must have been quite awful."

"Is Jasper really dead?" Aki asked, steering the conversation away from the topic of what he went through.

"He is. Unfortunately, he is." Master Wehr paused in his walking and stared out at the sea. "You know, he was my first student."

"I had no idea."

"Yes. My very first one. He wasn't unlike you. He always had a difficult time telling anyone no. I'm afraid he never learned to overcome that. I'd venture to say that's why he became entangled with Keziah Grimere's plot. That, and the debts he'd incurred and had no way of paying. Although, I suppose we'll never have the chance now to ask him."

Aki bit his lip. He'd never thought of Jasper being anything like him. It was an uncomfortable comparison given the events that had transpired in the last few months.

"What's going to happen to Kezi?"

"The girl? It's already happened. She was sentenced to death for conspiring against the crown. As the leader and instigator, she bore the greatest responsibility for the crime."

"It's already..."

"Yes. Before Sasha brought you back." Master Wehr realized Aki was no longer walking next to him and stopped. "I'm sorry, Aki. I had assumed you knew."

He was going to be sick. His face drained of all color and his body froze against his will. A cold wave of nausea swept through him and Aki swallowed hard to keep it back.

"Aki?"

"I didn't know. I..." words failed him.

"After what she did to you, I wouldn't have thought it would bother you quite so much."

"It doesn't. Not like that." Aki couldn't explain it. She'd betrayed him, used him, lied about him. Before that, though, she'd been his friend - one of the few people he could have called a friend. Now she was another death. And so many people in his life had died. He shut his eyes and forced his breathing to come back under his control. He'd thought he'd at least get the chance to talk to her again, to ask her why she'd done what she did. But it was gone. Any chance at understanding her was gone, lost forever.

"Are you alright?"

Aki didn't trust himself to speak, but he nodded.

"I'm sorry, Aki. Truly sorry."
Aki merely nodded again and started walking.

Chapter 56

AKI HADN'T REALIZED HOW LONG the road between Bren and home was until he had to walk it. The day was hot and the road was dusty from lack of rain. Slung over his shoulder, bumping against his back with every step, was the bundle that contained all of his possessions.

He'd stayed in Bren last night, putting off his homecoming one more day. Now, as the sun finally disappeared beneath the western horizon, he began to wish he'd put it off for just one more day. Sasha's home was tucked far back into the woods and he made it there without having to go past Stephan's. Now he stood, staring at the light that spilled out of the windows into the gray night.

His hand hovered in front of the door. Inside, he could hear voices. Someone, Ophelia, he realized, laughed. It was a sound he hadn't heard for so long.

"Aki?" Sasha answered the door when he knocked. "I thought you were with Stephan. I thought he was going to meet you."

"I didn't see him, so I just came here like you said."

"Come on. You walked all the way, didn't you?" Aki nodded, stepping past him into the room. "You've got to be tired then. That's a long walk."

The cabin was barely recognizable from when Aki had first seen it as a child. No longer was it a single room, sparsely furnished. Two doors led to bedrooms at the back, making room for a sitting area in the front. Here, both Lars and Ophelia were sitting. Aki lowered his head.

He didn't want to see the way Ophelia looked at him now, after what he'd done and after Dagmar's death. Perhaps coming here was a mistake.

"Welcome home, Aki," Ophelia's voice was warm as she rose to greet him. "You must be hungry."

And just like that, she lifted the weight of his guilt away. He looked up and her smile was genuine, and he managed to return it. "A little. Well, maybe more than a little."

He was starving, actually. When he'd left Bren that morning, he'd forgotten to buy any food to take with him. His murmured thanks was lost in a mouthful of the food Ophelia set in front of him. They gave him time to eat without pestering him with questions and Aki didn't waste it. He hadn't eaten this well since the night he ran away from Stephan's almost three months before. At last, he pushed his empty plate away.

Lars opened his mouth to say something but Sasha held up his hand to stop him.

"You look like you're about to fall over, Aki. We can ask our questions later. For now, you should sleep."

Aki nodded gratefully.

"You'll have to share a room with Lars for now, but thankfully there's more space now than when you two shared it with me before."

Aki was pretty sure he was asleep before he even laid down and he did not wake up again until sunlight poured through the single window of the room. He was alone, but by the sounds of it the others were just in the other room. The smell of food was enough to pull him out from underneath his blanket and out the door.

"You're just in time." Lars looked up from his food.

"For what?" Aki slid into a seat.

"You can help Sasha and I finish working on the new room."

"I think there's something else Aki needs to do today," Sasha said.

Sasha didn't need to say it, Aki already knew. His appetite abandoned him for a moment.

"I'll come with you."

"You don't have to," Aki said too quickly.

"But I still will. I won't make you do that alone."

338

"Thanks." Aki decided it would be a shame to miss out on good food simply because of who he had to see later that day.

"How was Halle?" Sasha's question caught him off guard and he looked up to find both him and Lars watching him curiously.

"He was alright." But that wasn't entirely true. "He's going to have a really hard time now that I'm not there, I think. I tried to teach him some, but he still couldn't really understand much."

"You tried to teach him?" The disbelief in Lars' voice was deserved, Aki supposed.

"We're not... we're not enemies anymore. I mean, we're not friends either, but I think we're done trying to kill each other."

Lars didn't quite believe him still, but Sasha gave him a small smile.

The distance between Sasha's and Stephan's was not nearly as long as Aki wanted it to be. The house and barn were already within sight and he still didn't know what exactly he was going to say. There was no speech, no apology he could make that could whisk the past away.

"This is a bad idea," he whispered as they approached.

"No, it's not. The longer you wait, the harder it will be."

"I could wait forever and then it wouldn't be hard at all."

Sasha just laughed and kept walking. Aki hadn't been making a joke, though. He half ran the next few steps to catch up.

The barn doors were flung wide open, letting in the daylight. Aki could see Stephan working inside. Stephan turned his head and then straightened as they got close. Putting down whatever was in his hand, he came out to meet them. He stopped a few feet away. Aki stared at the dirt he scuffed up with his foot.

"Well, somebody needs to say something," Sasha said from behind him.

"I'm sorry, Stephan."

"Why didn't you just tell us?"

"I told you why. I didn't want you finding out what I'd done."

"Aki, if you'd just told us instead of running away, I could have gone with you. None of this would have happened. And none of it would have happened if you'd just walked away from Kezi."

"I know."

"I just don't understand why you were so afraid of telling us. You didn't honestly believe it would change anything, did you?"

Aki thought he'd proved that belief so disastrously well that it didn't need to be questioned. He had nothing left to say, anyway.

"Come on, Stephan, stop. Give him a break," Sasha said. "Don't make it as hard for him as you did for me."

For a moment there was nothing but stunned silence. Aki wasn't sure he'd ever heard someone tell Stephan to stop. He waited for Stephan's retort, but it didn't come.

"It's alright, Sasha. He's right. I should have done it differently."

"But you didn't. And I'm pretty sure you've been punished more than enough for it. You don't have to keep punishing yourself over and over again. And no one else needs to either."

There weren't enough words to express the gratitude Aki felt for Sasha's words or for his presence. It was a good thing he hadn't talked Sasha out of coming with him. He lifted his eyes to meet Stephan's for the first time.

"I am sorry for everything."

"Come on," Sasha said, laying a hand on his shoulder and turning him away. "Let's go home."

They were no longer within sight of the house when Sasha spoke again. "He'll come round, you know. He always does."

Aki decided he'd just have to take Sasha's word for it. Such a change of heart didn't seem likely to him. At least it was over with, though he wished he'd had the chance to see Alina before they left.

It wasn't until after supper that Aki wandered out to the paddock Sky now shared with Sasha's own horse. She lifted her head over the fence as he ran his hand over her forehead.

"At least, you're not disappointed with me," he said with a slight smile. "I guess it helps that you have no idea what's going on."

Someone cleared their throat behind him. Aki jumped and spun around.

"Stephan?"

"I didn't mean to startle you."

Aki's eyes found the ground. "I'm..."

"Don't. You don't have to apologize again. Sasha was right about that." Stephan leaned his back against the fence rail, facing Aki. "You're feeling better? Sasha said you were almost dead when he found you."

"I'm still not sure how they kept me alive, but yes, I'm better now."

Stephan nodded for too long as if he wasn't quite sure what else to say.

"You're staying with Sasha?"

"I just thought it was best for now."

"Alina wants you to come home."

"Is it still my home?"

"Of course it is. If you want it to be, that is. Alina wants it to be. To be honest, she was very disappointed she didn't get to see you yet. And she might be a little furious with me for chasing you off."

Aki smiled at the idea of Alina being angry. It turned into a frown almost at once. "Do you want me to come back?"

With a sigh, Stephan ran a hand over his face. "I should have been there. I should have come to visit you, at least. It wasn't right to leave you to face everything alone. Yes, Aki, I want you to come home, too."

Epilogue

AKI HAD HEARD THE RIDER coming up the drive but hadn't bothered to step outside the barn. It was most likely a courier, and he didn't want to be reminded of what he'd lost. He went on with his work.

"Aki, come out here," Stephan called from outside the barn.

Running the brush down the horse's neck one last time, Aki set it aside and went outside. A glance at the rider made the blood rush to his face. Felix sat rigid on his horse, deliberately ignoring Aki's presence. He'd come alone, Aki noticed with a prick of jealousy and disappointment.

"This one's for you," Stephan said, holding out a sealed envelope.

Aki took it but waited to open it. Stephan waved him off. "Go ahead. You might as well see what it says."

Not wanting to read it in front of anyone, Aki found a spot behind the barn. Perched on an empty barrel, he broke the seal and unfolded it. The handwriting was familiar. It ought to have been, he realized. It was written by the man who'd taught him to write.

Aki,

I trust this finds you well. I will waste no time in getting to the purpose of this missive.

I am an old man. Old enough that I have decided it is time for me to move on from teaching and hand it over to younger men. That being said, I have spent a good deal of time in these last few days contemplating my life and my work. It has been my pride now for many years that no student I taught has failed. It would be a great shame for my last pupil to break such a perfect record.

And, I must be honest, there are times when I miss your endless questions and conversations. I've had few students as inquisitive as you and fewer still so eager to learn. It is perhaps one of your greatest strengths - one, I'm afraid, you often overlook in yourself.

Do you remember when we first spoke? You claimed you were no longer the person you used to be and I told you that you would always be something of that person. The same is still true. We are, all of us, a compilation of all our choices, both good and bad. You are more than your worst mistakes, Aki. You will forgive me, I hope, for the inquiries I made in searching for an answer to the decision I was compelled to make. However, I needed the whole picture.

Here I said I would get straight to the point and yet I've rambled on. I may be ready to move on and retire from my work - but there is still some unfinished business that I need to complete. I cannot bear the thought of ending like this. So, if you will humor the sentimental hubris of an old man, I look forward to seeing you at my door at 8 o'clock in two days' time.

Atticus Wehr

Aki reread the letter two or three times, trying to convince himself he wasn't imagining it. In the last week, he hadn't even allowed himself the temptation of hope. After his conversation with Master Wehr on the day of his release, he'd thought the man had already made up his mind.

"You are coming back?"

Looking up, Aki found Felix standing only a few feet away. He stood, stiff and uncertain, his hands fidgeting.

"You don't want me to, do you?"

"I," Felix started, finally clasping his hands behind his back to keep them still, "I haven't decided yet."

"You knew what this was?"

"Yes. I asked to be the one to bring it. And I spoke to Master Wehr before he wrote it. He told me everything that happened to you."

"Oh." Aki couldn't keep his face from falling. He hadn't decided himself how much he wanted people to know.

"You didn't want him to, did you? He said you wouldn't, but I insisted. I mean, I saw you when you first came back, so I already knew a little."

Shrugging, Aki folded the letter up and put it in his pocket. He jumped off the barrel.

"So, you are coming back?"

Aki gave him a sheepish smile, "Of course, I'm coming back."

Other titles by S. T. Hobbs

The Divalian Chronicles –

Prequel ~ The Thief and the Slave

Book 1 ~ The Traitor's Alliance

Book 2 ~ The Last Chief

Book 3 ~ The Courier's Apprentice

Book 4 ~ The King's Successor

The Oracle's Odyssey –

Book 1 ~ The Forgotten Curse

Book 2 ~ The Fallen Gates

Book 3 ~ (Coming soon) The Fates' Finale

www.ingramcontent.com/pod-product-compliance
Lightning Source LLC
Chambersburg PA
CBHW050545260626
47157CB00002B/437